THE MAGIC OF LAST RESORT

Book 6: The Western Lands and All That Really Matters

ANDREW EINSPRUCH

Cover design by Maria Spada of Maria Spada Book Cover Design.

Editing by Vanessa Lanaway of Red Dot Scribble.

Proofreading by Abigail Nathan of Bothersome Words.

Layout by Andrew Einspruch of Wild Pure Heart.

ISBN: 978-0-9806272-9-9

DEDICATION

To Billie and Tamsin

Thank you for everything on this long journey.

THE COUNCIL OF WAX FIGURES

ueen Eloise Hydra Gumball III sat at the table with her Privy Council, her face in her hands, and groaned.

It wasn't a my-haggleberry-tea-is-stone-cold-and-my-ginger-snaps-are-soggy kind of groan, a someone-tie-dyed-my-bathrobe-as-a-prank groan, or an I-really-shouldn't-have-eaten-the-entire-Fudge-Miracle-torte groan. It was a the-queen-in-the-realm-to-the-east-stole-a-village-and-its-surrounds-from-me-then-stonewalled-me-at-our-parlay-before-sending-me-and-my-entourage-of-soldiers-running-away-at-full-speed-and-then-threatening-to-take-another-chunk-of-my-land kind of groan. "This is a disaster," she said. "A true shemozzle."

She lifted her face from her hands and stared around at her Privy Council, expecting at least one or two of the dozen of them to have something useful to contribute.

Nope. They were as silent as the two empty seats at the table, those once occupied by the Supreme Magistrate and the Court Nominee, both of whom had resigned weeks earlier because they'd lost confidence in Queen Eloise. They hadn't been replaced yet.

The seventeen-year-old queen scanned them with her blurry, magic-tinged right eye, and listened with her buzzing, magic-distorted right ear. Nothing registered there, either.

Finally, one of them spoke. "Do you think you might be catastrophizing just a smidge, Queen Eloise?" It was Jerome Abernatheen de Chipmunk, Eloise's best friend, former champion, current Assistant Seer to the Court Seer, and one of the new members of the Privy Council. The chipmunk's fluffed tail and twitching whiskers betrayed the apprehension he felt at speaking. "We all got away from the parlay at Flachberg. Yes, there were injuries, some of them serious, but fortunately, no one died. Yes, Queen Aglandau tried to capture you, but you managed to escape. And she didn't launch a full-on attack while we were there, which she very much could have. Now, we're back here in Castle de Brague, safe and sound, ready to figure out what to do next."

Eloise stared at him.

"Goblet half full and all that." His voice squeaked a little at the end, and the statement came out more like a question.

A few of the others nodded agreement.

"Goblet half full," Eloise repeated. "Gotta keep a positive mindset and all that." She picked up the spoon and started rapping it on her saucer. *Rap!* "Tell you what." *Rap!* "I'll get Seamstress Linttrap to embroider 'Goblet half full' onto the front of a tunic for me." *Rap!* "In big letters, so everyone can read it." *Rap!* "On the back, it'll say something different." *Rap!* "'Ask me how my parlay went.'" *Rap!*

The saucer cracked on the last hit.

Eloise blinked at the damage, her cheeks flooding red. She set down the spoon. "Sorry, I didn't mean to do that. And I shouldn't have yelled. Jerome, you don't deserve me being snarky. None of you do. I think I'm..." She paused and swallowed. "I think I'm angry. And scared. And I don't know what to do."

From the far end of the table, Niville Numptorius raised a tenuous, fluttering hand. The Interim Other Places Advocate, who just about everyone (except Eloise and her First Advisor) called "Numpty," was thin, and wore an unflattering bowl haircut and wrinkled lavender robes. He wasn't much older than Eloise herself, and was perpetually nervous. "I'm, I'm sorry, Queen Eloise. As I didn't attend your parlay, perhaps you could color in some of the detai—in particular, the discussion between you and Queen Aglandau."

It was a reasonable request.

"Of course." Eloise tamped down her jumbled feelings and delivered a dispassionate summary. "You'll recall that having a parlay was our idea, and when Queen Aggie accepted, we were pleased at the possibility that it might turn into a useful dialog that kept us from going to war, something we're still utterly unprepared for. We met in Flachberg at her suggestion, which had historical echoes as that's where my mother and Queen Aglandau held their parlay a couple of decades ago. When we arrived, we confirmed the Easties had, indeed, moved a section of the Adequate Wall of the Realms to incorporate the stolen lands."

"That's..." Niville furrowed his brow. "That's amazing." He looked around to see if anyone else had reacted. No one had. His voice quietened. "They moved a section of the Adequate Wall. The thing's huge. That's amazing, isn't it?"

Eloise nodded. "Niville's right. It's a staggeringly huge thing to have done. The mind boggles. They didn't just use the materials and rebuild it. They actually reassembled it exactly like it was, worn stairs and everything. Other than new grout and mortar, it looked like it had been in that place for centuries, not just weeks. The relocation job, with its meticulous attention to detail, gave an overwhelming sense of permanence to the change. I guess that was the point—to make it seem like something you'd never undo."

"Would you?" asked Niville. "If you had the chance, would you undo it?"

A snort came from midway down the table.

"You have something to say, Exchequer?" asked Eloise.

Cyrus Snorklepipe Borborygmus, Exchequer of the Realm, was a gaunt man with almost translucent skin and a tidy, gray-flecked beard that did little to decorate his humorless mouth. He waved a hand as if granting Eloise permission to keep going.

"Please, Master Borborygmus," she said. "Have your say.

"I mean no offense, Your Highness," he wheezed. "It's just that, given the state of the royal coffers, the Adequate Wall of the Realms will have to stay where it is until further notice. Especially if you think you might need to take up arms against our neighbors to the east."

"They've already taken up arms against us. What choice do we have?" Eloise's shoulders drooped. "But you're right. We aren't exactly coming at it from a position of strength."

"And yet, we are better prepared than we were just a few weeks ago." It was Master Sergeant (No Longer Retired) Tiberius de Sphenodon. The ancient tuatara wore an extremely outdated soldier's uniform and sat in the spot previously occupied by a brigadier general, a third former Privy Council member who'd been relieved of his duties because of his differences with Eloise (specifically, his lack of respect for her, and his complete lack of any skills that met the queendom's current needs). The tuatara was unusually spry for someone well over a century old, and he was the only living person Eloise knew who had direct experience in war. He'd served in her great-grandmother's military, injured his foreleg in the process, and was now doing what he could to reshape her soldiers. He'd started with a group of parading fops in fancy duds, and was slowly turning them into several brigades worth of armed warriors who might actually cause damage. "There's no question we still have a long way to go, but with Mistress Cloisterfeld's help, progress is definitely being made. We just need time."

Sylvia Cloisterfeld, Eloise's late mother's former champion, nodded her agreement. "Definitely progress. If Queen Aglandau doesn't go all out attacking us right away, we stand a chance of being close to ready. That is, assuming we can get the training in, get re-outfitted, obtain adequate supplies—all of that."

Exchequer Borborygmus shook his head again, but held his tongue.

Niville raised his hand. "And the parlay itself, Queen Eloise?"

"Right. The parlay." She sighed, the memory as welcome as severe reflux. "Like I said, we arrived at Flachberg and the next morning, I went through the main gate at the Adequate Wall of the Realms to where the parlay tent was set up on top, making sure I was on time and ready. By contrast, Queen Aglandau was a couple of hours late."

"That seems rude," said Niville. "Why would she do that?"

Eloise lifted a shoulder. "I assume it was a not-very-subtle show of disrespect dipped in a thick coating of 'Go shove a grape up your nose.' Ultimately, we didn't talk for all that long. She had little to say that wasn't derisive, demanding, demeaning, or ludicrous. She disparaged my appearance, ate olives the whole time and lined the pits up on her leg, told me she hated my mother, which wasn't exactly news, said she had better things to do than be there parlaying with me, and essentially said it was long overdue that the Eastern Lands queendom claimed back its territory. What I saw as hostilities against my queendom, she characterized as righting an ancient wrong. Her position was that I should formally cede Flachberg, plus all lands within one hundred strong lengths, acknowledge the 'wrong-doings' perpetrated by the past queens of the Western Lands and All That Really Matters, and pay reparations. And she was extremely aware of the unprepared state of my forces and the state of my counting room."

"Gosh." Niville's fluttering hand settled in his lap.

"Oh, and when it was over, she had her archers shoot arrows at our encampment, and tried to have her soldiers capture me."

"No! You mean *capture you*, capture you? You mean Assistant Seer to the Court Seer Jerome Abernatheen de Chipmunk wasn't just being figurative?"

"No, he wasn't. And yes, capture as in detain me and keep me from leaving. The arrows and the attempted kidnapping were part of what she called her 'parting gift,' like it was some sort of party favor. I escaped thanks to the bravery of those who'd come with me, including some among us here." She nodded acknowledgment toward Sylvia Cloisterfeld, Jerome, and her champion, Lorch Lacksneck.

Niville gasped. "That's horrible! And grim. Anything else we should know?"

Eloise shrugged. "No, that pretty much covers it." She slumped back in her chair and looked at the faces of her Privy Council. To her right, Maybelle de Chipmunk, Jerome's mother and court seer, looked pensive. For her mother, Seer Maybelle had been incredibly effective. For Eloise? Not so much. The seer hadn't been able to garner anything from the Unseen for weeks. Which was too bad, because a few solid prognostications would have been rather useful just then.

Beyond Seer Maybelle, the Venerable Prelate Herself, an ancient tapir who was the highest-ranked Çalahtist figure in her queendom (save Eloise, of course, but that was more symbolic than religious) did what she usually did in these meetings—snoozed.

Eloise couldn't tell what the Speaker for the Land, Rölf de Phobaeticus, was thinking. Being a stick insect and at the far end of the table, his expressions were hard to read. He seemed to be slowly scratching his thorax; it wasn't clear if the gestured carried a specific meaning.

"Queen Eloise, if I may?" It was First Advisor Bërnädïce-Ändrëä Thëjëts, a mountain of a woman, three times the size and two heads taller than most. Since taking on the role of First Advisor, she'd toned down the outrageousness of her wardrobe, although she still wore scarves and robes that could be seen from two strong lengths away on a foggy day. "You should mention what Queen Aglandau said about Queen Johanna."

"Of course. No point in hiding it." Eloise swallowed the lump rising in her throat. This had been the most shocking bit of the parlay. "According to Queen Aggie, my sister has, on behalf of the Northern Lands, entered an alliance with the Easties."

The Venerable Prelate Herself coughed, opened her eyes, and raised a forepaw. So she hadn't been deep in slumber after all. "What sort of alliance, Your Highness?"

"The details aren't clear, although I've written to Johanna seeking clarification. What Queen Aglandau said was that Jo had tied herself to the Eastern Lands, and that she'd be in no position to take my side in any dispute."

The tapir curled her prehensile snout. "That doesn't seem right. You'd think sisterly loyalty would override political considerations."

"If what Queen Aggie said is correct, then the price of sisterly loyalty is, and I quote, 'A ridiculously small pile of coin.'" The words came out with the taste of vinegar and thistle.

"That's not good," said Niville.

"No, it isn't," agreed First Advisor. "In situations like these, a queen needs allies. One would have thought that the relationship of the Western Lands and All That Really Matters and the Half Kingdom—sorry, the Northern Lands; I'm still not used to that—would be one we could rely upon. I look forward to hearing what Johanna says in response to your letter, Your Highness."

"I do, and I don't. I may not have been overly diplomatic in my choice of words. And I guess it also depends on what she writes back. But if she's not on our side, that only leaves Queen Onomatopoeia of The South and Khan Nergüi Unbenannt Nimetuseta of the Central Ranges as potential close allies."

"I wouldn't expect much from the Central Carbuncle horses," rasped Cyrus Borborygmus. "In the past half century, they haven't done more than flick disgusted tails at anyone who wasn't one of their insular little herd. They're not exactly stellar inter-realm actors."

"We met them," said Jerome. "The queen, Lorch, and I did. The Us are fierce, proud warriors with strong hearts and incredible discipline. I wouldn't want to take them on and I wouldn't want to rule them out."

"But they keep completely to themselves," said the Exchequer. "Which doesn't do our queen much good. Plus, that whole thing about classifying people in the realms as 'the Us,' the 'Not Us,' and the 'savages?' It's insulting."

"Let's stay on track," said First Advisor. "The taxonomic systems of the dominant Central Ranges species aren't all that germane."

"Unless you're trying to count on them," said Borborygmus. "Unless you're thinking they might come to your aid."

"You're right, Exchequer Borborygmus." Eloise tapped her index finger on the table. "I might have a word with their ambassador. Actually, I should speak to all of them. And I'll send a note directly to Queen Onomatopoeia to feel out where things stand with The South. First Advisor is right. I really don't want us to face the Eastie soldiers all on our own. Not the way things stand. I mean, if we have to, we have to, but I don't relish the idea."

"Master Cloisterfeld and I will keep up our training," said Tiberius de Sphenodon. "We'll get both the metaphorical and literal blades of war as sharp as possible."

"I'll see if I can find any coins hidden in the counting house sofa cushions," said the Exchequer. "It sounds like we're going to need them even more than I thought."

Eloise nodded. "That would be good. If the rest of you can put your minds to solutions that don't involve slashing and bleeding, I'd be grateful. I'm sure not seeing any myself, and I fear the blood that might flow will mostly be ours. Let's meet again tomorrow."

BLÖDSINN. STUPIDITÉ.
IDIOZIA

As the group stood to leave, Eloise said, "Assistant Seer to the Court Seer, can you please stay a moment? There's something I'd like to discuss."

"Of course, Your Highness." Jerome climbed back up on his chair and stood with his forepaws clasped, waiting for the others to go. When the door closed behind them, he said, "What's up, El?"

Eloise sat down and indicated for him to do the same. She drummed her fingers, trying to figure out how to phrase what she had in mind. It was a terrible idea, and she needed to figure out a way to make it sound better than it was. "Jerome, I need you to keep researching the Star of Whatever."

The size and weight of a decent grapefruit, the Star of Whatever was an emerald-colored stone that was the most powerful and least understood magical object in all the realms. It seemed to suck the magic out of whatever it was near. Two centuries before, Melveeta the Elusive had used it to benefit her queen, Gwendolyn the Irritable, by casting a spell that laid waste to half the Northern Realm, turning it into the Half Kingdom. Ever since Eloise had taken possession of the stone and bonded to the spark of something inside it, she'd worn it in a box at her hip, making sure it didn't fall into anyone else's hands.

"Sure. Of course," said Jerome. "We've been trying to figure it out for months now and haven't really gotten far. But I'm happy to keep looking. Do you have anything in particular in mind?"

"I'm wondering if we can figure out how to use it."

Jerome lifted his head. "*Use it*, use it?"

Eloise nodded. "*Use it*, use it. As in, deliberately harness it for a specific purpose."

"El, that's... That's risky. You better than anyone know it's risky. Tell me, is your right eye still blurry?"

"Yes."

"And your right ear. Does it still have its constant buzz?"

"It does."

"And did they, or did they not, undergo those changes the last time you tapped into the Star of Whatever and used it in conjunction with the Orb of Alleged Omniscience?"

"What are you? A magistrate?"

"Answer the question, Your Highness."

"Don't go all formal on me, Jer. But yes. The blur and buzz are magical remnants from my use of the Star."

"Permanent magical remnants, El."

"We don't know that they're permanent."

"They sure seem permanent. But, OK, *persistent* then. Persistent magical remnants." Jerome hopped from his chair onto the table and walked over to her. "So why would you want to do that again?"

Eloise stood and paced the length of the table. "I'm thinking that it might…" She lowered her voice, even though no one was nearby. "I'm thinking that it might be necessary to use it."

"Necessary?" The chipmunk tilted his head. "Necessary how?"

"As a defense."

Jerome's tail fluffed and his eyes saucered. "You're kidding." He stared at her. "You're not kidding. Çalaht slurping a salad sandwich, El. That's a spectacularly bad idea. A stupendously bad idea. A catastrophically, monstrously, superlatively bad idea. *Blödsinn. Stupidité. Idiozia.*"

"Are you quite done yet?"

"Not quite. *Narishkeyt. Stultitia. Glupost. Dommheet—*"

"That'll do, Jer. I get the idea." She massaged her right wrist, a habit she'd gotten into on the advice of a healer after the second time it was fractured. "I'm not saying I want to use the thing."

"And I'm saying you don't even want to contemplate using it. Why even go there?"

"I may have no choice."

Jerome threw his paws up in the air. "Because that worked so well for Gwendolyn the Irritable. And even better for her champion, Melveeta. At least old Gwen didn't have to spend two hundred years living a painful half existence enthralled to a spell she'd conjured that both kept her alive and fed on her. But, hey. What's a couple of centuries of torment here or there?"

Eloise leaned over him. "At least Gwendolyn won that war."

Jerome matched her, leaning in. "For some values of 'winning.' I'm not sure Melveeta would agree that she'd won much."

"Melveeta stayed true to Gwendolyn to her last breath." Eloise paused, remembering. "It was both sweet and incredibly sad. She said I had Gwendolyn's eyes. Melveeta recognized my sister and me as relatives."

"Creepy. And yes, sad."

Eloise sat back down. "Look. It's like you said. More than anyone, I know this idea is as cracked as a tinker's teapot. But I'll need to do whatever needs doing to protect my queendom. The Western Lands and All That Really Matters comes first."

"But at what price? Because it seems like there's always some kind of price when you use that thing."

Eloise lifted and dropped one shoulder. "The Star of Whatever scares the stuffing out of me. It leaves me utterly stuffingless. But if Queen Aglandau is marching across my realm and my soldiers are beaten—which would hardly be a surprise, given the state of them—and I'm desperate, then I might have no choice but to use it. Believe me, I don't want to." She patted the box on her hip. "I want it to stay nestled in here. But I want using it to be a realistic option that won't leave half my queendom destroyed." She clasped Jerome's forepaws in her hands and gave them a little squeeze. "That's what I want from you, Jer. Help me at least keep it an option. Keep looking for information about it, and maybe we can find a way to practice without me getting maimed or permanently enslaved. Please?"

He squeezed back. "Sure. Of course I'll help. But can you promise me something?"

"Sure. Anything."

"If you find that you do need to use it, give me a couple months' warning so I can get as far away from here as possible."

"If it comes to actually using it, it'll probably be too late for you to escape. Most of us will already be under siege. Or dead."

"That's a chipper thought. Çalaht slinging saucepans, I hope it doesn't come to that."

"Me, too, Jer. Me very much too."

❧ 3 ❧

CORATINA

Her Imperialness, Queen Aglandau Gaeta Cerignola Ponentine, Shining Light and Sovereign Voice of the Eastern Lands, Plenipotentiary of Peace, She Who is Beloved by All Her Peoples and Who Brings Forth the Bountiful Harvest from the Olive Groves sat on a utilitarian throne in her private office, looked at her daughter, and felt irked. It wasn't a feeling she enjoyed, but it was a feeling she experienced often—more or less every time she cast eyes upon the nineteen-year-old disappointment.

Coratina Ponentine had arrived late in Aglandau's life. Almost too late, but not quite. For two decades, the queen had not found herself in the family way despite the attentions of the king. A month after that useless sack of liquid consolation-imbibing dung finally slugged down his last mugful and passed to stand with Çalaht (assuming the deity could overlook his smell and the advanced pickling of his liver), the queen announced to her Court that the old sot had left her a departing gift, which Aglandau dutifully delivered after the requisite nine months.

The fact that Coratina, with her long, blonde hair, oval face, and blue eyes, looked nothing like the king and only marginally like the queen was duly observed and reported by the gossip heralds. People were titillated for about a minute, but most shrugged it off. What's a monarch to do, eh? At least there was finally a successor, even if it soon became clear that she was—*gasp!*—violently allergic to olives, a strange fate for any Eastern Lands heir.

Aglandau just wished that Coratina showed even the tiniest inclination toward learning what it would take to assume the throne. An excellent step in that direction would be to pay attention when Court happenings took place, as they were at the moment. But no, her daughter was sitting in the corner reading. Again. "Coratina Frantoio Patrinia Ponentine."

The girl looked up, her thoughts a thousand strong lengths away. "Mmmm... Yes, Mother?"

"I need you to pull your nose out of that text and listen to what Seer Throumbolia is saying here."

The young woman arranged her face in an expression that came very close to feigning interest. "Yes, Mother."

"Don't 'Yes, Mother' me. This is important."

"Yes, Mother." Coratina marked her spot with a strip of linen and closed her newest favorite work of ecclesiastical exploration, *The Commentaries on the Commentaries on the Commentaries on the Scrolls of Çalaht*. "Apologies, Seer Throumbolia. I've just been so completely absorbed by a heretical exegesis put forth by Lipid the Elder. You have my full attention."

Aglandau wrinkled her nose. Where had her child's scrollish disposition come from? And for *theology*, of all things. Çalaht help them all.

Seer Throumbolia was a bearded, older man who wore drab olive-green robes and a stick pin shaped like a pair of divination twigs, and had the demeanor and flair of a broken lute string. He had a cleft chin and a matching cleft in his forehead, which, according to Court gossip, was the visible remnant of a childhood encounter with either a razordisc or an attempted axe murder. The reality was simultaneously much more ordinary and more strange—as a child, he'd tripped while running and slammed into the sharp edge of a table. It left his skull somewhat caved in and his forehead marred, but within days, he was tapping into the Unseen with freakish accuracy. With that unfortunate injury, a future Court Seer had been minted. Throumbolia coughed. "As I was saying, I can't see her, my queen."

"What do you mean, you can't see her? We know she exists. If she'd died, we'd have heard about it." Queen Aglandau scoffed. "But even if she had kicked the olive bowl, you'd still be able to detect her. You can see anyone in the Unseen, living or not."

"With respect, that's not strictly true, Your Imperialness. It requires a certain spiritual..." He paused, bouncing the tips of his fingers against each other as he sought the right word. "It takes a certain spiritual heft to be perceptible in the Unseen."

"That doesn't make sense."

"With respect, my queen, it does. You are correct in saying that everyone—every street urchin and every waif, every merchant and noble, alive or dead—is out there somewhere in the Unseen. But being able to perceive them rests on a combination of factors. How connected to the spiritual realms is the person? How well known are they among the people? More prominence and attention yields a kind of mass in the Unseen. Also, a factor is how talented the seer doing the perceiving is."

Coratina spoke up. "Excuse me, Mother."

Aglandau hid her astonishment. "Yes, my olive blossom?"

"Who are we discussing?"

"That bumfuzzled, snot-nosed, piffle-spouting brain-addled gubbins."

"I take it you're referring to Queen Eloise of the Western Lands and All That Really Matters?"

"Just say 'Western Lands,' dear. The rest of it is pretentious, offensive, self-aggrandizing twaddle."

"Yes, Mother. Although it's not like this Queen Eloise, or any of the previous Queen Eloises, is responsible for the name. They've been calling themselves that at least as far back as the cranky one, whatever her name was."

"That was Gwendolyn the Irritable," said Seer Throumbolia. "She ruled either side of 233 years ago, before and after the advent of the Purple Haze that devastated the Half Kingdom."

"That's right. Queen Gwendolyn," said Coratina.

"You're making my point for me, Cor. The Westies had their collective noses stuck up in the air for literal centuries, looking down at the other lands that dare exist on the same plane of existence." Aglandau gestured to her seer. "Keep going, Throumbolia."

"With modesty, Your Imperialness, I'd say my talents as a seer are as good as any and better than most." He unconsciously ran a finger along the divot in his forehead, like he was trying to activate it, or to ascertain its depth. "Much to my surprise, I simply can't see Queen Eloise in the Unseen."

"And why not?"

"It'd be speculation to say."

The queen gave him an annoyed flick of the hand. "So speculate."

"I would guess that, for some reason, she doesn't have enough heft, spiritually speaking, to make enough of a dent on the Unseen to register."

"She's the queen," said Coratina. "How can she lack heft, spiritual or otherwise? Everyone across all the realms knows who she is. She's responsible for the same number of lives as my mother. You can see my mother in the Unseen, can you not?"

"Yes, I can, when the Unseen allow me to glimpse their realm. But Queen Aglandau has been on her throne for decades. That's plenty of time to gain the needed spiritual density." The seer shrugged. "Perhaps this lack of heft is a function of Queen's Eloise's recent ascendancy to the Western Lands throne. She's only recently crown-plonked. The cushions on her royal seat would have barely molded themselves to the shape of her posterior."

Coratina shook her head. "I'm unconvinced."

"I'll tell you why she's not in the Unseen," snorted Aglandau. "I met the pipsqueak. She's nothing like her mother. Nothing at all. She's a fraction, a sliver, a flyspeck of a girl who has no more business wearing a crown and holding a scepter than a moldy papaya. Fuuuugh me, she is a bent coin quarter-wit. The Unseen surely has better things to do than register such a non-entity."

The seer pursed his lips. "If you say so, Your Imperialness."

"I do say so." Aglandau reached for the dish of olives that was never more than an arm's length away, day or night, no matter where she was. She selected a black Nicoise olive marinated in sunflower oil, thyme and sea salt, held it up to the light, and examined it. "Tell me, Throumbolia. Can you detect her sister, the one who failed upward onto the Half Kingdom throne?" Aglandau popped the olive in her mouth.

"Queen Johanna?" He shook his head. "I haven't tried."

The Eastie queen stopped chewing and stared at him.

"You'd like me to try now? Here? In front of you?" His cheeks pinched, and he tried to suppress a look like she'd stirred habanero juice into his custard. "I don't normally..."

"Seer away. Come on. I don't have all day."

He swallowed. "Of course, Your Imperialness." He looked around. "With permission, I'll need to sit."

Aglandau waved him to a chair by the wall. Throumbolia lowered himself onto it, stood, adjusted the cushion, sat, stood, adjusted the cushion some more, sat, wiggled, wiggled some more, closed his eyes, and deepened his breathing. He cracked one eye, saw that both women were watching him, pursed his lips, closed his eyes again, and took a series of increasingly long breaths. Two minutes later, the seer's face contorted—his dented brow tensed, his nose scrunched, and he snorted like the realm's worst snorer. On the exhale, snot flew from both nostrils, speckling the front of his robe. He drew a long series of loud, strained breaths through clamped, bared teeth, and drool bubbled from both corners of his mouth.

"You can see why he didn't want to do this in front of you," whispered Coratina.

Aglandau glanced at her, then returned her gaze to Throumbolia.

"Does this actually work?"

"He's my best seer by a hundred strong lengths. Now shush, please."

Throumbolia carried on for a full ten minutes like a hurdy-gurdy being played at a funeral. Finally, he let loose a belch that could have wilted flowers, took three more clenched-teeth breaths, and stilled. His eyes fluttered open, and he dabbed spittle from his face with his sleeve as he looked around, trying to figure out where he was. His eyes found Aglandau and Coratina and he jerked in sudden awareness. Deep red rushed his face and neck. Clearly, he knew what he must have looked like. "Your Imperialness."

"And?"

"And what?"

"Could you see her? The dandiprat's sister?"

"Oh. Queen Johanna? Yes. Yes, she was there. Nothing particularly significant was revealed. Apparently, she has an affinity for spring beans. But she was detectable."

"There you have it," said Aglandau. "Proof that the problem with the fopdoodle is she's heftless."

"As you say, Your Imperialness," said the seer, his tone hedging.

"That's all, Throumbolia. Keep an eye out for me and let me know if she pops up anywhere. I'll continue planning the next stage of the invasion."

"Yes, Your Imperialness." He bowed his way from the room.

Aglandau turned her full attention to her daughter. Her first advisor had been telling her for months that she needed to find a way to connect more closely with Coratina, to strengthen their bond. She'd suggested trying to take an interest in the things her daughter showed an interest in.

Ugh. That meant theology.

The queen forced a smile on her lips and pointed to her daughter's bound volume. "So tell me. What's the heretical exegesis about?"

Coratina lit up like a cracked oil lamp tossed in a bonfire. "Why, thank you for asking, Mother. You know how when one passes we always hope that they will be chosen to stand with Çalaht?"

"Yes. So?"

"Lipid the Elder's scholarly writings examine what happens if Çalaht deems a soul unworthy of being in her presence through eternity."

"They get an eternity of torment," said Aglandau. "That's no big mystery."

"Lipid doesn't think so. He cites some of the more obscure passages in the *Livre de Protocol* to postulate what he calls the Boredom Penance Principle."

This was followed by one of the most painfully dull explanations of inconsequential thinking the queen had ever come across. *Who cares?* she thought. *By the time you're standing with Çalaht (or not), you're dead. It doesn't matter.*

But it mattered to her daughter, which meant Aglandau paid attention with the front of her mind (or at least appeared to), while the back of her mind continued to scheme.

4

GNARLYWEED

Queen Johanna Umgotteswillen Gumball, Crown-Plonked Monarch of the Northern Lands, stuck her hands into the garden bed up to her elbows, and tried to find and yank out the taproot of a gnarlyweed plant that had sprouted. Gnarlyweed lived up to its name, and Johanna had found that the least bit of the plant left in the soil would, given time, take over the whole place. She was vigilant to remove all traces of it, and careful not to let her weak magic for growing things give it any encouragement.

Of all the nooks and crannies in Castle Blotch at Stained Rock (ugh, those names!), this garden was her favorite, especially in the morning like this, before the castle got too busy with demands for her attention. She'd commandeered the garden for her private use and forbade all entry without her explicit permission. The space reminded her of her late uncle, King Doncaster, because he'd asked for her help with his gardens, and that was the reason she'd strong-armed her mother into letting her leave home with him.

True, he'd asked for her help as a pretense for kidnapping her. And true, he and his jester had addled her brain with prattleweed and, in the resulting suggestible state, tried to get her to marry Uncle Doncaster (*yuck!*) in an attempt to take over the Western Lands and All That Really Matters. But if she skipped past all that, in the end, he'd died and she'd been able to take over the vacant throne with the support of her father.

So, there was that. She'd never have been a queen otherwise.

Being queen wasn't exactly a stroll in the park, Johanna was finding. Not that she'd thought it was going to be easy, but she'd had zero idea what it would really be like. In retrospect, she faulted their mother for that. The woman had done little to prepare her to rule, since Eloise was destined to be the one with the crown. Johanna was supposed to be diplomatically married off, not take command of a realm. When she'd maneuvered her way onto the throne, her thought was that if Eloise could do it, so could she. How hard could it be?

Turns out, super hard. And depressing.

Like realizing just how incompetent a king Uncle Doncaster had been, and what a shambles the Half Kingdom was when he carked it. The joint was a wreck. Not just the castle, but the whole queendom. A ruin. A dilapidated mélange of ennui and decay.

Still, if she hadn't left home with him, then the series of unlikely events that had left her with his crown plonked on her head would never have happened. Now the Northern Lands (Johanna insisted that the term 'Half Kingdom' no longer be used) was *her* dilapidated mélange of ennui and decay, and she loved the place.

And in particular, this small garden in the exact middle of the castle grounds, where she'd planted all the cuttings and seeds she'd brought with her from her private garden in Castle de Brague. Her study led onto it, and she'd walled off all other entrances, save one locked gate to which she had the sole key. By decree and design, the garden was her refuge, and she relished its isolation and solitude. It was a place where she could actually string two thoughts together without distraction.

She hadn't realized how important that was.

In Doncaster's honor, she'd planted a bed of carrots in a rainbow of colors. One of her last, fond memories of him was when he'd shown an unexpected interest in them, not believing carrots could be anything other than orange. The purple ones in particular made her think of him, more than just about anything else in the castle.

And thinking of him was good. It meant she wasn't thinking of her sister, and the poisonous letter Eloise had sent.

Johanna pulled out the gnarlyweed, checked that the tap root was whole, and that nothing was left behind. It was too bad the things tasted like week-old hankies from a cholera ward and, as far as she knew, had no medicinal value. The best use she'd found for them was drying them out and using them as kindling.

Johanna splashed water from a pitcher into a stone basin that looked like it had stood there for centuries, scrubbed her hands clean, and dried them on a towel hanging from a peg. She walked into her study, a well-lit, stone-walled room crammed full of tidy shelves and featuring a roll-top writing desk on a raised platform, positioned to give her a clear view of her garden. Before Johanna's arrival, the space had been a cobweb-choked informal dining room. She'd commandeered it, kept the table, brought in a desk and shelves, and turned it into a sanctum that wasn't unlike the Queen's Study back home, except hers didn't have the lived-in feel of the one Eloise had inherited from their mother. But building a study from scratch had saved her the effort of de-Doncastering the late king's study. Better a fresh start.

Johanna pulled Eloise's envelope from her apron pocket, bracing herself. It had hurt to read the hemp parchment pages the first time. It had hurt to read them the tenth time, and now, on what would be the twenty-third reading (not that she was counting), she suspected it would hurt again.

She'd had no idea that her decision would cause so much hurt.

But now she knew, and she felt a jumble of feelings.

The letter started OK.

Dear Jo,

It went downhill from there.

Are you out of your Çalaht-benighted mind? An alliance with Aggie? How could you! Really, Jo. How? Did you form the alliance before or after she invaded Flachberg? Because if it was after, then I can see no excuse other than you hate me.

JOHANNA SIGHED. THEY'D BEEN GETTING ALONG SO WELL, WHICH had been nice, after all those years of unpleasantness. Eloise was first born by only seventeen minutes, and allegedly their birth order was thanks to Seer Maybelle's interference. The fraternal twins had been inseparable until their Thorning Ceremony had cemented Eloise's status as Future Ruler and Heir to the Western Lands and All That Really Matters and Johanna's as "her sister." From that moment on, Johanna knew that she'd forever be the spare button sewn onto the inside hem in the tunic of the realm.

That disappointment had grated on her outlook and demeanor for years.

But then, everything that happened had happened, and *plonk!* A crown ended up on her head, pretty much at the same time as Eloise's. Enmity washed away, and they'd been trading missives and confidences once or twice a week ever since.

And now this.

Johanna slid the pages back into the envelope and put it in a cubby hole of the roll-top desk. She didn't need to read it again, having committed the entire invective to heart.

The thing was, Eloise was right. Johanna hadn't considered the implications of taking Queen Aglandau's coin. Not the short-term consequences or the long-term ramifications. When she discussed the offer of coin with her father, he didn't exactly raise any warnings, either.

Johanna had just been looking for a way to nudge her queendom toward improvement. Half the realm was still covered by the Purple Haze, and the queen's counting house had more echoes than coins. Aglandau's offer to finance improvements like roads and public buildings seemed a Çalaht-sent miracle.

Less so, now.

She was learning the hard way that all coin came with opinions attached, and that some of those were easier to ignore than others.

Eloise's letter deserved a response, and sooner rather than later. Johanna just wasn't sure what to say.

Well, no time like the present.

She reached for a sheet of hemp parchment, one of the nicer ones that had lavender petals pressed into it, and picked up a quill. She held it up to the light and couldn't help noticing that its quality was grossly inferior to the ones she was used to. The feather was too short, the shaft too narrow, and whatever curing process was used to make it suitable for writing left it too soft, meaning she went through many more of them than she should have, which was expensive. Did they even have a Quill and Quillery (Yes We Know They're Not Related Concepts) Guild in the North? If so, they could learn a thing or two from their Westie counterparts. And if not, maybe she could bring in someone to help raise the local standard. It was just one more example of the general malaise she faced in her queendom day after day.

It. Was. Exhausting.

Johanna closed her eyes, took a single long breath, then dipped the quill in her ink pot and started writing.

Dear El,

It was a completely adequate start. Dependable. Solid. Neither offensive nor obsequious.
The problem what should follow that.

Johanna paused, not sure what to write next.

I am...

Another pause.

I am so...

SHE STRUGGLED FOR THE RIGHT WORD. "I AM SO..." SO WHAT? I AM so sorry? So not going to apologize? So embarrassed? So angry? So frustrated? So looking forward to seeing you again so we can talk this out? So going to ignore your last letter and pretend it didn't arrive?

All of it was true.

A patterned rap on her door interrupted—her father's distinctive knock. *Thank Çalaht,* she thought. Then she hesitated. Was he having one of his good days? Or was he having an I'm-going-to-be-vague-and-sad-and-just stare-out-the-window day. The latter were becoming more frequent again.

Johanna put down her quill. "Yes?"

Chafed Motley Gumball née de Chëëëkflïïïnt poked his head around the doorframe, one eyebrow raised.

So, a good day, then. That was a relief.

She waved him in. "Should I say, 'Blessings of the day, Father' or 'Blessings of the day, First Advisor?'"

"Perhaps a bit both." He looked irritated. "He has requested another audience."

"Again? So soon?"

"Unfortunately, yes."

"Ugh."

"He" was Bosana de Coluber, who originally came to her court as Lead Trade Negotiator from the Eastern Lands, along with the Eastie Ambassador Picholine Manzanilla. When Queen Aglandau recalled Manzanilla back to her court, she granted de Coluber the ambassador's sash. Ever since, he'd been demanding an ear and a say in Northern Lands matters that were well beyond what he should have been involved in. De Coluber was a mesmerizing python with luminescent blue scales down his back and pure white ones underneath, and was as scary as they came.

It was his three eyes.

The snake had the usual two on either side of his head, which functioned as one would predict. But in the middle of his forehead there was a third eye that was fully independent of the other two. It would fix on her, unblinking, every time they spoke. The way he locked in on her gave her a feeling like he could look into her soul. She knew that made little sense, but he made her skin crawl.

Johanna wondered if he had some sort of weak magic for perceiving what others thought. She didn't know if such a thing was possible, but she couldn't dismiss the notion. The snake always seemed to anticipate what she was going to say.

Like the hurt being felt by her sister, the interference from the meddling python was an unexpected and inescapable consequence of having taken Queen Aggie's coin.

"I am really not in the mood," groaned Johanna. "Do I have to meet him? He makes me want to toss my biscuits. I can barely stand to be in the same room as him, much less converse."

"I tried to put him off," said Chafed. "He said, and I quote, 'I rather must insist.'"

"He insists." Johanna shook her head. "Well, that's about as compelling as it gets. Insisting is the corker. We're lucky more people don't show up at the castle insisting. It would be chaos. A chaos of insisters."

Chafed nodded with mock seriousness. "A mayhem."

"A bedlam of insisting."

"A turmoil of insistence."

"A pan-de-mo-ni-um of insisting insisters and their incessant insistences." Johanna picked up her quill and twirled it between thumb and index finger. "Do you know what he wants?"

"He didn't say," said Chafed. "Or more, he *wouldn't* say. I asked. He just did that thing that sort of looks like a shrug and remained silent."

"How can a snake shrug?"

"Exactly."

She stabbed the quill in her inkwell, splashing black. "Fine. Please inform Ambassador Bosana de Coluber that the crown will receive him at her usual receiving hours, two days hence."

Chafed quietly coughed.

"Tomorrow?"

He looked at her.

"Today? Really?"

"What can I say? He insisted."

Johanna snorted. "Then I look forward to seeing him this afternoon. Anything else?"

"Actually, there is."

"OK."

Chafed stood in silence, his face drawn into a frown.

"Father, just say it."

"I heard from your sister."

"Oh? So did I." She held up the envelope.

"It would seem she's agitated. Her language was... piquant." His frown deepened. "I'm pretty sure my eyebrows got singed reading it."

"You reckon neither of us should expect a Yule gift from her this year?"

"I wouldn't hold my breath."

"No. I suppose not." Johanna sank her face into her palms. "I thought..."

Chafed placed a hand on her shoulder and gave a small squeeze. "What did you think?"

"I knew being a queen would not be all gourmet Court dinners and fancy frocks. I'm not sure exactly what I expected. But this..." She waved her letter from Eloise, then indicated three eyes for the snake. "This is not what I thought being queen was going to be. It thought it would be more..."

"More what?"

"More fun. More fulfilling, maybe? Less stuff that makes me roll my eyes."

"There is a lot of eye-rolly stuff you have to deal with." He suddenly looked very sad. "Your mother was splendid at keeping the eye-rolly stuff at bay. She had a knack for cutting to the core of matters quickly and finding agreeable solutions. Plus, when she needed to be, she was as tough as century-old hardtack left in the desert."

"You miss her still?"

"With every heartbeat and every breath."

"Me, too." Johanna put a hand over his on her shoulder and returned his squeeze. "I spent so much time since our Thorning Ceremony feeling hurt and angry that I was blinded to the fact that she was actually very good at the queen thing."

"First, you were young. Second, until you had a crown plonked on your own head, you didn't have the frame of reference necessary to make that judgment."

"I suppose. Even so, I regret not learning more from her, even though I was never supposed to be the one with the crown. I could have been more appreciative of the way she conducted herself and managed her queendom."

"She thought there would be more time for that kind of thing," said Chafed. "You were both so young. She didn't want to burden either of you before she really had to. Turns out, that was a mistake."

"Yep." Johanna picked up Eloise's envelope again and tapped it on her desk. "What do I do about this? As searing as it is, there's truth to it."

"Acknowledge the truth. And maybe apologize. That's what I'll be doing."

Johanna allowed herself a shrug. "I guess. But her problems are not my problems. I have plenty of my own. She has a realm to run and political issues? Guess what? So do I. Her problems are tough? Hey! So are mine!"

"Well, you can say that to her. But, figure out a nice way to do it. The two of you are better off working together. The tensions between realms are high enough as it is."

"And whose fault is that? Not mine."

"No, but you don't want to make it worse. You have a role here, too. Let's not lose sight of that."

"I guess." She stood up. "I'll write her back later. Thank you, Father. Unless you have something else, I have some more gnarlyweed to deal with before my receiving hour this afternoon."

"I'll leave you to it."

5

THE PAIN OF MERINGUE

The training hall smelled of sweat and a lingering hint of the burned sage they used to cleanse the room ritually at the beginning of the daily Balancing Way dawn session. Eloise's muscles burned and juddered as she held a plank position. Next to her, Lorch did the same, the effort just starting to show in the tiniest quiver of his arm muscles.

Opposite them, their training master, Sylvia Cloisterfeld, also held herself in a plank, but showed no sign of strain. "Student Gumball," she said. "What value is there in holding a plank for ten minutes?"

Eloise relaxed her gritted teeth so her voice did not come out strained. "Building strength."

"Do you want to quit?"

Her muscles screamed. *Yes. Absolutely freaking yes. This is torture!* "No, Master Cloisterfeld."

"I'm not sure I believe you, but as you wish. We'll keep going. Another two minutes should do." Sylvia sounded almost bored, but Eloise knew it was an affectation. "Student Lacksneck. What do we wish to develop in addition to strength?"

"Flexibility. The Balancing Way requires strength and flexibility."

"Yes. Strength and flexibility are central to everything we do—in our fitness, in our choice and use of tools, and in our mindset." She nodded her chin to indicate the world beyond the hall. "I'm sure I don't need to point out the obvious extension of this. A queen must be strong and flexible in how she approaches everything—how she makes decisions, how she interacts with those around her, especially those who give her advice, and how she treats those under her rule. Similarly, a champion must be strong and flexible in how they ensure the queen's safety, and in defense of her person and her honor."

"Yes, Master Cloisterfeld," said Eloise and Lorch together.

After two minutes more agony, they eased themselves to the rush-covered floor mats with controlled movements. No collapsing allowed.

"Stand, please," said Sylvia. "Grab an iron staff."

No! No! No! No! No! screamed Eloise's muscles. "Yes, Master Cloister-feld," she said. Eloise never let her muscles have the last say in things when it came to her training with Sylvia.

A dozen iron staves sat in menacing silence, stacked on a wall rack, the lightest one at the top, the heaviest at the bottom. They looked innocent enough, poles that came to her mid-bicep when stood on end. They were the same length and thickness as the wooden ones they used for weapons training. But the mere thought of working with them made her want to run as far away as she could.

It was their weight. After three minutes, the top one felt like swinging a tree trunk. She'd never even tried to lift the lowest one.

That one was the one both Sylvia and Lorch reached for.

"Apologies, Master Cloisterfeld," said Lorch, gesturing to the staff. "Please."

Sylvia's eyes crinkled in suppressed mirth. "Be my guest, Student Lack-sneck. If you think you're ready to get to know Berthilda, then please do."

Berthilda? thought Eloise. *The iron staves have names?*

"If you don't mind, I'd like to try."

"By all means."

Eloise was tempted to take the top one, but the previous week, she'd forced herself onto the next one down, and her pride wouldn't let her regress. "Master Cloisterfeld, does this one have a name?"

"Yes. Meringue."

Eloise looked at her. "Meringue?"

"Obviously, it's meant to be ironic."

"Of course, Master Cloisterfeld."

"Let's cycle through the five thrusts. Slow movements, please." Sylvia took a triangular stance and stood Berthilda's slightly lighter cousin to her right. "As slow and controlled as you can make them."

Eloise and Lorch matched her stance and stood with their rods at the ready. At Sylvia's nod, they began. Direct thrust. Counter thrust. Rear thrust. Thrust, low counter. Thrust, high counter. Repeat.

Repeat.

Repeat.

Eloise kept her movements steady and her iron staff controlled and free of tremors. Sweat soon soaked her training tunic and breeks as she moved the iron staff weak length by weak length in lunges and arcs from one motion to the next.

"Student Gumball," began Sylvia. "Why do we train slowly?"

"We train our muscles with slowness so they know what to do at speed."

"Student Lacksneck, what is true victory in the Balancing Way?"

"True victory is the victory you experience over yourself."

"Student Gumball, what does that mean?"

"It is about control," said Eloise. "You have to control yourself before you can control others."

"*Harmonize with* and control others."

"Harmonize with and control others," she repeated. "It requires balance and self-control to first, avoid attacks and, second, respond effectively to the ones you can't avoid. That self-control is central to both the Balancing Way and a harmonious life."

"Correct."

Direct thrust. Counter thrust. Rear thrust. Thrust, low counter. Thrust, high counter.

"Student Gumball, what role does sacrifice play in the Balancing Way?"

This one was new. Eloise had no idea. She gave the only acceptable answer. "Apologies, Master Cloisterfeld. I require you to repair my ignorance."

"Sacrifice is central to the Balancing Way. This can manifest in an infinite number of ways. For example, it requires sacrifice to show up here every day to train. It requires a sacrifice of one's previous world view and mindset to embrace and embody the teachings of the Balancing Way. One may need to sacrifice one's position to create space for an attacker to lose their balance. One must sacrifice comfort and ease to build strength and flexibility." She cut and thrust in silence for a minute, then added, "Sometimes sacrifice is easy. There isn't all that much sacrifice, really, in waking up a little early every day to be here. But sometimes sacrifice is the hardest thing in the world. Sometimes that which must be sacrificed is precious beyond words, and yet, it must be yielded because you know it is the right thing to do. Such is the Balancing Way."

"Such is the Balancing Way," repeated Eloise and Lorch.

"Student Lacksneck, what is the Balancing Way's Principle of Grand Unity?"

"The Balancing Way requires an attitude of oneness, of unifying with everyone and every situation. That means respect for all things, all people, always. Enemy or friend, one must be ready to come into harmony with them."

"Student Gumball, does the Principle of Grand Unity apply when someone is coming at you with murder in their eyes and a hatchet dripping blood?"

Eloise hedged. "The Balancing Way would say 'yes.'"

"Why?"

"It says that by harmonizing with the murderer, you act with economy and rightness."

"You don't believe it?"

"I feel like I understand the theory, but don't know what I'd actually do if it really happened."

Sylvia thrust and swung, thrust and swung. "Student Gumball, have you ever been in a fight?"

Eloise thought about it. There was the time she'd barreled Gouache Snotearrow McCcoonnch into the Purple Haze. And the time Turpy had run over her and she'd ended up burned by a campfire. And the time Turpy had knocked her into the Whacking Great Hole. She'd told Sylvia about all of those before, but none of those seemed like the kind of situation that Sylvia seemed to be talking about. So she said, "Does scrapping with my sister count?"

"Did either of you bleed or break a bone?"

"Bruises only."

"I'm not sure that counts. Have you ever seen a fight with actual blood and damage?"

"We once had traveling pugilists come to court."

"Traveling pugilists," Cloisterfeld scoffed. "They're more about enter-tainment than anything else. You can't even be sure that any blood you saw wasn't corn syrup mixed with chocolate syrup and berry juice. But let's take it as real for the sake of discussion. Was it always the bigger, stronger person who won?"

"Not always."

"What happened when a smaller, weaker person won?"

Eloise tried to remember back to the fights she'd seen, the men and women punching, kicking, scratching, and grappling. There was one man in particular who faced someone twice his size. The man should have lost. His opponent could have tossed him aside or just sat on him. But the other man barely touched him. The small man ducked, wove, and darted, evading and confusing his opponent.

"The smaller man knew where to go," she said. "He anticipated what would happen and put himself somewhere to take advantage of it."

"Yes. Despite our training to build strength, what counts more is how correct we are. Grand Unity helps you be correct, efficient, and effective in your actions."

Cloisterfeld let those thoughts settle.

Lorch looked like Berthilda was going to make him weep. He was finding it hard to keep his movements precise and smooth.

Eloise knew how he felt. Practicing with Meringue was like... well, it was like flailing around with a heavy iron rod. Her arms, shoulders and chest ached like Çalaht's own impacted tooth. The pain of Meringue was almost overwhelming.

Almost.

There was no way she'd quit.

After what felt like ten thousand years, Sylvia said, "Let's move on to hand-to-hand techniques."

Eloise and Lorch alternated with stylized attacks. The defenses all started with some version of "get the heck out of the way" followed by "turn what your attacker has done against them." Eloise found that training as the attacker was just as important as defense, as it taught a different kind of resilience, like learning how to roll gracefully after being thrown, landing hard without breaking bones and, more than once, how to take a punch.

Because the Balancing Way did not involve projectiles like spears or knives, Eloise didn't have to be careful that her weak magic for throwing things might hurt someone. She could participate with complete abandon.

And she did. She could ignore the pain and relish the physicality of it, the ritual, the repetition, the way it slowly, but definitely, changed the way she moved through the castle. If it weren't for being queen, she'd spend hours each day doing Balancing Way training. She could imagine dedicating her whole life to it.

But she *was* queen.

That meant their morning sessions had a strict end time. When the horological cuckoo called the top of the hour, they bowed to each other and finished. Feeling tapped out, but with a happy soreness, Eloise went to find the hot bath that Odmilla de Platypus, her handmaid, would have waiting for her.

6

NOT A FANCY LADY

Eloise emerged from her hot soak ready to break fast and seek what the day would bring.

Instead, the day found her before she'd even had a chance to schmear brunchberry jam on her toasted half bagel. Lady Seneschal Läääcy de Aardvark scuttled into the Salle de la Famille, her expression pinched and her brow knotted. Eloise didn't think of aardvarks as a scuttling, scowling species, but Läääcy was definitely scuttling and scowling. She set down her unschmeared bagel. "Blessings of the day, Lady Seneschal."

The aardvark froze, hunched her shoulders, and looked around behind her, the habits of her years in service kicking in. Then the hair on her cheeks twitched and flattened, and she looked embarrassed. "Oh, I'm still not used to that, Your Highness, and I'm not sure I ever will be. My whole life, 'Lady Seneschal' was Lady Seneschal Älphonsinä Póöòmáäädéëè, and I never wanted to spend more time in her line of sight than I had to. If she was around, the odds of getting more work, a scolding, or both were so high as to be a certainty."

The aardvark smoothed the sides of the black outfit she wore. Póöòmáäädéëè had always worn black robes buttoned up the front from her ankles to collar, decorated only with the barest hint of lace. Läääcy was trying to affect a similar look, possibly to engender a sense of continuity, or maybe a sense of gravitas. But as an aardvark, she just looked awkward buttoned into a tight robe, and it impeded her movement in a way that the former Lady Seneschal never had to tolerate. With an effort, Läääcy forced her shoulders to relax and straightened to her full height. Pinching the seams of her robes, she hiked them a little and curtsied. "Blessings of the day, Your Highness."

"You'll get used to it all, Läääcy. You've only been Lady Seneschal, what, three weeks?"

"Three weeks, two days, and five hours. Give or take. Not that I'm counting or anything. You asked me to take on the role just a little before you went for your parlay in Flachberg."

"You don't feel like you're settling into it?"

"No, ma'am. It's not natural."

"What's not natural?"

"Me running the castle. It's about as unnatural as it gets. I never ran much more than a cleaning crew before. And now I'm in charge of everything? Lady Seneschal Póöòmáäàdéëè used to always point to the sign in the handmaid's gathering room that says, 'Help the queen be the queen.' It was everyone's motto. She said it a hundred times a day. What I didn't know was just how much was involved with that simple phrase. I'm surprised my fur isn't gray from worry." Läääcy stopped, her expression anxious. "Apologies, Your Highness. You don't need to hear me complaining."

Eloise shook her head. "If we're going to make this work, you've got to be able to talk to me. Go ahead."

"Yes, ma'am. If you insist. I really don't think this is working out very well. I'm overwhelmed. I'm in so far over my head that I'd have to hire a troupe of acrobats to toss me up to reach bottom."

"It can't be that bad. Things seem more or less on track."

"It's kind of you to say that, Your Highness. But I'm scrambling from one end of the day to the next, careening from concern to problem to disaster and back. There's all this stuff I didn't know that anyone even had to think about."

She looked at Läääcy. Had she repeated the mistake she'd made with Jerome? Eloise had made the chipmunk her champion because he was her friend and she trusted him. Plus, his mother, Seer Maybelle, had come to her with a vision that she interpreted as meaning Eloise needed to marry her son. The seer's visions were impossible to avoid, but their interpretations were malleable. Naming Jerome her champion had been a dodge, but one that had worked, more or less—until it didn't.

Eloise's decision to appoint Läääcy as Lady Seneschal was, in retrospect, feeling awfully similar. She'd chosen someone she liked and was comfortable with rather than thinking through who might be most qualified. "Maybe you can give me an example of something you didn't realize needed thinking about."

"An example?" The aardvark closed her eyes, curled her snout, and thought for a moment. She opened them again and said, "Radishes."

"Radishes?"

"Radishes. Did you know that radish farmers are a shifty lot?"

"Are they? I hadn't heard."

"They are, Your Highness. Shifty and full of themselves, like if we don't have their precious radishes, the sun will fall out of the sky. Three times now, I've had them deliver a load of radishes and insist that the price they'd been promised—and that they'd agreed to—was much too low, given 'circumstances.'" Läääcy assumed the posture of a radish monger on a cart. "'Oi, m'lady, these 'ere radishes be the best in the queendom. The price was based on yer average-type radishes. But these be supreme quality radishes, which I couldn't but know until they came out of the ground. They're fit for a queen's radish-topped soup, a queen's radish dip, a queen's radish and potato salad with onions, or even, dare I say it, a queen's roasted radishes. Plus, me cart wheel flew off into a ditch on the way 'ere and we was attacked by flying radish-eatin' monsters, which I risked life and limb to fend off. You're lucky we made it 'ere at all. That's worth ten coin more per half strong weight, or my old granny tweren't never born and me ol' grandad never planted a seed.'"

Eloise laughed. "Did you give them more coin for their load?"

"I did not, Your Highness. I told them that if their radishes were so staggeringly fine, then I'm sure there would be a castle somewhere in one of the other realms that would overpay for them. But I would not."

"Well, it seems like you handled that OK."

"I guess. But I'm not comfortable with it. I've never had to haggle with radish mongers before. Or harangue kitchen staff to support Chef. Or decide which silversmith needs to be contacted because some nong knocked over a candelabra and dented it. Or, or, or... There's so much to do, and so much to know."

Eloise gave the aardvark's forearm a gentle, encouraging squeeze. "But you're learning, Läääcy. Aren't you?"

"Somewhat." The aardvark thought for a moment, trying to get the words right. "The problem runs deeper than haggling with the radishers or calling in the silverers. Things are slipping, Your Highness. Things that used to get done aren't getting done, and things that used to get done quickly are getting done slower. Nothing too big. It isn't a catastrophe, or not yet, anyway. But the little things matter and are indicative. Like, I see things that used to get dusted have a layer of dust on them. Scraps that should be taken out for compost are left half a day longer than they should be. And underneath it all, I fear the problem is me."

"You?" Eloise shook her head. "How could someone not dusting or leaving scraps be because of you?"

"Because of who I am." Läääcy curled her snout, a gesture Eloise recognized as her not wanting to let her words out.

"Go on. Help me understand."

"I'm not a fancy lady or a high-born whatsit-hoosie. I'm just an aard-vark from a nowhere backwater called Dudgeon Spit who knows a lot about polishing brass and cleaning out hearths, but not a lot else. Not long before you asked me to be Lady Seneschal, my most important task was to not drop your breakfast, and even then, I wasn't always successful." She opened her claws and mimed dropping a serving tray, mouthed, "Oopsie," then mimed cleaning it up. "Now, I know I'm not dim. I know I can pick new things up and I'm learning all the time. But there's a perception issue. The others don't see me as someone they need to pay much attention to. I'm just that cleaner who for some crazy reason, Three—sorry, Your Highness, no disrespect, but the others sometimes call you that—put in charge of everything. They think I've been put well above my station, and they're right. They're not scared of me the way they were Lady Seneschal Póöòmáäàdéëè. And I don't want them to fear me. I just want them to do their jobs and then look around, see whatever else needs doing, and then go do that next. When I see a mantle that hasn't been dusted for three more days than normal or that dirty linens are piled up, it's a sign that there are cracks in the way of things. It doesn't bode well. And that scares me."

"I see what you're saying." Eloise unconsciously did her wrist flexing exercise, a habit built after the fracture healed and she got her cast off. "Let me ask, do people say things to your face? Is there direct disrespect?"

"Often enough to make it uncomfortable, but not so often that it's a genuine problem. Not yet, anyway. There are a couple of problematic cleaning wenches, and I've heard a few of the lackeys sniggering behind my back, but it isn't widespread."

"Hmmm... I'm going to have to think about this and figure out what to do. Is there anything else?"

Läääcy did her snout curling thing again.

"Please, Läääcy. I need to know."

"Yes, Your Highness. It's your coronation."

"My coronation? What about my coronation?"

"It's apparently my job to organize it. I've never even been to a formal coronation. I didn't even get to see your Crown Plonking Ceremony because I was in the kitchens. How am I supposed to know what to do? I have a strong weight of questions, starting with who gets to be invited and how much fancy food I'm supposed to have prepared?"

"Wait a second. I might be able to help you with some of that. Come with me." Eloise stood and walked through the Salle de la Famille back into the Queen's Bedchamber. There was a stack of scrolls and pieces of hemp parchment on her bedside table, items she was supposed to read before falling asleep in a pile that never seemed to get smaller. She rifled through the materials until she found a dozen pages scrawled front and back in crimped handwriting and pinned together with a straight pin. She returned to Läääcy and handed them to her.

The aardvark took them, glanced at the first one, furrowed her brow, and flicked through the rest. "They're in Lady Seneschal's handwriting."

Eloise nodded. "Lady Seneschal Póöòmáäàdéëè spoke to me about my formal coronation. I have to admit that I had trouble mustering much enthusiasm, but she convinced me of its importance. I asked her for a list of items that needed a decision from me, and that's the result. I'm sure it doesn't cover everything, but it might help you get across some of it."

Läääcy went back to the first page and began reading more carefully, mumbling as she went. "Number of formal balls... Color palettes... Dress code... Dignitaries... Laudatory speeches... Feast food for towns and villages... Musical acts... Non-musical entertainments..." As she read, the aardvark started blinking and snuffling, then she wiped her eye with the back of her forepaw.

"Läääcy, what's the matter? Why are you crying? This is supposed to help."

"Your Highness, I can't do this. Like, musicians? I have a niece who's learning to play the snout lute, so that might be entertaining. But I don't know any others, or where I'd go to find some. And the rest of it?" She waggled the pages. "Having me do this has disaster written all over it in gold ink and letters with all those fancy curlicues. I'm just not ready to do this kind of thing."

Eloise realized she knew just how Läääcy felt, because it was exactly what she felt about herself. "I'm too young." "This is too much." "I'm not ready." "Can't someone just give me some Çalaht-cursed answers?" Those were all things she'd thought over and over since her Crown Plonking. Those thoughts and others like them gave expression to the many, many doubts she had about wearing the crown—doubts she felt every day.

She held out her hands to her Lady Seneschal, took her forepaws, and gave them a little squeeze. "I hear what you're saying. Look at me, Läääcy. Look me in the eyes."

The aardvark raised her head until her gaze got to Eloise's nose. Close enough.

"Läääcy de Aardvark, I believe in you. I believe you will rise to this moment. I trust you. That's why I want you doing this. But I don't want you to be miserable. If it really isn't working out, then we'll be honest with each other and change what's going on. Please do the best you can for a couple more weeks. If we both think you're the wrong person for the job, then we'll find someone else."

"Truly, Your Highness?"

"Truly." Eloise gave her paw a little more of a squeeze, then let go. "But I need you to promise me to try your hardest and do your best. I know you always do your best, but you know what I'm saying. Keep trying your hardest and keep doing what you can to get better."

"Yes, Your Highness. I understand. My hardest. My best. I will."

"And I will do the same. I'll try my hardest and do my best. We'll support each other that way. OK?"

Läääcy nodded.

"And maybe we can find someone to help with the whole coronation thing. A party planner or someone."

"That... That would be most welcomed. It's just not something I know, and I don't want to have you embarrassed in front of all of the queendom just because I'm ignorant of what a good coronation needs." She hesitated. "Do you know anyone who does that kind of thing?"

"No. Not at all. No idea. How about you?"

"Oh, Your Highness." The aardvark laughed like it was the most ridiculous idea ever. "Not in the slightest."

"Well, I'll see what I can do. And if you come up with someone, please let me know."

"I will, I will." But she was still chuckling when she said it, so Eloise did not hold out much hope. "I'd best get on with the day. Thank you, Your Highness, for your confidence in me." She went to leave, but paused at the door. "Oh, First Advisor asked me to tell you she'll be waiting for you at the Queen's Study when you've finished breaking fast."

"Thanks. I'll scarf this down and get going."

Läääcy put her forepaws on her hips. "You'll do no such thing, Your Highness. You'll break your fast at a proper and reasonable pace. No one's attacking Castle de Brague. No one's dying. There's nothing going on in all the queendom that's stopping you from having your bagel with brunchberry jam. I'll let First Advisor know you'll be in your study in 45 minutes."

Eloise grinned.

"What?" asked Läääcy.

"That, right there, is helping the queen be the queen."

"I suppose it is, ma'am." With a small smile, she was off.

❧ 7 ☙

OLIVE ALLEY

As a rule, Älphonsinä Füüürchtbarkeit Póöòmáäàdéëè was entirely unimpressed by castles and completely blasé about the trappings of royalty. After all, her entire working life had been spent in a castle, her days filled with helping, cajoling, directing, or disciplining one person or another in support of the Gumball family (and sometimes doing exactly that to the Gumballs themselves, if subtly). It had started on her twelfth birthday. That was the day her mother had walked her into Castle de Brague, found her second cousin, who was a Lady in Waiting in Waiting (the castle service equivalent of sitting on the bench at a hockey sacking game) and, using the full force of her will and family pressure, practically forced her relative into giving young Älphïë a trial run at being her assistant. Älphonsinä had immediately taken to life at Court and service to the crown. Competence and hard work saw her rise through the ranks, reaching Senior Lady in Waiting, and finally, toward the end of One's disastrous reign, Lady Seneschal.

And she'd done a pretty admirable job, if she didn't mind saying so herself. And it had gone just fine, more or less, until the day she'd packed her bags and left the flibbertyqueen to her own devices.

46

So walking toward Castle Lucques in Gordal, the center of the Eastern Lands queendom and the residence of Queen Aglandau Ponentine and her family, should have been no big deal.

And yet, Lady Seneschal (Retired (in a Huff)) Póöòmááàdéëè felt an unexpected jumble of emotions as she approached the line at the castle gates. Sure, there was excitement in anticipation of seeing her friend Picholine Manzanilla again, the first time since the Eastie had left Brague and her role as an ambassador for the Eastern Lands. There was also a vague sense of "wrong" about being in Aglandau's realm at all. The flibbertyqueen's late mother and the Eastie queen were famous for not getting on, which meant that for decades, "us" had been the Western Lands and All That Really Matters and "them" had included anything east of the Adequate Wall of the Realms.

Póöòmááàdéëè shook that off. She wasn't doing anything wrong. Not at all. She was having morning tea with her friend, whom she hadn't seen for weeks. It was something she was allowed to do. Just as she was allowed to travel to the Eastern Lands and not have her mind filled with worry from dawn until candle snuff that Queen Eloise (the late one, not the flibbertyqueen) would be discomfited, inconvenienced, or distracted from the important work of ruling her realm. Whether or not that particular household fell apart was no longer her concern.

And the coronation! She was especially glad to no longer be responsible for planning for the flibbertyqueen's enthronement and associated balls, parties, and receptions. The wee sniveler had been obstinately uncooperative every time Älphonsinä had brought the matter up. She didn't seem to grasp the simple concept that a formal coronation was a Big Deal. It was much bigger than a mere Crown Plonking Ceremony, and even that, the stupid zounderkite had ruined with her clumsiness.

Shedding all those burdens had made her feel two decades younger, even if it left her completely unsure what to do with her life.

Which is why she'd jumped at Manzanilla's invitation to visit her realm.

And now she was here.

It was something she had every right to do and not feel odd about.

Not at all.

Before she knew it, Lady Seneschal (Retired) reached the front of the line at the castle gate. Three guards at desks ensured that the line moved quickly and efficiently. A strapping, angel-faced Eastie guard fifteen years her junior wearing a bottle green uniform, epaulets and a ceremonial sash waved her forward to the middle desk. "Name?"

"Älphonsinä Póöòmáäàdéëè."

He looked for her name on his scroll. "Not here, sorry."

"No?"

"No. Sorry."

Her shoulders sagged.

"Keep your olives on your branch, love," said the guard. "You said it was 'Älphonsinä Póöòmáäàdéëè?'" His thick Eastern Lands drawl gave her name several syllables it didn't normally have.

Utterly charming. She suppressed a smile. "That's right."

"And what was your business today, Mistress?" (This came out, "Ay-yund whay-ut ee-yuz yur bee-uhz-ness, too-uh-day, Mee-uh-stress?")

Again, absolutely charming.

"I'm supposed to be meeting Picholine Manzanilla."

"Ah. Right. Apologies." He turned to the guard on his right. "Jeffers. You have the VIP list?"

"I've got it." The guard to his left picked up a scroll and handed it to him. "Fresh from the scribe."

"Ah, here you go, love. The VIP list is your friend. All good, love." He smiled, and with a wink, waved her through.

A wink?

A wink!

No one had winked at her like that in yonks. A decade of yonks. An eon of yonks. She had to purse her lips to keep a girlish giggle from bubbling its way out. Plus, he'd called her "love." Three times.

How unexpected. As was the tingle she felt in response.

Well, Älphïë, she said to herself as she nodded a thank you and stepped through the gateway. *Apparently, you're worthy of a wink from a handsome guard. Not dead yet, then.*

Just beyond the gates was a large piazza surrounded by grand buildings. The castle proper was at the far end of the open space, and between her and the heavily guarded door was a swarming market humming with commerce.

But what a castle! Póöòmáäàdéëè guessed the main part of it rose to an incredible 65, maybe 70 lengths above the market square. Even more impressive were the towers. The tallest was twice that high again. They seemed to touch the sky itself. The phrase "high enough to see Çalaht's knickers" came to mind, but she pushed it aside as blasphemous.

The castle's stones were in a graduated pattern of olive hues—shades blending from brown at the bottom to green at the top. The effect recalled an olive orchard on an autumn day when olive fruits hung heavy on their trees.

"Stunning," muttered Póöòmáäàdéëè. "Just stunning."

A horological cuckoo called the quarter hour, which meant she had time to wander the market before meeting Manzanilla. Like the castle, the merchants were all dressed in olive hues. One sold crockery and cooking utensils, a second had open piles of spices on ceramic plates, and a third seemed to specialize in octagonal fruits. Póöòmáäàdéëè found she could buy toys that looked like they'd been rescued from children who'd grown up and lost interest, wine glasses whose stems were all bent at strange angles, and a pair of shoes with ridiculously high heels. One vendor had bags full of short segments of string.

When Póöòmáäàdéëè asked what one did with lots of short pieces of string, he replied, "Whatever you fancy, ma'am. Whatever you fancy." Perhaps strangest of all was a teapot with seven spouts arranged in a circle around the top, like the fingers of an upturned hand holding a small melon. What kind of tea party required a pot with seven spouts? She was tempted to buy it just because of how odd it was.

When Póöòmáäàdéëè saw a sign shaped like an arrow that read "Olive Alley," she knew she had to go that way. Olive Alley was known as the most olive-y place in all the realms. Since she was a little girl, she'd heard of the olive treasures one could find there—decorative olives, large olives, tiny olives, hundreds of flavors of olive oil, rare olives, common olives, olives with healing properties, olives that claimed magical properties, olives favored by collectors, pots of perfect olives, barrels of malformed olives, and speculators who sold olive futures—all crammed together like olives in a jar. She couldn't wait to see the marvels of the place for herself.

She turned left into Olive Alley and idled her way from one stall to the next. Póöòmáäàdéëè had expected to be overwhelmed. She wasn't. Quite the opposite, in fact. It seemed strangely empty, both of customers and vendors.

She stopped at a stall where a heavily pregnant young woman in a dark green dress sat knitting. A child at her feet was engrossed in forming geometric patterns using sliced olives.

"Excuse me," said Póöòmáäàdéëè. "Is the Olive Alley market not on today?"

"No, ma'am, it's open," said the woman, setting down her needles. She heaved herself up from her seat and stood with her hands resting on her belly. "This is it."

"Hmm. Not what I expected."

The young mother nodded. "You were expecting it to be cheek to jowl with olives and olive sellers?"

"Yes."

"That's the way it was a few years ago. Much less so today."

"Really?"

"It's the blight, ma'am."

"Blight?"

"The olive blight. Terrible thing, it is. Devastating to so many groves. That's why it's so empty here. For most folks, it's not worth making the trip these days, as they don't have the olives to sell."

"That's... That's awful."

"Yes, ma'am. The blight is awful, and the olives that come out of it are horrible. Scrawny, scrunchy, measly little things." Then she waved her hands over her wares. "But not mine, ma'am. None of my olives have come anywhere near any blight. They're certified blight-free. And you can see it." She took a toothpick from an olive-shaped dispenser, lifted the lid of one of her pots, stabbed an olive, and handed it to Póöòmáäädéëè. "Have you ever had a Thassos, ma'am? Straight from my grandfather's orchard. It's the only olive you can eat straight from the tree when ripe."

"An olive that doesn't need brining? I've never heard of that." She took the toothpick from the woman and bit into the olive, then raised her eyebrows. "It's not bitter."

"No, ma'am. All the Thassos needs is sun and hot temperatures to reduce the bitterness. That, and my grandfather's love. That seems to help. Also, keeping my grandma out of the grove. It's like the olives can feel her bitterness and absorb it. But that's enough about my life. So, how many jars would you like? Two? Three? Tell you what, I'll sell you three for the low price of two."

Póöòmáäädéëè considered the state of the woman's middle, the daughter at her feet, the paucity of offerings on her table, and the meager presence in Olive Alley. "Three for two sounds nice. How much?"

The woman said a number.

Póöòmáäàdéëè froze in the middle of digging coins out of her purse. As Lady Seneschal, she'd been responsible for procuring plenty of olives. The young woman's price was three, maybe four times the amount one would expect, even for a rare species of olive. Was the woman trying to dupe her? Did she take her for a rube, or maybe just an ignorant tourist?

"I see you've hesitated," said the woman. "What can I say? It's the blight. Supplies are tight and prices aren't what they were even a month ago. Or last week. That's why I offered you the three-for-two deal—to lessen the sting somewhat." Unconsciously (or perhaps consciously), she rubbed her blossoming middle.

"I see," said Póöòmáäàdéëè. "I guess a spike in prices makes sense if there's a blight on." Given how much the Easties loved their olives, she was surprised they weren't rioting in the streets.

"I can throw in a string bag to make them easier to carry, if that helps."

The former Lady Seneschal hesitated a few moments more. It really was a steep price.

But...

But here she was in the Eastern Lands for the first time. She was on vacation, so expenses were to be expected. Easties were obsessed with olives and she'd regret not having some of them while she was here. Plus, the young woman seemed nice enough, and being that far along in the family way was its own kind of tribulation (not that Póöòmáäàdéëè had personal experience). With three jars purchased, she could give one to her friend Picholine.

She poured out the requested number of coins and handed them over.

"You won't regret it, ma'am. These are truly wonderful olives. Why, just last week I sold some to a woman who said she worked for the queen and would pass some on. I doubt it was true. She was probably just trying to get a better price. But still, you might be eating olives that Queen Aglandau herself has had."

"That would be something." Póöòmáäàdéëè heard the horological cuckoo call three-quarter hours. "I need to be going, but thank you for this." She handed over her coins and picked up the net bag with her jars. "What is it you Eastern Landers always say? Something about drought?"

"We say, 'May you be forgiving like a grove in drought, resilient like branches in the wind, and may Çalaht bless your harvest with bounty. All these things I wish you.'"

"I wish them to you as well."

"Thank you ma'am. Enjoy your olives while you still can. Who knows what it will be like a year from now."

Riots, thought Póöòmáäàdéëè. *There will be olive riots.*

❧ 8 ❧

HAMSTER CEMETERY
VOLUNTEERISM

"**Ä**lphïë, Älphïë, Älphïë." Picholine Manzanilla stretched out her arms—not for a hug (she wasn't a hugger), but in general welcome. "I'm so glad you could make it to Castle Lucques. How was your trip to Gordal?"

Actually, it had been a misery. Póöòmáäàdéëè had shared a public carriage with a chittering bilby who was heading east to a convention of Protocol scholars, hoping to convince them to revise the *Livre de Protocol* to remove the many clauses that slandered bandicoots. *Good luck with that one*, Póöòmáäàdéëè had thought, nodding as the bilby cited, chapter and verse, each of the offending passages. On her own, the bilby would have been tolerable, but the two of them had also shared the carriage with a family of flatulent fruit bats who hung from the ceiling and fouled the air as they slept.

"It was fine, just fine," said the former Lady Seneschal. "I'm so glad to see you again. I've brought you a small something." She removed one of the olive jars and handed it to her. "Purchased here in the market, so you know it's the real deal."

"Oooh, Thassos. My grandmother had a fondness for them. I shall think of her, and of you, as I eat them. Thank you." Manzanilla air-kissed Póöòmáäàdéëè's cheeks. "Now, I hope you also brought your appetite, as I have a surprise for you."

"A surprise?"

"We won't be having morning tea on our own."

"No?"

"Her Imperialness, Queen Aglandau, has said that she'd like to meet you."

"Really? Whatever for?"

Manzanilla shrugged. "Who knows why a queen does what a queen does? I mentioned to her that I knew you, and that was enough for her. Now, come, our queen awaits."

Póöòmáäàdéëè followed Manzanilla through halls that were as grand as those at Castle de Brague, but in a completely different style. The Gumball queens had varied and eclectic tastes over the centuries, so the rooms, halls, walls, and chambers veered from the ornate to the austere. Castle Lucques looked like a single architect and a single designer had worked hand-in-hand to create the entire building. It went without saying the colors were shades of olives and the art was all olive-themed. She wouldn't have expected anything different. But there was a unity of vision that had been executed with grace and flair. One hall had decorations that made her feel like she was walking through the trunks of a giant olive grove, while another had olive leaves of every shape and variety, almost as if it were a historical record or a botany text. There were olive jars on plinths, ceramic olives, and examples of both ancient and modern tools of the olive trade—clippers, cutters, rakes and nets for harvesting, pitters for the kitchen, presses for extracting the oil, and pots and urns for brining. It was impressive, elegant, historical, educational, and testified to the significance of olives in the Eastern Lands psyche and way of life.

This, more than anything, made her feel as far from home as she'd ever been.

"Picho," said Póöòmáäàdéëè. "How is it that you're back in the Eastern Lands?"

"Travel did not suit me, and home is home." Manzanilla reached over and touched Póöòmáäàdéëè's arm as they walked. "And you, more than anyone, know what it is like to serve a queen. There are demands to be met and orders to carry out. One meets those demands and carries out those orders to raise her up to glory above all else."

Póöòmáäàdéëè wasn't sure she'd ever raised a Gumball queen to glory above all else, but she got the gist. There was stuff to do. You did it, and you didn't spend too much time thinking about it.

"And you, my Älphïë? Now that you are no longer subject to the whims of a child, how are you?"

"It is odd to have one's time be one's own after so many decades. But overall, I'm better, I think."

And that was more or less true. She thought back over the days and weeks since she had relinquished the title of Lady Seneschal. There was the initial rush of excitement when she quit—no longer being subject to the whims of a child was the perfect way to put it. And the flibbertyqueen hadn't even *tried* to talk her into staying. No, she just let her walk away without so much as a note to say, "Thanks for the help all these years. You'll be missed." That had confirmed that she'd made the right decision.

She'd had to find a place to live and move her things (such as they were) out of the castle. Póöòmáäàdéëè had stayed with a second cousin and her wife for a week, but after the third day, she'd felt like an intruder. It took her that full week to find a pleasant cottage to rent, with the cutest window trims and the sweetest sconces she'd ever seen. That gave her a place to be while she figured out if she wanted to remain in Brague, the place she'd lived her whole life. There wasn't much tethering her there, save momentum. Once she had the keys to the cottage in hand, she'd turned her attention to preparing to travel, followed by the travel itself, and the newness of being in the Eastern Lands.

With so much going on, Póöòmáäàdéëè hadn't had much time alone in her own head. If asked, she might have expressed some trepidation about what it would actually be like in that nice little cottage, there on her own with nothing to do but stare at its cute window trims and sweet sconces. She had no idea how she was supposed to fill her days. It's not like she was inclined to knit or volunteer her time at a Çalahtist hamster cemetery. The castle and Court had been her life, her work, her relationships, and her hobby. Well, not her hobby. She didn't believe in hobbies. You either did something for real, or you didn't bother. But it had been everything else.

Maybe hamster cemetery volunteering wasn't a bad idea. At least if she was hanging around with hamsters, she might keep the loneliness at bay.

Póöòmáäàdéëè came back to the moment and found Manzanilla ushering her into an intimate space with walls of carved wood fashioned to look like one was standing in an olive grove. "We call this Ethel's Room."

The room was dominated by a massive olive tree that grew from below the floorboards and crowded a large window. Manzanilla walked over to it, stroked one of its leaves and, in an accent so heavy Póöòmáäàdéëè thought she was making a joke, said, "Good morning, Ethel. How's my favorite? You'll be blossoming soon, won't you? Who's a clever girl? Who's a clever girl?"

This took Póöòmáäàdéëè by surprise. It was the most animated, unreserved moment she'd ever seen from her friend. Odd that she could be so unguarded with a tree. It seemed so out of character.

Manzanilla gestured to a rectangular table large enough for six, but set for five. "This will be us once—"

"I'm here, I'm here," came a heavily accented Eastie voice from an entrance on the other side of the room.

TEA WITH THE QUEEN

The Eastern Lands monarch burst forward like a distracted, olive-green wind. She was about the same age as Póöòmáäàdéëè, but a full head taller, and her braided hair was deep black, despite her years, and oiled to a shine. Aglandau wore a simple silver crown fashioned to look like a wreath made of olive branches. This drew attention away from a wrinkled face and eye make-up so heavy she looked like an actor in a third-rate stage play. Her clothes nodded to the simple garments worn by olive growers, but even the briefest glance at her breeks and tunic revealed cloth so expensive and stitching so fine that it would have been a crime to take them within an olive pit's throw of an actual grove.

Most striking were her teeth, which were stained a brownish green that made her look like she'd requisitioned them from a crypt.

Behind her came a young woman dressed much more conservatively. Her blonde hair was pulled back into a braid that echoed the other woman's, but she had deep blue eyes, unstained teeth, and a way of carrying herself that was studious and sober. She trailed the queen by exactly seven steps, the number Protocol allowed for family members. A niece? Maybe a cousin?

And behind the young woman was the three-eyed snake she recognized from back home. He'd been Picho's offsider. The trade delegate, maybe? She'd been glad that Manzanilla hadn't brought him along to their morning teas together, thinking him the less trustworthy of the Eastern Lands representatives. He'd always given Póöòmáäàdéëè the creeps, and she couldn't help feeling somewhat disconcerted that he was here.

Manzanilla dropped into a curtsy and said, "Your Imperialness. It is an honor to be in your presence once again."

Póöòmáäàdéëè pulled her attention away from the snake and curtsied as well, going much deeper than Protocol specified, despite the protest of her knees. "Thank you for having me in your home, Queen Aglandau."

"Good that you could make it to my fair queendom." She turned her palm upward. "Arise." She gestured to the other woman. "My daughter, Coratina."

This surprised the former Lady Seneschal. She'd heard of a daughter, but the young woman had been kept well away from the gossip heralds. In the absence of details, speculation filled the void, and the gossip herald consensus was that there was something not quite right about her. But, at first glance, nothing struck Póöòmáäàdéëè as particularly amiss.

"And you've likely met my ambassador to the Half Kingdom, Bosana de Coluber," said the queen.

"In passing, yes," said Póöòmáäàdéëè. "Nice to see you again." Even though it wasn't.

As the second round of curtsies with Coratina (but not the snake) took place, Aglandau stepped to the tree and touched one of its leaves. Like Manzanilla, the monarch dropped into what, to Póöòmáäàdéëè's ears, sounded like a mockery of an Eastie accent. "Good morning, Ethel. How's my girl today? You're looking very good. No spots. That's what we want."

This made the former Lady Seneschal wonder if everyone in the Eastern Lands talked to their olive trees, or there was something special about this one, but she held her tongue, worried it might be rude to ask. However, the daughter didn't follow suit, nor did de Coluber, so who knew?

The queen turned back around. "Fuuuuhg me, I'm fuhgging starving. Let's have some food."

The five of them took their seats, Aglandau at the table's head and de Coluber to her right. As soon as they were settled, two serving wenches and a serving lackey came through a side door with covered dishes on trolleys. The lead wench came over to the queen, ducked a small bow, and lifted the cover, revealing an artistically arranged assortment of foods. She gestured to each as she named them. "Black olive cake made on spelt, featuring pomegranate molasses. Olive oil breakfast cake made with applesauce and topped with fresh mint and blackberries. If you prefer savory, there's olive focaccia with an olive tapenade. As a standalone sweet, we have Kalamata olive brittle. For Princess Coratina, a strawberry aquafaba mousse." She indicated the teapot. "The tea is made from a combination of olive leaves and olive tree bark. And for the princess, haggleberry."

The queen nodded, apparently disinterested. The serving wenches and lackey scurried to portion out food to the four women, then left the remaining food on serving trays in the middle of the table. The snake's plate remained empty.

"I hope you don't mind, Your Imperialness," said Manzanilla. "I organized these Eastern Lands specialties for morning tea today. This is Lady Seneschal's first trip to our realm, and I know she has a penchant for sweets and delicacies."

"That I do," said Póöòmáäàdéëè. "Ambassador Manzanilla and I bonded over the Ultimate Delicacies Selection at my favorite café, On Golden Scone."

Manzanilla picked up a slice of focaccia. "I miss their mushroom barbecue burgeritos. Those were Çalaht-kissed. Also, Älphonsinä, I'm no longer an ambassador. For me, that title exists as a memory on a history scroll somewhere. Her Imperialness has honored me by naming me her Fourth Advisor."

"My congratulations." Póöòmáäàdéëè hoped her smile came across as sincere. Had her friend done something wrong? If the setup in the Eastie court was anything like back home, a Fourth Advisor role had the same level of responsibility as a shoeshine lackey. She hoped Manzanilla was OK. "As you know, I'm in a similar position. It's 'former' Lady Seneschal for me now. Or perhaps, at best, Lady Seneschal (Retired). My use of that title is also relegated to the history scrolls."

Aglandau grunted and furrowed her brow. "You're telling me your queen did not allow you to keep your title when you left her service?"

"To be honest, Your Imperialness, it wasn't even something that we discussed." Póöòmáäàdéëè set down her fork and dabbed the corners of her mouth with her napkin. "The young queen and I parted ways rather abruptly. My emotions were rather..." She sought an appropriate word. "They were piquant in the moment. I was ready to never see her again, and I suspect she shared the sentiment. Residual use of my title might have come up for discussion had things been amicable. But they weren't. Instead..." She smoothed her napkin back onto her lap, then gestured toward the room around her. "Instead, here I am in one of the finest buildings I've ever had the chance to see, enjoying a splendid morning tea in amiable company. It's an honor I would otherwise not have had. So, silver linings." The last three words came out a little sadder than she'd intended.

"Yes, yes," said Aglandau, waving her fork like she heard that kind of thing all the time. The queen turned her full attention to her olive cake, shoveling down several mouthfuls. "Tell me," she said, chewing. "What do you think of her? I mean, beyond the obvious fact that you left her service."

"What do I think of Queen Eloise? I couldn't possibly say."

"Why not? Why should you feel any allegiance toward the woman you no longer answer to, whose service you so abruptly left?" The queen stabbed another piece of cake. "I'm not asking you to dish on her mother, whom you served so loyally for so long. For that matter, I'm not asking you to dish at all. I'm simply asking for your professional opinion of the current monarch."

Póöòmáäàdéëè felt put on the spot. She glanced at Manzanilla, who was carefully cutting up her focaccia, at Princess Coratina, who was looking at her mother, face blank, and at de Coluber, who sat coiled on his seat, his weird third eye unblinking. Was this whole invitation to morning tea just a setup? Or had Queen Aglandau imposed herself on the situation opportunistically? "With respect, Your Imperialness," she said, "how could my opinion of the young queen possibly make any difference?"

"My information sources—"

"Spies, I think you mean," said Póöòmáäàdéëè. Then her cheeks reddened. "Apologies, I shouldn't have interrupted."

Aglandau made a peculiarly Eastern Landish noise in her throat, like she was trying to clear an olive seed. Póöòmáäàdéëè had heard Easties use the sound over the years to convey everything from disinterest to disdain, or, as the queen seemed to use it now, to accede a point. "Spies then, if we're being blunt. The Westies have them here. They're part of doing a queen's business." She tilted her head toward Manzanilla. "Once upon a time, Picholine was one of them. A pretty decent one, if I may say so."

Póöòmáäàdéëè wasn't sure what to make of that. Had Manzanilla culti-vated her as an intelligence source? She would have expected it from the snake, but from her friend? She felt the tips of her ears turning red. Had her friendship with Picho been nothing more than a ruse?

The queen put down her fork. "Spies are an odd breed, and the communications they provide are, given the secrecy they require, heavy on facts and light on color. Those facts always strike me as having come from a long way away, like someone yelling across a canyon." She stood, went back to Ethel the tree, and put a fingertip in the soil, testing its moisture. With her back turned, she said, "I met your child queen at our parlay, but we didn't speak all that long. I don't mind telling you, I was singularly unimpressed. She struck me as a lightweight." The queen gestured toward Manzanilla and de Coluber. "That's what these two had led me to expect. But..." She let the word linger as she turned back around. "Maybe I was hasty. Perhaps I rushed to conclusions." Aglandau considered the dirt on her finger, seemed to approve of what she saw, and took a cloth from a table next to the tree and wiped it clean. She looked straight at Póöòmáäàdéëè and softened her tone. "Our queendoms need to coexist in peace. Any insight that I can garner from you that might help make that happen would be a blessing for both realms."

This pronouncement sounded distinctly like blown smoke to Póöòmáäàdéëè. If she'd had even a soupçon of affection for the third Queen Eloise, she might have leapt to her defense.

But she didn't, so she didn't.

Instead, she let the statement stand at face value. "That's a sentiment we can all agree on, Queen Aglandau."

"Good. I'm glad we can see eye-to-eye on that." Aglandau lifted a serving tray toward her. "Have another piece of black olive cake."

It was a gesture of peace, and Póöòmáäàdéëè acquiesced. "It's certainly very good."

Aglandau herself put the slice on her guest's plate. A second gesture of goodwill. "So, anything useful, any color you can provide... You have our full attention."

The former Lady Seneschal took one more bite of cake to buy a few moments, then began with less care than she would have three months before. "Queen Eloise the Second was hard-working and honorable. She had a good grasp of what it took to be a queen. This new queen, not so much. Eloise the Third was an obstinate, self-absorbed, high-maintenance child. She was not my favorite of the twins, although that's something you've probably already heard from Picholine. With Princess Johanna, you knew where you stood. She was clear about her likes and dislikes. Like, she loved strawberries and hated asparagus.

You knew about both. And she could make a decision, even if it rubbed you the wrong way. And she was tractable. Still is, I think. I could always achieve an outcome by bargaining with seeds she could plant in her garden. Princess Eloise was much... how to put it... odder. I just never warmed to her."

"Odd how?" asked the queen.

"She was very particular, but in a persnickety way. She had these habits, and everyone had to accommodate them. For example, her gowns all had to be stored in order of hue, or the items in her room had to be placed in specific locations and at exact angles. Little things, small deviations, could send her into a near panic, or she would become petulant or dysfunctional. Another example was that she had issues with needing to be clean, and what could, or couldn't, come in contact with her skin. That the girl got through her Thorning Ceremony was a minor miracle."

De Coluber spoke for the first time. "My sources said she cheated." His tone conveyed accusation rather than information.

"I'd heard she'd been clever." That was Princess Coratina, also speaking for the first time. "I hated my Thorning Ceremony. Loathed it." She shuddered visibly at the memory.

"Everyone hates their Thorning Ceremony, Cora. That's sort of the point."

"I wouldn't say she cheated," said Póöòmáäàdéëè. "But I also wouldn't say that what she did was in the spirit of the ceremony. Call me a traditionalist, but finding a loophole to deal with the thorns seemed... I don't know... Not quite right. The Thorning Master let her get away with it, and the late queen accepted the results. But the Thorning Master was new to the position, and the late queen just wanted the thing done. The current Queen Eloise is more grown up now, of course, but in the weeks that I served her as Lady Seneschal..." Póöòmáäàdéëè trailed off, her decades-long habit of never speaking ill of her monarchs lingering. She cleared her throat and continued. "Suffice it to say, I'm here now, not there. The child did not inspire confidence. Nor did she seem to have much confidence in me. All that goes to the larger issue with the current Queen Eloise. She waffles about, muddling through from one end of the day to the other. She's hardly a strong queen. About half her Privy Council vacated their chairs within a week or two of her assuming the throne, and the ones who are left are not the sharpest arrows in the quiver. Maybe it's too soon, but she doesn't convey a sense of having any kind of agenda. If we are being honest, I have profound worries for her reign. And yet..."

Aglandau leaned forward, eyebrows arched. "Yes?"

"Those closest to her are devoted. They give her fierce loyalty, whether or not she deserves it. Clearly, I am in the 'not' category, but there are those who disagree."

"Why?" asked de Coluber.

"I don't know for certain. If one bothered to ask, they might cite things like the fact that she allegedly broke the spell that caused the Purple Haze. But I've seen no evidence that she had anything to do with anything. It makes me wonder what they see in her. Evidently, it's something that I don't."

"Nor do I," agreed Aglandau. "Perhaps you can continue telling us about the twins when they were girls?"

Another forty-five minutes passed with the former Lady Seneschal relaying key moments from Eloise and Johanna's childhood. As she spoke, the others gave her their full attention.

Perhaps she was a bit more free with details of the inner workings of the Western Lands and All That Really Matters, but it was just nice to actually feel valued. And heard.

Such a change from that flibbertyqueen.

Eventually, the food had been eaten and the tea drunk. Somewhere in the castle, a horological cuckoo called the hour.

Aglandau slid her chair back from the table and the other women immediately stood. "Fuuuuuuuuhg me, I'm stuffed." She belched without restraint, then stood and offered Póöòmáäàdéëè the back of her hand to kiss. "Your insights have been so incredibly valuable—all received in the name of peace, of course."

"Of course," said Póöòmáäàdéëè. "It's wonderful to have met you, Your Imperialness. And you, too, Princess Coratina."

Aglandau gave a regal wave of the hand. "The rest of the day calls, my lovelies. Delighted to have met you, Lady Seneschal."

She, the princess, and the snake, were gone before Póöòmáäàdéëè could say another word.

When they'd left the room, Manzanilla turned to her friend with a big smile. "You were stupendous, Älphïë. Just splendid. I hadn't planned this, but it couldn't have gone better."

"Thank you, Picho, for your hospitality. It was a morning tea like none other."

As Póöòmáäàdéëè made her way out of the castle and back toward the gate, she noticed she was feeling unsettled. "You've done nothing wrong," she muttered to herself. "Nothing."

But still, the taste that was left in her mouth wasn't exactly pleasant.

❦ 10 ❦

A SIMPLE ASK

While her former Lady Seneschal sipped tea with her rival, Eloise sat in Castle de Brague's Receiving Room wearing the Come On, For Çalaht's Sake, Be Reasonable Cape. The doors, normally kept open when the queen sat in attendance, were closed. No herald announced supplicants and petitioners, no scribe took official notes, and no gossip heralds scavenged for tidbits that could be reshaped into something scandalous. Not even First Advisor was there.

It was just Eloise and Naranbaatar Enkhtuya, Ambassador for the Central Ranges. The mare stood tall, proud, and with the haughty formality and complete stillness she always displayed. Her glossy coat, with its draftsman's precise delineation between white in the back and black in the front, was immaculate and dust-free, meaning she'd not been traveling recently.

The horse chortled.

An actual chortle.

"You want what?"

"An alliance," said Eloise. "It's a simple ask. I'd like to establish a formal alliance with the Us, as the ruling species of the Central Ranges and representing all people of that realm."

The mare snorted this time—a wet snort that left no doubt as to her opinion of the idea. "That's hardly a simple ask. His Alacrity Khan Nergüi Unbenannt Nimetuseta is disinclined to form alliances. You have spent time with the Us. Do we strike you as an alliance type of people?"

"No. You don't."

"The problems of the Not Us and the savages do not concern the Us overly much. Such has always been our way. That is unlikely to change because you have some sort of need."

"I know that I'm asking you to consider going beyond your normal proclivities."

The mare's ear twitched. "So, why ask it of us when you know we won't?"

Eloise allowed herself a sigh. "Because I need the help."

"I could convey that to the khan, but you know the first question he'll ask me? 'What's in it for the Us? What value would we derive from such an arrangement?'"

"Peace in the realms?" Eloise's voice was smaller than it should have been.

"We have that already. None in the Central Ranges dare go against us."

"The threat you need to worry about will not come from within the Central Ranges. It'll come from without. From the east. You share a border with the Eastern Lands, just as we do."

"Maybe you're right, although the border between us and the Eastern Lands is an impassable nightmare, even for the Us." Enkhtuya shook her head slowly. "Look at it from our point of view. There are a lot of strong lengths between Flachberg and the Central Ranges, both physically and strategically. And it's not like our lands are exactly sought after. There's a reason the savages call our realm the Central Carbuncle. I ask you, Queen Eloise, what value would Queen Aglandau derive from instigating aggression against us?"

"I don't have a good answer for that, beyond if she is willing to take territory from me, she will be willing to take it from you."

"That's flimsy and simplistic. But at least it's honest." The mare shifted her weight, resting her opposite back leg. "What would such a pact with you entail? Do all your fights become our fight? Do all your slights and diplomatic tussles drag us into the same arguments and quagmires?"

"No, nothing so sweeping. The terms of the pact would need to have clear triggers to avoid minor events cascading into major ones. But, yes, coming to each other's mutual aid in times of difficulty would be part of it."

"'In times of difficulty.' The more I hear, the less I like." The mare licked her lips, a mannerism that Eloise knew from Hector and the Nameless One was a sign she was thinking through something. "I recognize that my role as ambassador is to represent a channel of communication—us to you and you to us. Please, put together the details of your proposal and I will take it to the khan. You can't expect me to advocate on your behalf, but I won't obstruct or try to sway the khan. Not that I could, anyway."

"I appreciate it. Thank you, Ambassador Enkhtuya."

"You're welcome. But I'll say it to you straight. I dislike your chances of success."

Two hours later, a squat, beautifully-berobed Southie sat before Eloise. In keeping with her request that the meeting be as private as possible, Ambassador Gléëëngarland Póöòíïíntilist arrived at the Receiving Room without the two ferrets he normally had on his head in place of a toupee, sporting instead a knitted cap that had the same pattern (a much less successful look than the pair of mustelids). "Her Majesty Onomatopoeia understands your situation, but our diplomatic relations with the Eastern Lands are already incredibly fraught without openly declaring ourselves against them."

"Are you referring to Southie guest workers being accused of propagating the olive blight, as well as taking work away from Easties?"

"First, 'guest worker' is an offensive euphemism. 'Temporary, exploitable, fungible, seasonal, ill-treated labor' would be more accurate. Also, the line that Southies are taking away work from Easties is made-up nonsense designed to stir up some sort of realm-istic fervor. Southie olive pickers have been helping the Easties harvest their olives for decades, and they do it with no protections or rights, and at wages that are well below what anyone might call fair or just."

Eloise furrowed her brow. "Why do they do it, then?"

"Our people need the work. The Easties need the labor. The arrangement suits both sides, if uneasily. There are those among the Southies who try to demand higher wages and better conditions, but with the number of willing workers outstripping the positions, they have little bargaining power or success with organizing the workforce."

"I can't imagine Queen Onomatopoeia putting up with anything like that."

Póöòíîntilist shrugged with open palms. "What is she supposed to do? Refuse to let the workers migrate to where the work is? They bring sorely needed coin back into her realm, some of which flows into her purse as tithes. Regarding an alliance, you can see things are already tense enough without throwing that particular burning branch onto the fire."

"I guess I had hoped our interests aligned enough that Her Majesty would find it advantageous to side with us. You also share a border. You must be worried that you'll have your own Flachberg."

"The queen is alert, but not alarmed. Openly aligning with you would make it look like she's alarmed. That's not what she wants to convey. I'm sorry, Queen Eloise."

Eloise blew out a breath. "I understand. Perhaps you can do me the kindness of conveying my proposal anyway."

"Of course. I'll take it to Her Majesty myself. But please don't hold your breath. These are delicate times."

"Thank you. I look forward to hearing what she has to say."

The Southie ambassador took his leave just as her next appointment arrived—a capybara dressed in purple robes and a deeper purple fez. He was barrel-shaped, with tidy reddish-brown fur and a regal bearing.

"Ambassador Ziïimmëëërmäään," said Eloise, standing up to welcome him. She'd become fond of the capybara when he was just a trusted messenger between her and Johanna. She hoped that fondness would make the coming awkwardness of their conversation a little easier.

"Greetings, Queen Eloise," said the capybara with a graceful bow and a deep, cultured voice. "I hope we're still on good enough terms that you can call me Ziïimmÿÿÿ."

That was a good sign.

"Of course, Ziïimmÿÿÿ. Good to see you again."

"It's my first time to have been summoned before you. I was apprehensive, but I see you have on your Come On, For Çalaht's Sake, Be Reasonable Cape. I was afraid you'd be wearing the Cape of Unreasonable, Painful, and Slow Wrath."

"I don't think anyone has worn that one in a long time," said Eloise. "Although I've considered it—it's a lovely turquoise."

"Ours is more of a maroon," said Ziïimmÿÿÿ. "Some of the fiercest capes are the prettiest. However, I'm guessing we're not here to discuss sartorial messaging. To what do I owe the honor of being called before you?"

"I'm hoping you can fill in some detail about the arrangement that Queen Johanna has struck with Queen Aglandau."

The capybara coughed, taken by surprise. "Ah. Well, I'm not sure how much I can say. For one, Queen Johanna has not brought me into her confidence on the matter. For another, even if she had, I'm sure those details are supposed to be kept strictly between those two contracting parties. Is there anything in particular you want to know?"

Everything, thought Eloise. *Every sordid, horrid detail, including why my twin sister stabbed me in the back by taking coin from a queen who's attacked my realm.* Eloise forced a smile. "Just a general outline might suffice."

"I should be able to do that. Broadly speaking, the arrangement between the Northern and the Eastern Lands has to do with financing some much-needed infrastructure improvements."

"Infrastructure. Really? Infrastructure? Like aqueducts and cisterns?"

"More like roads."

"Roads?"

"Yes, roads. Have you traveled the roadway between Stained Rock and Brague?"

"Yes, I went on that road at least part of the way from the Half Kingdom coming home last year. It wasn't that bad."

"You rode on horseback?"

"Yes."

"On the Western Lands and All That Really Matters side, it's fine. But on the Northern Lands side of the Adequate Wall of the Realms, it's a very different story. If you use one of the transportation guilds, that road is adequate. I, myself, have traveled it by guild-approved donkey several times. But by carriage, it is an absolute penance—a tooth-rattling, wagon-breaking misery. I know for a fact that on King Doncaster's last trip to Brague, the axle of his carriage broke twice, they used both spare wheels and were lucky they didn't need a third, and they lost half a day to clearing a fallen ironwood tree that blocked the road."

"I didn't know it was that bad."

"It's worse now. Or it was, before Queen Johanna instigated a program of repair and improvement."

"So why didn't she just pay for it herself? Why involve Queen Aglandau?"

Zïïimmÿÿÿ's jowls drooped. "Queen Johanna has not said. Would you like me to speculate?"

"Please."

"We're off the record?"

"There's no scribe here, so sure."

The capybara lowered his voice and leaned in. "At the risk of speaking ill of the dead, King Doncaster was a miserable financial manager. He had no mind for matters of coin at all and could hardly bring himself to give it any attention. The Purple Haze wiped out half the realm, including the bulk of its productive land, and two hundred years later, we're still suffering. My guess is that Queen Johanna went inside her counting house and saw a lot of nothing, but still needed to start implementing programs as queen. There weren't many options. It's not like she could set up a GoCoinMe campaign. I further speculate that Queen Aggie figured she could toss a few coins toward the Northern Lands as a goodwill gesture."

"And what do the Eastern Lands get in return? Interest?"

"Perhaps she expects to be repaid, and perhaps she's charging interest. But I suspect that wasn't the goal of the exercise."

"What was the goal, then?"

"To counteract the natural proclivity of one sister to side with the other. If you are sitting on opposite sides of a political scale from Queen Aggie, it's reasonable to assume she's going to try to add weight to hers. But again, this is pure speculation on my part."

"It makes sense." Eloise leaned back on her throne. "It's not the only explanation, but it's a sound one. I wonder what it would take to confirm it."

"I could query Queen Johanna. I can say that the matter was raised, and that I'd like to represent the situation accurately. Would you like me to do that?"

"Yes, please." Eloise hesitated. "I should probably warn you that I raised the matter directly in a letter, but I've not received a response yet."

"No?"

"My language was... let's call it tart."

"I see. I appreciate the heads up. I'll ride for the Northern Lands today."

MAYBE A CHARM OFFENSIVE

"Well, that went about as we thought it would." First Advisor Thëjëts came into the Receiving Room from her hidden listening post in an adjoining room.

"It went exactly as you said it would," said Eloise. "Essentially, a probably not, a probably not, and an I don't know very much."

"At least you've raised the possibility. Negotiations have to start somewhere. We'll see what the ambassadors say when they get back from conferring with their monarchs."

"It will be interesting, but we can't wait for them. We'll have to continue planning as if we're going through this alone," said Eloise. "And maybe see if there's some other incentive for alliance that we can conjure up, other than 'peace in all the realms.' If the situation with the Eastern Lands is my problem only, we're stuffed. If we can somehow get them to see it as 'our' problem, there might be hope."

"Yes," agreed First Advisor. She shifted uncomfortably. "So, closer to home, I need to raise another matter."

"Oh? That sounds ominous. Do we need to repair to the Queen's Study, or is here OK?"

"Here is going to be fine. It is private enough, and this is really just for your information."

"Please, go ahead then."

"I have concerns about the gossip heralds," said First Advisor.

Eloise stuck out her tongue like she was gagging. "I thought you advised me to ignore them."

"I did. And you should. But that doesn't mean they don't exist, or that they don't have influence. So, I have someone who listens to them and reports the tone and substance of what they're saying."

"Jerome does that for me, somewhat informally. He said that Headlong Helda's coverage of my parlay with Queen Aggie was pretty positive."

"I'd agree. On the whole, it was, save for a few blips. But that was then, and this is now. The conversation has moved on."

"It's only been, what, a week? Week-and-a-half?" Eloise pressed her lips together. "I just can't catch a break with them."

"Gossip heralds rely on volume, not quality. If they aren't commanding attention, they're not doing their jobs. And what do people pay attention to? Disaster, outrageous wrongdoing, titillation, the appalling, the horrifying, the breaking of laws, the meting out of punishment, the carriage and miscarriage of justice (often the same story and in the same sentence), and who's doing what to whom with appendages that aren't discussed in polite company. Your parlay with Queen Aglandau stands no chance of staying in the gossip heralds' version of public discussion when there's so much scandal and sensation to get through."

"But so much of what they say is made up of nonsense."

"Which brings me back to your original point. Don't pay them much attention."

"Then why are we discussing them?"

First Advisor frowned. "Because the general tone of what they're saying about you and your reign continues to decline precipitously."

"It can't be worse than calling me 'the flibbertyqueen.'"

"It can be. And it is. We're in a tricky situation regarding the Eastern Lands. How people perceive what's going on affects how much latitude you have to act. For example, you probably can't just say, 'Hey, Aggie, Flachberg's yours.' People would see that as exceptionally weak. But more to the point, if you want to do something about it, especially militarily, then having public opinion behind you makes it easier. While there's not a huge amount we can do about it, the mood of your people matters, and it's something we need to be at least somewhat aware of. The general perception should be that you're doing what's best for the queendom."

"Surely, people think I'm trying to do what's best for the queendom?"

"You can't assume rationality. Or truth. Or fairness. 'She's hard-working and doing a good job' won't get a gossip herald a lot of listeners."

Eloise thought for a minute. "Is that true what you said about not being able to do much about it? Can we at least try?"

"What are you thinking?"

"I don't know. Just tossing this out there, but we seem to have done OK with Headlong Helda. Why not bring in the biggest of the gossip heralds? Let them ask me some questions. Maybe do what we did with Helda and feed them some morning tea. Make them feel like they're getting a peek behind the scenes, but use the opportunity to conduct a kind of charm offensive. Try to get them more on my side."

"That is a very dangerous idea, Your Highness. I can think of ten thousand ways that could go wrong for you."

"Come on. How bad could it be? At worst, they keep saying terrible things about me. At best, they can see I'm a person with feelings who's doing what you said, trying her hardest to do what's best for the people of the realm."

"I don't know."

Eloise stood. "Let's at least try to shape the narrative a little. Can you please put together a list of who you think we should invite? Let's see what we can do to win the gossip heralds back."

"If you think that's wise, Your Highness."

"'Wise' is probably too strong a word, but let's give it a go."

"Yes, ma'am."

12

MIRACULOUS THUMBS
THEORY

Queen Aglandau stood in her private office and stared at the tapestry that took up the entire wall. It was a map of the four and a half realms, rendered in exquisite detail and accurate in scale to within half a strong length, or so she'd been told by her mother when she was a girl. A stretch of purple-dyed linen covered up the top-most part of the tapestry, where the Purple Haze sliced off half the Half Kingdom. When she was eight, she'd gotten a ladder and spent an entire afternoon looking underneath the purple bit, trying to imagine what had happened to all the people and towns beneath it. Were they lavender-colored ghosts floating in a purple fog? Was it more like an impenetrable curtain that one could enter, but not cross back through, and everyone on the other side was living their lives as before?

That was one mystery that had been solved. If the information coming from the Half Kingdom was right, everyone in that fog, no matter the species, was dead and dust, wiped out over two centuries before.

That this was now known struck her as astonishing. Something in the fog had changed (her spies couldn't seem to figure out what), and it wasn't killing anymore. The fog was supposedly as thick as ever (although there was conflicting information about this), and Queen Johanna was sending in explorers to see if anything that remained was salvageable, and if the land could somehow be used again.

Aglandau grunted to herself. Johanna was doing the same thing she'd done as a child—peering beneath the fog and trying to figure out what was there.

Maybe when she finished conquering the Western Lands (or at least the more useful bits) and turned her attention toward the north, there would be more up there that was worth seizing.

The queen moved to a different part of the tapestry and traced her index finger across a newly restitched area. She'd had the map altered to reflect the changed location of the Adequate Wall of the Realms at Flachberg, showing the town back in her realm. Given the scope of the tapestry in front of her, it was a minor change compared to what she had in mind overall. But it was nice to literally put her finger on progress and feel it manifest in thread. If things went according to plan, the tapestry would soon need a lot of alterations. She wondered if it would be simpler to have a new one made. But no, it appealed to her to cover over the representation of old wrongs and the past queens' lack of ambition with new stitching.

There was a knock at the door, breaking her reverie. Aglandau sighed. "What?" she snapped.

"Mother, it's me. May I come in?" Coratina's voice was soft through the door, and more tentative than normal.

"Enter."

The door opened and clicked closed as her daughter curtsied. Aglandau noted it was about twenty percent more curtsy than Protocol required, which meant her daughter was nervous about something.

The queen flicked her hand. "Arise, arise. No need to grovel."

Coratina moved forward and stood next to her mother. She considered the map and saw the changed spot. "You've had it altered."

"I wanted it to match current circumstances."

"I see. That makes sense." She considered the map. "Do you know what you're going to do next?"

Aglandau shook her head. "I'm still considering options. I'm thinking we should push as far as Lower Glenth."

"Lower Glenth." Coratina touched the tapestry. "Here? Why?"

"It's relatively close, and I like radishes."

"Radishes?"

"Radishes. Lower Glenth is famous for them."

"I didn't know that."

"Now you do."

"If I may be so bold, Mother, isn't it strategically frivolous to base a military operation on a love of radishes?"

"You're right. It would be frivolous to do that. But radish considerations aside, I've asked my generals to develop contingencies for movements all along the shared border. I'm trying to figure out what would be most effective against the fustilarian—repeated small nibbles that will nip at her, but won't provoke her to respond, or larger strikes that she won't be able to ignore and will be unprepared to meet."

"How will you decide?"

"I'll see what they come up with, gather more information, and then work out which combination of options I think is best. It's still early days. I have time."

"If you delay, don't you give Queen Eloise a chance to organize herself? Surely she's spending her days trying to prepare her defenses, or perhaps to do something about Flachberg itself. It's what you would do, isn't it?"

"Fuuuugh me, you're darn right it's what I would do. And if I've taught you anything, then it's what you would do, too. But while the scobberlotcher seems to have taken some steps toward preparing her soldiers, she does not seem to have much of a sense of self-preservation. I mean, she came to the Flachberg parlay with that tiny little contingent, leaving herself and her people absolutely wide open. She practically had a sign on her backside that said, 'Kick me.' I delayed my talk with her for two hours trying to figure out what kind of trap she was setting, but there was no trap. She, honest to goodness, expected a good-faith discussion. Can you believe it?"

Coratina lifted a shoulder. "Actually, I can. You heard how Lady Seneschal Póöòmáäàdéëè spoke of her. She was frustrated and disappointed with her experience serving the current queen, but other than describing some personality quirks, she had little to say that was solid or recent enough to be of much use. From what I can gather, Eloise the Third is inexperienced, but basically good-hearted."

"Good-hearted? *Good-hearted?* Fuuuuuugh me, Cora. That and half a coin will get you a cup of olive leaf tea."

"If you say so, Mother, although that statement betrays a lack of recent visits to our local market."

"Don't."

"Yes, Mother."

That took Aglandau by surprise. Coratina, even with her scrollish ways, was not one to back down. It almost certainly meant she wanted something.

Aglandau cut to the chase. "Tell me, Cora, what are you here to ask me?"

Her daughter's eyes went wide. "Am I that obvious?"

"In a word, yes,"

"I see." Coratina straightened, readying herself for a confrontation. "An opportunity has presented itself."

"Oh? What kind of opportunity?"

"You may or may not be aware that at the Studium Gymnasium of The South, they have an entire, hundred-strong faculty devoted to Çalahtic Studies. I've been corresponding with Professor Orbisculate Ineffable Béëëtwîîïxt, whose area of expertise is the theological examination of the Divine One's various tribulations and, more specifically, her thumbs."

"He specializes in Çalaht's thumbs?"

"*She* does, yes. You're familiar, I'm sure, with the controversy between Thumbs Dislocationists and Thumbs Elongationists."

"Of course." Aglandau wasn't, but she wasn't going to admit it.

"Good. Well, Professor Béëëtwîîïxt's work seeks to reconcile those two opposing theological positions, proposing a unifying Miraculous Thumbs Theory that—"

"Cora, is there a point to this?"

Coratina coughed and cleared her throat. "Yes, Mother, there is. Professor Béëëtwîîïxt has invited me to attend the Studium Gymnasium of The South for a semester or two, three at the most, to help her research Çalaht's thumbs, helping her codify her Miraculous Thumbs Theory, and ensuring it is supported with theological rigor."

"We have a Studium Gymnasium of the Eastern Lands. Surely that's good enough. You can study the thumbs thing here."

"Our Studium Gymnasium does not have such a grand Çalahtic Studies faculty. It does not have the same level of expertise concentrated in one place. Mother, this is an incredible opportunity for me to—"

"No."

"I—"

"I said no."

Coratina's face flashed from disbelief to disappointment to anger to a stony blankness. "Mother, I implore you. Please consider—"

Aglandau raised a hand, cutting her daughter off. "Here's what I'm considering. One, my health is what my health is. Two, you're next in line for the throne. Three, I have been lenient with you until now, indulging your scrollish ways since they kept you occupied. You seemed genuinely interested in them and they didn't seem to hurt anyone. It's not like you were studying torture techniques for marsupials. But enough is enough, because four, things are about to heat up more. And five, have a look at the dalcop sitting on the Westie throne. She's completely out of her depth and it shows in every word she utters."

"There's still time for me to—"

"Don't interrupt. Here's what I don't want: I don't want you to find yourself suddenly crown-plonked and looking like a loiter-sack. People will think I failed to prepare you to be queen. That. Won't. Happen." Aglandau stepped toward her daughter, leaning forward so they were nose-to-nose and eye-to-eye. "From now, from this moment, Coratina Frantoio Patrinia Ponentine, you need to devote your time and attention to preparing to sit on my throne. I fully plan to rule for years to come, but one of these days, you will wear the crown, and by the Çalaht you are so interested in, you will be ready."

Coratina, eyes wet, swallowed back her rage and the retorts she'd been composing. "Yes, Mother."

"Do you have any questions?"

"No, Mother."

"What is the first thing that you will do when you are done here?"

"I—" She clamped her jaw shut, let a wave of emotion pass, then relaxed and said, "I'll quill a letter to Professor Béëètwîîîxt letting her know that I'm incredibly grateful for her kind and generous offer, but circumstances are such that I cannot take it up. However, I would be grateful to continue our correspon—"

Aglandau raised her hand again.

"Just that I cannot take up her kind offer."

The queen nodded.

Coratina dropped into a curtsy so she could break eye contact. "Thank you for hearing my request and for giving me such a clear response."

"My pleasure. If there's nothing else, you're dismissed to go take care of that errand."

"Yes, Mother."

Aglandau watched her daughter depart and hoped that, for once in the child's life, she'd start paying attention to things that actually mattered.

13

TOY SOLDIERS

Eloise studied a financial report from Exchequer of the Realm Borborygmus on the state of the queendom's coffers and tried not to swear. To her relief, a knock on the Queen's Study door interrupted her. "Come on in. It's unlocked."

First Advisor entered carrying a single piece of hemp parchment.

"I hope you're not coming to tell me I've been given the wrong version of the coffers report and that the reality is worse." Eloise tapped the scroll in front of her. "Because this one's pretty bad."

"The news is not good, Your Highness, but it's on a different matter. I've received intelligence that there are two separate massings of Eastern Lands troops near two more gates at the Adequate Wall of the Realms."

Eloise stood and went to the table that dominated the middle of the room, which was covered by a massive, detailed map of the four-and-a-half realms. "Show me, please."

First Advisor opened a drawer, fiddled for a moment, then put down two rows of toy soldiers as markers. "Here, and here."

Eloise shook her head. "This doesn't make sense. The only thing near that first spot is Lower Glenth. There are just a bunch of radish crofters down there. The land would hardly be ideal for olives, and there's no cultural tie like there is in Flachberg." She moved to the second spot. "This makes even less sense. Is the map out of date? Is there something up there that's not represented here?"

"Nothing that I know of."

The two of them stood staring at the map table. "So, what do you think she's doing?" asked Eloise.

First Advisor considered the map from all angles, then said, "What do we know about the current situation? Queen Aggie has superior numbers, superior equipment, and superior preparation. If I were her, I would split my forces, so that you had to make a choice. You either choose to focus on one area and hope for the best for the others, or spread your resources thinner at each place, reducing your chances of success at any of them."

"Divide and conquer."

"Yes, with the emphasis, in this case, on the conquer bit."

Eloise stared dully at the marked positions, her mood plummeting. "What am I supposed to do?"

"Prepare to fight and defend your territory as best you can, and keep looking for a solution that does not involve bloodshed."

Eloise felt her spirits droop further. "This is not a very hopeful position be in, is it."

"No, Queen Eloise. It's not."

"There really aren't many options here."

"Unfortunately, no."

Eloise drew a breath and straightened her spine. "Then it is time to hunker down and do the best I can. I just hope that, somehow, that's good enough."

14

SYMBOLS AND SQUIGGLES

Jerome whooshed into the doorway of the Queen's Study running full pelt. "El! El! I found them! I found them!" He skittered to a stop when he saw Eloise and First Advisor were in deep discussion. "Whoops! Sorry. I mean, g'late afternoon, my queen." The chipmunk dropped into a paw-wavy bow.

"What did you find?" asked Eloise.

Jerome looked from Eloise to Bënnïë-Änn Thëjëts and back. "Uh, nothing. Gotta go." Without another word, he sprinted from the room.

"That was odd," said First Advisor.

"Jerome is Jerome. What can I say? I might need to go figure this one out. Do you mind if we call it a meeting?"

"Everything else can wait."

Eloise waited while Thëjëts gathered her scrolls and documents and put them back in the royal boxes. She accepted a curtsy and said, "I'll see you in the morning?"

"Yes, Your Highness. Have a good evening."

Eloise found Jerome standing on a bench in the Culpability Courtyard waiting for her and practically jigging with excitement. "Are you OK?"

"Sorry, I didn't mean to be so weird just then. I didn't want to talk in front of Bënnïë-Änn, and I panicked. Do you think she noticed?"

"What do you think?"

"Right. She noticed."

"That's OK. I told her you were emotionally distraught because your third cousin twice removed hid your teddy bear."

"Really?"

"No, but I can next time, if you want."

"Thanks. Hard pass."

"Your call." Eloise sat down on the bench. "So, what did you find?"

"Melveeta's notes from working with the Star of Whatever."

Eloise leaned back and looked at him. "You're kidding. Really?"

"Really."

"Where did you find them?"

"They were in That Room We Don't Talk About Because We Don't Want People to Know About It."

"We looked in there before. We scoured the section on Gwendolyn the Irritable from top to bottom, front to back, side to side."

"They weren't in that section." Jerome puffed out his chest, proud. "They were misfiled as an artifact from the reign of her daughter, Queen Aubrey the Parasitic."

Eloise jumped up, extended her arm to him, and patted her shoulder. "What are we waiting for? Hop up and let's go look at them."

Jerome looked up at the darkening sky. "The Bibliotheca de Records and Regrets is almost certainly closed by now. They were shuffling the scholars out as I was leaving."

Eloise pointed to herself. "Queen, here. Surely they'll keep it open for me."

"Are you kidding? Have you met Head Scribe? He wouldn't stay open late if it was his own mother returned from the dead and bribing him with two baskets of brunchberry muffins."

"OK, good point. I'll free up tomorrow morning and we'll go have a look then." She sat back down on the bench. "How do you know what you have is from Melveeta, and that it has to do with the Star of Whatever?"

"I know it's Melveeta because the handwriting matches. I cross-checked with three other documents she wrote. After two centuries, the ink has faded a bit, but it's her alright. And I know that it's the Star of Whatever because she calls it that. The first sentence is something like, 'Being explorations on the Star of Whatever (we really need to get a better name for this thing).'"

"So tell me, tell me, tell me, what does it say?"

"First, I just found it this afternoon, and most of my time was spent verifying what I thought I had. Second, there are several scrolls worth of the stuff." Jerome's tail flicked in impatience. "And third, it's kind of cryptic. It's not like it's a recipe or a guidebook or anything. It's more like a set of notes. I'm guessing it has things she tried, things that seemed like they might have worked somewhat, things that failed—that sort of thing. But, like I said, I've had little time with it yet, and parts of it are also in what looks like a kind of code."

"A code? What kind of code?"

"Symbols. Numbers. Squiggles. I don't know. You'll have to see for yourself tomorrow."

⚜ *15* ⚜

BROOM CLOSET DWELLER

The next morning, Eloise and Jerome were standing at the doors of the Bibliotheca de Records and Regrets, waiting with a basket of still-warm-from-the-oven chai-spiced muffins when Head Scribe Bernardo Speculum Twiddle arrived with the keys. The ancient, glasses-wearing raccoon was dressed in a fresh-pressed, dust-gray cloak that picked up the gray in his snout and around his eyes.

As he fiddled his keyring out of his cloak pocket, Eloise said a bright, "Blessings of the day, Head Scribe. Lovely to see you again."

"Blessings of the day, Queen Eloise." He turned, bowed to her, then went back to looking for the correct key. "It's been a while."

"Yes, Jerome's been doing the bulk of the research for me while other things have taken my time."

"Yes, I heard about the parlay. Disappointing result all around, or so the gossip heralds would have one believe."

"Surely you don't pay attention to them, Head Scribe," said Jerome. "They're scurrilous."

"No, I don't make a habit of listening to them. However, we do have scribes attend a representative sample of the more important ones and copy down their ravings so they can be entered in the Bibliotheca's permanent record. As such, I do come across what they have to say."

Jerome frowned. "Why would you want that in your archives?"

"Because, young chipmunk, the mission of the Bibliotheca de Records and Regrets is to be an accurate representation of the history and dealings of the realm, and they form part of that record. Like it or not."

"Do you also get the more reputable non-gossip heralds?" asked Eloise.

"All of them."

"Oh, well, good then."

"And Queen Eloise, if I may be so bold..."

"Yes?"

"You don't need to bribe me with baked goods. We've been enjoying them, but I've put on a weight or two, which my missus is chiding me about." He inserted a key, and the lock clicked. "Both you and Assistant Seer to the Court Seer Abernatheen de Chipmunk have proven yourselves careful users of our archives. You've handled the babies with care. I trust you to do the right thing."

"Thank you, Head Scribe. We appreciate that very much. So, what should I..." Eloise waggled the basked she held.

"I'll be grateful for one last muffin indulgence, but after that, no more, please."

"I'll leave them on your desk."

"Thank you, Your Highness. At the rate I move, you'll be long gone by the time I get there, so all the best for your research today."

"Thank you, Head Scribe."

Eloise and Jerome walked to the front desk, where they found Head Scribe's apprentice, Jóöôáäàqúüùĩĩn. The short, rotund teenager wore ill-fitting apprentice scribe robes and looked like he'd just rolled out of bed.

"Blessings of the day, Jóöôáäàqúüùîîn." Eloise set the basket on Head Scribe's slanted desk. "Can you take care of this for me?"

"Of course. And blessings of the day, Queen Eloise." His nose twitched, sniffing the air. "Chai spice?"

"Very good. That's spot on." Eloise looked at the apprentice and narrowed her eyes. "You're not sleeping here in the Bibliotheca de Records and Regrets, are you?"

Jóöôáäàqúüùîîn's eyebrows shot up to the middle of his tonsured forehead. "Sssshhhhh! Don't let Head Scribe hear you!"

"Why not?" asked Jerome.

The apprentice launched into a rushed, stage-whispered explanation. "He thinks I'm living at home, and that I'm just super dedicated. And my mother thinks I have a place here in the castle. It's all fine. The broom closet on the second floor is more than adequate for my needs. Please, don't..." Jóöôáäàqúüùîîn straightened and deepened his voice. "Ah, blessings of the day, Head Scribe. I trust the morning finds you well."

"As well as can be expected," grumbled the raccoon. "I see you've taken possession of our latest bribe."

"Yes, Head Scribe."

"Head Scribe," said Eloise. "Jerome and I had a question about correctly storing a document we found in one of Gwendolyn's rooms. Could you please spare Apprentice Jóöôáäàqúüùîîn for a few minutes to clear up the matter?"

"You want *him*? How odd. I mean, yes, of course, Your Highness. Jóöôáäàqúüùîîn, please see to the queen's needs, then come right back. There are ledgers from one hundred and sixty years ago that need copying."

"Yes, Head Scribe." The apprentice's head bobbed like an over-eager buoy on rough seas. "I'll be back in a jiffy."

"We do not say 'jiffy' in the Bibliotheca de Records and Regrets," humphed Head Scribe. "This is a 'jiffy'-free zone."

"Apologies, Head Scribe. I'll be back *presently*."

Eloise led Jerome and Jóöôáääqúüùíîìn to the hall that led to Queen Gwendolyn's archive rooms. As soon as they were out of earshot and in a secluded spot, she stopped and looked hard at the apprentice. "This is absolutely ridiculous. The Bibliotheca de Records and Regrets is not a dormitory. You cannot dwell in a broom closet. Plus, you're lying to both Head Scribe and your mother."

The apprentice looked at his feet and mumbled, "I'm not lying. I'm just letting each of them believe what they want to believe."

"You've heard of lying by omission, right?" said Jerome. "That's a thing."

Jóöôáääqúüùíîìn looked even more embarrassed.

"Why?" asked Eloise.

"Because I'm an apprentice scribe. The role is an incredible opportunity, and I'm so grateful to be here, but it barely pays two coins. If I'm going to make it all the way through the process—apprentice scribe, journeyman scribe, junior scribe, full scribe, senior scribe—a bit of scrimping is required."

"Why don't you just live at home?" asked Jerome.

"I love my mother, but I can't live with her. If you'd met her, you'd understand. She's... uh... very clear in her opinions. About everything, from how you hang a washrag over the side of the kitchen bucket to how many buckles are acceptable on shoes."

Jerome nodded in sympathy. "So why doesn't Head Scribe have a place for you to live?"

"Because my accommodation is not his problem. And I don't want it to be. That's just how these things are. So I took some initiative, rearranged some brooms and buckets, and found a relatively comfy place to sleep. Plus, the walk to work is a breeze."

Eloise shook her head. Was that really how things worked in the castle? "If there was a room in the castle, what difference would it make to you?"

"I can't ask that of you, Queen Eloise. It's not my place, and it's not my desire to be a burden. On anyone."

"Let me ask, are you dedicated to becoming a full scribe?"

"Yes, ma'am."

"Can you promise me you will work even harder than you already do, and that you'll do as Head Scribe says without question?"

"Of course. I want nothing more in the world than to be a full scribe. I want to be the best scribe anyone has ever seen."

Eloise turned to Jerome. "Can you please speak with Lady Seneschal de Aardvark? See if she can find a spot for Jóöôáäàqúüùíîìn in the castle."

"Certainly."

She turned back to the apprentice. "Consider it handled."

"Thank you! Thank you so very much, Queen Eloise." Jóöôáäàqúüùíîìn grabbed Eloise's hands and shook them, then realized what he'd done, gasped, and dropped them. "Sorry, ma'am. I get excited."

"It's OK." Eloise avoided wiping her hands on her cloak. "That's all for now. Jerome will be in touch, and we'll see you later."

Jóöôáäàqúüùíîìn's eyebrows met in the middle. "What about correctly storing the document you found in one of Gwendolyn's rooms? I'm still happy to help you with that."

Eloise looked at him and said nothing.

The apprentice's eyes went wide. "There is no document in Gwendolyn's rooms. That was pretextual." He gasped again. "You lied to Head Scribe!"

"Yes, I did. Let's keep that one between us, shall we? Now get back before your jiffy is up."

"Yes, ma'am." Jóöôáäàqúüùíîn bowed one last time, and as he walked away, she could hear him repeating to himself, "Presently, not jiffy. Presently, not jiffy."

16

SECRET CYLINDER

Eloise and Jerome headed toward That Room We Don't Talk About Because We Don't Want People to Know About It. "That was a nice thing you did just then. Plenty of people would have found the awkward, somewhat bumbling apprentice not worth much of an effort."

"He's been helpful to us, and his heart is in the right place. I'd hate for him to get turfed out by Head Scribe because his best living option seemed to be a Bibliotheca broom closet."

"Well, good for you."

"And what does it say about the apprentice system that it doesn't pay enough to live on? I might need that looked into when things settle down. If they settle down. Or if I'm queen long enough."

"Stop it, El. You've got to stop thinking that kind of thing."

"You're right, you're right."

They reached That Room We Don't Talk About Because We Don't Want People to Know About It, where Jerome drew a key from his tunic and unlocked the door.

"You have your own key?"

Jerome shrugged with his tail. "They're convinced I'm here on the queen's business."

"Which you are."

"Which I am. And I don't steal or hurt the babies. So it's easier to let me come and go with less involvement from Head Scribe."

"Makes sense. And I think it's funny that we're still calling everything in the archive 'babies.' It's not like Head Scribe is checking up on us or anything. So where's this scroll from Melveeta?"

"Scrolls. Plural. Over here."

Jerome led her to a bin on the opposite side of the room from where all of Queen Gwendolyn's artifacts were. There was a single, smallish document cylinder sitting by itself in the corner. Eloise and Jerome pulled on cotton gloves used by archivists, a habit drummed into them by Head Scribe himself. She nodded toward the tube. "May I?"

"Be my guest."

It was heavier than she expected and unlike anything they'd come across before in the Bibliotheca. The rosewood container was ornately carved, the pattern dominated by thistles and the Gumball coat of arms, with its weasel on a bushel of onions and one-eyed otter holding a fire poker. The quality of the craftsmanship was superb, giving it the feel of something officially commissioned.

Eloise looked at it from every angle. "I can't tell how it opens."

"It took me a while as well. Someone obviously designed it for secrets. You want me to tell you, or do you want to try to figure it out?"

"No, give me another minute."

Eloise tried pressing the family crest. Nothing. Twisted the ends. Nope. Compressed the cylinder. She poked, prodded, picked, pecked, turned, and pressed. Nada. "I'm not getting it."

"It's OK. I sort of lucked into the solution. You'll want a hat pin or sewing needle." Jerome held up a claw. "I used this. The secret is in the family crest." He took the cylinder, laid it on the floor with the Gumball coat of arms facing upward, and stuck his claw in the eye socket of the one-eyed otter.

The tube clicked, a latch releasing. A curved panel retracted three weak lengths, exposing three nubbins of a darker wood. "What are these?" asked Eloise.

"I think it's a second layer of protection. I pressed right, then left, then middle, and it opened. My guess is that if you did it in some other order, something would happen to the contents inside. But I got it open and didn't want to risk the contents by trying anything else."

"Two things. First, you just happened to get the right combination on the first try?"

"Yep."

"And you were worried about the babies inside if you got it wrong?"

"That's right."

Eloise gave him a palms-up shrug. "Weren't you worried about the babies being destroyed if someone else opened this thing wrong?"

"Yes."

"So, why didn't you just leave the babies out of the tube? You could have found some other container to put them in."

Jerome looked at her for a long, slow moment, whiskers twitching. "Yeah. That might have been a good idea. I'll keep that in mind for next time." He coughed. "Sorry. Anyway, you should be able to remove the end piece. The scrolls slide out easily, so be careful."

Eloise took the open cylinder to the table in the middle of the room, got some weights ready to hold down the corners of the pages, and tilted them out.

They smelled of dust and history, and looked like a prop someone would fabricate for a play. Instead of being made of hemp parchment like most scrolls, the pages were thin, like onion skin. It didn't surprise her that they were in such good shape; she'd seen lightweight, bound, travel copies of the *Livre de Protocol* and the *Scrolls of Çalaht* made from this kind of material. So she knew it could be durable, although she hadn't known they could last centuries.

A sense of reverence came over her. "Melveeta the Elusive definitely wrote this," whispered Eloise. "I recognize the quillmanship from that list of magical items we found before. Holy Çalaht sitting on a surprised supplicant, this is amazing. Well done, Jer. Well done."

She eased the rolled-up sheets apart and carefully, one by one, laid them out, weighing them down. There were twelve scrolls, but the last one was only partly used, so eleven and a half, really. Only one side of each was written on, which made sense as the ink bled through the thin pages.

The handwriting was cramped, and in an archaic style of script that had been out of date when her grandmother was a girl. She could make out some of the words, but it was soon clear why Jerome couldn't tell her what the scrolls said. It would take a fair bit of work to parse their contents.

Eloise stood back from the table. "Are we allowed quill and ink in here so we can make notes?"

Jerome shook his head. "That was one of the first things Head Scribe said to us. 'Don't bring in anything that, if it spills, might damage the babies.' He specifically listed ink pots, along with cleaning fluids, anything you can digest that requires chewing, hot beverages, cold beverages, warm beverages, cool beverages, tepid beverages, and fondue."

"Like we'd have fondue in here."

"It might be fun, though. Chocolate fondue, nibbled while surrounded by the ghosts of all these scrolls and the people who created them."

"Pass. I get enough communing with those who've passed at Afternoon Tea for the Dead."

"Yeah, me too."

Eloise stripped off her cloth gloves. "I'm going to ask Head Scribe how one is supposed to take notes in here."

Fifteen minutes later, Eloise was back in That Room We Don't Talk About Because We Don't Want People to Know About It, and she and Jerome were being lectured by Jóöôáäàqúüùíîn. "Herewith are Head Scribe's Edicts on Note-Taking. Part One: Graphite Sticks," he said. "You're allowed to use graphite sticks on hemp parchment to make notes, under the following conditions." He recited the edicts like he'd said them a bazillion times. "One: one must always leave the note-taking materials on the far side of the table from where one has the babies. Two: one is to work in pairs, with one person taking the notes and the other person saying what the notes should be. Three: the person taking the notes may eschew the cloth gloves to facilitate note-taking, but must not touch the babies." This went on for forty-five minutes, including having both Eloise and Jerome report back the key points of what he'd said.

When he was satisfied that Head Scribe's Edicts on Note-Taking had been conveyed, he left them to it.

"Forty-five minutes," moaned Jerome. "Just to say, 'You sit over there, take notes in graphite, and don't touch anything.' Once you finish looking at the apprenticeship system, maybe you can look at the Bibliotheca's edict system."

"I'll put that on the list." Eloise pointed at the graphite sticks and hemp parchment pages that Jóöôáäàqúüùíîn left behind. "Do you mind taking the notes?"

"First, your hands are bigger than my paws, so it's easier for you to hold the graphite sticks. Second, there's no way I'm missing out on reading Melveeta's scrolls."

"We'll share the duty, then?"

"Deal."

"I think what I'd like to do is make a copy of it," said Eloise. "That way we can take it with us, and it might help us figure it out as we go. Read me the first line, and I'll write it down."

Jerome peered at the first page scroll. "I got it a little wrong when I quoted it to you yesterday evening. It says, 'Star of Whatever' at the top, then on the next line, there's a parenthetical quote. '(We need to get a better name for it)'. Then it goes to the next line, which says, 'Examinations thereof.' Her quillmanship really is terrible. I thought mine was bad, but hers is appalling."

"Good idea to try to get the words and lines to be the same. That will make the copy more faithful." Eloise wrote down what he said, walking back and forth to double-check spelling and the positioning of the words.

It was tedious, but fascinating work that involved weighing each word, making sure they transcribed it in the correct position, and cross-checking the shape of letters to resolve illegibilities. And it took much, much longer than Eloise would have guessed. After two hours, they'd finished most of a page.

"I can't spend any more time on this today," she said. "I'll block out another chunk tomorrow. At this rate we'll be here for weeks."

"With no guarantee that we'll actually learn anything."

"True. So, let's summarize what we've learned so far."

Jerome looked thoughtful. "Melveeta tried a few things and nothing worked the way she expected it to. She was cagey about what she said to the Court mages, as though she didn't trust them. The few straight-up spells she tried didn't do anything."

"Those are my takeaways as well. I'll send a page to let you know when I'll meet you tomorrow. First Advisor won't want me spending too much time on something secret like this."

"You don't want me to keep going?"

Eloise shook her head. "It really is a two-person job. Plus, this is what passes for fun for me right now. This and training with Sylvia Cloisterfeld. Please don't take this from me."

"That's a bit sad."

"That's reality. See if you can find a proper storage box so we don't have to worry about Melveeta's tube."

"Will do. See you tomorrow."

17

A NOT SO MODEST PROPOSAL

Eloise felt like her Privy Council meetings were less intimidating and more useful now that some of her own appointees were there, people she knew and trusted. She no longer dreaded them, which was good.

After getting the latest depressing update on the queendom's finances from Exchequer of the Realm Cyrus Borborygmus, and giving Seer Maybelle de Chipmunk, the Venerable Prelate Herself, and Niville Numptorius, the Interim Other Places Advocate, a chance to raise any issues (they didn't), she asked, "Can I please get an update on how our military improvements are going?"

Tiberius de Sphenodon and Sylvia Cloisterfeld exchanged a glance. The tuatara raised his uninjured forefoot. "I'll field this one. On the matter of military preparedness, there's somewhat good news and somewhat not-so-good news."

"Give me the somewhat not-so-good news first, please."

The tuatara stood on his hind legs on his chair to address Eloise and the room. "Well, I have conducted a careful analysis, and have considered a plethora of factors, like number of soldiers, their level of training, the state of our armament stores, and the level of success we've been having with turning what are, essentially, ceremonial weapons into actual tools of war that might cause damage. I have come to the conclusion that, if we were attacked today by foes from the east, our forces would crumple like a used hanky."

Eloise winced. "It's still that bad?"

"Probably worse," said Cloisterfeld. "I think Master Sergeant (No Longer Retired) de Sphenodon has gilded the proverbial lily somewhat."

"Right." Eloise suppressed the urge to sigh. "And the somewhat good news?"

The tuatara cleared his throat. "It has become clear that the number of self-inflicted injuries during training is way, way down. The troops are much less likely to hurt themselves with their weapons than was previously the case."

Eloise slumped and let out the previously suppressed sigh. "This is hopeless, isn't it?"

"It is," agreed her mother's champion. "But, if I may say so, it is slightly less hopeless today than it was yesterday. The trend is definitely in the right direction. We just need more time. It took decades for things to reach this state. It will take more than a few weeks to right them."

Eloise looked around the table. "Anyone have any suggestions on how we can gain the time we need?"

"Try another parlay, perhaps?" said Jerome. "Maybe Queen Aglandau will be more reasonable the second time."

Eloise looked at him. "Is there any reason to think she might be?"

"No."

She turned back to the table. "Any suggestions that might actually work?"

"Actually, I do have one. It's a not-so-modest proposal." It was Rölf de Phobaeticus, the Speaker for the Land. This surprised Eloise. It was, perhaps, the first time the stick insect had shown enough initiative to join in the conversation. He got up on the table to make sure he could be seen and heard. "If you had the support of the other realms in pushing back against the aggression (and possible future aggression) from the Eastern Lands, then that unity of opposition might help dissuade Queen Aglandau from pushing forward."

Eloise gave a two-palm shrug. "I tried that. None of the other realms are interested in anything formal. I spoke with all the ambassadors, save anyone from the Eastern Lands, since we no longer have a representative from there. I asked each ambassador to put forward the idea of forming an alliance with the Western Lands and All That Really Matters. The all came back with some polite version of 'meh.'"

De Phobaeticus shook his antennae. "I was thinking of something different. Not a formal alliance like you've been trying to set up. Rather, something more in the direction of a meeting of equals. A kind of Grand Council of the Realms, whose purpose it would be to have the leaders of each realm meet and discuss problems affecting their realm, as well as matters affecting all of the realms, with the aim of trying to resolve matters peacefully."

"A Grand Council of the Realms," repeated Eloise. "It sounds impressive, anyway. But what's in it for the others? Peace in the realms doesn't seem to be much of an incentive."

"It would be a forum for high-level concerns, one of which would be the relationship between the Eastern Lands and our fair queendom. But the discussion could be had in the context of other matters that need discussing. Say, the way Southie guest workers are being treated, or the need for the Northern Lands to determine what, if anything, can be done with the area previously lost to the Purple Haze and still shrouded in mist. If one engenders a spirit of mutual respect and cooperation, then we may not need to sharpen so many ceremonial weapons. Mind you, I'm hardly suggesting that we stop our preparations, but getting ready for war is one of those things that one hopes is ultimately a wasted effort."

The room was quiet as everyone considered the stick insect's proposal.

"Do you think anyone would actually listen to me if I put up a proposal?" asked Eloise. "I think my sister hates me. I know Queen Aggie does. Her Maj Ono and I get along OK, as do the khan and I, but the Us are incredibly insular and disinclined to engage outside their herd. There'd be no point attempting something unless we're all there. A Grand Council of the Realms (Except for a Couple of Them) wouldn't fly."

"I think you hit on the solution to that already." It was Seer Maybelle this time. Generally, she hadn't had much to say since she'd worked out that Eloise was opaque to her in the Unseen. "Start by getting Her Majesty, Queen Onomatopoeia on board, as well as the khan. If they are amenable, then have them spearhead the effort to get the others, with them able to say you are happy to be a part of it. If The South and the Central Ranges are willing participants, then it's just a matter of Queen Johanna and Queen Aglandau."

"What do you think, Niville?" asked Eloise. "And you, First Advisor. You were the Other Places Advocate for my mother. Do you have any thoughts on the Speaker for the Land's proposal?"

"Niville, you go first," said Bënnïë-Änn.

"Really?" squeaked the Interim Other Places Advocate. "I'd be more comfortable—"

"Niville!" snapped First Advisor. She pounded the table hard enough to rattle the glasses. "Own it. Or leave. We spoke about this. Now is not the time for your timidity."

The room quietened. It was the harshest Eloise had ever heard Bënnïë-Änn speak to her protégé. Or anyone. It seemed out of character.

Almost.

Before Eloise could say anything, First Advisor broke the uncomfortable silence. "Apologies, Your Highness. It is not my place to decide whether or not the Interim Other Places Advocate stays or leaves. Obviously, that call is yours and yours alone. But, my point holds. I am not understating it that the queen and queendom face a crisis. Your Highness needs people on your Privy Council to give free, fair, and frank advice. Otherwise, what's the point? So, Niville, please give our queen your opinion on the proposal."

The young man looked like he wanted to cry. Or bolt. Or both. To his credit, he mastered himself and kept his normally fluttery hands under control. His voice, however, betrayed him with an adolescent crack. "There is precedent," he squeaked. Niville stopped, cleared his throat, and tried again. "There is precedent for attempting these kinds of high-level talks. Shortly after the Purple Haze devoured half the Northern Lands and Gwendolyn the Irritable proved victorious against King Brüüütus, the ruling monarchs, save the Northern Lands, gathered to assess the threat to their own realms posed by the Purple Haze. Some years later, there was a gathering for the three hundredth anniversary of the opening of the Adequate Wall of the Realm that was attended by all five monarchs, although discussions were limited to matters regarding the wall itself, and a small number of minor cultural matters. There was also an attempt to have a political meeting during the reign of your grandmother, however she was..." Here Niville faltered.

"What?" said Eloise. "Standoffish? Politically unconcerned? Playing her cards close to her chest?"

"Preoccupied with One's Great Mistake to the exclusion of all else." Niville's face went pink. "With respect, the record shows that she received the invitation but ignored it. The other monarchs decided there wasn't much point without her, and figured they'd take the matter back up once Queen Eloise the First had resolved her situation one way or another."

"But she didn't ever really resolve it. Not until he died, and then, as you know, she passed shortly thereafter." Eloise drummed her fingers.

"So no one has really done this kind of thing with any success. There have been feints in that direction, but no real progress. Is that a good summary?"

"Yes, Your Highness," said Niville.

"In your opinion, should I attempt to organize such a meeting of the monarchs? Do you think there would be appetite for something like this?"

"That's two different questions, ma'am." Niville's voice broke again on the last word. "To the latter, I can't say. To the former, I say, absolutely."

"Based on what?"

"Based on what Master Sergeant (No Longer Retired) de Sphenodon said earlier—that our forces would crumple. Anything would be better than finding out if he's right."

"Thank you, Niville." Eloise addressed the rest of the room. "Let's try it. If the Speaker for the Land, Interim Other Places Advocate, and First Advisor could stay behind, we can sketch out the best way to approach. And you, Jerome and Lorch, please stay as well. With any luck, we're onto something."

Seer Maybelle raised a paw. "I have one last suggestion, if I may?"

"Of course."

"I suggest that you reach out to your sister directly. Don't do it through an emissary. I would be surprised if she wasn't more amenable than you think."

"I'll keep that possibility in mind, but things really aren't great between us."

"One might suggest that they need to be. And that one might need to do whatever needs to be done to foster a renewed sisterly spirit."

"Seer Maybelle, did you just politely tell me to get over myself?"

"I would never presume to do so, Queen Eloise." But the chipmunk's smile said otherwise.

18

LACK OF ASSUMED
KNOWLEDGE

It was the fourth day of working with Melveeta's notes in That Room We Don't Talk About Because We Don't Want People to Know About It. Their copy of Melveeta's scrolls was looking more like a copy of the *Scrolls of Çalaht*, with text in the middle that was as exact a copy as they could make, and commentary, questions, and notes surrounding it as they tried to puzzle through what she actually meant.

"Here's part of what I'm tripping over," said Eloise. "Assumed knowledge."

"What do you mean?"

"Well, Back When, there was strong magic everywhere, before Melveeta's spell sucked it all in."

"OK. So what?"

"So, what's not in Melveeta's notes because it was assumed knowledge —stuff everyone knew, so there was no point mentioning it."

"I get what you mean. Like, if I'm making an almond meal cake." Jerome mimed a mixing bowl and spoon. "If the recipe says to mix almond meal with olive oil and a teaspoon of lemon juice, it doesn't need to tell me to take the almond meal out of its bag, to pour out the olive oil from its jug, or to squeeze the lemons. I know to do those things without being told."

"Exactly. And it's like we're in a world where no one has mixed almond meal with olive oil, or squeezed lemons for more than two centuries, and all those assumptions have been lost. So, what did Melveeta omit because everyone just knew it?"

"That, Queen Eloise, is a most excellent question."

"Thank you, Assistant Court Seer to the Court Seer Abernatheen de Chipmunk."

They stared at their copy of the notes, thinking.

Jerome broke the silence, stroking his chin. "You know what the problem with that question is?"

"What?"

"You'd have to go back a couple of hundred years to answer it."

"Hmmm... That's not likely to happen, is it?"

"No. I don't think so."

Eloise nodded. "And even if we researched what life was like Back When, we'd still have the same problem. Anyone writing back then would have the same assumed knowledge. No one would want to read a document that said, 'First, pour the almond meal from its bag and decant the specified volume of olive oil from the jug.' They'd be bored to tears."

"I'm falling asleep just listening to you say that."

"But I still think the lack of assumed knowledge is something to keep in mind. Like, when she says, 'I cast a concealment spell and it was ineffective,' we get that she was trying to hide either herself or something, but we don't know how the concealment spell was cast, the purpose of it, or what we'd need to do if we wanted to replicate it.

You'd have to study strong magic techniques from back then to even be able to approach the problem. That's a lifetime's work right there."

"Time we don't have."

"My point precisely. So, maybe in our Çalahtic commentary around her scrolls, the points of assumed knowledge are something we should call out."

"Works for me."

19

TOKEN CONSIDERATION

Johanna stood at the window of the Peacock Room and watched heavy rain clouds deciding if now was the time to let loose their torrent or if they needed to stay pent up a bit longer.

She knew how they felt.

One of the things that surprised her about being queen was how little latitude she had for expressing her emotions. She still felt them all, of course, but everyone around her seemed to take the least little nostril flare or arched eyebrow and blow it completely out of proportion. A harsh word she failed to suppress made its way to the gossip heralds. A tear of sadness from the lingering grief over the death of her mother prompted the nearest handmaid to reach for a clean hanky. Çalaht forfend that she express frustration, lest someone cower away from her like they were about to get fifty lashes.

Her Uncle Doncaster really had messed these people up.

But it was her father who was becoming one of the worst offenders. Less and less did he seem to be giving her fair and frank advice. More and more, it appeared that the darkness of his own grief was reclaiming him. When it came to interacting with her, he tiptoed like a nervous mouse instead of striding like the first advisor he was supposed to be.

She glanced at him, standing at the far end of the Peacock Room, looking like he wanted to be anywhere but where he was.

Mind you, at that particular moment, she could relate.

All her practice at suppressing feelings was coming in very handy just then. Bosana de Coluber, the three-eyed Eastie snake, was freshly back from a trip to his home realm. The moment he'd arrived at Stained Rock, he had, for what felt like the thousandth time, "requested" an immediate meeting. And now, he sat coiled in the middle of the room, waiting.

Johanna could feel his strange third eye boring a hole into her back.

She stared out the window, working hard to tamp down her irkedness. Was "irkedness" even a word? Irksomeness? Irkitude? The fact that she was standing there thinking about variants of "irked" irked her even more.

Deep breath taken. Smile plastered onto her face. Then a graceful about-face toward the snake. "How lovely to have you back with us in the Northern Lands. I trust your travels were comfortable?"

"I do not overly concern myself with comfort," said de Coluber. "What concerns me more is bringing greetings directly from Her Imperialness, Queen Aglandau, long may she flourish in the sacred olive groves of her realm."

Johanna once again marveled at how he managed to speak without the lisp that so characterized his species. Learning that must have taken incredible discipline. "Your queen is well?"

"She and the queendom thrive. Thank you for asking." He nodded toward a burlap sack to his right. "I've returned with a present, Your Majesty."

Johanna stifled a groan. It would be something olive-y, presumably. Easties were complete dullards when it came to gift-giving. She looked at her father, who was staring blankly out a window of his own. Another one of his bad days. "First Advisor?"

Chafed jerked to awareness. "I agree, Your Majesty," he said.

Johanna frowned. "Agree with what?"

"With your opinion on the matter at hand." His face struggled not to betray just how pathetic he knew the comment to be.

She pointed. "If you could please bring me the ambassador's gift."

"Of course, Your Majesty." Chafed walked forward, stumbled a little, righted himself, nodded to de Coluber as he picked up the sack, then bowed as he handed it to Johanna.

The sack was big enough to house a family of gerbils and weighed much more than she'd expected. "Thank you."

"I know you like things for your garden," said the snake.

"Oh, that's kind." She set the bag down on a side table and untied its strings. Inside were numerous plant crowns, their long roots radiating from a central nubbin. They were too large and knobby to be strawberries. "Rhubarb?" she asked. She liked rhubarb, and hadn't gotten around to planting any yet. Johanna could almost taste the rhubarb pie in her future.

"Asparagus," said de Coluber.

Ugh. Just ugh. Johanna had never found an approach to asparagus that was palatable to her. Not baked, grilled, steamed, or pan-fried. Not sauced, chopped, or quiched. The plants would grow and thrive and she'd have to give their efforts away. They would be an intruder in her garden, which was filled only with plants she loved.

Johanna forced another smile. "That's wonderful. I've never attempted to grow them, so I appreciate the opportunity. My thanks to you and Queen Aglandau for your thoughtfulness."

"I shall convey your gratitude. The carriages with Queen Aglandau's coin have been parked at your counting house. Unloading has begun."

"I see. Again, thank you. My realm is grateful for the support."

It was the fifth delivery of coin to arrive from the Eastern Lands. The first one had been a Çalaht-sent miracle. It had provided Johanna the capability to begin making improvements in her realm. It had been desperately needed and very welcome. The second was the same. The third seemed more like an indulgence than a necessity. By the fourth, she was starting to feel uncomfortable. Chafed waved off her concerns, saying free coin was free coin, and immediately turned the discussion to what might be achieved with it.

Now here was the fifth. She and her father had argued vehemently over this one. She felt like they were taking it out of habit or convenience, rather than need. Chafed had pointed to the continuing dismal state of the royal coffers—a valid concern—and Johanna had allowed herself to be persuaded.

The snake shifted his coils. "I have one other matter to raise, if I may."

"Of course." Johanna sat on her throne and gestured for him to continue.

He fixed all three eyes on her. "My queen is grateful that she has been of assistance in helping you find your financial feet in these early days of your rule."

"And I have been grateful, as I've said on several occasions."

"I was hoping that your gratitude might find expression in a small concession."

Johanna frowned. "A concession?"

"A trade concession."

"What sort?"

"You know that Eastern Lands merchants favor Northern Lands wart creams above those of other realms."

"That's true," agreed Johanna. "I'd have to check, but I suspect we export more wart cream to your realm than any other."

"No need to check," said de Coluber. "We're your biggest consumers by a factor of three. As such, given the volume that we purchase and the fact that Queen Aglandau has been so supportive, it is my hope that we can reach an arrangement where our merchants can be favored somewhat with pricing."

"I don't set the price of wart cream. It's not something I've seen any need to get involved with."

"But you could. You're queen. It would be well within your rights to decree that a small concession be allowed for Eastern Lands merchants, to be applied to all purchases."

Something about him sat oddly with Johanna. "How small of a concession did you have in mind?"

"Thirty percent."

"What? You want me to order that prices be chopped by a third?"

De Coluber tilted his head to the side. "Not quite a third, Your Majesty."

"The Wart Creamers' Guild is a very strong presence in my queendom. I can't imagine they'd react to such a decree with anything less than pitchforks."

The snake looked at Chafed. "What do you think, First Advisor Gumball née de Chëëëkflïïïnt?"

Her father had returned to staring out the window, and looked surprised to have been called back to the conversation. "I... Uh... Well..." His cheeks went pink. "Apologies, but what was the topic?"

"Ambassador de Coluber has asked for an across-the-board thirty percent concession on all wart cream purchases by Eastie merchants."

Chafed's eyebrows arched. "Really? Our most important export? Whatever for?"

"As a token of gratitude to Queen Aglandau," said the snake. "For her continuing and generous support of the young queen's reign."

"I see." He paused, considering. "Well, I guess a concession doesn't seem completely unfair. If it was your mother, I think she'd consider it." Chafed shrugged, looking like he'd engaged enough on the topic, and that his window and his sadness were calling him back.

Johanna shook her head, and returned her attention to de Coluber. It seemed like she was going to have to give some kind of ground. "I could possibly accept First Advisor's position that a concession could be considered. But thirty percent is hardly a 'token.' Maybe three percent."

"Twenty-five," countered the snake.

At that point, it was just market haggling. They ended up at 12.873 percent, a ridiculous number that would take a lot of time, hemp parchment, and quills to calculate.

The snake bowed and took his leave. Johanna was left with the feeling of having been badly done by, especially since her next task was going to involve placating a lot of angry wart creamers.

20

MY DEAR ONOMATOPOEIA

Eloise sat alone in the Queen's Study, a pile of hemp parchment before her and a quill poised in her hand.

Words did not flow. She was paralyzed with uncertainty. She wasn't even sure how to start.

After the Privy Council meeting, it was agreed that Eloise should reach out to Her Maj Ono first, as the most senior monarch and the one whose cooperation was crucial if the idea was ever going to work.

But what should she write?

Eloise had already written and scratched out "Dearest Queen Onomatopoeia," "Hi Ono," "To Her Majesty, Onomatopoeia," "To Whom It May Concern," and "Yo There!"—all of which failed to strike the needed balance between formality and familiarity.

The context of her writing was also somewhat complex. This was an official representation from Eloise as queen, but it also needed to be persuasive, so the language couldn't be too dry. Further, she and the Southie queen had spent a couple of days together and had gotten reasonably close then (as close as one could with the difference in their ages and the fact that Eloise had accidentally gotten out of her noggin on prattleweed at a Çalahtist devotional), but it wasn't like they'd become quill pals. Her representation to Onomatopoeia through her ambassador had politely gotten nowhere, which felt like a rejection. And yet, Her Maj Ono had called her "her little song bird" when she'd assumed the throne and given Eloise a playful present of three bags of groats. These now had pride of place in the Queen's Chambers.

Eloise put the quill back in its stand and picked up the document that outlined the proposal. First Advisor had drafted it with help from Niville, and to Eloise's eye, it read pretty well. It kept to the spirit of what the Speaker for the Land had originally said—it would be a meeting of equals with the purpose of airing concerns and seeking mutually supportive ways of helping each other.

Jerome had sniffed at it when he first read it, calling it the Grand Council of Kumbaya. But even he had come around by the time he'd gotten to the end of the scroll and the principles were laid out.

So, the idea was to send a messenger directly to Onomatopoeia with the proposal scroll and a cover note.

It was the note she was stuck on. She wrote, "Hi there! It's Your Little Songbird!"

Nope. Too familiar. *Scratch*.

"Being a formal representation to Her Majesty, Queen Onomatopoeia from Eloise Hydra Gumball III..."

Too formal. *Scratch*.

"My Dear Onomatopoeia." That would have to do.

She wrote:

I hope this finds you well, healthy, and happy.

I haven't written to you directly since my Crown Plonking Ceremony, but I have received your well wishes through Ambassador Gléëèngarland Póöòîïn-tilist. Please allow me to personally thank you for your kindness and the gift of prattleweed seeds, stems, root shreds, and leaves that Ambassador Póöòîïntilist presented to me along with his credentials.

All very much appreciated.

You are undoubtedly aware that I've been having problems along my eastern border. This letter comes to you with a proposal, which I hope you will give your due consideration and support. It comes from a place of wanting to foster cooperation between the realms, and it strikes me as somewhat obvious that if we all sit down and talk, maybe we can find common ground and help each other out. Better that, than ramping up armaments production and shedding blood, which appears to be the way things are headed.

It is my hope that you will find this proposal appealing, and will take a role in helping to make it happen.

That was the core of it. When Eloise was happy with the words, she got a fresh quill and hemp parchment, copied it over without any of the mistakes a first draft inevitably had, then folded it and sealed it with her signet ring.

She needed to figure out who she could use to send it. Someone who was trustworthy. She couldn't send Lorch, who needed to stick around as her champion. And she needed Jerome to continue his research efforts. Hector de Pferd, perhaps? It would probably be too noticeable for him to be absent from the Horse Guards. She didn't like sending the Nameless One anywhere, as she didn't want to leave Lorch without a ready mount.

There was a knock at her door. "Princess Queen Eloise, is there anything you be needing?"

It was the wombat, RoyLee, wearing his Senior Page-In-Training livery.

Eloise looked at him—young, eager, healthy, and devoted. She knew he was comfortable on the back of a horse, so long as he had a basket to ride in. His bad eyesight wasn't helpful, but he was fiercely loyal and would carry out an instruction to the best of his ability. Having grown up in a gang of wombat ruffians, he was used to being stealthy and to traveling long distances.

But could he be trusted with a confidential message for Her Majesty, Queen Onomatopoeia?

Of course he could. It was RoyLee. She'd trust him with anything that didn't require keen visual perception.

"Actually, RoyLee, please come in. There is a task I'd like to discuss."

Half an hour later, fully briefed, RoyLee burst from the Queen's Study, yelling, "Secret mission for the queen! Secret mission for the queen!" Perhaps that wasn't quite in the spirit of the discretion that Eloise had in mind, but she was confident he was up for the task. The wombat carried with him her note to Her Maj Ono, the proposal document, and authorization to Ferdinand de Pferd, the royally appointed leader of the Queen's Stables, to assign RoyLee a transportation and protection horse so he could get to the Sclerotic Wold in The South as soon as was practicable.

That left Eloise just one more task—reaching out to her sister, walking back her accusations and invective, and trying to enlist her support for the Grand Council idea.

She'd use the private code they'd developed when they were nine—a substitution cipher they both knew how to crack. That way, Johanna would have to pay attention to the letter to understand it, and she could dispatch it using whichever trusted courier was at hand.

But she had to draft it before she could encode it.

Another blank page. Another fresh quill. A deep breath.

Dear Jo,

I wish humble pie could be baked in a way that tasted better. The one I'm currently eating tastes of salt, vinegar, and disappointment. While I still don't understand the decision you made, I can see that there's more to it than I perceived at first glance, and I should never have assumed or implied that you had anything other than the best interests of your queendom in mind.

Still, there are implications that perhaps bear discussion.

Which brings me to a proposal I hope you'll consider...

21

STILL LIKE A WEDDING

Lady Seneschal Läääcy de Aardvark stopped Eloise in a corridor. "May I have a word, Your Highness?"

"Of course. Do we need the privacy of my study?"

"No, ma'am, I don't think so." The aardvark curled her snout, like she was trying to decide how to approach the matter.

"Go ahead, Läääcy. Just say it."

"Yes, ma'am. You remember a few weeks back when we were talking about finding a coronation planner to organize your formal coronation?"

"Yes, yes. I do. Sorry, I haven't... I mean, I still don't..." Eloise let out a breath. "To be honest, I haven't even looked for one yet. It's very likely that conversation was the last I thought about it."

"That's OK, Your Highness. I think I may have found someone."

"Oh? Wow. That's good. Who?"

The aardvark whispered a name.

"Sorry, I didn't catch that," said Eloise.

She tried again, louder this time. "Helda de Anatidae."

Eloise's eyes widened. "Headlong Helda? You're kidding, right? This is a joke?"

"No, Your Highness. Not a joke."

"You're suggesting that I hire a gossip herald as my coronation planner? I should put a gossip herald in charge of all the pomp and ceremony, as well as all the celebrations that follow? It will be the biggest diplomatic event of the year, possibly of the decade, and I should have a gossip herald running it?"

"I think it could work," said Läääcy. "This wasn't a random suggestion. Mistress de Anatidae has a reputation for throwing massive, successful parties that have food, entertainment—the works. It's part of her business, because she has to foster good relationships with both her contacts and potential contacts. The parties have, if I may say so, quite the reputation, although, of course, I've never actually been to one. Mistress de Anatidae prides herself in throwing 'jaw-dropping' parties. Those were her words, not mine."

"This is an unexpected idea. Of all the people, Headlong Helda would never have occurred to me as a possibility. I'll have to give it some thought."

"Your Highness, I've spoken with First Advisor, and she says you have a break in your schedule now. As such, I took the liberty. Or maybe I took initiative. Sometimes it's hard to tell the difference. Anyway, I hope it's OK, but Mistress de Anatidae is in the Salle à Manger."

"I... Um... Do I really have to—"

Läääcy didn't let her finish. "Thank you, Your Highness. I'll have a pot of haggleberry tea brought. And New Chef just baked some crullers."

"Are they any good?"

The aardvark curled her snout to one side. "They're in line with most everything else he bakes."

"Well, an adequate cruller. That's so very tempting. But, sure, I'll talk to Helda."

"Thank you ma'am." She sent a page to the kitchens and led Eloise to the Salle à Manger. Stepping across the threshold, Helda stood, and Läääcy announced "Her Highness, Queen Eloise Hydra Gumball III."

"Thank you, Lady Seneschal," said Eloise. "Mistress Helda. So good to see you."

The goose was as primped as ever, with her gray wings and white body shining, although it appeared she'd eschewed the tail feather plumage extensions. The last time Eloise had seen her—in Flachberg, at her preparation session before the parlay with Queen Aggie—she'd not been wearing the mesh of gold links around her neck, but now they were back, encasing her from chin to breast. A quick glance at the claws on her webbed feet revealed rubies, instead of sapphires, pasted to the tops in a surprisingly fetching way. As Eloise approached, the goose did the waterfowl version of a curtsy. "Your Highness, I'm sure you don't really think that, but it is good of you to say."

Helda's directness was always a little disarming. "Shall we sit? How have you been since Flachberg?"

The goose settled onto her chair. "Busy, busy, busy. There was all the reporting that came out of your parlay with Queen Aglandau. May I say that the dramatic nature of your escape was incredibly popular with my audience. I barely had to embellish."

"Thank you, I think?"

A serving wench arrived with a tea service and crullers. She poured two cups, served Eloise a cruller, cut another into small pieces for Helda, and left. Eloise blew across the rim of her cup, then sipped. Either New Chef was getting better at the tea, or she was getting used to the way he made it.

The goose nipped a segment of cruller, swallowed, then said, "I have a confession, Your Highness."

Eloise set down her cup. "Oh, what's that?"

"It was me who suggested to your Lady Seneschal that I organize your formal coronation. She didn't come up with that one on her own."

"You did? I guess that's not surprising. How did that come about?"

"Your Highness, I simply identified an obvious need. It's what I do—spot needs, then do something about them. Usually, that 'something' has to do with me telling others about them. In this case, I thought I'd step in to help."

"Läääcy said you give 'jaw-dropping' parties?"

"I'll allow it's possible that you've not heard of my annual Grand Goose Gala, as we move in somewhat different circles. I never managed to entice your parents to attend, although I did invite them, as I will invite you later this year when it comes around again. My goal with the Grand Goose Gala each year is to get everyone who attends to say 'wow,' and for good reasons, not bad. That requires a carefully executed blend of food, drinks, costumes, and entertainment. Now, Queen Eloise, does that remind you of anything?"

"A coronation?"

"A coronation. Exactly. Your coronation needs to leave the punters saying 'wow,' but for all the right reasons. Unlike... Well, we don't have to go there."

"Go ahead. You can say it. Unlike my Crown Plonking."

"Your formal coronation will be a way to wipe that incident from their memories, and give everyone a chance to glory in the spectacle that is their monarchy. It's a way to say, 'Look everyone! You're in safe hands! This particular queen is one you can be proud of!'"

"You've thought a lot about this."

"Yes, Your Highness. I have. A lot. But this is ultimately simple. You have a requirement, and I have the means to help you meet it."

Eloise and the goose both sipped their tea, letting that sit between them.

"Tell me, Helda. Why would you want to do this? What's in it for you?"

The goose honked a laugh. "Isn't that obvious? Access. This is pure self-interest on my part. In my business, access is everything. If I'm in charge, then who, other than me, will have the full inside scoop? It isn't just that I *can* help you with this, I *want* to help you with it. This is a once in a lifetime chance for someone like me."

This sounded awfully mercenary to Eloise, but she had to give the goose credit for directness. And if she really did know how to organize a big bash, then giving her inside access might be a price worth paying. "What about the actual formal coronation part of it, rather than the receptions and parties afterwards? There's a lot of Protocol that needs to be respected and carefully followed."

Helda curled her neck and lifted her head. "Believe me, I know my Protocol. I've been snarling at royals for years about various breaches, both minor and profound. I study the *Livre de Protocol* the way the Venerable Prelate Herself supposedly studies the *Scrolls of Çalaht*, although I suspect my devotion to my source material is greater than hers."

This was straight-up blasphemy, and, Eloise suspected, also likely to be true. The Venerable Prelate Herself had always struck her as singularly disengaged.

Eloise picked up a spoon and drew circles on the tablecloth with it. "I'm not quite sure how to ask this next question, but here goes. The coverage of me and my reign has been... mixed at best. Much of it has been downright unkind. How do I know that inside access won't lead to the stories being scurrilous and scandalous?"

Helda nodded. "It's a fair question. Look at it this way. If I control the planning, you can rest assured that I'll want the coronation to be seen in the best light possible. Consider that a side benefit of me taking on this task. My reporting will glow so much, everyone will want to be here. Everyone will want to bask in the glory. I can promise you that, at least."

"Sure, sure, sure. I get how that works for you. But what about your competitors? Won't they be jealous of your access? Isn't there a risk that your coverage will be one way and theirs will be the exact opposite, out of spite, if nothing else?"

"Yes, that's a real risk. But I've been dealing with my colleagues for years and years. I know how to drip out enough exclusive details for them to use to keep them on side." She sipped her tea, then continued. "What I'm about to say may sound like boasting, but it's a simple fact: most of my colleagues are neither particularly smart nor particularly innovative. In fact, they are downright lazy. That means, Your Highness, that they are followers, not leaders. They often take their cues from me. So if I start going in one direction with my coverage, most, if not all, will come along with me. That one I can't promise, but I can be fairly confident of it."

Eloise looked at her. "Well, that sounds good."

"Of course, you have to do your part."

"What's my part?"

"First, you have to give me a sufficient budget to do a good job. And second, you have to avoid doing anything so monumentally stupid that it would be negligent of me not to report on it."

"Pardon? Monumentally stupid?"

"The big stuff, like getting snockered in public; blatant, overt corruption and self-dealing; finding yourself in the family way without having first chosen a spouse—that kind of thing."

"That all sounds avoidable. I can promise you I won't get in the family way between now and my coronation, and I'm unlikely to get hammered in public or get caught acting corruptly. As for the budget, we'll have to negotiate that one, but I understand that we don't want it to look like the coronation cost less than a used dray from Lurid Eddie."

"Good. Good, good, good," said Helda. "Now, I think of a coronation as being a bit like a wedding."

"Really? Wow. That's what Lady Seneschal Póöòmáäàdéëè said. She said, and I quote, 'Wedding planning follows the Golden Rule of Weddings. The person with the gold makes the rules.' She also said, 'What works best is that the happy couple has the wedding *they* want to have. They don't try to meet someone else's expectations. They don't fulfill someone else's vision of a wedding. They think, 'This is who we are. This is what we want.'"

The goose nodded. "That was sound advice from your former Lady Seneschal, and mirrors what I was about to say. So have you worked out who you are and what kind of coronation you want?"

Despite herself, Eloise felt her cheeks flush. "Not exactly, no. My former Lady Seneschal gave me a list of things that she wanted me to decide, but I gave that list to Lady Seneschal de Aardvark."

"Oh, I have that." Helda pecked at a pouch around her neck, pulled out Eloise's list, and beaked it to her. "It was a good starting point then, and it is a good starting point now. Have you reached any conclusions about any of the items?"

Eloise unfolded the note and read off some of the items. "Color palette, choice of portrait artist, number of receptions, distribution of food in Brague, distribution of food outside Brague, overall theme... There really is a lot here to think about."

Helda tilted her head. "But no decisions yet? Guests? Entertainments? Musicians?"

"Actually, there, I do have a few ideas, and a couple of promises I've made. Have you ever been to the Velvet Cask?"

"I have. Some good acts perform there." The goose suddenly stopped and clacked her beak together several times, completely interrupting the conversation. "I just remembered something. Your First Advisor invited me to a gathering of gossip heralds. She gave me an invitation and said I was the first to be invited. May I give you some advice on that?"

"Certainly. I'd love to hear it."

"Don't. Don't even think about it."

"Why not? I thought it might be a good way to maybe get on their good sides. Or at least help them realize I'm a person with feelings."

"Bad idea. Very bad idea. You might think you will be able to control the conversation, but you won't."

"What do you mean?"

"Tell me, Your Highness, when do you plan to take a spouse? Or are you more partial to taking a husband, wife, or less-specific partner? What are you wearing to the wedding? Who are your bridesmaids?"

"I—"

"Is it true that you no longer beat up your sister every time you see her? I hear your running sores are getting worse. What creams do you use to treat them?"

"I don't—"

Helda stood and leaned forward, as close to Eloise as she could get. "What did you have for breakfast? What did you have for lunch? What did you have for dinner? What are your dieting tips for the goodmen and goodwomen out there? How do you stay so thin? Why have you put on so much weight?"

"I don't... I haven't—"

"Why not?"

"Why not what?"

"I'll take that as a yes. No more questions."

Eloise felt her heart racing and her mouth go dry. The goose's sudden viciousness floored her. "That was uncalled for. And totally unfair."

"Your Highness, they will eat you alive. I know I would. Don't. Just don't."

"Point taken. I'll have First Advisor call it off. Consider your invitation rescinded."

"Good." Helda waddled backwards and settled back into her chair. "Now, what about the Velvet Cask?"

22

WHAT'S NEXT?

Eloise left Helda and the Salle à Manger after another forty-five minutes of wide-ranging coronation-centered discussion. She felt like she was finally in capable hands for her big, formal event. It was a relief.

She turned a corner and saw two figures at the end of the corridor facing away from her—a cleaning wench and a cleaning lackey. Nothing unusual there; cleaning staff were all over the castle at that time of day. The one on the left carried a bucket of dirty water that sloshed dangerously close to the edge and she seemed to be gesturing with a sponge. The one on the right had an ash bucket full to the brim in one hand and a fireplace shovel, brush, and long-handle dustbin tucked under his other arm.

"I don't want to," said Sponge. "And you can't make me."

"I'm with her," agreed Ash Bucket.

They weren't talking to each other. There was a third figure, occluded by the other two.

A smaller figure in a black robe.

Läääcy de Aardvark.

"I tasked you with cleaning the Receiving Room. Her Highness will be in there tomorrow and it—"

"What's the point? What's the absolute bleedin' point?" said Sponge. "We cleaned it last week. Surely that's good enough."

"'Do this. Do that.'" Ash Bucket was mocking Läääcy's aardvark voice. "Well, I'm sick of it. I'm sick of being told what to do."

"You are cleaning staff," said Läääcy. She was clearly trying to keep her voice calm, but there was too much pleading in it for Eloise's taste. "Your role is to clean. And I need you to clean the Receiving Room."

"And we do clean." Sponge waggled her sponge. "See this? It's not been idle. But I say that the Receiving Room is just fine as it is."

This won't do, thought Eloise. *Not at all.*

She walked toward the group and in her most pleasant voice, said. "Why, g'mid-arvo to you all."

The two cleaners froze in mid-sentence and spun around. Ash Bucket fumbled his bucket and barely avoided dumping it. Sponge was less agile and there was an explosive *splort!* as it hit the flagstones. A bow and a curtsy quickly followed.

"Is everything OK?" she asked. "Lady Seneschal?"

The fur on the aardvark's face bristled in embarrassment. Läääcy looked at her, mortified. "Everything is fine, Your Highness. No problems here. But thank you for the inquiry."

Good. She was protecting her staff.

"Please be at rest."

The cleaners relaxed, but kept their eyes firmly on their feet.

Eloise stepped closer and straightened into her most regal pose. "May I ask your names, please?"

"Tïîm, ma'am," said Ash Bucket.

"Gurt, ma'am," said Sponge.

"Hi Tĩĩm. Hi Gurt. I'm Eloise."

"We know that, ma'am," said Tĩĩm.

"Tell me, Tĩĩm and Gurt, which one of you do you want me to appoint to be in charge of running the castle?"

Both of them gasped, horrified.

"Tell me. I'm going to need it to be one of you."

Neither said anything.

"Come on. I don't have all afternoon. Don't you want to be in charge of everything and everyone?"

Gurt mumbled something.

"Sorry, I didn't quite catch that."

"I said, no thank you ma'am. If it's all the same to you, I don't want to be in charge of everything and everyone."

"Why not? All that power to make decisions. All that telling everyone what to do." Eloise took another step closer, which they matched with a shuffle backwards. "Why wouldn't you want that?"

"It is a thankless task," muttered Tĩĩm. "Everyone is always mouthing off. Everyone is always being disobedient. Having to wrangle everyone all the time. It'd be a terrible burden."

"Tĩĩm's right. It'd be a hard and miserable job," said Gurt. "I wouldn't do it for all the radishes in Lower Glenth."

"I see. You know what?" There was a pause, while Eloise waited for one of them to actually respond.

"What, ma'am?" said Gurt.

"You're both right."

"We are?" said Tĩĩm. He looked a bit confused not to have been contradicted. Or reprimanded.

"Yes, you are. It's a hard and miserable job. A terrible burden. I wouldn't want to do it either. I'm incredibly grateful that I don't have to, and that Lady Seneschal de Aardvark is willing to take it on. You should be, too."

"I am, ma'am," said Gurt.

"You know how I show her that I'm grateful?" Another pause, while they worked out that she was still expecting an actual answer.

"No ma'am," said Tim.

"I listen to what she has to say. And when she asks me to do something, I do it, right away and without complaint."

Both of them looked confused. "But you're the queen," said Gurt.

"True. I am."

"And she asks you to do things?"

"All the time. It's part of her terrible, burdensome job that she has to ask me to make decisions that affect the running of the queendom, like who to keep on staff, and who needs to be sent away from Castle de Brague with the next tinker's cart to come along." This was an exaggeration—Läääcy would hardly bother her with that kind of thing, unless the circumstances were extraordinary, and tinker's carts would never be involved—but Eloise felt the veiled threat was pertinent.

"I didn't know that, ma'am," said Tïîïm.

"That's OK. Not many people do. So, from now on, I need you to do something for me. Can you promise me that?"

"Yes, ma'am," said Gurt, nodding, not waiting to know what she was promising.

"I need you to show your gratitude to Lady Seneschal the way I do—by doing what she asks, when she asks it, without complaint. Can you do that for me?"

Both nodded.

"And there's a phrase I keep in mind while I'm doing it. Do you know what that is?"

Head shakes.

"What's next?"

"I don't understand, ma'am," said Gurt.

"I look around and think, 'What's next?' I figure out what the next thing is that needs doing, and you know what I do?"

Tiïm's voice was small. "You do it."

Eloise beamed at him. "Exactly. Say it with me. 'What's next?'"

"What's next?" they both said. To her surprise, Läääcy joined them.

"That was great," Eloise said. "I need you to do one other thing for me. Tell the rest of the staff about our conversation. Let them know that the queen does what Lady Seneschal requires right away and without complaint, and that you've promised me to do the same. Can you do that for me?"

"Yes, ma'am," they both said.

"And you'll tell them about 'What's next?' I want to hear people murmuring 'What's next?' as I go through the halls."

"Will do, ma'am," said Gurt, and Tiïm nodded agreement.

"Excellent. I'll leave you to your afternoons. Tiïm, Gurt, lovely to have met you. Lady Seneschal, I'll see you next time you need me to do something."

"Yes, ma'am," said Läääcy.

She walked away, leaving them to their tasks.

Eloise didn't know if this would make a difference to Läääcy at all, but she sure hoped it would.

❧ 23 ☙

GLORIFIED KAFFEEKLATSCH

Dear Queen Eloise,

I have received your latest message, and acknowledge receipt of the previous one, as well as the representation made to me through my ambassador. I am responding to them in aggregate.

I'm not sure why I had to decode that last message, given what you had to say. An official messenger would have sufficed. I assume you had your reasons, but forgive me if I don't have the time to reciprocate by encoding this response. Matters of the realm are pressing and there is much to do here in the Northern Lands.

You're right. My decision to take Her Imperialness, Queen Aglandau Ponentine's coin was fully pragmatic. I wanted to get some capital improvements underway, the financing of which was proving most challenging. When Queen Aglandau's offer came along, it would have been foolish of me to turn it down, given the needs of my queendom.

That you are having problems with Queen Aglandau is hardly my concern. Contrary to what we were taught as girls, the Western Lands is not the center of the world. I no longer treat it as such.

As for your suggestion of a Grand Council, I'm not so sure there's a genuine need for it. I mean, if the others are coming, then perhaps I'll make the effort to be there, too. But I'm unconvinced that it would be more than a glorified kaffeeklatsch, and so am disinclined. I would need convincing assurances that things would be otherwise.

Yours,

Queen Johanna

PS. Father's usefulness as First Advisor is waning. He's proving very set in his thinking, and more to the point, grief continues to dominate his mind. There doesn't seem to be much I'm able to do for him. If you'd like to invite him back to your realm, feel free.

❧

"So much for sisterly love," muttered Eloise. The tone of Johanna's letter practically froze her eyebrows off.

Perhaps she deserved it, given what she'd written previously.

But perhaps she didn't. Johanna's involvement with Aglandau was almost certainly more problematic for her than she realized. What Johanna had done would, sooner or later, come back to bite her in the tuchus. Eloise was sure of that.

She called for a page and sent for First Advisor. When Thëjëts lumbered into the Queen's Study, Eloise handed her Johanna's note.

First Advisor read it, her frown deepening with every word. "Well, it isn't exactly 'Get lost and shove it up your nose.' But it's far from 'I'd love to be part of it.'"

"It has been years since I've been able to count on her. This is just further proof of that." This wasn't exactly a fair thing to say, but it was how Eloise felt, so fair could get stuffed.

"It seems clear that if we can get Queen Aglandau there, your sister will follow." Thëjëts handed back the letter. "Have you heard from any of the others?"

"No. Not yet."

"I thought not. So…"

"So," said Eloise.

"It's still down to Her Maj Ono and the khan. No change there, really."

"No. Johanna's response does not materially affect what's going on. It just hurts more than it should."

❧ 24 ❧

UNEXPLAINED JUMP

The next morning found Eloise and Jerome hunkered down yet again in That Room We Don't Talk About Because We Don't Want People to Know About It, hunched over Melveeta's scroll. As Jerome finished reading a paragraph, Eloise wrote. "'... whereupon Her Majesty expressed displeasure at the rate of exploration with the object. I promised to redouble my efforts.' And that, my queenly friend, is the tenth page done. Shall we take a break before we tackle page eleven?"

Jerome stepped away from the table so he was safely away from the babies, and stretched his tail, back, and neck.

"No, I'm good," said Eloise. "I need to keep going. It's hard enough for me to get here, and I've got to get this thing done before First Advisor thinks I've skipped town."

"Fair enough. Let's push on. Want to swap and let me take notes for a while?"

"Sure." Eloise stood, stepped back, stretched, massaged her wrists and shoulder, and moved to where she had a clear view of the next page of scroll. "Ready?"

Jerome took a fresh sheet of hemp parchment from a stack on the table and picked up Eloise's graphite stick. "Ready."

Eloise covered her blurry eye and read slowly so Jerome could transcribe. "'Decided to try more radical test of object's dampening effects. Put in a hemp bag at waist height and walked into main office of the Mages' Guild.' Caused chaos, but went undetected.'"

"Does she say what kind of chaos there was?"

"No, unfortunately not. That would have been useful."

"You have to give the old girl credit. She was clever."

"And she had nerve. Can you imagine deliberately walking into a guild hall of mages with the explicit purpose of disrupting all the magic you found there? I don't think I could do it."

"Me either. And yet she did."

"Yes, indeed, she did." Eloise paused, thinking. "There's one big problem I'm having as we read through her notes."

"Just one? I have about a thousand, but go ahead."

"How did she get from ascertaining that the Star of Whatever could dampen magic to using it to amplify magic? It seems so counter-intuitive. Amplification is the polar opposite of what she was observing. So how did she make that jump?"

"So far, that's not in her notes at all."

"Not that I've been able to tell." Eloise pointed to the random array of symbols around the page. "Unless it's in these things, somehow. I mean, what in the name of Çalaht's impacted wisdom teeth are they? Are they doodles? Some sort of code? They have no rhyme or reason, and there's no legend or explanation."

"They don't make sense at all," agreed Jerome. "And they're all through the pages in the margins, but at the end..." He pointed to the last sheet, which was only half full. "Here, there's a whole cluster of them."

"It looks like a paragraph mark. See, that and that look like punctuation."

Jerome peered closer. "I hadn't noticed that, but now that you've said it, it seems obvious. Which makes me think 'code' again." He paused. "I just realized that we haven't been including those symbols in the transcription. Maybe we should."

"That's a good idea. Let's finish doing all the words," said Eloise. "Then we can do another pass to put the symbols in. After we have a complete copy with our notes and all her symbols, we can take a step back and look at it all as a whole."

"That's a plan, Queen El." Jerome went back to their transcription spot. "Go ahead and read the next bit. We still have a lot to do."

❦ 25 ❦

AVAILABLE LEVERS AND BUTTONS

Queen Onomatopoeia's reply came that afternoon, hand-delivered by RoyLee. The wombat looked absolutely exhausted. He must have been traveling at full speed for days, given how fast he'd returned.

"Thank you, RoyLee," Eloise said, taking the message from him. "How was your journey?"

"I no be complaining, Princess Queen Eloise, but the Southies be having some right strange ideas about us non-human folk."

"That they do. Did you run into any problems?"

"I be good at keeping my mouth shut, so I no be having problems. But, I no be in a rush to go back there, either."

She leaned toward him and whispered, "To be honest, neither am I. Thank you again for doing this for me."

"My pleasure, Princess Queen Eloise." Then he bowed and said, "Despite what I just be saying, it would be my pleasure to be doing so again."

"You're a good wombat, RoyLee."

144

"And you're a good human."

"Thank you. I appreciate your saying so. Now, go get some rest."

She watched him go, then took the letter into the Queen's Study to read.

Dear Little Songbird,

How lovely to receive your message. Çalaht knows, I understand how busy things are for a new queen, so it was particularly pleasing to hear from you.

Let's skip any other niceties and get straight to the crux of your missive. I think something like what you propose is long overdue. I know you have ongoing challenges with Queen A, and I'm sure you know our guest worker situation with the Easties is particularly (and unnecessarily) fraught—but, fortunately, not subject to military measures (yet). Getting together and sitting around a table like adults to discuss the issues facing us sounds civilized and needed. So please count me in.

Would it be too bold of me to make three suggestions?

First, leave it to me to get Queen Aggie there. If you're the one who approaches her, she'll say "no" before she's finished opening the envelope. But I have some levers available to me, buttons I have been holding off pushing, which I can now deploy. So figure that, barring my levers breaking (metaphorically speaking), she and I will both attend. That leaves your sister (sisterly support can be assumed) and the khan (always a mystery—I've never even met him).

Second, I have a suggestion of where "there" should be.

You're perhaps familiar with the Midpoint of All the Realms in the Central Ranges? There's a seminary there, which has facilities that would suit such a gathering well enough. The location is equally annoying for all of us to get to. It's in the khan's realm, and he'd be as neutral a host as we could choose. I'll leave it to you to convince him of that role (since you know him better than I do).

Third, pick a date and stick to it. If you're agreeable, then let us set a date for four weeks hence from the date of this letter. That gives everyone time to prepare and travel, but keeps it soon enough that it is imminent.

I do hope this initiative works. I'd hate to see your queendom overrun (the threat of that is real, and don't kid yourself that it isn't). That's a very self-interested statement to make—that outcome would be bad for all of us. The threat from Aggie to the rest of us is quite real.

Yours in Çalaht's embrace,

—O

P.S. Is what my sources tell me true, that your sister took A's coin? If so, what a curious decision. So many downsides, and other than some coin, so few upsides. I'd love your opinion on why she did it. It seems... Well, it seems naïve.

THAT WAS A YES, THEN. AN ENTHUSIASTIC YES, EVEN.

What a relief to have something actually go right for once.

And Queen Onomatopoeia had addressed her as a peer. Also a relief.

Eloise set the letter on her desk and asked a page to find First Advisor.

Ten minutes later, Bënnïë-Änn Thëjëts was knocking on the Queen's Study door, and two minutes after that, she'd read the letter from the Southie queen and handed it back to Eloise. "That's about as good a response as you could have hoped for. And I like her suggestion of the Midpoint of All the Realms." First Advisor walked to the map table and pointed to a spot right in the middle. "It's there."

"I didn't realize that was a place name," said Eloise. "I thought it was more like a geographic marker."

"It's a place alright. There's a small tourist village there that sells a lot of kitsch, like embroidered garments that say, 'My noble lord went to the Midpoint of All the Realms and all I got was this stupid tunic.' That kind of thing. Just outside the village, up a steep hill, there's a seminary. They have a history of scholarly work and an enviable library called the Bibliotheca de Çalaht, and they've long hosted gatherings of monks and religious organizations. I wouldn't call the facilities uncomfortable, but there's a sparseness to them. It's a savvy suggestion from Her Maj Ono. The choice conveys a neutrality of location and host, and the surroundings would signal a seriousness of purpose."

"Sounds good. I guess we leave Her Maj Ono to communicate with Aggie. I'll put the idea of hosting to the khan, and we'll start making plans for traveling there."

First Advisor chuckled.

"What?"

"Oh, there's so, so much more to do than that. This is one of those things where there will be chaos if everything isn't agreed to in advance."

"Like what?"

"Just off the top of my head?"

"Sure."

"How many people are allowed in the entourage? How many meetings will there be? Over how many days? Are meetings to be held at night? Where will they be? How many soldiers are allowed to accompany each monarch? How close are they allowed to be to the meeting facility itself? What shape will the table be? What color and material will it be? What table arrangements will there be and how will they be placed? Who will sit where? What's the color scheme of the room? Will there be a theme? Will there be windows? Will it just be the five monarchs around a table or are assistants allowed in the room as well? Will there be sidebar, one-on-one meetings? Who gets to speak first? Who gets to speak last? Can one choose not to speak? Will there be voting or is unanimity required? Who pays for it? How much will be budgeted overall? If the costs are to be split, what percentage will each realm be responsible for? Who does the catering? How many meals will be planned for? Will the doors be sealed and locked? How long will the sessions be? Will the monarchs be forced to submit to a search for weapons on their persons? What will the agenda be? Will there be an agenda at all? Will there be a joint communique released at the end? If so, who will draft it? Will it be drafted in advance? Will there be entertainments? How many entertainments per day or night? Is the khan the official host or an unofficial host? Will the monarchs stand for a portrait? If they do stand for portrait, will they be asked to wear outfits that reflect some aspect of the host realm? How stupid are those outfits allowed to be? Hats or no hats? Does everyone need to bring their own chair? Are there limits on how big the chairs can be? Will there be an exchange of gifts? Is the—"

"OK, OK, OK." Eloise rubbed her temples. "I get it, I get it. You're saying that four weeks is barely enough time to pull this thing off?"

"It may as well be tomorrow. There's no doubt that a lot of people are going to be very busy in the coming days and weeks, myself and my counterparts among them."

"Do we need to change the timeline?"

First Advisor lifted a shoulder. "I like the idea of putting a time pressure on it. The situation is urgent, so the meeting should happen urgently."

"Is it doable?"

"Do you want it done?"

"Yes," said Eloise. "Definitely, yes."

"Then it's doable. But if you'll excuse me, I'll need to get to it."

"You'll keep me in the loop?"

"Much more than that. I'll make sure you are core to the planning."

"Good. I don't want to be surprised."

"Good diplomacy does not allow for many surprises. Surprises mean that planning has failed somewhere along the line. What you want are solid expectations and a framework that actually lets things get done."

❧ 26 ☙

BOARD BEFORE YOUR HEAD

Naranbaatar Enkhtuya, the Central Ranges ambassador, snorted with profound derision, a sound that echoed in the Receiving Room, where Eloise sat on the Listening Throne wearing the I Know These Are Delicate Matters cape. "You want the khan to do what?"

Eloise smoothed the cape over her legs in a conscious effort to keep her composure. "I would like His Alacrity, Khan Nergüi Unbenannt Nimetuseta, to attend the inaugural Grand Council of the Realms as the head of his realm. Further, I would like him to act as the gathering's host."

The mare raised her head and arched her neck, making her even taller. Then she neighed out an explosive laugh. "You've met the khan. You've met the Us. Why would he possibly even consider doing such a ridiculous thing?"

"Well, with permission, we would like to meet at the facilities at the Midpoint of All the Realms."

"You wish to meet at Dundad Baigaa Ter Tseg? At that place where the religious fanatics congregate and Çalahtist reprobates gather?"

"I don't know that I would use the word 'reprobates,' but, yes, Çalahtist scholars convene there to discuss religious matters. My point is, we'd like to convene all of the monarchs there to discuss a more secular topic—inter-realm relationships."

"So there will be bloodshed."

"No. No, the point is to avoid the bloodshed."

"And all the queens will be there? That's confirmed?"

"Not quite. We definitely have two on board, a third is considered highly likely, and the fourth is a probably. With the khan, that would be everyone."

"Don't you have more comfortable places to go than Dundad Baigaa Ter Tseg? It really is a most unappealing pit. Perhaps you could host it here? Or find a location that's a bit less in the direction of, say, my realm?"

"Dundad Baigaa Ter Tseg—that's what you call it?—has the advantage of being more or less equidistant for each of the queens. Plus, and I say this with respect, the deeply unaligned nature of the Us means that we would be meeting somewhere none of the queens might have the home paddock advantage."

The mare shook her head. "You saw how little traction your alliance idea got. And here, you're asking for more engagement between the Us and the savages, since none of the queens are even equines of the Not Us. I really don't care for your chances of having the khan agree to this."

Eloise looked at her hands, clasped carefully in her lap to avoid any tells that her gestures might betray. How could she convince the mare to take the idea to her khan and then advocate on its behalf?

She stood, took off her cape, hung it on the back of her throne, and said, "I feel like a walk. Ambassador Enkhtuya, would you do me the kindness of coming with me?"

The mare licked her lips twice, thinking about it, then said, "It would be my honor."

"If you'd be so kind as to follow me."

She led the mare out to the Culpability Courtyard. Instead of walking its perimeter, the path she took for her morning runs, they strode out into the grassy middle, where a bright patch of sunlight bathed rose bushes that were showing an enthusiasm for the emerging spring weather. Eloise walked to one in particular. "You know what this particular bush reminds me of?"

"No, Your Highness. I don't."

Eloise pulled up her sleeve to reveal a recently-healed scar. "An attempted assassination. A crossbow bolt pierced my arm. That was after one pinged off my crown, missing my skull by short lengths. I fell into this bush, but at least I didn't become rosebush food."

"I didn't know there'd been an attempt on your life. Did you crush the one who assailed you into dust?"

"They managed to kill themselves, which saved me the effort and any associated moral quandary. But that's not the point I'm trying to make."

"What are you saying?"

"I'm saying that someone tried to have me killed, and the clues are vague enough that I can't tell you who it was, although I have my strong suspicions. But whoever organized for it to happen, they're putting me in a situation I don't want to be in. I'm not a fan of using crossbow bolts to settle disputes or score political advantage. That's not the world I want to live in." She turned to the horse. "Ambassador, I understand that the khan and the Us are fundamentally uninterested in that which happens beyond your herd. Otherwise, you wouldn't use the terms 'Not Us' and 'savage,' both of which, I'll add, are deeply offensive."

"Your offense is not my problem."

Eloise pointed at her. "That right there—that's what I'm talking about. You don't give two bent coins about anyone else. And I get it. It has served you to be this way. You train in your ways and you set yourselves apart, and you leave the rest of the realms to each other."

"Correct."

"I think the time for that has passed."

The mare flapped her ears back, wary. "Who are you to decide that for the Us?"

"I'm not deciding anything for you. I'm pointing to trends. The political winds are shifting around you. There are two new queens on half your borders. A third queen who has already acted aggressively against one of them and apparently co-opted the other. If she's willing to send troops against me, what's to stop her doing the same to you?"

"We have trod this ground already." Ambassador Enkhtuya flicked her tail. "Our lands are a midden heap compared to yours. There's a reason the savages call our realm the Central Carbuncle. Our realm suits us and our existence, and not much else. If one wants to grow olives or radishes or whatever, one doesn't hunt for land where I was born, ignoring the fact that if you tried to, we'd hunt you back to where you came from."

"With respect, Ambassador, that is still a naïve position." Eloise clasped her hands behind her back and resumed walking. "The Eastie queen isn't just looking for land, she's looking for distraction and diversion, for scapegoats, for any short-term advantage she can find. You don't think she's trying to figure out how to march in the Central Ranges? She's like a conjurer waggling the fingers of one hand to draw your attention while she steals your coin purse with the other."

"We do not wear coin purses."

"I'm being metaphoric. I'm saying that being disinterested in the affairs of the 'savages' and 'Not Us' is short-sighted. I'm saying that your khan—out of a sense of self-preservation and for the protection of the Us—needs to step onto the stage of the realms and demand some of the attention. The easiest way to establish himself as an equal and interested party who has a people to protect and help prosper is to host this meeting of the monarchs on his lands and on his terms. It's a way to make a statement of self-determination to the others and to his own people. It's a way of saying, 'We of the Central Ranges matter, we take ourselves seriously, and we speak with one voice, as you speak in one voice for your own realms.'"

"But we don't speak in one voice for the people of our realm. We speak in one voice for the Us."

"That is to your disadvantage. Are you telling me the only people in the Central Ranges who have any value, who have something to contribute, are those with four legs, a mane, and a tail?"

"Yes. That has always been our way."

"Then you may as well walk around with boards before your heads." Eloise mimed a piece of wood in front of her face.

The hair rose on Enkhtuya's withers. "You are saying we're stupid."

"I'm saying not looking beyond your own herd is to your detriment. It's an own goal. I'm saying that my problems may not be your problems today, but that doesn't mean they won't be your problems tomorrow. There's a solid chance that one of these days, some unnamed queen is going to show up on your border thinking it might be worth quelling some alleged internal unrest. That's the day you might find it useful to have us 'savages' and the 'Not Us' on your side and interested in a mutually self-preserving outcome."

The mare was quiet. Idly, she reached down and took a mouthful of the lawn, chewed twice, then jerked up, eyes wide, one ear flapped back, one ear forward. "Sorry, Your Highness. I was lost in thought. I eat when I'm preoccupied. Apologies. I don't even know if this area is allowed for food or not."

Eloise spread her arms to take in the Culpability Courtyard. "My lawn is your lawn."

"That's generous of you, Queen Eloise." The mare slowly chewed her mouthful, but did not take another. She swallowed and said, "Much of what you say would be considered heretical if spoken in the gathering of the Us. But I fear what you say also has truth in it. I will take your words to the ear of the khan, and will return with his words."

"I would be grateful. We are hoping to meet in less than a month. How soon do you think you'll return with the khan's response?"

"Less than a month? Truly?"

"Truly."

"I would normally say ten days. But I'll leave immediately, and endeavor to be back in five. You have to allow that His Alacrity will want to connect with the Purity before he replies. That takes time."

"That would be great. And thank you for hearing me out. You'll give my personal regards to the khan?"

"I will. It will be up to him to accept them or not."

❦   27   ❦

NOT. THE. ORIGINAL

Once again, sleep wouldn't come for Eloise. Instead of fighting it, she surrendered to wakefulness. She popped her head out of the door to find RoyLee on duty (if curled up and snoring could be considered on duty).

"RoyLee?" she whispered. "Are you awake?"

The wombat jolted from slumber, shouting, "We are the Wombanditos! The fiercest gang with bad eyesight in all the realms! Heeyahhhh!" Then he woke up enough to squint around and remember where he was. "Apologies, Your Highnessness. I no be doing that for a very long time."

"That's OK. I was wondering if you could organize a pot of haggleberry tea, and have someone stoke the fire in my hearth."

"You no be sleeping again, Princess Queen Eloise?"

"Unfortunately, no."

"That be OK. Will you be needing anything else?"

"Not at the moment."

The wombat bowed, then ran toward the kitchens, calling, "Tea for the sleepless queen! Tea for the sleepless queen!"

Fifteen minutes later, she was blowing across the lip of a cup of Conk Out tea, a combination of magnolia, chamomile, valerian, and passion-flower. She was back in bed, propped up by a pile of pillows filled with buckwheat hulls, which she found much more comfortable than the ones filled with kapok (which she suspected she was allergic to) or cotton (which mushed together badly).

Eloise sipped until the cup was drained, set it aside, then covered her blurry eye with her hand. For what felt like the thousandth time, she read the transcription of Melveeta's scrolls she and Jerome had made . She was confident that the copy was a good and accurate transcription of the original, but reading it wasn't bringing her any new insights, nor any closer to knowing how to reliably control the Star of Whatever.

She'd thought she might draw on the Star of Whatever to help solve the crisis with the Eastern Lands, but those hopes were now almost completely gone. Melveeta's scrolls had added a little insight to her understanding, but nothing that didn't fall into the "cute but useless" category.

Eloise set down the last half page and refilled her teacup. The Conk Out tea would eventually work, but a second cup might speed things along.

She was starting to feel tired when she picked up the last page, covered her eye, and looked at it again.

Eloise gasped.

Suddenly, inexplicably, the symbols looked like words.

Then she realized what she'd done. She'd covered her clear eye and looked at the page with her blurry one.

Through the magic-tinged eye, the symbols changed. They became words. Sort of. They were somewhat legible, but appeared unskillfully written—like a child's first barely coherent scrawl. The words weren't in any language Eloise had ever seen, and she had no idea how she could read what she was able to make out. But there were definitely words there. "Talk," "puzzled," and "essence" were pretty clear, but the words around them looked broken and distorted.

Was it because she was tired and having trouble focusing?

Why would her blurry eye make them look like that?

She set the page down, closed her eyes, rubbed the lids, then tried again. The clear eye just saw unintelligible symbols. Both eyes together saw the same. Only the blurry eye could make out the few words.

Definitely magic of some sort involved. What else would explain it?

Excitement warred with the soporific effects of the Conk Out tea. Part of her wanted to leap out of bed, grab Jerome, have Head Scribe sent for, and rush to That Room We Don't Talk About Because We Don't Want People to Know About It. But the dozy part of her thought, *It'll wait until the morning. Besides, you have your copy. What's wrong with studying the transcription?*

What was wrong, indeed?

Eloise assembled the pages, set them in the folio she used to protect them, blew out the candles, and closed her eyes.

Her last thought as she fell asleep was, *The copy is not the original.*

The thought clanged in Eloise's head like a gong, and sleep was banished for good. She sat up, got out of bed, pulled on her robe and slippers, and went to stand by the fireplace.

The. Copy. Is. Not. The. Original.

She and Jerome had no idea what the symbols were, so when copying the scrolls, they'd only made rough approximations. Certainly, they hadn't used magic to create them. Maybe that's why she could only read some of the words. If the symbol they duplicated was close enough to the original, then it conveyed the underlying word. If it wasn't, then she got an indistinct impression.

Eloise took off her robe, pulled on a simple day dress and shoes, grabbed the transcript folio, and walked out of the Queen's Chambers. Again, she found the young wombat dozing. "RoyLee?"

"Fiercest gang with bad eyesight in all the realms!" He spluttered. "Heeyahhhh!"

"RoyLee, are you awake?"

"Yes, Princess Queen Eloise," he yawned. "I am."

"Can you please wake Jerome and have him meet me at the Bibliotheca de Records and Regrets. And find out where Lady Seneschal put Apprentice Scribe Jóöôáäàqúüùíîin, and wake him up as well. Have him meet us there, and make sure he brings his keys."

"Right away, Your Highnessness."

As RoyLee ran off in the other direction, Eloise headed for the Bibliotheca.

28

MIGHT BE RAMBLING

As Eloise arrived at the foreboding door of the Bibliotheca de Records and Regrets, a horological cuckoo called 2:15 am.

Jerome arrived twelve minutes later, fur unkempt and eyes puffy. "Hey, Queen El. What's the matter?"

"An insight. I'll talk to you about it inside."

Jóöôáäàqúüùíîìn shuffled toward them three minutes later, looking like he was still three-quarters in the La La Realms. "Blessings of the day, Queen Eloise, Assistant Seer to the Court Seer Abernatheen de Chipmunk," mumbled the apprentice scribe. "Although, I'm not sure I'm allowed to say that yet. It's still pretty early. Is there a rule for when 'Blessings of the day' kicks in? Does the sun need to be up yet? I'm never sure, but then, I'm never awake at this time. By the way, my room is very nice. Thank you for that. Much bigger than a cupboard. It's possible I'm rambling."

"Blessings of the day, Jóöôáäàqúüùíîìn," said Eloise. "Sorry to drag you out of bed, but I needed to see something and I didn't want to disturb Head Scribe at this hour. Thank you for meeting me."

"M'pleasure, ma'am." He rubbed his face, trying to wake up the rest of the way. "You're wanting to get in the Bibliotheca at this hour?"

"Yes."

"You'd need a key for that."

"Yes. That's why you're here."

"I see." Jóöôáäàqúüùíîin yawned and patted his pockets. "I'd like to help you, but..." He yawned again, which caused both Eloise and Jerome to yawn as well. "Sorry, but I don't have a key to the door."

"You don't?" said Jerome.

"Head Scribe said I'd get one..." Jóöôáäàqúüùíîin squinted, like he was trying to remember the words exactly. "'When I stop acting like a thundering dunderhead.' Mind you, I'm not exactly sure when that will be, as that's a rather unspecific bit of feedback. What constitutes thundering dunderheadedness? How would one recognize if one had exited the state of thundering dunderheaditude? 'Dunderhead' obviously implies stupidity, but the qualifier 'thundering' seems to imply that the degree of stupidity is exacerbated, heightened, and magnified in some vague way. Is it possible for someone who is legitimately a dunderhead, and therefore stupid, to recognize not just that they have left the realm of stupidity, but also that they had exited the subset of stupidity occupied by the modifier 'thundering?' It seems like a logical impossibility. I might be rambling again."

"So you can't get us in," said Eloise.

"Not through this door." He yawned again. "No."

There was a pause as Eloise and Jerome both yawned in response.

Jóöôáäàqúüùíîin stood there, bleary-eyed, perhaps lost in the world of dunderheadedness.

"You're saying there's another way in," said the chipmunk. "Another door."

"Not another door, no."

"A window, perhaps? A crack in the wall? A secret passage?"

Jóöôáäàqúüùíîìn yawned once more. "There's a secret passage into the Bibliotheca? I didn't know that."

Jerome yawned back. "No, I didn't say there was a secret passage. I was asking if there was a secret passage."

"How would I know? Apparently I'm a thundering dunderhead."

Eloise stifled her yawn. "Jóöôáäàqúüùíîìn. Focus. How can we get in?"

"Window. Second floor. You have to climb up there, but it's left open because one of the scholars who works in that room eats onions and Brussels sprouts for lunch every day, and his officemate can't stand the smell."

Which is how Eloise found herself scaling a wall behind Jóöôáäàqúüùíîìn and Jerome. It wasn't the most challenging climb she'd ever made (it would have been laughed off the obstacle course out in the Drill Paddock), and in a matter of a few minutes they'd made it to the ledge and clambered inside.

Still, Jóöôáäàqúüùíîìn was wheezing when they made it. "I assume you want That Room We Don't Talk About Because We Don't Want People to Know About It. I'm guessing you're still looking at Melveeta's scrolls?"

They looked at him.

"You know about that?" said Jerome.

"Of course. You work away, day after day, in secret in That Room We Don't Talk About Because We Don't Want People to Know About It. You don't think you'll generate at least a little curiosity among the scribe-ishly apprenticed? One such scribe-ishly apprenticed person might know the Biblioteca well enough to be able to tell which babies have been examined, or at least moved. I must say, it's a fascinating document. I can see why you might be interested in it. But I also can't help but wonder, why that particular document? Why that particular ancient allegedly magical object?"

Eloise and Jerome exchanged a glance.

"Melveeta the Elusive was a fascinating historical character," said Eloise, trying to say nothing.

"Is that what's in the box?" asked Jóöôáäàqúüùíîìn.

"What box?"

"The one you wear at your hip. I've never seen you without it. At first, I thought maybe you had some sort of weird hip-based variation in the way you were born. But I've glimpsed the box from time to time, so I know it's there. Plus, I started my apprenticeship when the late queen, may she stand with Çalaht, was still on the throne, and I had occasion to see you from time to time, especially in the Bibliotheca. You didn't have it back then."

Apparently the apprenticed scribe was more cluey than he seemed.

He bobbed his chin toward her hip. "Don't people ask you about it?"

"Surprisingly, they don't. My handmaids are trained not to notice these things, or at least not to say anything about them." She rapped a knuckle on the box, the sound muffled by her clothing. "But I can neither confirm nor deny that the alleged object you're referring to is in my possession."

Jóöôáäàqúüùíîìn frowned and nodded. "I get it. Fair enough. Part of me hopes that it is in there, because how amazing would that be? But part of me hopes it's nowhere close to Brague, because remnant strong magic can only be dangerous in today's world."

"That, Apprentice Scribe Jóöôáäàqúüùíîìn, is one of the smartest things you've ever said. Now, can you lead us to That Room We Don't Talk About Because We Don't Want People to Know About It?"

Twenty minutes later, they had the room lit and ready. Eloise could tell that the apprentice wanted to stay in there with them as they took out and examined Melveeta's scrolls, but she wasn't sure what she'd discover and didn't want him knowing more than he'd already put together. "I don't think we'll be all that long," she said. "Where will we find you when we're done?"

"At my usual post at Head Scribe's desk. I'll copy some ledgers or something to pass the time."

"Very good. And Jóöôáäàqúüùíîìn?"

"Yes, Your Highness?"

Eloise reached out and gave his forearm a small squeeze. "Thank you."

The apprentice's cheeks flushed the color of a mandrill's nose. "Th-th-thank you, ma'am."

And he was gone.

29

TEN THOUSAND WAYS NOT TO
MAKE AN OIL LAMP

"I think young Jóöôáäàqúüùíîn is sweet on you," said Jerome.

"Don't be daft."

Jerome responded with loud smooching sounds.

"You know I can have you banished to the Elegy Swamps and sentence you to making mud angels for the rest of your life."

More smooches.

"Jerome."

"Alright. I'll stop. But I think it's cute."

"So, do you want to know why I called you out in the middle of the night, or not?"

"Of course I do. What's up?"

She told him what she suspected about the symbols.

"That's amazing," said Jerome. He found the first symbols in the scrolls. "Can you tell what that means?"

Eloise covered her good eye and looked with the blurry one. The difference was immediately obvious—the revealed writing was much more distinct and legible than their transcript, as clear as if it had been written by a Language Arts instructor schooled in old-school calligraphy. "It says, 'G. putting on pressure. No obvious way forward with this.'"

"Wow," said Jerome. "I can't see that in the symbols at all. 'G' is presumably Gwendolyn. Why would Melveeta feel the need to hide that? Nothing particularly mysterious there."

"She wasn't 'Gwendolyn the Irritable' for nothing. Maybe Melveeta was worried that the queen would demand to see her notes. And maybe it was risky not to be completely positive. Who knows?"

"So some sort of magical cipher was the only way to record her true thoughts and feelings. The logic of that holds. What's the next one say?"

Eloise found the next set of symbols. "This is next to the bit where she's trying to crack it using an elixir. 'Another disappointment. Had high hopes for potion. No clues revealed.'"

They stepped through Melveeta's scrolls, writing down each marginal comment. Together, the coded symbols pointed to a woman desperate to find a key to unlocking the stone, and becoming more and more frustrated and depressed at the complete lack of progress.

"I feel for her," said Eloise. "It looks like she's trying really hard here, and Gwendolyn isn't exactly helping. Or supportive."

"Do you get the sense that she feels like she's making progress?" asked Jerome.

"Only in that she's able to rule out possibilities. It's that ten thousand ways not to make an oil lamp thing. But, you're right. Nothing in what she has here feels like any kind of big step forward."

"Well, all we have left is that big paragraph on the last page."

"Are you ready? I'll read it out."

"Ready."

Eloise cleared her throat. "She's written, 'I would not go so far as to call it a breakthrough, but there is certainly a change to the way that I work with the object. It seems to be facilitated by direct connection. Maybe it's all in my head, but there seems to be a palpable back and forth. Enough progress seems to have been made this way that I carry the hope that, Çalaht willing, I can do my part in this desperate gamble of G's.'" Eloise uncovered her eye. "That's it. There's a lot there, I think."

Jerome wrinkled his nose. "Is there? It didn't strike me as such."

"No?" Eloise tilted her head. "For one, the 'desperate gamble' could well be the mission Gwendolyn sent her off to do that ended up with the Purple Haze eating half the Northern Lands. For another, that 'direct connection' sounds a bit like what I do. I've told you about the spark of something in the Star of Whatever."

"The naked mole-rat thingo? Yeah, you've spoken of it once, maybe twice. 'Sparky,' right? But to be honest, El, I'm not quite sure what to make of it. Like, I can't tell if you're being metaphorical, if something is really going on, or if you're having a prattleweed flashback of some sort."

"If we're being honest, I couldn't tell you for sure, either. It certainly seems real to me when I talk to him. But then, my dreams seem pretty real to me also, and we know they often aren't more than nighttime brain burps."

"Mine aren't. Mine are jewels cascading down from the Sleep Lords." Jerome straightened. "And as your Assistant Seer to the Court Seer, I can testify to the fact that dreams can be a valuable portal into the Unseen."

"Maybe so, oh great and wise Assistant Seer to the Court Seer. But Jer, you've told me enough of yours. If they're jewels, then yours are costume jewels made of paste and loud colors."

"Ouch. Just for that, I'm going to record all of my dreams and read them out to you at breakfast every day."

Eloise shook her head. "Remember what I said about mud angels?"

The chipmunk gave her one of his overly ornate bows. "I acquiesce to the power vested in you by your dented crown. But cut me some slack. It's late..." He glanced at the window. "It's early, and I'm running on acorn fumes. Can I give you an opinion?"

"Sure."

"It doesn't matter what Melveeta did or didn't do."

It was Eloise's turn to wrinkle her nose. "Why would you say that?"

"Look, we're both pretty certain that you have used the magic in the Star, right? Getting out of the Whacking Great Hole. Ruining that brunchberry paddock. Seeing what you saw with the Orb of Alleged Omniscience. All that involved the Star."

"Yes."

"And in your experience, that's facilitated by you talking with the spark of something inside it."

"Yes."

"So I say, so what if Melveeta hit on the same thing or not. At best, it's confirmation of what you already know."

"I guess."

Jerome pointed to Melveeta's scrolls. "I think we've learned about as much as we're gonna learn from the old girl, especially now that you've figured out the symbols. Don't spend any more time on them or on her. I reckon you'd be better off having another chat with Sparky. Find out more, if you can."

"What do you mean?"

"Find out what it—"

"He. Sparky is a he."

"Sorry. Find out what he and Melveeta talked about. If you can get insight directly from the source you'll be better off. Can you figure out how they worked together? Was it similar to what you do, or different? Did Melveeta bring anything to the working relationship that was valuable? Something like that."

"Huh. You could be right. I haven't talked about that kind of thing with Sparky. Let me think that one through, though. I'll need to handle it right."

"Well, think quickly. I reckon you're running out of time to get a handle on this if you want to deploy the Star's capability for the ends you originally mentioned."

"You mean deploy it as a defensive tool."

"Whatever you had in mind, Queen Eloise. Just give me a heads up before you do."

"Why?"

His tail twitched. "Isn't that obvious? So I can be somewhere very, very far away when you do."

30

FIFTEENTH DRAFT

D ~~ear Jo,~~

~~Stop being a prat. I said I was sorry, so get over yourself.~~
~~Also, you do have some responsibility here as well.~~

~~Come to the stupid meeting of the monarchs. We can work out what-~~
~~ever this is there.~~

~~—El~~

❧ 31 ❧

TWENTY-SEVENTH DRAFT

Dear Queen Johanna,

I would like to formally invite you to attend the first Grand Council of the Realms. Your ambassador to the Western Lands and All That Really Matters has conveyed your reluctance to attend. I will be there. Queen Onomatopoeia will be there. Khan Nergüi Unbenannt Nimetuseta will be there. And Queen Aglandau will, I have on good authority, also be there.

Please do me the kindness of making it the full set so we can try to achieve the best good for all involved. If not as a personal favor to me, then perhaps for the betterment of inter-realm relationships and your own queendom.

Wishing you all the best. I apologize again if need be, and I look forward to seeing you in the Midpoint of All the Realms in just over three weeks.

With love,

Eloise

32

FAITHFULLY RECITED WORDS

RoyLee found Eloise coming out of her morning training session with Sylvia Cloisterfeld and Lorch. "Princess Queen Eloise, Princess Queen Eloise! You be telling me to watch out for that horse with the black in front and the white in back?"

"Yes. Is she back?"

"Yes. And she called for a page, so I spoke to her. Her Ambassadorness be wanting a meeting with you as soon as possible."

"Oh. Good. Well, I hope it's good. Can you please let her know I'll see her in an hour in the Receiving Room, and let First Advisor know as well."

"Yes, Princess Queen Eloise."

And the wombat was off, calling, "Receiving Room for the queen! Receiving Room for the queen!"

Fifty-eight minutes later, Eloise was bathed, dressed, breakfasted, and sitting on the Listening Throne wearing the C'mon Give Me Some Good News cape, which, she noted, didn't get a lot of use.

Harold Hairauld the herald proclaimed the mare's entrance as she stepped into the room. "Ambassadorrrrrrrr Narrrrrranbaatarrrrrrrrrrr Enkhtuyaaaaaaaaaaa of the Centrrrrrral Rrrrrrrranges!"

The mare strode into the room looking exhausted but tidied up. Her coat was glossy and her mane brushed, but she looked like she needed a solid two days' rest.

"Welcome back. How was your journey?"

The ambassador ignored the small talk. "I have a message to convey from the khan."

"Very good. Are you sure you don't want to rest up first?"

"No, I'd best relay his words while they are fresh in my head and I can be as accurate as possible. I am not the herd rememberer, so I must take particular care to ensure accuracy."

"As you wish." Eloise leaned back, readying herself for what was likely to be, knowing the khan, an involved and nuanced diatribe.

The mare drew several long, calming breaths, then cleared her throat twice. She struck a pose that was both regal and studious, apparently ready to launch into a great oratory. When she spoke, her voice was deep and clear. "What follows are the direct and faithfully recited words of His Alacrity, Khan Nergüi Unbenannt Nimetuseta, this being a message to Her Highness, Eloise Hydra Gumball the Third." The mare paused dramatically, letting tension build. She cleared her throat a last time, then declaimed, "His Alacrity said, and I quote, 'Yeah, sure. Why not?'"

Eloise waited for the rest of the message.

The ambassador just stood there.

Silence stretched.

"That's it?"

The mare nodded once. "That's it."

"So, that's a yes?"

"Yes."

"No speech? No conditions? No diplomatic haggling?"

"No. He thought it was a good idea. He checked with the Purity, but that was just a formality. He's in."

"Well, what a pleasant surprise. Please be at rest. You're sure there's nothing else?"

"No. I mean, he had extensive discussion with me with regard to facilitating arrangements. But otherwise, he will see you on the full moon."

Having expected a battle and not gotten one, Eloise wasn't sure what to do next. So she punted. "I'll have First Advisor get in touch with you to coordinate. And Ambassador Enkhtuya?"

"Yes?"

"Thank you."

33

EVEN

Princess Coratina Ponentine found her mother in Ethel's Room using a delicate pair of shears to trim their favorite olive tree. She knocked on the doorframe. Aglandau glanced at her, nodded that she should enter, then turned back to the tree.

"You had me sent for, Mother?"

"Yes. Have a look at the scroll on the table."

Coratina sat down and read through the document. It was a proposal for a meeting of all the realms' monarchs. Not just a meeting, but regular, coordinated, high-level discussions, at what it called the Grand Council of the Realms. Coratina knew her mother could tend Ethel all day, so she took the time to re-read the scroll. "It's an interesting idea."

"It's a stupid idea."

"Then it's a stupidly interesting idea."

"No, just stupid."

"If you say so, Mother."

"I have nothing to gain from this. *We* have nothing to gain from this. Fuuugh me, they can all shove olives up their noses. If they can find any."

Coratina set down the scroll and leaned back in the chair. "If you feel that strongly, then tell them that. It's not like you have to go."

Aglandau's grip on her shears tightened. "It's not like there isn't enough to do here without me having to take, what, ten days to schlep across the realm to go to some Podunk spot in the Central Carbuncle so I can listen to three queens and a pony complain."

"You don't have to go."

"Actually, I do."

"Why?"

"Because of this." She pulled an envelope from her pocket and handed it to her daughter.

The seal was broken, but Coratina lined up the pieces so she could see who it was from. "Is this... Is this from the Southie queen?"

"It is. Go ahead. Read the note."

Coratina slid out the folded piece of hemp parchment and opened it. There was a single word inside. "Even." She looked again at the back and front, then at her mother. "'Even?'"

"Even."

"What does that mean?"

"It means Her Majesty Onomatopoeia has called in a debt."

"I don't understand." Coratina returned the note to the envelope and handed it back. "What debt could you possibly owe her?"

Aglandau put down the shears, stroked one of Ethel's leaves, and in the heavy accent everyone used when talking to the tree, said, "Stay healthy, my sweet." She moved to the table and flopped into a chair next to the princess. "Fuuuuugh me."

Coratina knew the thing to do was wait, so she folded her hands in her lap and stayed quiet.

Aglandau spent long moments in thought, then slapped the table with her palm. "Fuugh me, twice." She cleared her throat. "Suffice it to say, before you were born—like, decades before—Her Maj Ono helped me out of a jam, I guess."

"What kind of jam?"

"A jam of my own making." Aglandau drew a deep breath and let it out. "My mother was queen, and Ono had not been on her throne all that long, and I… Let's just say that I was seventeen, had too much time on my hands, and not as much sense as one might have hoped. I was not averse to dressing down, sneaking out of the castle, and spending time in the public inns down at the docks."

Coratina's jaw dropped. "Mother!"

"There was one place called the Scabrous Wound (formerly the Running Abscess) that served the most delicious beer with olives in it. One night, I met a rather fine-looking first mate named Stúüùbing. Fuuuuuugh me, he was a looker. Tall, dark, handsome."

"Mother!"

"It's OK. He was an alpaca. Not my type. But he was huge and had this dark charcoal gray fleece, except for a perky white tuft that peeked out from under his hat. He always wore this midnight-black sombrero with a flat brim. And a spyglass. He wore this spyglass around his neck on a lanyard. Also, I remember he always had a chaw of something in his cheek, so he was constantly spitting. Fuuuuuugh me, he was amazing."

"Mother?"

"So, anyway, we got to be drinking buddies and I had this idea for smuggling a shipment of prattleweed into The South—"

"Mother! That's a capital crime. They'll hang you for that."

"Cora, if you're going to interject this often, I'll never get through the story. And they don't hang you down there. They behead you."

"Mother!" She covered her mouth. "Sorry."

The queen put both palms on the table. "So, like I said, I had no sense and a fantastic idea to smuggle prattleweed into The South. It's not like I needed the coin or anything. It was my idea of adventure. Stúüùbing said he could get a boat, and I knew from skulking around the castle that there was a substantial load of prattleweed in a warehouse that someone had gifted my mother, or her mother or someone. They didn't know what to do with it, so they locked it up and left it to rot or cure or whatever for a decade or two. I ascertained that it was still in good shape and would have value to someone. And what better someone than someone in The South, where they value it so highly? It'd be pure profit."

"It'd be stealing from the queen and the realm."

"You know, funny how I'd think that now, but didn't take that point of view back then. I wonder what's changed?"

"No need for sarcasm, Mother. I'm just pointing out that you were not engaging in a victimless crime on your home soil, regardless of the crime you intended to commit on foreign soil."

Aglandau furrowed her brow. "One, I know. And two, not really the point here, Cora."

"Fine. Keep going."

"So, Captain Handsome secures a ship and finds hands to sail it and help move the prattleweed from the warehouse to the dock. We disguised the bales of prattleweed by relabeling them as 'guano samples' and perfuming them appropriately. I told my mother that I was visiting a cousin and would be away for a week. Everything was smooth and easy."

"She let you go?"

"I was seventeen, and allegedly capable of good decisions. I doubt she would have even considered the possibility that I might be going off on a smuggling jag with a not-quite-pirate."

"So what happened?"

"The first thing that happened was I got horribly seasick about forty-five seconds after we left port. I spent the next four days leaning over the rail or clutching a bucket. It. Was. Awful. I had no idea one could feel so bad. But worse, we landed at a secret cove that First Mate Stúüùbing had heard about from a couple of his mates. Turns out, it wasn't so secret. As soon as we'd unloaded on the beach, ready to meet the team that would transport the items to our buyer, two dozen customs inspectors swooped in. We were caught guano-handed. Stúüùbing didn't help; he started mouthing off at the customs team, unaware of The South's edicts against non-humans speaking in public."

"Those rules are barbaric. And antiquated. And stupid."

"It was worse back then. Much worse. Anyway, they confiscated our prattleweed as evidence, put all of us in chains, and hauled us to the Sclerotic Wold to face the queen's justice. I don't mind telling you I was petrified."

"I would be. I'd be wetting myself. What did you do?"

Aglandau went to a sideboard and found a dish of olives. "Want some? Sorry, you're allergic. Want something else?"

"No, thank you. Come on. How did you manage to keep your head on your shoulders?"

"My first inclination was to lie about who I was and what I was doing. But the magistrate was this stern old codger with this ominous look, and from his first question, I cracked like a half-coin teapot. I flat out told him the whole story, from who I was to what I was doing. And because he had two brain cells to rub together, he threw me and Stúüùbing back in the clink and kicked the case upstairs."

"By upstairs, you mean to Her Maj Ono."

"Precisely." Aglandau picked an olive from the dish, considered it, then ate it and spat out the pit. "She did this weird thing where she had me and Stúüùbing brought into the throne room, and then she ignored us. She did some paperwork. Had a nap on her throne. Ate some soup.

That kind of thing. It completely rattled me. My alpaca friend seemed rattled as well, but he did a better job of hiding it. I think it was the first time I'd ever seen him without his chaw in his mouth. Eventually, Her Maj Ono says, 'You know why you're here?' I said, 'Yes.' So she says, 'You have thirty seconds to convince me that you should retain your head on your shoulders.' I said the first thing that came to mind, which was, 'Because my mother would rather you let her behead me instead.'"

"You didn't."

"I did."

"What did she do?"

"The old bat—well, she wasn't an old bat back then. She was young and reasonably pretty, but already had a reputation for fierceness, so she was like an old bat before her time. Anyway, she stared at me hard for so long, I thought I'd faint. And then she laughed. It was the loudest, longest laugh I've ever heard in my life. When she finally recovered, she wiped the tears from her eyes and said, 'I had no idea what it was that might change my mind, but you seem to have hit on it. Shall I make you an offer?' I said, 'Yes, ma'am.' She said, 'If I make you this offer, you can't refuse it. You realize that, yes?' I said, 'Yes, ma'am.' She said, 'I'm going to pretend that you didn't smuggle a queen's ransom of prattleweed into my queendom. Instead, I'm going to purchase it from you at fair market value, less ten percent as a PIB tax.'"

"PIB?"

"'Pain in the behind.' She said, 'I'll forward the payment to your mother with appropriate paperwork legitimizing the sale, and a polite note of thanks. I'll also let the two of you and your crew return home and not sink your ship. You'll have to explain your end of things to your mother, but that's not my problem. You'll be home and out of my hair.'"

"Wow," said Coratina. "You got off easy."

"Yes, I did. But now we're getting to the bit that brings us to today. Queen Onomatopoeia walked over to the two of us, leaned forward, and whispered. I had to listen hard to hear her. She said, 'I'm doing this for you today, but some day, there will come a time when I will need you to make us even. I don't know when, what, or how, but there will be reciprocity. When that time comes, you will act appropriately and without hesitation. You owe me that. Do you agree?' I really had no choice, so I nodded. She said, 'Say the words.' So I said, 'I agree,' and Stúüùbing did the same."

"And?"

"And she let us go and that's the last I ever heard of the matter."

"What did Grandmother do?"

"I got home, caught Çalaht's own fury from her, was punished in some way that I can't remember, and the matter passed and was forgotten."

Coratina pointed to the letter with its one word. "Until today."

"It arrived yesterday, but yes."

"That's a spectacular story."

"I've never told it to anyone. It shames me on so many levels, but I can't say I didn't learn any lessons." The queen ate another olive and put the pit neatly next to the first one. "Anyway, that's why, even though I'd rather pluck my eyebrows out with a pair of blacksmith's tongs, we're going to this idiotic Quarter-Wit Council thing."

"'We?'"

"Yes, 'we.' You're coming with. You read the document. I'm allowed one accompanying advisor. That's going to be you."

"Me? Why me? Why not First Advisor or that Manzanilla woman, your Fourth Advisor? Or Seer Throumbolia? Surely they'd be of more use to you."

"Look at my skin."

Coratina's eyes went wide. She stood and offered her hand to her mother, then led the queen to a window so she could see better. Her skin and face had a yellow sallowness that was, indeed, worse than it had been.

"It's getting worse," said Aglandau. "It's subtle, but the trend is in the wrong direction."

"Maybe you really shouldn't go. We can come up with a suitable excuse."

"That's exactly what we're not going to do. I'm going, and so are you."

"Yes, Mother."

"I'm putting you in charge of the arrangements. Work with First Advisor. I'll expect you to report on progress at dinner each night. There's not much time. We'll need to leave soon. And it'll be cold there, so plan for that."

"Yes, Mother." Coratina stood. "And thank you."

"'Thank you?' Whatever for?"

"For sharing that piece of your life. For helping me know you a little better. And for your confidence in me to be your advisor at the Grand Council."

Aglandau waved her off. "Go. And let's not mention it again."

"Yes, Mother."

FIFTH DRAFT

D~~ear Queen Eloise,~~

~~It is with regret that I inform you that you can take your stupid Grand Council and shove it in~~

NON-NEGOTIABLE

Johanna knelt at the end of a row of freshly turned dirt in her garden and contemplated the asparagus crowns she was about to plant. "Are you guys ready to go into the soil?"

She didn't expect them to answer, but she did get a strong sense of their spirit, and their desire for water and nourishment. That's why she'd decided to plant them, even though she couldn't bear the thought of eating them. She just couldn't, in her heart, deny the dormant crowns their lives.

Maybe she'd discover a way to prepare them that crossed the line into palatable. Or maybe she'd just let them be decorative. Either way, she figured she wouldn't have to worry about it for a few years. All of the writings she had read said they would need at least two to three years to get established. Johanna figured she could stretch that to, maybe, seven years without feeling bad about it.

In other words, harvesting them was a problem for another day. In the meantime, she could admire and learn about them.

A cough came from the direction of her courtyard gate.

Anger flared. No one was to disturb her in her garden. Not unless fire rained from the sky or enemy troops had broken through the castle gates. Her mother's study had been a sacrosanct place, and Johanna had decreed her garden to be the same.

Yet, someone was there.

"Go away," she said without deigning to see who it was. "Whatever it is, it can wait."

"G'mid arvo, Queen Johanna."

It was de Coluber.

Of course it was him. The belly-crawler never seemed to think that rules or boundaries applied to him.

Once again, she swallowed back her emotion. "Yes?"

"There's a small matter I'd like to raise with you. May I come in?"

The last small matter had turned out to be, effectively, a kind of self-imposed internal tariff on wart cream exports, except none of the coin flowed into the queen's coffers. Johanna's meeting with the Wart Creamers' Guild had featured a lot of purple faces going as purple as their wares. She'd chivvied and cajoled them into accepting the hit on their profits for the good of the queendom. But then gossip heralds had got wind of the story. It had been the first time they'd really turned on her.

It hadn't been pretty. Or nice.

"I'd rather you didn't. I can hear you just fine from here."

Johanna took her spade, dug a hole, then backfilled it to create a mound in the middle of the hole. She took the first asparagus crown, placed it on top of the little hill, spread out its roots so they sloped down the mound, and covered the whole thing with dirt. Sprinkling water from a can, she patted the soil to help settle it, then covered it with straw mulch.

The snake hadn't spoken again, and she looked toward the wrought iron gate to see if he'd left her in peace.

He hadn't. He also hadn't heeded her request that he not enter the garden. The snake had slithered through the wrought iron and wound himself into a coil just this side of the entryway.

What a jester, she thought. Johanna moved to her right and dug a second hole. "I'm listening."

"I trust you've received your invitation to the bombastically named Grand Council of the Realms?"

"I have, yes. I suppose you're going to suggest that I not go."

"Quite the contrary. It is a minor matter, but I think you should attend."

"Oh? I wasn't going to bother."

"I think you should. In fact, I'm going to insist that you go."

"You're going to insist. Really."

"Yes."

Johanna stabbed her spade in the dirt and turned to him. "Why? What's it to you?"

"It's nothing to me. But it is something to my queen. She wants you there, therefore I want you there. And her wanting you there should be adequate motivation for you."

"I can't say I care for your tone," Johanna said. "Or the implication of your reasoning."

"Then you'll like even less that you're going to have me there as your advisor."

"Oh, come on. That's ridiculous. You certainly don't think of me as your queen, and you hardly represent the interests of my queendom."

De Coluber said nothing. He fixed her with all three eyes, flicking his forked tongue once, twice.

"No," said Johanna.

He kept staring.

"Absolutely not."

More staring.

"I will not be bullied into—"

"This matter is fully non-negotiable."

"Is it now?" Johanna clenched her jaw, holding back a torrent of barbs and insults.

"Yes. Non-negotiable. Certain considerations between you and Queen Aglandau should render you amenable to this suggestion."

She went back to her soil, jabbing violent stabs that flung dirt much farther than necessary. "I'll give the matter my due consideration, and will have my answer conveyed to you."

"Within the day, please."

Splurgle you. Splurgle you and anyone who looks like you. "Yes. Within the day."

"Very good. Thank you for your cooperation in this small matter, Your Majesty." The snake bowed the minimum allowed by Protocol. "And may your asparagus grow in abundance."

EIGHTH DRAFT

E—*Fine. Whatever. I'll show up.*

—*J*

A CERTAIN CONVERSATION

A week later, Castle de Brague was a flurry of preparations for Eloise's journey to the Central Ranges. From Seamstress Lint-trap making sure Eloise had appropriate outfits, to First Advisor and the Interim Other Places Advocate trying to cram years' worth of knowledge into Eloise's head, she barely had time to blink. After a two-hour history lesson on the various interactions between the Northern Lands/Half Kingdom and The South, Eloise stood to stretch her back, neck, and wrists. "Do I really need to know all this stuff?"

First Advisor also stood to stretch, and Niville followed her example. "It's up to you, Your Highness," she said. "My feeling is that the more prepared you are, and the more context you have for the discussions, the less likely it is that you'll be surprised or caught out. The last thing you want is to be blindsided by something you should have known."

"Like what?"

"We're not sure," said Niville. "That's what makes this so difficult. It's hard to know what's going to be relevant."

"So we're just going to cover everything."

"As best we can, yes."

"Right. Do you think we could pick it up tomorrow?" said Eloise. "My head is so full that if you jostled me, everything would probably spill out of my ears."

"Of course, Your Highness," said First Advisor. "I'll leave you some scrolls to study before we resume in the morning after your training session, and before you meet with Master Sergeant de Sphenodon and Former Champion Cloisterfeld to get an update on military preparedness."

Eloise faked a happy smile. "Goody!"

"I understand your reluctance, but time is short, and once we're on the road, we won't have access to the Bibliotheca de Records and Regrets. So we need to do what we can now."

As Bënnïë-Änn Thëjëts and Niville bowed their way out of the room, Jerome appeared. "You have a minute?"

"If you can lend me a few of yours, then sure. Come on in."

Jerome entered the room and scampered up onto the chair next to hers. "Oooh. It's still warm. Was First Advisor sitting here?"

"Yes."

"Good to know, in case we're ever caught in a snowstorm." Jerome tilted his head. "You look tapped out. Are you OK?"

"I guess. I don't have anything to compare it with. You're coming with us to the Central Ranges, right? Lorch spoke to you?"

"Yes, he did. Lorch is riding the Nameless One, and Hector will be there if you don't want to ride in the carriage."

"I already don't want to ride in the carriage, and we haven't started yet."

"We're concerned that riding Hector the whole way will be too tiring for you. We need you to arrive as fresh as possible."

"You may have a point. We can play it by ear. It might be nice to spend time with the four of you so I can feel a little normal."

Jerome held up his forepaw, claws extended. "Five of us. RoyLee is coming as well."

"Oh? I guess that's OK."

"What can I say? RoyLee is RoyLee. He's strangely helpful in unexpected ways."

"I think of him as being a bit like a good-luck charm," said Eloise. "Things tend to happen right for him."

Jerome wagged his tail in a "maybe" motion. "One way or the other, it seemed wrong to leave him behind. He's part of the gang."

"Agreed. We just need to remember that only fifty people are allowed across the border into the Central Ranges. Lorch worked that one out as a security measure, and the khan's people are set to enforce it."

"If you need the slot, say so. But I like the idea of him being there. I like the idea of *all* of us being there to support you."

Eloise reached out and squeezed his elbow. "I like that idea, too."

Jerome's ears drooped a little.

"What? I said something nice."

"No, no. I just need to ask you something and I'm not sure I want to, because you've been busy."

"Go ahead."

The chipmunk looked around to see if anyone was listening. "There was a small matter of you having a certain conversation based on a particular set of scrolls that I can neither confirm nor deny that you and I were working on together."

"What conversation? I don't remember saying I'd see anyone."

Jerome pointed at the box on her hip. "That someone. Have you had that little chat yet?"

"With Sparky? No, not yet. I've been kind of busy, you may have noticed."

"I know, I know."

"Is there a rush?"

Jerome raised one shoulder and let it drop. "I'm worried that you're going to need to do that something that we don't want you to have to do, but you'll need to do it anyway, and my fear is that you won't be ready to do the thing you're trying to avoid."

"Right. I get it. That thing I don't want to do but might have to involves processes and understandings that I'm nowhere close to having. And you still think that talking to the spark of something in a certain object will make the difference?"

"I can't say for sure if it will or won't. But it continues to be the smart next step."

Eloise nodded. "Fine. I'll talk to him. I'll do it this afternoon."

"OK. Good. I'll go, then. Let me know if you need anything or want me there or something."

"I should be good. Can you please tell First Advisor I'll be off to the La La Realms for a bit later on?"

"No worries. I'll do that."

❧ 38 ❧

THE THREE PHASES OF MELVEETA

Jerome was right. She did need to speak to the spark of something in the Star of Whatever. She hadn't exactly been putting it off, but she also wasn't rushing toward it. She enjoyed her time with Sparky; it was more that she was afraid of what the conversation might reveal. She was worried she'd be tempted to do something that was well beyond her capability, and that—either accidentally or deliberately—something would happen that was on par with what Melveeta the Elusive and Gwendolyn the Irritable had done to the Northern Lands. She didn't want anything like that on her conscience.

Part of her could barely resist diving in with both feet. And part of her —probably the more sensible part—wanted to run screaming from it.

She didn't know if a middle ground was even possible. Not with the way magic was in the world these days. And not with the Star of Whatever being what it was.

Eloise slurped down the rest of her haggleberry tea and walked through the door from the Salle de la Famille into the Queen's Chamber, put up the Do Not Disturb sign, and closed the door behind her. There was no guarantee this would provide her uninterrupted time, but it was the best shot she had at an hour or two alone.

She hoisted up her robe and skirt, untied the box at her hip, sat down in the comfy chair by the fireplace, and placed the box on her lap. Using a smidge of will and intent, she opened the box and took out the Star of Whatever. It had been a while since she'd held it, but it looked the same—an emerald-green stone the size of a prize-winning grapefruit, lit from within by a delicate glow.

She put the box on the floor next to her, cupped the Star in her hands, leaned back in the chair, and closed her eyes.

Eloise no longer had to go through the whole process of traveling down a staircase of rough-hewn steps through profound darkness. She'd done the inner journey often enough that now that she could just think of the green-lit underground space and she'd be there. And she no longer thought of the being she met there as the ugliest creature she'd ever met. Now, he was just Sparky, with his hairless, mole-shaped body about ten weak lengths long, his squinty eyes, his thin, short legs, his bare, stumpy tail, and four massive incisors, two above and two below, that protruded like a beaver's nightmare and moved independently. It had weirded her out the first time they'd met, but now it was just how things were.

"Hey, Sparky," she said.

"Hey, Loulou!" He waved his tuber at her. "Long time."

"Sorry. It has been a while. Did you really notice?"

"Naw. Figure of speech. Time has no meaning to me. It's all one big, long hanging out. What can I do you for?"

Eloise paused. "What does that phrase even mean? I've never understood it. I mean, I know how people use it, but it always struck me as odd."

"No comment. I just found it in your head."

"Yeah, I know. Hey, can I ask you some questions?"

The naked mole-rat gestured grandly. "Ask away."

"Did you talk to Melveeta like you talk to me?"

"Yes and no."

"How so?"

"Yes, in that it started out similarly. She figured out how to form a connection with me, and we engaged in communication that was similar to this."

"What did you talk about?"

"The use of magic, although she had a much better frame of reference than you do. I mean, no disrespect, but you truly have no clues at all. None. Zippo. Zilch. Melvee she seemed to know a fair bit more about it than you. Although, to be honest, a lot of her thinking was very rigid. Calcified. Your ignorance means you don't have the same sort of preconceptions that she did, for what that's worth."

"There was a lot more magic around back then."

"So I gather."

Eloise pondered for a moment. "You know what happened to the magic, don't you?"

"Why don't you tell me."

"I'm pretty sure you absorbed it."

"Yeah, again, so I gather." Sparky took a bite of his tuber. "Want some?"

"What does it taste like?"

"It tastes like tuber. It's tuber flavored."

"Could I get one you haven't already chewed?"

"Nope." He held it out to her. "Go ahead. It'll help you grow up big and strong."

"I might pass, thank you."

"At some point, you're going to want to eat the tuber." Sparky nibbled the frayed end of it. "Maybe not now. Maybe not today. But someday, you're going to want to eat it."

"I'll keep that in mind. Can you tell me more about Melveeta?"

"There were three phases in my interactions with your predecessor. The initial phase, which I just described, was a lot like our interaction here. Questions. Answers. A bit of getting to know you. That kind of thing. Then came the middle phase, where she cast that spell that you refer to as the one that created the Purple Haze. That phase was important, but short, relatively. And then there was the long, tedious, final phase that ended when you came along."

"You want to tell me about the second and third phases?"

"The second phase was a matter of a minute or two. Five minutes, max, although like I said before, I'm not very good with time. When she cast her spell, it was one for the ages. Out it went. *Fffffooooom!* I can tell you, I'd never been a part of anything like that before. She put absolutely everything into it. Didn't hold anything back.

Eloise nodded. "When I found her, her left arm had bone poking out of the skin in three places, and her left leg was completely disfigured, twisted around into a painful, unnatural angle. She fell off a cliff, and was not the better for it. Not to mention, she was enslaved to a spell and her hand had become physically attached to you, or your stone, or whatever. I think the intensity of her pain, the fact that she thought she was going to die, and her deep desire to help her sister with her last living act, all coalesced into the spell that was the Purple Haze."

Sparky spat out some of the tuber's fibers and piled them to his left. "Well, it was a doozy."

"You're not wrong there. Two hundred-plus devastating years of 'doozy.' Tell me about phase three."

"After she cast her spell, Melvee went a little strange. She was constantly mumbling incoherent nonsense about someone named Gwendolyn, who I took to be her sister, and someone named Brüüütus, who I took to be some sort of bastard. It was never very clear to me what exactly had happened, but as the years went by, the sentience left her and the babble-to-coherence ratio deteriorated. To be honest…" The naked mole-rat looked chagrined.

"What? You can tell me."

"Oh, Loulou! It was dull. *Dulll!*" Sparky shuddered. "Phase One Melvee was fine. Charming, even. Phase Two Melvee was a little odd and strained, but it didn't last all that long. Phase Three Melvee was tee-dee-ous. Rambling about the same stuff over and over and over and over. Eventually, I just had to do my best to tune it out, but it's not like I had a lot of options. I don't mind telling you, there was a measure of relief when it finally stopped. Thanks to you."

"It stopped because she died."

"I know, I know, I know. Well, it stopped because you broke the spell."

"I broke the spell that was keeping her alive. So, what you're saying is it stopped because I killed her."

"I'm not sure that's the most helpful way to think about it. Also, she was stuck in a kind of semi-life. Don't you think you did her a favor?"

"What can I say to that? I don't regret having done it. She did, after all, try to drag me and Johanna into the madness of feeding her spell. But I don't feel great that I was the cause of her passing."

"Understandable."

They sat quietly for a few minutes, each lost in thought.

Eloise broke the silence. "Feel like playing a bit of whist?"

The naked mole-rat didn't answer, but a deck of cards appeared from nowhere and he began shuffling.

As he dealt, Eloise asked him the question she'd been puzzling over since she and Jerome had their discussion in the Bibliotheca de Records and Regrets. "Hey, Sparky. Can you please tell me, do you know how Melveeta made the logical leap that she did with regards to you?"

"What do you mean?"

"How did she get from observing the dampening effects of the Star of Whatever to knowing she could use it to amplify other magic?"

The naked mole-rat began arranging his cards. "She didn't."

"What do you mean, she didn't. She used you to cast the spell that caused the Purple Haze. She must have worked out that you could make her magic bigger."

"You have it completely backwards, Loulou."

"What are you talking about?"

"Tell me, what was what you call the Purple Haze?"

"It was a honking great spell that wiped out half a realm."

"How?"

"I don't know. By sucking out all the magic, and then sucking out all the life."

He waved his cards. "There you go. She didn't make any logical leaps."

"I don't understand."

"All Melveeta did was a big version of what she already knew I could do. Wasn't the plan to suppress the magic in the Northern Lands castle and make it vulnerable to attack? As we just discussed, she was under extreme duress when she cast the spell. Her intention was so powerful that the spell was bigger and more effective than she ever could have dreamed. That's what wiped out half the Northern Lands. The thing you call the Purple Haze was a supercharged dampening spell."

Eloise looked at him. "I never thought about it that way."

The mole-rat scratched an underarm with his back foot. "That's the only way to look at it."

"So if she didn't figure out that you could be used to amplify a spell, who did?"

Sparky chuckled. "Isn't that obvious?"

"No, it's not."

Sparky laughed even more.

"Who? Who figured it out?"

The naked mole-rat reached over and patted her knee. "You did, Loulou. You did."

"Me?"

"Yeah. You figured out something no one else ever did."

"Oh." She wasn't sure what to make of that.

Sparky cackled away, chewing his tuber, wobbling his weird front teeth, and waiting for Eloise to take her turn at whist.

39

GOODWOMAN MOUNTEBANK
AND THE WIDOW COMELY

Eloise was finding it hard to concentrate during her early evening briefing. Her conversation with Sparky had left her feeling perturbed and she kept coming back to his words about her figuring out something new. How could that possibly be? She had no training. Any skill she had was either natural, or the result of surviving dumb luck.

Plus, First Advisor's report on the difficulties that the members of the Chain Mail Tailors Guild were having with a new design of hauberks was not holding her attention. "They made some advances in the metals, which allow for a lighter hauberk that's more comfortable to wear. But, when tested, these designs are proving to be brittle."

Eloise suppressed a yawn behind a cupped hand. "What, so they break if they're struck with a sword?"

"Correct. The test subject had to have twenty-seven stitches across her arms and chest."

"Ouch."

"Exactly. I've told them to—"

Eloise held up her hand. "Can we pause for a second?" She put down the scroll with the report in it and rose from her chair. First Advisor immediately stood as well. "I'm not really taking this in very well. Is there anything particularly pressing?"

"Everything is pressing, Your Highness, but I can see you're tired. May I make a suggestion?"

"Please. First advise away."

"Have the rest of the night off. Give your mind a break."

"A night off sounds like a luxury. Don't we have numptizillion things to do?"

"Yes. Numptizillion and twelve. But fatigue leads to bad decisions. How about I let Lady Seneschal de Aardvark know that you'll sup alone in the Queen's Chambers. Shall I have her organize a bath?"

"That sounds decadent. But yes..." She put on a mock orator's voice. "I hereby declare Executive Time for the rest of the evening."

"Very good, Your Highness." Thëjëts gathered the scrolls and put them back in the royal boxes used for official documents. "These can all wait for tomorrow."

An hour later, Eloise was soaking in a tub. Odmilla had lit half a dozen candles and—to her surprise—added bubbles. She hadn't had a bubble bath in over a decade, and popping them proved strangely relaxing. She stayed there in the bath enough for her fingers to prune, then dried off, slipped on a robe, and had a light supper of roasted potato and pumpkin seasoned with basil and rosemary. Perfect comfort food.

Bathed and fed, Eloise headed to bed, but it was earlier than she was used to and her mind was racing. Sleep wouldn't come.

Don't fight it, she thought. *A mental break doesn't have to mean slumber.*

Eloise shrugged her robe back on over her nightclothes, re-lit her oil lamps, and looked around the room for something to do. She didn't have any sedentary hobbies, like knitting or embroidery—both of which she'd always been terrible at.

Her eyes landed on a scroll that had been sitting on a table in the corner for months. It was the one she'd found in the Queen's Study among her mother's possessions—the romance scroll *The Most Torrid Trials and Tribulations of Goodwoman Mountebank*. Lady Seneschal Läääcy de Aardvark had read it and found it compelling. A romance scroll seemed like the perfect way to spend an evening not thinking about the world crashing in around her.

The fruit bowl on her vanity was filled with grapes and berries (where had grapes and berries come from so early in the season?). She plunked the bowl on her bedside table, got back under the covers, and settled in to find out what she thought of Goodwoman Mountebank. If her mother had liked the story enough to keep the scroll around, maybe Eloise would like it also.

Having never read a romance scroll before, she didn't know what to expect—a bit of froth, perhaps, and unspectacular writing.

She couldn't have been more wrong.

From the first paragraph, Eloise was absorbed, enthralled, and enchanted. The writing sang. The story captivated.

She. Was. Completely. Sucked. In.

Eloise fell for the characters instantly, and kept scrolling down because she just *had to know* what happened next.

Goodwoman Mountebank was a young noble by birth, but ignorant of such origins. She passed her days running an inn in an out-of-the-way village called Hillview Bluffs. The village was full of talented artisans and craftspeople, and Goodwoman Mountebank sold their wares in the lobby of the Mountview Inn, in addition to providing excellent meals and lodging in splendid but homey rooms featuring beds made up with sheets of astronomical thread counts, weighted, comfy blankets, and thousands of throw pillows.

One afternoon, an independent-minded merchant, the Widow Comely, was passing through the village when one of the wheels of her carriage broke just outside Goodwoman Mountebank's inn. The Widow

Comely made her fortune selling unusually scented candles to nobles and royals (her three most successful lines were candles that smelled of rice malt-sweetened popcorn, candles with the scent of a patch of bamboo growing wild in a rainforest, and one with the odor of a scrollarium).

When the wheel came off Widow Comely's cart, Goodwoman Mountebank rushed to the rescue. She fetched the wheelwright, who said he'd have it fixed and fitted the next morning. Mountebank provided the Widow Comely her best room and a simple but elegantly presented meal.

Sparks flew, and after an amount of will-they, won't-they, they found themselves in a passionate embrace (the saucy description of which caused Eloise's ears to go pink—her mother had read this?).

Heartbreak followed, when it turned out what to Goodwoman Mountebank was a meeting of the souls was a mere fling to the Widow Comely. Devastated, the goodwoman shed copious tears when, three-quarters of the way through the story, the now-fixed carriage rolled out of town and out of her life.

Eloise was just winding the scroll to the next chapter when she noticed a quill-scrawled note in the margin. The ink was faded, but still, this irked Eloise. Why couldn't they make their note on a separate piece of hemp parchment? Some people had no respect.

Then realization struck.

The handwriting it was her mother's.

How odd. She didn't think of her mother as a defacer of scrolls.

Eloise leaned in toward the oil lamp to get more light on it.

"Just like at the parlay with Aggie," it read. "To give one's self so completely, and then be cast aside. How mortifying. I was so young and stupid."

Eloise gasped.

Mother!

She rifled through the rest of the scroll to see if there were any other notes, then rescrolled to the beginning and looked all through it again. Nothing. That was the sole bit of marginalia.

That's really all you're going to write?

She set the scroll down, leaned back on her pillows, and hugged her knees to her chest, thoughts racing.

Twenty-six words.

A wagonload of questions.

Eloise thought about her mother and Aglandau pulling a stunt like King Brüüütus and Queen Gwendolyn. It wasn't exactly the same—Gwendolyn ended up in the family way, and when King Brüüütus dumped her, she went to war and ended up wiping out half the Northern Lands.

There was none of that.

But emotionally, it could well have been very similar.

Çalaht suffering suppurating sores and severely seeping psoriasis! This is huge!

Had her mother cheated on her father with Queen Aglandau?

No, no. That wasn't right. First Advisor had told Eloise she'd asked Chafed about the parlay, and he'd responded that it was "before my time" and that her mother refused to talk about it. Eloise remembered, because she'd thought her parents had no secrets between them, and this ran counter to that narrative.

The thought of her mother being intimate with the old bat made Eloise a little queasy. Aggie was so incredibly unpleasant to be around. Plus, the age gap was creepy.

Or was it?

She'd have to check the exact dates, but if the parlay happened before Chafed, then her mother would have been in her mid-twenties. That meant Aglandau would have been in her mid-thirties-ish. Call it a ten- or twelve-year gap—not enough to raise eyebrows. The fact that they were both monarchs would have been much more noteworthy.

Eloise knew from portraits painted around that time that her mother had been a looker. She could also imagine Aglandau with two-and-a-half decades less age and anger, and she, too, could easily have been, well, more attractive than she was now.

This was so, so possible.

And it explained a lot.

If her mother had fallen for Aggie and felt spurned, if her heart had been broken, if she felt "mortified" like the note in the margin said, then she may well have wanted to shut that whole part of herself away and never, ever talk about it.

If the result of the parlay was a weird awkwardness between the two queens, then a state of "live and let live" was a logical result. Have trade, but keep your distance and stay out of each other's way. That could certainly have held while her mother lived, and changed with her passing.

Also, who knew what Aglandau really felt about the situation with her mother. Was there residual affection? Did she feel it was her mother who ended things badly? Did she consider herself the aggrieved party? Who was to say she didn't identify with the role of Goodwoman Mountebank and not the Widow Comely.

Then there was the open question of whether or not the Eastie queen was involved in having her mother murdered. Eloise's vision hadn't tied her to it—pointing instead to the three-eyed snake. Now, more than ever, if they'd been that close, Eloise was inclined to give Aggie the benefit of the doubt.

She rubbed her temples. Of all the things that might have happened at that parlay two-plus decades before, this had been nowhere on Eloise's list of speculative possibilities.

The real question was, did this change things now or was it an historical blip of no consequence?

She had no idea.

But she spent the rest of her waking hours that night puzzling over it.

40

EGGPLANT EXTRAVAGANZA

"The traveling party will leave for the Central Ranges several days earlier than we really need to," said First Advisor at the last Privy Council meeting before the journey. "I want to keep the pace restrained so it is less tiring for all involved. Plus, since Queen Eloise is going to go through her realm with a largish group, she needs to interact with her subjects."

Eloise raised her hand. "Can we not use the word 'subjects?'"

First Advisor looked at her. "Why not?"

"It seems demeaning."

"Demeaning? Really, Your Highness? You are their queen. They are subject to your rule. 'Subjects' perfectly describes their relationship to you." She put down the scroll with her planning notes. "What would you prefer?"

"How about 'people?'"

First Advisor looked like she'd never considered such a possibility, but seemed amenable. Others around the table kept their faces carefully blank. Perhaps they were getting used to Eloise's ways, or knew when it wasn't worth the fight.

"As I was saying, Her Highness will be traveling through her realm, on a route that's the most direct possible. I have organized half a dozen public appearances for her subjects—sorry, people—on our side of the Adequate Wall of the Realms. Your Highness, you should be able to give the same speech at each location, but I suggest you vary it a bit because Headlong Hilda is going to be with us and she likes things kept fresh."

"Headlong Helda is coming? Isn't she busy organizing my formal coronation?"

"I raised that with her, and she said that, for one, things in that department were well in hand and that you would be pleased with the arrangements being made—she wants another meeting with you, by the way—and two, she wouldn't, and I quote, 'Miss an event like this for all the leafy greens, watermelons, and insoluble grit in all the realms.'"

"Right. Well, having her come with us to Flachberg worked well enough. I'm sure it will be fine." Eloise pointed at Jerome. "You should ask Assistant Seer to the Court Seer Abernatheen de Chipmunk if there are going to be any local festivals when we pass through the various locations."

"Local festivals?" said First Advisor.

"That's right," said Jerome. "You know, like the Celebration des Pamplemousses held in For The Love of Çalaht Cut It Out You Two, the Aloe Vera Jamboree at Inevitable Splat, the Eggplant Extravaganza at New That Place Shaped Like a Kumquat, which is fantastic and is not to be confused with the much sadder Eggplant Exhibition at Old That Place Shaped Like a Kumquat, or the Rootin' Tootin' Royal Radish Revel at Lower Glenth—"

"I think I see."

"These festivals are the best."

"I gather."

"Like, at the Eggplant Extravaganza, they'll have eggplants everywhere —in shop windows, at the Mister Eggplant and Miss Aubergine Pageant, at the Eggplant Muster (which is kind of like a parade), and at the Aubergine Hoedown. Eggplant fritters. Eggplant and sarsaparilla cordial. Eggplant tossing. Eggplant juggling. Eggplant stacking. Largest aubergine. Sweetest aubergine. Funniest-shaped aubergine. Feats of strength involving weights (and even strong weights) of aubergines. There will even be an eggplant poked onto the spire of the local Çalahtist devotional house—"

"Jer," said Eloise. "I think they get the picture."

"But you're right to look into them," said the chipmunk. "We don't want to arrive unannounced mid-festival and throw everyone off because Protocol gives royalty the preference."

"Point taken," said First Advisor. "I'll liaise with you to ensure we don't inadvertently ruin someone's event. So, continuing, in addition to a public appearance, at each venue we will also have a Meet the Queen event that will be a mix of local nobles and self-selected VIPs, and subjects—sorry, *people*—chosen at random by a lottery system to ensure we have a wide representation from the local community. These will be catered events that feature local entertainments."

"Sounds like fun," said Eloise, almost meaning it. "Let me ask a different question. How do we know that each party from each realm will only be fifty people? What's to stop Aggie from bringing a battalion? The Adequate Wall of the Realms is little more than an idea in certain places over there."

"Khan Nergüi has assured us that the Us will have ample border security."

"If anyone can do it, I guess he can." Eloise turned to the rest of the Privy Council. "Anyone want to raise any concerns? Interim Other Places Advocate Numptorius and Seer Maybelle, you're coming with us, as are Master Sergeant de Sphenodon and Former Champion Clois-terfeld. Speaker for the Land de Phobaeticus, this all started with an idea from you. Do you or anyone else want to bring anything up before we leave tomorrow?"

There was a general shaking of heads.

Finally, Exchequer of the Realm Cyrus Borborygmus raised his hand and Eloise nodded for him to speak.

"I'd just like to say..." The gaunt man trailed off into a fit of wheezing, which he eventually got under control. "I'd just like to say, good luck, Queen Eloise. Çalahtspeed to you, and may peace come somehow home with you."

"Thank you. I hope so too."

41

ETHEL

Queen Aglandau felt her frustration bubbling as she strode down the main hall of her castle. She was two days away from leaving for the stupid monarchs' gathering, and her meeting with Seer Throumbolia had been a waste of time yet again. What use was a seer if they couldn't actually *see* anything useful? He'd gotten wrapped around his own axle again, this time about a green presence or force. A vague, unspecific green presence or force, shrouded in mist. But a *helpful*, vague, unspecific green presence or force shrouded in mist, apparently.

Aglandau had practically ground her molars into dust. Why did she bother? It was the Eastern Lands, for Çalaht's sake. Everything was a shade of green. He couldn't say what the presence or force was, where it came from, or in what way it was supposed to be helpful. It could just as easily be a drunken tithe collector with a cartload of coin tarnished green with age as it could a jester dressed in green harlequin carrying a platter of olives. She hoped it was the latter. At least she could eat the olives.

What a waste of time. What a waste of space.

She stopped when she saw her daughter sitting on a bench in the hall outside Ethel's Room looking down at her hands. Unusually for her, she didn't have a scroll or bound volume open on her lap.

"What's the matter, Coratina?"

"It's Ethel."

Aglandau blanched. "No. No, no, no. Not Ethel. That's not possible." She rushed into the room.

It was true. Ethel was suffering.

All the precautions, the isolation, the quarantining of the castle area—it had all been for nothing. She had the spots. She had the first stages of wilting.

She had the blight.

"No, Ethel. Not you."

The Eastie queen stood at the tree and stroked the spotted leaves, forcing herself to keep her tears in check. Anger warred with sadness, and both battled with fear. What would become of her queendom when all the olive trees were dead?

For surely, that's the direction in which everything was heading.

Aglandau plopped down on a chair next to the tree and willed back her emotions. Nothing was going to get the better of her. Nothing. If she had to conquer every other realm and smash them to the ground, well then, that's what she'd do.

"I'm so, so sorry, Ethel. I can't tell you how sorry I am."

She lit a fire in the fireplace and did what had been done to every other blighted olive tree in the realm. Despite herself, tears streamed as she broke off the branches and fed them into the flames, destroying all traces of the blight. Each branch she broke off was a rip in her soul. Each leaf devoured in fire was seared into her memory.

When all that remained was a bare trunk too big for her to break up with her hands, she took an ornamental sword from the wall and hacked the rest into pieces down to floor level. These misshapen chunks she also burned, feeding in dry wood to help consume the green.

When Aglandau was finished, she stood still for a moment, sweating and drained. Then she stripped off her clothes and threw them into the flames as well.

She walked out of the room not caring who saw her. Aglandau gestured to her daughter, who still sat there, mind-numb and shocked, indicating that she should go in and burn her clothes. Then the Eastie queen went to find the nearest bucket of clean water so she could begin scrubbing herself raw.

42

NOVEL STUMBLING

The morning was overcast, gloomy, and unseasonably cool as the traveling party assembled in the main courtyard. Eschewing more elaborate dress, Eloise wore practical clothes—green travel breeks, a gray tunic with the Gumball crest embroidered in green thread, and her favorite dark indigo travel cape, which Seamstress Linttrap had restored, more or less, to its original glory. Eloise mounted Hector, then helped Jerome up to sit in front of her. Lorch hopped on the Nameless One, and then helped RoyLee into a specially-made wombat-sized pannier. Sylvia Cloisterfeld sat atop another of the nameless Guard Horses, as did Tiberius de Sphenodon. They'd originally planned to share a single horse, but decided against it for security purposes. Around them gathered First Advisor, Niville Numptorius, and a retinue of soldiers and support staff much larger than the group that would eventually cross into the Central Ranges, the idea being that most would travel with them to manage logistics, organize the local events, and generally support the core travelers. Eventually, they'd camp out at the border and await Eloise's triumphant return.

She hoped it would be triumphant, anyway.

Making the travel party a grand affair was First Advisor's idea. "You need to be perceived as actively doing things for the benefit of the queendom," she'd said. "Yes, what I'm suggesting is showy, but there's a point to a show, sometimes. We'll make sure everyone knows why you're going and the stakes involved, and try to raise public support that way."

"Aren't we lying to everyone by inflating the size of the traveling party?"

"With respect, Queen Eloise, you are the sitting queen, not a wayward, escaped princess, and queens don't move without large retinues. You need to look the part. You're only doing what everyone expects you to do. And in this case, that's appropriate."

"I guess."

The Venerable Prelate Herself and half a dozen acolytes shuffled out from a side door and headed to a raised platform for the traditional benediction. The tapir waddled up onto the platform, adjusted her vestments, and began to speak. "May the road be smooth, the weather pleasant, and may Çalaht light your path with her gap-toothed smile."

Everyone waited for the rest, but it didn't come. Murmurs broke out.

Jerome turned to Eloise and whispered, "What happened to the next bit—'May you not be accosted by wild, marauding, bloodthirsty, ravenous bandicoots?'"

"I asked her to leave it out. Bandicoots have suffered enough, and there is a time and a place to break with tradition."

"How did you get the Venerable Prelate Herself on board? She's such a stick in the mud traditionalist."

"I might have suggested that, while she would be a crucial member of the party going to the Central Ranges, if she didn't respect my prefer-ence, she'd be urgently required to stay behind and tend to the spiritual needs of the good people of Brague. That seemed to do it."

"No! And she agreed?"

"Yes, eventually, after curling her snout and mumbling about whipper-snappers."

Jerome nodded. "Clever." He looked around. "You should probably say something to everyone."

"Right." Eloise straightened on Hector's back and said, "Everyone!" All eyes turned to her and the murmuring ceased. "Let's give a big thank you to the Venerable Prelate Herself for blessing our journey." She clapped, and everyone joined in. After a suitably long time, she held up a hand. "And with that, let me say two things. First, thank you to everyone who helped make this journey happen so quickly, and thank you to those who will accompany me on this trip to the Central Ranges. And second..." She paused, and smiled. "Let's get going."

The parade of carriages, carts, Horse Guards, Guard Horses, and Transportation Guild donkeys wound its way through the streets of Brague along a circuitous route designed for maximum visibility. Calls of "Boring travels to you" echoed around them, mixed with "Go, Three, go!" and "Good luck, Yer Highness!" It seemed everyone in Brague knew where she was headed, and, as First Advisor had wanted, why. Eloise smiled, waved, nodded acknowledgement, and mouthed, "Thank you" for the couple of hours it took to reach Brague's main gate.

With a final fanfare from a dozen brass horns, they were on the road and moving at a good pace. The day's riding was uneventful, and around dusk, they made it to the place where they always stayed, the First Night Inn (formerly the First Knight Inn).

"G'early evening to you, Your Highness," said the innkeeper, Halcyon Spleenfluke, a rhubarb stalk of a woman with eyes like a surprised owl and hair molded into an unnatural, but impressive, beehive. "It seems strange referring to you as such, as I still think of that as being your late mother, may she stand with Çalaht. Condolences on your loss."

"Thank you, Mistress Spleenfluke. I appreciate it very much. And how lovely to be staying with you again."

"I've got the Queen's Suite ready for you. Would you like a bath before dinner?"

"That would be splendid." She slid off Hector and followed Spleenfluke into the building.

Washed and refreshed, Eloise sat down to supper with just Jerome, as everyone else seemed to have matters to attend to. "Are you going for the fermented morel and fenugreek soup or the three bean soup?"

"I'm leaning toward the three beaner, but she keeps changing the spicing. Once when we were here, it was three bean soup with curry, cumin, and chilies. Another time it was cold broccoli and three bean soup."

"She told me that the three bean soup has fire-roasted tomatoes, red wine vinegar, bay leaves, and red pepper flakes. Who could resist that?"

"Not me, I guess," said Jerome. "Are you having the apple cider or the warm mulled cherry cider?"

"I always get the apple. I might go for cherry this time."

"I might do the same."

"By the way, I had that chat with that someone you and I discussed a few days ago."

The chipmunk's ears pricked forward. "Oh?"

"Yep."

"And?"

"Interesting."

"Interesting how?"

"Interesting in a way that we're not going to want to discuss in a place that's anywhere close to public."

"Right. Later then, perhaps?"

"We'll have to see. There might be activities planned."

But there weren't. As the First Night Inn (formerly the First Knight Inn) was essentially a way-station, there was no speech or Meet the Queen event, although First Advisor set her up with an impromptu receiving line (mercifully short), so that Eloise could practice saying not very much to a lot of people. Headlong Helda made an appearance in a different room and did her gossip herald performance. As far as Eloise could gather, Helda was fairly gentle on her, which was a relief. She also drew a much larger crowd, which left Eloise with mixed feelings, but ultimately she was relieved not to be the sole point of attraction.

The bed in the Queen's Room's was incredibly comfortable, and Eloise managed to get a decent night's sleep.

Before she knew it, RoyLee was knocking on her door. "Princess Queen Eloise? You be wanting me to be waking you for training. You be saying so last night."

"Mmmph."

"Shall I be telling Champion Guard Lorch that you'll be seeing him in fifteen?"

"Hmnumph."

She was up, dressed in her training gear, had mumbled, "Blessings of the day" to a couple of people, and was in the middle of a stable yard warming up her wrists in thirteen and a half minutes.

Exactly an hour later, the Balancing Way training session was done, and thirty minutes after that, she was back on Hector holding a folded napkin containing four brunchberry breakfast muffins. The muffins were so delicious that it was a good thing Jerome had his own supply or there might have been trouble.

Halfway through the morning, Eloise tapped Jerome's shoulder. "Tell me, Assistant Seer to the Court Seer, is this fully adequate weather we're having an omen?"

"Everything is an omen. You just have to be open to the message."

"Have you been practicing that one?"

"Yes. How did it sound?"

"Unhelpful."

"Right."

"Keep practicing, though."

"That's what my mother keeps saying to me."

"Seer Maybelle is wise."

"Hmmph."

They stopped at a clearing for lunch. While everyone was setting up and the perimeter was secure, Eloise announced, "I need a private word with Assistant Seer to the Court Seer Abernatheen de Chipmunk." Then she extended her arm for Jerome, let him clamber up onto her shoulder, and strode to the middle of the clearing, well away from everyone.

She found a friendly elm tree and let Jerome hop onto a branch so they could speak face-to-face. "So, it turns out, we were wrong."

"Oh? About what?"

"You remember we were wondering how Melveeta made the jump from ascertaining that the Star of Whatever could dampen magic to using it to amplify magic?"

"Uh-huh."

"She didn't."

"Of course she did. Purple Haze? Voom!"

"Sparky said that was the wrong way to look at it." Eloise described how the Purple Haze was a souped-up version of the dampening quality she already knew the Star had. "He said I was the one who figured out it could be used to strengthen other spells."

"You? No disrespect, El, but all you've done is bumble along with the thing. We're lucky the Star of Whatever hasn't eaten you."

"No offense taken. You're right. But apparently, that bumbling has stumbled into a novel understanding of its capabilities."

"Huh." Jerome scratched his chin and flicked his tail. "Huh."

"Exactly."

The both stood under the elm's cover, thinking.

"So, Queen Elnormous. Where does that leave us?"

"As First Advisor would say, I have no flopping idea."

❧ 43 ☙

RETRIBUTION-FREE ZONE

Their route toward the Central Ranges was, for the first two-and-a-half days, the same one that Eloise had taken when she'd returned home from there months before to find her mother dying. She kept recognizing landmarks that took her back to those hectic days. Her wrist had fractured and her shoulder dislocated when she'd gotten herself out of the Whacking Great Hole, and her rushing homeward had been painful and fraught. She was surprised at how emotional the memories made her feel.

In the middle of the third day out, they turned left onto the less-traveled That Other Reasonably Good Road, which wended its way toward a part of the Adequate Wall of the Realms that was closer to their destination. After a long day of riding, they reached Proboscis Bluffs, where they were booked to stay at the best accommodation in the village, the Occluded Nostril. Eloise slid off Hector with a thank you, and entered the front door behind First Advisor and Lorch.

She was immediately struck by the inn's decor, which was dominated by odd shades of green and yellow.

"Welcome, welcome to the Occluded Nostril," said a gaunt, red-faced man with blotchy skin and a febrile nose. He came around the reception desk with an arms-open-wide bow. "I'm Devia Ted Septum and we're thrilled to have you staying with us, Your Highness. You, and your companions. It's our first royal entourage here in decades."

"Thank you for having us, Master Septum," said Eloise. "I look forward to enjoying your hospitality. First Advisor tells me that you've organized the reception?"

He beamed. "With the inestimable aid of your forward staff, yes, I have. I think you will find the good people of Proboscis Bluffs are stuffed with pride, and ready to meet you and share with you our little corner of the world. I'm sure you'll find their enthusiasm infectious."

"I'm sure I will."

"My wife, Rhinop Lasty Septum, will show you to your room. If there's anything you need, anything at all, please let me know."

Rhinop Septum was as thin as Devia, with consumptive cheeks, a ghostly pallor, and a handkerchief that was never out of her hand. But her good humor and twittering laugh were both contagious, and Eloise found herself warming to her.

Rhinop unlocked the door to the second story room, curtsied, and let Eloise enter before her. "I changed the sheets this morning myself, Your Highness." She sneezed twice. "The water in the ewer is from our well, which is supposed to have health-giving qualities. And we put you here because you've got the best view of any of the rooms."

Eloise walked to the window and took in the view, which was pleasantly bucolic. She nodded toward the landscape. "What am I seeing here?"

Rhinop pointed. "That's Schnoz Hill. Just beyond it is Snout Peak, and that over there, that's Proboscis Bluffs, from which our village derives its name."

"Lovely. I'll enjoy the view as much as I can."

"We'll have dinner for you in about two hours," said Septum. "I'm proud to say our kitchen has a well-deserved reputation for excellence in warm, viscous soups."

"That sounds like..." Eloise hesitated. "Like something you don't hear every day. What's the specialty of the house?"

"The house specialty?" The innkeeper laughed and waved her hanky. "There are those who swear by the creamy fennel and leek soup or the lemon, ginger, and onion soup with rice. And they may be right. But my personal favorite is the purple soup."

"You have a purple soup?"

"Yes, we do. It was created two centuries ago by Devia's many times great-grandmother. She had kin who disappeared behind the Purple Haze, so his gran invented a purple soup made from cabbage and cauliflower with garlic and celery in an effort to appease whatever spirits or forces took her family."

"It didn't work though, did it?"

"No." Rhinop sighed. "Of course, it didn't. Not at all. But the soup was a hit, and the kitchen has been making it ever since. If you have a bowl, you'll see why."

"You've convinced me. I'll have the purple soup tonight, regardless of what other temptations lurk on the menu."

Two hours later, Eloise was pleased to find the purple soup simply delicious, despite a thick, slippery consistency that was definitely an acquired taste. She was half way through a second helping when First Advisor appeared at her table.

"Yes?" said Eloise.

"Your Highness, in an hour, your first formal public appearance is scheduled to start. Are you happy with your outfit, or shall I organize a handmaid to help you freshen up?"

"I should be good, thank you."

First Advisor Thëjëts stood there silently, as though Eloise hadn't said anything.

"I take it your question was rhetorical."

"Yes, Your Highness. The handmaid is waiting outside your door. May I suggest the green dress and robe, to go with the overwhelmingly green color scheme we find ourselves surrounded by?"

"I was thinking more the cream one."

Once again, First Advisor just stood there with an anticipatory expression.

"The green dress, then," said Eloise.

"An excellent choice, Your Highness. I'll pick you up in fifty-five minutes and guide you to the marquee."

"I'll see you then."

Fifty-two minutes later, Eloise had had the road dirt washed from her and was wearing a sea-green collared dress with a light robe over the top in a complementary deeper hue embroidered with a pattern of interlocking knits. The handmaid, a chatty teenager five years Eloise's junior named Turbina Ted Septum, was Devia and Rhinop's daughter, and she showed no signs of discomfort grooming and dressing Eloise. She even brushed her hair and massaged her scalp, which Eloise found incredibly relaxing, to the point that she dozed off for seven of her fifty-five minutes.

First Advisor knocked on the door at exactly five minutes to the hour. "Are we ready?"

"Yes, we are, thank you, First Advisor."

"We should go then."

"Be there in a second." Eloise turned to Turbina. "Thank you so much for your help. I appreciate it very much. Will you be joining us at the reception?"

"I would, ma'am. Truly I would. It's just that..." She stopped, and her cheeks flushed.

"Go ahead. You can tell me."

"It's just that Helda de Anatidae is also here in the village."

Eloise tried not to raise her eyebrows. "So I've heard."

"I... I couldn't pass up the chance to see Headlong Helda declaim her gossip-heralding. For someone like me, this is truly a once-in-a-lifetime opportunity. To see someone like her at the height of her gossip heralding profession? I wouldn't miss it for all the cream of broccoli soup in all the realms."

"I see. Well, I can certainly appreciate that."

"Can you? Really? I do so appreciate your understanding."

"You go ahead. First Advisor is waiting. Thank you once again for your help, and I hope you enjoy your evening."

"Oh, I will, I will." She curtsied and sped out of the room as Bënnïë-Änn Thëjëts entered.

"Problem?" asked First Advisor.

"I don't think so."

"No?"

"No. But we'll see."

A group of fifty people awaited her under a marquee in the inn's courtyard. Candles lit the space, illuminating a hundred or so chairs in a semicircle, and in the front, there was a low-rise dais for her to stand on. She stepped up to a wave of bows, curtsies, and people standing up from their chairs. The faces looked friendly and eager to hear what she had to say.

She started the way her mother always did, with words specified by Protocol. "My friends."

"Our queen," came the reply, also decreed by Protocol.

"Please be at rest."

With a rustle of clothing, everyone took their seats. Definitely at least half remained empty.

Eloise touched the scroll tucked in her pocket, which held the speech she and First Advisor had written. It was a reasonably elegant statement that said almost nothing. It was designed to be a series of non-specific pronouncements and non-core promises that no one would remember or be able to follow up, and that was supposed to leave the audience feeling good.

The speech bored Eloise to tears. She was almost certain it would have the same effect on her listeners, but had given First Advisor the benefit of the doubt and agreed to deliver it.

She retrieved the scroll, unrolled it, and launched in. "Ladies, gentlemen, and otherwise of all species, I thank you for welcoming me here this evening. I can say from the depths of my heart that it has been a delight to visit..."

Eloise froze. She was blanking on the name of the village. Apparently, she was more nervous than she'd realized. It was Nose Something? Maybe Nostril Something? No, no, Nostril Something was the name of the inn.

Eloise suddenly became hyper-aware of the buzzing in her ear and the blurriness of her eye. How was she supposed to give a speech with this racket going on in her head and an inability to read her notes? She felt her breath quicken. Her mouth was doing its best imitation of a desert.

Mercifully, her brain finally got there. "It's been a delight to visit Pro Bono Beach."

As soon as the words were out, she knew they were wrong. The muffled gasp from the audience confirmed the faux pas.

"Sorry, sorry, sorry," she said. "I meant Protuberance Butte." She wrinkled her forehead. "That's not right either. Procrastination Basin? Probationary Berm?" Frustrated, Eloise shoved the speech back into her pocket and looked around. There was a beautiful family of swans sitting in the front row. She leaned down to a cygnet sitting between her pen and cob, and stage-whispered, "Çalaht slipping sideways in sawdust, could you please remind me the name of this beautiful place I'm so delighted to visit?"

"Proboscis Bluffs," cheeped the young swan.

"That's it!" Eloise straightened. "I can say from the depths of my heart that it has been a delight to visit Proboscis Bluffs. Well, thank you everyone for coming." She feigned heading off the dais, and got the round of chuckles she was hoping for. "Would you mind if I started over?" The room full of nods gave her the strength to keep going. "Perhaps everyone could stand, like I'd just come into the room?"

More rustled clothing, and all the heads bobbed up.

"My friends," Eloise said.

"Our queen."

"Please be at rest."

The room sat back down.

"This is where things went off the rails for me about two minutes ago. So, let me start that bit again as well. I truly am delighted to be here in Proboscis Bluffs—I got it that time! Yay!—and I truly am grateful for the warm reception you've given me. I'm supposed to make a speech about us being at a crossroads, something about standing at the corner where the trails of the past meet the main street of tomorrow's possibilities. It's not a bad speech, really. Well, maybe it is. But you know what? I don't think we'll ever know, because it doesn't say much and it uses a lot of words to do so. I'd rather not inflict that on you tonight."

"Thank Çalaht for that," said someone in the back. "I was dozing off already, and you weren't two sentences into it."

"It's OK," said Eloise. "So was I."

This, also, got a laugh or two.

"Let me propose something different. How about we skip the speechifying. Instead, I'd like you to talk to me. This is your chance to say whatever you might like to your queen. The odds of me being back here any time soon are pretty low, so I invite you to take advantage of this limited-time offer."

"You might not want to hear it, Your Highness," said the wag at the back. "Or I might not want to spend the rest of me days in a dungeon."

"Tell you what, good sir. I'm queen, right?"

"So it seems."

"I hereby declare the next half hour to be a retribution-free zone. So long as you are polite, stick to issues, remain in good faith, and avoid any and all slander of me or anyone else, then you can say what you want. Not only will I listen, but..." She waved Bënnïë-Änn Thëjëts forward. "First Advisor will be at my side taking notes so that if something needs to be acted upon, then we can do so." She motioned for Jerome to come up. "And so will Assistant Seer to the Court Seer Abernatheen de Chipmunk. I'm not promising I'll fix everything immediately, or even that I'll be able to address every concern. I'm just promising to hear you out. Does that seem fair?"

There were nods and grunts of assent.

"I'll make you one more promise, then. If anyone wants to escape what might be a dreary conversation with your queen in favor of what I'm sure will be a more entertaining presentation by Helda de Anatidae, then I promise you I won't take offense. Feel free to preference Headlong Helda's gathering to mine. Does that work for everyone?"

More nods and grunts.

"To those who'd like to leave, please feel free to go now, and thank you for coming. And to those who want to stay, allow me to say, from the depths of my heart, that it has been a delight to visit Proboscis Bluffs and thank you for welcoming me." There were a few more low laughs. "Now, can someone please do me the kindness of bringing me a chair and maybe a haggleberry tea, and let's get started."

44

LEGENDARY FALLS

A little more than an hour and a half later, the last citizen of Proboscis Bluffs—a merchant with a business called The Root, The Whole Root, and Nothing But The Root, specializing in kohlrabi, rutabagas and turnips—bowed and said, "Thank you, Queen Eloise, for letting me bend your ear."

"The pleasure is mine," she said. "And First Advisor has made a note to have me chat with Chef about increasing the castle's consumption of brassicas. But no promises, right?"

"No promises," agreed the merchant. "Just like you said. I'll leave you to your evening."

When Eloise and her party were finally alone in the marquee, she said, "What did you think?"

First Advisor bobbed her head side to side. "It was risky, but it seemed to work."

Jerome fluffed his tail. "When you first said what you said, I thought you were going to end the evening with a pitchfork protruding from your backside. But everyone was polite. So that was good."

"Yes. I think setting ground rules the way you did worked. Also..." First Advisor hesitated.

"Go ahead," said Eloise.

"I think you're lucky that Headlong Helda is such a draw."

"There's no question that she's much more of a draw than me."

At that moment, the two hundred-plus people crammed into the Occluded Nostril's main dining room burst into raucous laughter, drowning out whatever Helda was saying.

"At least they're all pleasantly distracted," said Eloise. "I hope it isn't at my expense."

"You'll be able to tell by the looks they give you afterwards," said Jerome. "If they all give you the side eye, I'd be worried."

"You'll be fine," said First Advisor. "Helda seems to be pretty much on the team at this point. Having her coordinate your coronation looks like a winning decision." She checked over her notes. "Did any of these issues particularly catch your fancy?"

"I don't mind trying to source a few more brassicas from this region, assuming the prices are reasonable and the quality is good. Could you please give Lady Seneschal de Aardvark the details and ask her to look into it?"

"Noted. Will do."

Jerome was also looking at his notes. "What do you think of this request for royal patronage for the Proboscis Bluffs hockey sacking team? Instead of..." he raised his fists in a mock cheer, "'Go, Honkers,' it would be 'Go, *Royal* Honkers!' It sort of has a ring to it. Maybe?"

Eloise took another sip from her teacup and made a face. It was her third cup, and had gone tepid. She slid it aside. "How would royal patronage be helpful to the team? Prestige? It's not like I'd give them coin or anything. I can't really favor them as a fan, because a) I don't, and b) I tend to like my own team best. Plus, it doesn't strike me as fair to the other teams. What's distinctive about the Honkers that they might deserve royal patronage over any of the others? Or am I supposed to provide patronage to all of them, every hockey sacking team in every hamlet from one edge of the Adequate Wall of the Realms to the other? That would devalue the patronage and render it worthless. No, I don't think so. I'll give that idea a miss."

"I agree," said First Advisor.

They spent another twenty minutes discussing the complaints, requests, and issues that Eloise had heard, making decisions as needed, noting where research was needed, and writing off the couple of cranks who'd had their (very long-winded) says.

"Overall, I think this was a useful exercise," said Eloise. "Maybe we can give the boring prepared speech a miss at the other venues and just let me hear what people have to say."

First Advisor scrolled up her notes. "I agree. Let's give it a try. And maybe we coordinate with Helda so that everyone has the same kind of out they had here, so that only the people who really want to talk to you do."

"Good idea."

The next morning they were on the road an hour after sunrise and arrived at Legendary Falls in the late afternoon.

"Where's the waterfall?" asked Eloise as they entered a hamlet surrounded by completely flat land.

"There isn't one," said Lorch.

"But there's a legend about one," added Jerome. "Apparently that was enough for the people who named the place."

That evening's Meet the Queen was rockier than the one at Proboscis Bluffs. Perhaps it was the fact that Eloise didn't have the botched attempt at a speech, so people hadn't felt endeared to her. But when she announced that she'd rather just hear what people had to say instead of delivering a speech, the audience grumbled and wandered over to the free buffet to fill their plates. Only one person dared approach her, a six-year-old wearing what must have been her best yellow frock, which beautifully set off her dark eyes and her dark hair, pulled back into an unruly ponytail.

"Hi there," said Eloise. "I'm Eloise."

"I know who you are," giggled the girl. "You're the queen."

"That's right. I am. Who are you?"

"Fengella. Fengella Thereisreallynofallsbutkeepthattoyourself. But people call me Gel. My mom's head of the village council and my dad's family founded the town."

"Pleased to meet you, Gel. You have an impressive family."

"Can I be queen someday like you?"

What was Eloise supposed to say to that? *Sorry, sweetie, but entrenched hereditary power structures mean that a lot of people would have to be dead for you to get anywhere near the throne.* She decided to leave the truth out of their conversation. "I think you'd make a marvelous queen."

Gel's eyes went big. "Really? Why?"

"Well, let me ask you. Are you smart, brave, able to learn new things, and dedicated to helping others be the best they can be? Do you care what happens to others and want to protect them? I think that's you. Am I right?"

The girl's face fell. "I don't think so." Tears welled, and the father, who'd been listening, scowled.

Eloise thought she'd been giving a pep talk, not crushing dreams. "Uh... Would you like to be those things?"

Gel blinked. "Uh-huh."

"Are you willing to try your hardest every day to be smart, brave, able to learn new things, and dedicated to helping others be the best they can?"

"Uh-huh."

"Well, there you go. Do that every day, and you'll be queen material before you know it. I can't *promise* you'll be queen, but if it ever happens, that will mean you're ready for it. And if it doesn't, well, then you'll be the best person you can be. How does that sound?"

"Good." It looked like the tears might stay in her eyes.

Eloise squatted down so she was at the girl's eye level. "Tell me something. Do you have your letters yet?"

"I know A, L, X, B, and N. But not Q. I don't like Q."

"Those are very useful letters. When you learn the rest of them, can you do something for me? Can you write to me and tell me how you are doing at becoming smart, brave, able to learn new things, and dedicated to helping others be the best they can?"

"Will you remember me?" She frowned. "I don't always remember people after a while."

"Of course I will. With a wonderful name like Fengella Thereisreallynofallsbutkeepthattoyourself, you bet I will."

Gel seemed to accept this. "OK, I'll learn the rest of my letters, even Q, and write to you."

"I'd like that."

Eloise extended her hand and the two of them shook on the deal. Then Gel curtsied as Protocol required with a surprising amount of accuracy. She ran to her father, who scooped her up. He nodded once. "Thank you, your highness. That was generous."

"I look forward to hearing from her, Goodman Thereisreallynofallsbutkeepthattoyourself."

"I'll make sure she holds up her end of the bargain."

45

OLD ONES' RISK

The pattern of getting up early, training, cleaning up, eating, traveling, arriving, kibitzing, then going to bed was well established by day six of the journey. The meet-the-queen sessions had become familiar, and Eloise's crowds paled in comparison to Helda's, which suited both of them fine.

The extra members of the traveling party had been slowly sent home, so that by the time they reached That Other Xrossing on the ninth day, they were at exactly one hundred. Fifty of these would stay at That Other Xrossing on the Western Lands and All That Really Matters side of the Adequate Wall, and the other fifty would cross through into the Central Ranges.

The last time Eloise had crossed the border between the two realms, it was at a Royally Designated Border Xrossing Checkpoint heading into the Western Lands side. It was hardly impressive. The border was represented by a precisely placed row of stakes, there was an unmanned information box instead of border guards, and it lacked even the barest hint of Adequate Wall construction.

That Other Xrossing couldn't have been more different. It was a bustling border town awash with commerce and travelers, dominated by a fully staffed gate at the Adequate Wall of the Realms.

They stopped in front of the gate. "It looks exactly like the one at Flachberg," said Eloise. "Down to that squiggly pattern carved into the keystone."

"It also looks like the one we went through going into The South when we were looking for Princess Johanna," said Jerome.

"They used a standard design for all the gates," said First Advisor. "It was part of the cost-saving measures implemented back then."

"OK, now I'm confused." Jerome turned and looked at Eloise. "Should I have said 'Queen Johanna,' because she's queen now, or 'Princess Johanna,' because she was a princess at the time the event took place?"

"Queen Johanna," said Lorch.

"Princess Johanna," said Hector.

The Nameless One snorted.

"What did he say?" asked Eloise.

"'Either can work,'" interpreted Hector. "'And no one cares.'"

"I care," said Jerome.

"I think that's his point."

"Don't be snarky," said Eloise. "We're supposed to be having a good time here. Or at least a serious one."

Lorch, Sylvia Cloisterfeld, and Tiberius de Sphenodon went up to the gate to make sure all was in order. They spoke to five guards wearing Western Lands and All That Really Matters colors, each signed a scroll, then passed through to check out the other side. Five minutes later, they returned.

"All good," said Lorch. "No surprises. We all need to sign at the desk—well, those of us who can hold a quill—and we'll be on our way."

"Sounds good." Eloise got down from Hector's back. "I'd like to walk this stretch. Is that OK?"

Sylvia took a look around. "I don't see why not."

The party of fifty made their way through the gate and emerged in the Central Ranges.

The difference was striking. Not in the terrain, but in the number of people. There must have been several thousand in That Other Xrossing. On the other side? A dozen at the most, and all of them were equines of the Us.

Jerome squinted at the small herd. "I thought The Us were supposed to ensure that only fifty of us came through."

Sylvia nodded at the horses. "That's them."

"What, a dozen of them? What if Queen Eloise had charged through here with a thousand screaming, armed berserkers?"

"They would have been stopped."

"By a dozen of the Us?"

Sylvia motioned to different points in the landscape. "A dozen of the Us. The additional several dozen of them there, there, there, and there." She looked at the ground. "The booby traps there, there, there, and especially over there, which would hurt—a lot." She nodded toward the wall behind them. "Plus the mercenary archers up there."

"You're saying that rushing in with a thousand soldiers would..."

"It would have made quite a mess."

"I see. Good to know."

As soon as all fifty were through the wall, the twelve horses trotted forward in a V formation. They stopped, as one, ten lengths in front of Eloise. Lorch moved to stand in front of her, but she said, "It's OK. I got this." Eloise took five steps forward so she was ahead of the others. She was wondering what to say, when she realized that she recognized their lead mare. "Alana, daughter of Ganbaat and Altan. That's you, isn't it?"

The mare's dark bay coat was so glossy it practically glimmered in the afternoon sun, and the shine was accented by the ochre splotch she wore where a blaze might have been. "Yes, it is I."

Without hesitation, Eloise stepped toward her, then leaned forward, offering her face. Alana extended her neck and offered her right nostril for the traditional greeting of the Us. She blew a puff of air into Eloise's face as Eloise did the same into her nose. They switched sides, touched noses again, and puffed into each other's left nostrils. Just as she had been when she first saw the Us perform this greeting, Eloise was struck by the intimacy of it.

"Queen Eloise Hydra Gumball the Third, I bring greetings from His Alacrity, Khan Nergüi Unbenannt Nimetuseta, and on his behalf, extend welcome to you and your fellow Not Us and savages. May the Purity infuse your time in the Central Ranges with clarity, and may your thoughts and actions here be conducted from a profound sense of purpose and duty."

Eloise still didn't care for their casual use of the term "savages," and "Not Us" wasn't that great either, but this was not the time or place. "Thank you, Alana, daughter of Ganbaat and Altan. On behalf of the people of the Western Lands and All That Really Matters, I express my gratitude for your hospitality. May our business be conducted in good faith, and with a sense of benefit for all the peoples in all the realms."

The mare nodded. "Spoken like one of the Us. I have been charged with your safe conduct to the Midpoint of All the Realms. Are you ready to depart?"

"Let me double-check that no one got left behind at a gift shop on the other side of the wall. We'll be with you in two minutes."

"It would be better if it was sooner."

Eloise hurried everyone and ninety seconds later they were heading toward the heart of the Central Ranges.

The terrain soon rose, and showed how the realm had earned its nickname of the Central Carbuncle. The path into the khan's lands was rugged and inhospitable. Rugged buttes, stark cliffs, and treeless plains surrounded volcanic mountains that had blown into the sky at least once in the past, and their rising smoke gave promise of future eruptions.

They followed the trail that Alana led them along, which soon veered away from anything looking even vaguely like a roadway. Eloise trusted the khan's intelligence officer to take them on an efficient and direct route to their destination. But it was hard going and she kept their pace brisk. The gain and loss of elevation as they wound their way into the mountains was particularly exhausting.

That night was the first they spent under the stars and not in an inn. They found their way to a large clearing, and soldiers immediately began setting up camp under Tiberius de Sphenodon's quiet directions.

"It's freezing," said Jerome, fluffing his fur and rubbing his arms. "I was expecting it to be colder than at home, but I'd forgotten what it is like up here."

"You will not lack for warmth," said Alana. "Queen Eloise, if you and your savage companion have a few minutes, I'd like to show you why this spot was chosen." She nodded her head toward a path. "Follow me that way when you're ready."

"Sure. Three minutes," said Eloise.

The horse turned and went the way she'd pointed.

Eloise drew a heavy cloak from her pannier and threw it over her shoulders, adding a layer to her travel cape. She turned to Jerome and patted her shoulder. "Want to walk or ride?"

"I'll walk. I've been riding all day."

They set off after Alana. The path left by the mare's hoof prints was easy enough to follow in the soft ground, and a carpet of pine needles hushed their steps as they moved through the unfamiliar terrain. They'd been walking less than ten minutes when a rapid thumping came from behind them.

"Queen Eloise! Queen Eloise!" It was Lorch, running at full speed, sword drawn, eyes wild.

Eloise looked at Jerome and saw the alarm on his face. "What's the matter with Lorch—" And then she realized exactly what she'd done. She'd gone off without telling anyone where she was headed, and she didn't have her champion with her. Blood rushed to her cheeks. "I'm here!" she shouted. "Lorch, it's OK. I'm here!"

Lorch slowed, and jogged the rest of the way to join them. "Thank Çalaht, you're OK," he panted. "I thought... I thought that maybe..." Lorch slid his Champion's Sword back into its scabbard.

"I'm so, so sorry. I didn't realize... What a stupid mistake. I'm truly sorry."

"When I couldn't see you, Queen Eloise, I just... I—"

"No, no. You're right. It's completely my mistake. Of course I should have told you where I was going. Please forgive me."

"I'm sorry, too," said Jerome. His whiskers were flattened back and his tail was fluffed. "I should have thought about what we were doing. It was inexcusable."

There was another sound from up the trail—more thunderous running. The three of them turned to see Hector and the Nameless One galloping toward them. They stopped moments later. "Oh, good. Lorch found you," said Hector. "We saw him pelting off at full tilt, and feared the worst. What's wrong?"

"Nothing, nothing," said Eloise. "I'm sorry. It's my mistake. I failed to tell Lorch what we were doing. Alana wanted to show me and Jerome something. It was stupid of me to just go off."

"At least you're OK," said Hector. "A thousand scenarios ran through my head. Most of them included blood loss."

"I was imagining arrows," said Lorch. "Or sacks over the head. Or throwing stars. Or ropes tied around the ankles, followed by being dragged behind a cart."

"Great," said Hector. "Now I have that in my head."

The Nameless One snorted and pawed the ground a few times.

"What did he say?" asked Eloise.

Hector interpreted. "He was thinking a noose and a tree limb."

She grimaced. "Again, I'm so very sorry. It won't happen again."

There was an uncomfortable silence as they all took a moment to calm down.

"Maybe you can come with us," said Eloise. "We can all see whatever it is."

"We won't be intruding?" said Hector.

"Not on me. If she'd wanted a private conversation, she wouldn't have included Jerome in her invitation. And if there's something nefarious afoot, which I don't think there is, then the more of us, the better."

The horses nodded, and with Lorch leading, the five of them walked single file down Alana's path.

The trail ended at the mouth of a cave, but the horse was nowhere to be seen. Lorch poked his head in. "Hello?"

"In here," said the mare from what sounded like a long way inside. "Come on in, but step carefully. It can be slippery, and it's dark. If you need support, stay in contact with the wall to your left."

Lorch turned and looked at Eloise. "I don't like this. I haven't had a chance to run reconnaissance. I'm concerned—"

"I understand," she said, then walked past him into the darkness.

The others followed.

Eloise counted her steps to get a sense of distance. At around step forty-five, there was a hard turn, a slight downward slope, a sudden increase in temperature, and the sound of water dripping.

"I'm over here." Alana's voice came from Eloise's right, accompanied by the sound of movement in water. "I hear that there are more of you than I expected."

"Jerome and I have been joined by my champion, Lorch Lacksneck, as well as Hector de Pferd and the Nameless One, both of whom you've met."

"That's fine. The hot spring is directly in front of you. Please join me. If you wish to remove clothing, there is an alcove to your right. Be warned, the water is hot. Tolerable, but hot."

"You don't have to ask me twice." Hector walked forward with the Nameless One right behind, and the two of them eased into the pool. Moans of delight soon followed. "My goodness," he said. "Your Highness, on behalf of the Horse Guards and Guard Horses, I hereby request that all of the queendom's resources be immediately devoted to getting one of these in the stables. Çalaht blessing bags of barley, this is amazing."

"Your request is duly noted." Eloise followed the cave wall by touch toward the right, trepidation growing.

"We call this place the Old Ones' Risk," said Alana. "In days of less sophistication, our elders came here to soak in the heat and get comfort for their aches as they prepared for death. It was considered unlucky if you didn't get here at least once before you passed. It was considered even more unlucky if you passed away while in here. They had to be careful about what they did."

"So the old ones' risk was the risk of dying?" asked Hector.

"Somewhat. They also felt there was a risk just being in here."

"How so?"

"They did not fully understand the ways of our mountains. They knew, for example, that the heat came from within, but were ignorant of the characteristics that made a place like this possible. They were fearful that the mountain would explode or collapse, as happens here in the Central Ranges. They considered it a hazard to come in here, but they took that risk because it just feels so darn good."

"Is it a hazard?" asked Jerome.

Alana snorted. "Waking up in the morning is a hazard."

That didn't really answer the question, but Eloise trusted the mare and figured she was just being glib.

"Good enough for me," said Jerome. There was the rustle of small pieces of clothing, then a quiet *bloop!* as Jerome got into the pool. Moments later there was an uncontrolled chittering, a sound Eloise had only heard once before, when she'd scratched a particular spot on his back.

Apparently, the water was nice.

Jerome coughed. "Sorry. That wasn't very dignified. But..." There was a splashing sound, like he was paddling. "Your Highness, on behalf of the of the Court Seer and myself, the Assistant Seer to the Court Seer, I hereby second Horse Guard de Pferd's request that all of the queendom's resources be immediately devoted to getting one of these, so long as I have equal access to it."

"Again, noted."

Feeling her way in the blackness, Eloise found a ledge that was a suitable height for a human to sit on and disrobe. She wasn't exactly sure what to do about going in the water. The thought of sinking into its heat appealed hugely after so much cold.

But there was the matter of getting undressed. She wasn't comfortable with that at all. The thought of dropping her duds made her stomach tighten, even in this extreme darkness. She'd never been unclothed in the presence of someone who wasn't her handmaid, her parent, or her sister. And certainly not in this kind of proximity to someone like Lorch.

Actually, thinking about it, she realized that wasn't true. When she'd suffered the soldiers cold below Mortimer Falls, there had been some degree of undress involved with saving her life. Lorch, Jerome, Hector, and the Nameless One had been involved, and none of them had ever made any kind of deal about it. The difference was, then she'd been mind-numb and had no say in the matter.

Here, she was going to have to make a conscious decision. That's what made her uneasy.

And she realized it was Lorch who was the problem. It was something to do with him being her species, coupled with being part of a society that followed Protocol, which clearly dictated that clothes were to be kept on except in very specific circumstances and within a tightly prescribed set of relationships.

She felt mortified just thinking about undressing, and she certainly hadn't done anything as definitive as starting to unbutton.

"Your Highness," whispered Lorch to her left. Her sense was that he was at least four or five lengths away. Good.

"Yes?"

"May I come closer for a moment?"

"Um, sure. I'm still decent."

She heard his footsteps approach. He lowered his whisper even further. "Your Highness, I feel I should remove myself, but I don't want to offend our host."

"Oh." It was like he'd read her mind. "Lorch, you don't need to..."

"With respect, I think it would be best for all involved if I do. I..." She heard him swallow, then slightly clear his throat.

"What?" whispered Eloise. "Say what you need to say."

"I... I include myself in that group of 'all involved' that would benefit from me leaving."

That surprised her a little, but not a lot. He'd always been very careful with her. "I see. Very well, then. And thank you for... For understanding."

"It is my pleasure to serve, Your Highness. Now, I need you to send me on an errand."

"What kind of errand?"

"That doesn't really matter. Just one that does not involve me being here."

"Right. I get it." She raised her voice so it was loud enough that the others could hear. "Thank you for reminding me, Champion Lacksneck."

"Of course, Your Highness."

"Can you do me the kindness of making sure those, uh, those water filtration systems are adequate to the needs of the soldiers and, uh, the others who are with us?"

"Pardon me, Your Highness, but you don't require me here?"

"No, no. Thank you, though. Much appreciated."

"Then I'll go do my sworn duty and check the water filtration systems. Please let me know if you require anything upon your return."

Eloise could have sworn he bowed to her, even though no one could see it, and within seconds, he was out of the hot springs area and heading for the cave mouth.

Relieved, she began undressing and was soon in water up to her chin.

Ten minutes later, Jerome muttered, "What a lunkhead."

"Who?" said Eloise.

"Lorchorino."

"Oh? Why?"

"Prioritizing duty above this luxury." His paw trailed through the water's surface. "I'm going to live the rest of my life right here."

The Nameless One snorted.

"What?" said Jerome. "Hector, what did he say?"

"He said that you're being oblivious, and therefore have earned yourself that selfsame 'lunkhead' moniker."

"Sssshhhhh," said the mare. "You Not Us and savages talk too much. Be quiet and listen."

"Listen for what?" asked Eloise, grateful that Alana had diverted the conversation.

"For the voices of the old ones who came here before us. Sometimes they have wisdom to share, but not if you're yammering."

So they were quiet, and enjoyed the heat and its relaxation for what seemed to Eloise like a very long time.

❧ 46 ☙

STRANGE DAYS INDEED

Another day and a half of travel brought them to the outskirts of their destination.

"We stop here," said Alana as they entered a large field from its western side.

"What are we doing?" asked Eloise.

"Waiting."

"For what."

"You'll see. But make yourselves comfortable. We are the first to arrive. I will return. Be patient."

So they waited for an hour, then two, then three. Around mid-afternoon, a party of the same size as theirs arrived, led by one of the Us, and took up a position along the southern end of the field. Eloise thought she could see Queen Onomatopoeia among them, but wasn't certain. Part of her wanted to wander over and say hello, but it didn't seem like the right moment. Like Alana, their guide left them where they were.

No more than ten minutes later, the Northern Lands delegation took their place on the northern edge. Johanna was clearly at the lead, side by side with their Us escorts, and with their father just behind them. It seemed to Eloise that her sister was deliberately not looking in her direction. Fine. Whatever. At least she was here. That counted for something.

Then the waiting resumed.

Another two hours stretched by before the Easties deigned to appear behind their guide from the Us. They took up their position on the eastern side of the field.

Alana trotted up from behind. "Please form a line with your queen in the middle, everyone facing inward.

They did, and Eloise saw the other groups mirroring their own movement. A hushed anticipation blanketed the paddock.

Alana spoke just loud enough for Eloise's group to hear. "As a sign of good will, His Alacrity, Khan Nergüi Unbenannt Nimetuseta has chosen to share one of our most private rituals with the assemblage." She looked straight at Eloise. "As for you, Queen Eloise, it is an honor that you see this welcoming for the second time. That is an unheard-of gift with regard to the savages, save our dream wife."

Eloise nodded an acknowledgement.

From the corners of the field, four precise lines of horses appeared, moving to the center of the field and forming an outward-facing square. In the center was a horse Eloise recognized from the last time she had seen a display like this—a Pinzgauer stallion, his black spots on a white coat reminding her of the pattern found on giant leopard moths.

The square of horses numbered at least two hundred and fifty to a side, and the thousand of them stood with unnatural stillness for a full three minutes, their faces stern, almost angry. The only movement was the spotted horse, who moved in a deliberate circle, looking like a warrior sizing up the attackers around him.

Jerome, sitting on Eloise's shoulder, tugged her collar. "Look over there," he whispered.

"Where?"

"I don't want to point. Uh... One, two, three... Seventeenth horse from the right."

Eloise counted along the line. "Oh, my. Is that... Is that Kïïït?"

"I think it is. She looks amazing. And..." Jerome squinted. "I think she may be expecting. As in, with foal."

"Wow. That didn't take long. I mean... Sorry, I don't mean to imply... I mean to say, I can't believe it has been so long already, and I'm glad she's so settled in. She certainly looks happy, if someone pulling a fierce face like that can look happy."

"Fierce-happy. That doesn't sound like the Kïïït we knew."

"No. Not at all."

Alana looked around, silencing them with a glare.

Suddenly, the Pinzgauer reared up with a yell, and the entire square of horses joined him. They cut loose an agony of blood-curdling neighs, accompanied with flailing forelegs like they were striking out in the midst of battle. Then, as one, their forefeet smashed back to the ground, and with a "Huh!" they grimaced, baring their teeth and hissing.

The black and white horse shouted something in a language Eloise had only heard once before, a deep, ancient, equine tongue that called forth ancestors and harkened to battles won over centuries past. As one, the thousand horses slammed down their right, front hoof. The Pinzgauer yelled something else, and the horses around responded with a left-right *stamp-stamp*.

Next came a call-and-response chant in the equine tongue. The call from the Pinzgauer sounded like an exhortation to war, and the thousand responses echoed a willingness to fight and die.

In unison, the horses began their posture dance, a mix of stylized head-weaving, kicking, and stomps. The choreographed aggression looked heart-stoppingly lethal. Eloise had seen this display before, but even so, the performance sent chills up her back. Their precision, their intensity, and the complete abandon with which they threw themselves into the dance was captivating. With deliberate movements, the lines of horses stomped and kicked forward, their square breaking into individual lines that moved away from each other and toward the delegations. The overall impression was that the equines would gladly bite out your heart then kick it into the next realm.

The call and response chant went back and forth, until the lines were within four horse lengths of their targets, when all at once, with a final *stomp-stomp-stomp-stomp*, they stopped, their eyes bulging and wild, their necks tight with strain, their tongues sticking out to the side. It felt like staring a declaration of war in the face.

Which is exactly what it was.

Or would have been, were it not ceremonial.

Then the four lines of horse warriors relaxed and moved back, reforming their square, resuming their stoic silence.

Minutes stretched.

To Eloise's right, Alana took four steps forward, reared, and let loose a neigh so loud and so ferocious that it seemed it would split open the heavenly realms. The other three guides from the Us responded with the same. The mare yelled something in the equine tongue, which the others repeated.

Then all four broke into song. Their voices harmonized, and despite the foreign tongue, the sense of longing for home and a yearning for peace was palpable. Their response, presumably meant to represent the other realms, met the earlier declaration of hostility with love and acceptance. The contrast was stark and brought tears to Eloise's eyes.

The four finished, and the square of horses let loose a cheer. Eloise and her companions couldn't help but join in.

Then a figure appeared from the edge of the clearing—an exceptionally small horse with a barrel body and blotches of hair in white and russet. The Us immediately snapped to attention. Like all the equines in the Us, an ochre smear marked his wisdom eye.

It was the khan.

When Eloise had first met him, he'd been carried from place to place by one of the other horses. Here, he moved on his own, his painful left foreleg barely used in his progress. Ten paces behind came the dream wife, an older woman who was the only human tolerated to live among the Us. She acted as healer and spiritual facilitator to the khan and the herd.

Eloise felt a fondness for them both swell in her chest, a feeling that surprised her in its intensity.

The khan reached the center of the square, accepting a bow from the Pinzgauer who'd led the welcoming chant. As one, the Us did an about-face so they were looking at their leader, and the dream wife found a spot to the side where she folded her legs and sat, back straight, on her calves. The khan slowly turned and looked in the direction of each contingent, his head tilted like he was trying to figure out why all these savages were here.

Then he seemed to make a decision, and spoke. "G'late arvo."

"G'late arvo," echoed the crowd.

Another pause and another full circle looking around. "Strange times, are they not? You here at Dundad Baigaa Ter Tseg. The Us hosting. The Us even acknowledging such a thing to have value. Strange days, indeed."

"For such a small person, his voice carries incredibly well," whispered Jerome.

Eloise nodded and whispered back, "I wonder if he has a weak magic for oration, or for making quiet things louder. Either would work in this circumstance."

This exchange earned them another glare from Alana.

"There has never been a meeting like this before. It is arguable that there has never been a time of greater need, but we can all point to our histories and find dire times, so who knows if that's true. What's different is that today, we have actually made the effort to gather here, to try our best to improve things in our world. Shortly, while the rest of you remain here, ten of us will make our way over that hill to the religious campus here at the Midpoint of All the Realms and we will spend however many hours and days it takes to come to an understanding between us. It *is* strange. But it is exciting. It is historic. It is unique to this time and place. I pray to the Purity that we act in good faith and accomplish something worthwhile, for the good of all involved, so that our children, their children, and theirs, out to seven generations and more, will look back at what we have done here with a smile in their hearts and complimentary words on their lips. May the Purity be our inspiration and, for those for whom it is appropriate, may Çalaht guide your thoughts and deeds.

47

VETCH HEDGE

The Pinzgauer lay down in the paddock and the khan slid onto his back. The dotted horse rose and carried his monarch from the field. When they were gone, the horses in the middle of the field relaxed and began milling about, a clear signal that the ceremony was over.

One of them broke from the group and trotted toward Eloise.

It was Kïïït, her smile wide and her gait sure. She stopped an appropriate distance away, did the horse equivalent of a curtsy, and said, "May I approach, Your Highness?"

Eloise waved her forward. "Kïïït, how lovely to see you. You look well."

"Thank you, Queen Eloise. I just wanted to come say hello while I still could, and to once again say thank you."

"Thank me? For what?"

"For taking me away with you from the Half Kingdom. For bringing me to the Us. For letting me stay with them."

"My pleasure on all counts," said Eloise. "If I may say so, you seem to fit right in, down to the ochre dot on your blaze."

"The Us is more home than any home has ever been for me. I can see why my Uncle Dougie left us to be with them."

"I'm glad you're happy."

"Happy would only start to cover it. I haven't said this in a long time, because the Us don't care for the phrases of the Not Us nor of the savages, but being with them is the total and complete grass strudel. Oh, and I'm with Malakai," said Kiïit.

"Malakai? Really? The one who thought we were spies when we first encountered them? I'm a bit surprised."

Kiïit nodded. "Me, too. But we got to chatting not long after you left. I told him I thought he was rugged. He told me he found me confusing. Then His Alacrity saw us and said he thought we'd be good for each other. I smiled at Malakai. Malakai scowled at me. And that was about all it took. We've been together ever since." She moved so her swollen belly was accented. "You can see the result."

"I saw. Congratulations to you both."

Eloise was struck by how profound Kiïit's transformation was. Gone was the chatty, over-awed scullery mare desperately trying to escape her life at Stained Rock and see something of the world. She seemed so much more grounded, so still in herself, so assured.

"Oh, look. There he is now." She nodded toward a horse twenty lengths away. "Malakai! Malakai! Over here, my barley button, my oaten overlord, my wheaten sweetie." She winked at Eloise. "He hates it when I do that. Isn't he just the grass strudel?" Kiïit sighed. "Mal! Mal! Come say 'Hi' to the queen!"

Malakai frowned, but did as she asked, trotting over wearing his usual haughty look. Eloise immediately recognized the interesting combination of a stock horse build, a palomino-gold coat, and white Clydesdale's hoof feathers. What was completely different was his mane. Last time she'd seen him it had been long, messy, and knotted in ochre-stained ropes. But now, it was washed, combed, and white like his hoof feathers—giving the impression that maybe, just maybe, he was trying to look nice for someone.

"Your Highness," he said. No bow, and no reaching over to exchange nose puffs. That stand-offishness fit with Eloise's memory of him. "I see my mate is bending your ear. Do you need me to remove her?"

Kiiit snorted. "Like you could if you wanted to, my vetch hedge."

Malakai looked at her, unsuccessfully masking frustration. "I could ask nicely. There is some possibility that you might comply with that. Maybe."

"Maybe," agreed Kiiit. She bumped him with her hip. "Depends on what's in it for me."

"My sweet Not Us, that is hardly a discussion to be had in front of the Western Lands queen, now is it?"

She bumped his hip again, this time more gently. Kiiit put a bit of gravel in her voice. "I like it when you call me that."

There was no doubt they were besotted with each other. It was so unexpected, and so lovely to see.

A horological cuckoo called the top of the hour. Eloise looked around and saw First Advisor heading toward her.

"My apologies, but I need to take my leave. I'm expected at the Grand Council of the Realms soon."

"Of course. I'm so glad I had a chance to say thank you."

"It was lovely seeing you again, Kiiit."

The mare dropped into an equine curtsy. When Malakai didn't move, she gave a sharp throat clear. The stallion jumped like he'd been goosed with a pointy stick and looked at her. He mouthed, "What?"

Kiiit nodded at Eloise.

He looked at the mare, then Eloise, and back to Kiiit. A small shake of the head. "Huh?"

Kïïït nodded at Eloise more emphatically, then exaggerated her curtsy.

"Oh! Right. Sorry. It is strange for me to give any kind of deference to the savages." He bowed like he was the first horse ever to do so. "Your Highness. Best of luck to you and the other monarchs."

Eloise had to press her lips together to keep the smile from her face. "Thank you, Malakai. I hope to see you both again soon, and good luck with your..." She lifted her chin in the direction of Kïïït's belly. "With your impending event."

"Thank you, Your Highness," said the mare. The two horses turned and walked back toward the Us. Eloise could just hear Kïïït say, "That wasn't so hard, now was it?"

To which Malakai answered, "You are the most Not-Us Us I've ever met."

"You say the nicest things."

"It wasn't meant to be nice."

"Well, it was." And she bumped his hip once more.

First Advisor reached Eloise, curtsied (always an awesome act from a woman the size of a small mountain) and approached. "Well, it's show-time, Your Highness."

"Yes, it is."

"Our things have been transported to the facility for the duration of the Grand Council of the Realms' meetings. RoyLee took charge of that."

"That's the sort of thing he's good at."

"He gets nervous about doing a good job, but he gets it done," said First Advisor. "Shall we start walking, Queen Eloise?"

"We won't arrive too early?"

"Not at all." First Advisor pointed to a path at the edge of the clearing, where two of the Us stood sentry. "That's the way."

Eloise took a deep breath and let it out slowly. "I'm nervous."

"Of course you are. I'd be worried if you weren't. After you, Your Highness."

48

CLIMB

They began the steep climb toward the seminary. Eloise found it fairly easy-going, but First Advisor apparently didn't go for that many mountain walks and was soon sweating through her garments.

"Are you OK?" asked Eloise.

"Fan-flopping-tastic, Your Highness. Never better."

That appeared to be the end of the discussion, and First Advisor continued huffing up the incline. Eloise slowed her pace to make it easier for her.

"The agenda has finally been agreed," puffed Thëjëts.

"Oh, good," said Eloise. "Care to run me through it?"

"First we settle in, then tonight is supposed to be an informal dinner, a chance to get to know each other a little better, and maybe take some of the tension away. It is supposed to help us remember that we are all people who are responsible for other people."

"Sounds awkward."

"It might well be. Or, perhaps, a bond or two might be formed or strengthened."

"One can hope." The thought of eating a meal with the likes of Queen Aggie or her sister sounded like one of Çalaht's tribulations. Maybe she could fake a gastric illness and give it a miss.

First Advisor stopped and leaned against a tree to catch her breath. "Tomorrow's first session will be formal opening statements. I have the final draft of the one we worked on in one of my trunks. I'll give it to you when we are up there."

Eloise really was getting worried about First Advisor. Her face looked a worrying shade of red. "Can't I just say to Aggie, 'Stop being an aggressive cabbage head' and be done with it?"

"Of course you can, Your Highness. And then you can walk out of the room and we can pack up and go home and wait for the battle to start. That's a very efficient approach."

Eloise grunted. "That's a 'no,' then."

"I'd never presume to tell you what to do."

"You tell me what to do all the time."

Thëjëts heaved herself from the tree and they continued the climb. "I'm the advisor. You're the decider. There's the difference."

"I know." Eloise wrinkled her brow. "Are you sure you're OK?"

"Absolutely, Queen Eloise. Never better." They took another fifty steps in silence, the agenda discussion paused for the moment. Then First Advisor stopped again. "Your Highness, may I say something?"

"Of course."

"Regardless of the outcome of these Grand Council meetings, I'd like to say how proud I am of you."

"Oh." The compliment caught Eloise by surprise, as did the lump in her throat that quickly followed. "That's... Thank you. That's kind of you. I'm bouncing between hope and despair. I can't tell you how much that means to me."

"I honor you for taking this path of engagement and discussion. It is an historic achievement to have come this far."

"We may still end up shedding blood. More blood, that is."

"True, but at least you did not reach for your swords first, something that a certain other queen can't say. You may not feel that you had much choice, but you did, as did she." Thëjëts gestured toward the top of the hill, which still loomed quite a distance ahead. "We are here because of you. That deserves acknowledgment, a recognition that I don't know you'll get in there from the others."

"Thank you, First Advisor. I appreciate your saying that. It gives me heart." The two of them turned to the path, and took another fifty steps. Then Eloise touched First Advisor's sodden sleeve and they stopped again. "May I ask you a question?"

"Always."

"Do you think this gathering will actually achieve something?"

Chest heaving, Thëjëts laughed. "Oh, Queen Eloise. I have no idea. No flopping idea whatso-flopping-ever."

An odd look came into First Advisor's eyes, like she was just remembering an important point she wanted to make.

Then Bërnädïce-Ändrëä Thëjëts, Eloise's only close political confidant and the person she relied on more than anyone else in the world, crashed forward, her nose slamming into a large stone on the ground.

The impact didn't hurt, however.

She was dead well before her face collided with the rock.

Eloise screamed.

❦ 49 ❦

DREAM WIFE

I t took eight monks from the seminary to lift the former first advisor's body onto the back of a Percheron from the Us, who was large enough to carry the woman's bulk. Eloise led the procession up the hill to the complex buildings, where they brought her into a nearby hut and laid her out on a sturdy table. Eloise sat with her while a healer was fetched, not that a healer could do any good.

It was the dream wife who appeared at the doorway. "I'm here to examine and anoint the body. May I come in?"

"Yes, yes," said Eloise, standing up to give her space.

The dream wife looked exactly like she had the last time Eloise saw her—dark eyes, hair a ropy chaos of tangles, breeks and knee-length tunic that wouldn't provide much warmth, and the ochre splotch worn by all the Us at her wisdom eye. She stepped inside, hesitated, then said, "You are a queen now. Presumably I should bow."

"It's what Protocol would have you do, yes. But under the circumstances, I think we can dispense with it, since no one else is here. Thank you for coming. It's good to see you again."

"And you." The dream wife briefly looked over the body. "It has been a while since I dealt with a lifeless form that had fewer than four legs. It is a novelty, in an odd way." She looked straight into Eloise's eyes. "You appear pale. I suspect you'll be in shock. Please sit down. Have you had any water? Maybe a tonic?"

"No, I haven't. And you're probably right that I'm in shock."

The dream wife poked her head out of the doorway, said something to someone Eloise hadn't known was there, and moments later, handed Eloise a mug of water. She pointed to a stool at the side of the room, had her sit, and motioned for her to drink.

The older woman began a closer examination of the body—lifting eyelids, palpating her chest, and loosening her clothing to look for who knew what.

Eloise stared at the body, and let her attention drift to her blurry eye. The corpse didn't trigger any reaction. It gave her the sense that nothing nefarious had happened.

As if reading her mind, the dream wife said, "Not much mystery. I could tell from a glance that it was her heart that gave out. The strain was too much. My condolences, Your Highness, for your loss."

"Thank you." Eloise took a sip. "What will be done with the body?"

"I will get some of the monks to help me wrap it and prepare it for transport. I assume you'll want her returned to your realm for burial or burning. Does she have family?"

Eloise's face reddened. "I... I don't know. That's terrible. I've worked with her every day for weeks and weeks, and I don't know if there's anyone back home to grieve for her, besides me." She dropped her chin to her chest and felt her cheeks burn. "What kind of person doesn't know about the family situation of those closest around her?"

The dream wife gave Eloise a moment to feel her feelings, but didn't let her wallow. "She was your offsider for the conference."

"That's right. First Advisor is… was… across all the details. She knew all kinds of things about the different monarchs, which she's been schooling me on for weeks. She was good with strategy. Good with seeing what was going on. I don't mean to make her passing about me, but it leaves me alone up here."

"You don't have any other advisors in your party?"

"I do, but none with her skills and her understanding of the realms. I left my Interim Other Places Advocate at home as he's new and I had her." Eloise swallowed. "What am I going to do without her?"

"Isn't that obvious?" said the dream wife.

"No. No, it's not. Not at all."

"You're going to sit down with the other monarchs and talk. Her presence, or lack thereof, doesn't change what you are here to do. It just means that you now have to rely on yourself instead of her."

"Oh. I guess that's the simple version of it."

"Do you need a more complex version?"

"No," said Eloise. "I guess not."

"May I say, Your Highness, that from the little time we've spent together previously, I think you're up for the task."

"That's kind of you to say."

"I'm not saying it out of kindness. That is not the way of the Us. I'm saying it because I think it is true. May I offer one small piece of advice?"

"I wish you would. It will be the last that I get, I suspect."

The dream wife stepped to where she could look Eloise in the eyes. "Keep your ears open. Try to listen more than speak. And try, if you can, to keep your heart open as well. You might find that helps in ways you don't expect."

"Thank you. I will."

There was a knock at the threshold. "Excuse me?"

Eloise turned to see a monk just beyond the doorway. The man was of middle years, wore a full-length, faded-brown, freshly-washed cassock, and was thin and pointy like an upside-down garden stake. His black hair was tonsured, and he stood, hands laced in front of him, like he could have done so until the end of time.

"Yes?" said Eloise.

"I am Sibling Nichtsdabei. If you are ready, Your Highness, I will show you to your room, then once you've freshened up, take you to the gathering."

50

TWO SIBLINGS

Eloise took one last look at Bënnïë-Änn Thëjëts's body, swallowed back her feelings, and stepped out into the early night. The monk led her past a long series of huts nestled among conifers. Some were dark, and others lit. One had a particularly noxious smell coming from it and Eloise wondered if there was another, older dead body stored there. But for the most part, they were nondescript. Occasionally, she glimpsed a scholar at a writing table and more than once, someone on a porch kneeling, head bowed, silently praying to the light clack of prayer beads. The sound made her reach for her own, and she pulled them from a pocket in her travel cape. Odmilla had given them to her, and they'd helped keep her calm on her journey to find Johanna. She found comfort in their familiar smoothness.

Sibling Nichtsdabei interrupted her quiet. "Is this your first visit to the seminary at the Midpoint of All the Realms?"

"Yes, it—"

"Or Dundad Baigaa Ter Tseg, as the Us call it. I try to respect their traditional stewardship of the land. We are, after all, in their realm and not the other way around. It does us Not the Us good to remember that."

His use of "Not the Us" was interesting. The Us used the term "Not Us" to mean equines who are not of the Us (which he wasn't), and "savages" for everyone else (which he was). "Not the Us," with a "the" in the middle, was absolutely not in their common usage. Had this monk made up a term that was less offensive than "savages," had he misheard, was he ignorant, ignorant but trying, or maybe he was—

Her mind had latched onto triviality. Was it a stress reaction? A form of grief?

"Do you know that 'Dundad Baigaa Ter Tseg' means—"

Eloise stopped, and Sibling Nichtsdabei did the same. "I'm sorry, this is all very interesting, but I've just had a bad shock, and I'm about to have the most important meetings of my life."

"Oh. Of course."

"Please understand that I'm a little preoccupied, and can't really take in all that much. Is the information you wish to share crucial for me to know right now, or can it wait until later?"

"Not crucial, no. I was attempting small talk, hoping to make you feel at ease here."

"Thank you. I appreciate it. But would it be possible for us to walk in silence for now?"

Sibling Nichtsdabei mimed pinching his lips shut and gave her a small bow. He gestured for her to follow him.

"Obviously, you can tell me things I need to know. But thank you for understanding."

They left the line of huts and made it to the main seminary campus, which was built around a grass mall and featured a mix of wood and stone buildings that were dominated at the far end by a four-story building with towers and turrets, like a repurposed castle.

The only problem that Eloise could see, even in the dim light, was that everything looked a little shabby. The grass mall was speckled with weeds, the wooden buildings sagged, and more than one roof canted at an odd angle. Even the main building looked like it needed a lot of love —a place well past its glory days, living on memories and inertia.

Sad, thought Eloise. *Also, not my problem.*

Arriving at the main building, Sibling Nichtsdabei gestured Eloise toward the worn stone steps and bowed. "Good luck with everything, Your Highness. And may Çalaht guide you in the hours and days to come."

"Thank you. I appreciate your help."

At the top of the stairs, the front door opened, revealing a smiling woman with a strongly masculine appearance, who looked like she could have been either Sibling Nichtsdabei's father or mother. "I'm Sibling Superior Nichtsdestotrotz, the abbot here," she said. "Welcome to our humble corner of the realm."

"Thank you for hosting our gathering," said Eloise. "It's very kind of you."

"It's our pleasure. The loftiness of the participants is a bit more than we are used to, but I am at your disposal should you need anything to help you achieve a peaceful result." She bowed again. "Also, may I say, I'm sorry for your loss. I met Bërnädïce-Ändrëä Thëjëts more than once. She was an impressive woman in so many ways." The abbot gave a crooked smile. "Or, perhaps one should say in her memory, 'in so flopping many ways.'"

"She'd have flopping appreciated it," said Eloise. "But it only seems right when she said it. It sounds odd coming from anyone else, doesn't it?"

"You're right. It does. Let me show you to your room. The others have begun to gather, but I've let them know why you're late. Can I suggest you take a few moments for yourself, then join the others in the drawing room."

"I'll also need access to Bënnïë-Änn's room as she would have had things ready for me. I'll need to find them."

"Yes, Your Highness."

51

IRONWOOD TRUNKS

Eloise's room was clean, reasonably large, and looked comfortable, in a spare kind of way. She wanted nothing more than to pull back the covers, sink into the bed, and sleep for a year. Or maybe grieve for an hour.

Neither was going to happen.

Her travel items had been laid out, so it didn't look like she needed to settle in much. She adjusted half a dozen things—her brush and comb, the pillow on the bed, the slippers at the side of the bed, the position of the other clothing trunk—so they felt more "right," then poured water from a ewer into a basin and washed road dirt from her hands. She dumped that into a bucket, tipped out a fresh lot, leaned over, and rubbed her face clean. She dried, straightened her travel clothes, grabbed an oil lamp, and walked next door to First Advisor's room.

The first surprise was that the room was bigger than hers. This shouldn't have bothered her, but it niggled, which, in turn, annoyed her. It seemed petty to be thinking like that. What made her think that she deserved the privilege of a larger room? Why should she be a bit miffed at the size of the room that wouldn't be occupied by a dead woman?

Then she took in just how much stuff First Advisor had traveled with and the choice of room made sense. There were at least two dozen trunks stacked head-high along three walls, leaving barely enough room for an oversized bed and an undersized desk. All of it was marked with loud, red letters that said, "Official Business. Do Not Open Under Penalty from Queen Eloise Hydra Gumball III."

The one trunk that wasn't like that was open, with clothing folded neatly, ready for use. The top layer looked brand new, and Eloise could see the distinctive style of quill-sewn embroidery favored by Seamstress Linttrap.

Clothing that would never be worn.

Eloise held the lamp high to get the maximum spread of light. She knocked on the closest trunk. It had a muffled, full sound, like you would expect from a wooden box filled with pages and scrolls of hemp parchment.

If there was a system among the trunks, it wasn't obvious. They weren't labeled like the bins in the Bibliotheca de Records and Regrets. *How am I supposed to find anything in all of this?*

Unconsciously, Eloise started stretching her right wrist as she tried to think through what she might need from First Advisor's stuff. Her opening remarks, for one—that carefully crafted speech designed to express hope and say almost nothing that would commit her to anything (she really did loathe that kind of thing). Maybe there were current intelligence documents on the other monarchs, especially Queen Aggie. Those might be handy. She should probably go through the trunks and see what research documents were there, just in case she needed to look something up.

In her heart, though, she knew that she would almost certainly not have time for that kind of thing. It's not like she could duck away from a negotiation with a quick, "Pardon me. I have to check on something." She'd been relying on First Advisor to have all that in her head. She swapped to her left wrist and sighed. She was going to miss First Advisor's extensive other places knowledge, and no amount of cramming facts and figures into her head was going to make up for that gap.

Plus, she was upset at what had happened. Rummaging through First Advisor's stuff wasn't going to help her manage those feelings at all.

Then she noticed something else: everything was locked. The trunks were solid ironwood, and their locks were the big, sturdy, "You really don't want to mess with me" kind. First Advisor had always been big on document security, so this wasn't surprising. But, where were the keys?

Probably on the corpse.

Ugh. Just ugh. Hard pass.

She could try to find a hammer and chisel, or maybe a crowbar or an axe. Or a sword. A sword might work. She was definitely stronger now that she'd been training with Sylvia. But ironwood? Her chances at getting through them were slim at best.

Maybe I'll just wing it.

There was a rap at the door frame. "Is everything OK, Your Highness?" It was Sibling Superior Nichtsdestotrotz, looking concerned.

"I was just here to check on our documents. They're all locked safely away." She didn't feel like admitting that meant she couldn't get into them.

"I see. Good then." The abbot frowned. "I'm here to take you to the gathering, but I see you've not changed. Do you need a few more minutes?"

"I probably shouldn't go dressed like this. Or, are the others casual as well?"

"I think you can get away with what you're wearing, assuming you're comfortable."

"I probably shouldn't try to get away with anything. Let me change. Five minutes?"

"I'll come back in ten."

❧ 52 ❧

DRAWING ROOM

I t took more like fifteen minutes for Eloise to freshen up. In honor of her late first advisor, she chose the sea-green dress with the light green robe that Bënnïë-Änn had liked. She felt more than presentable as Sibling Superior opened the door to the drawing room and gestured for her to go in. "Enjoy yourself. And please help yourself to the repast."

Repast, thought Eloise. *Not food. Odd.* She nodded. "Thank you."

The drawing room was painted white with polished wood beams spanning the roof. Tapestries decorated three of the walls, and the main dining room table was pushed against one wall and covered with a variety of foods in silver serving dishes. Upholstered chairs were clustered in groups around the room. For such a small gathering, the drawing room was much larger than was needed.

There were both more people than Eloise had expected, and fewer, and they looked to be clustered by realm and not interacting much. Five monarchs, each with a plus-one advisor, would have been ten people. But First Advisor Thëjëts was not there, and at a glance, neither was Queen Aglandau. That should have given eight. But eleven faces turned to look at her as she walked in—the khan, the dream wife, and a horse she recognized, but couldn't place. Her Majesty Onomatopoeia with two people she'd never seen before, a young woman and an older man dressed in Eastie green. Her sister, their father, and, to her shock, sitting with them was Bosana de Coluber, the trade negotiator from the Eastern Lands. No, wait, he was an ambassador now.

Eloise clenched her teeth and her stomach roiled. How could her sister have him anywhere near her? Just seeing him there made her want to run, or scream, or both. He was treacherous, murderous, mendacious, and dangerous, and her sister was a jester-level fool to have anything to do with him. It was all Eloise could do not to find the closest blunt object and go after him hammer and tongs.

But that wasn't really an option in this context.

Eloise mastered herself and approached them. "Good evening, everyone," she said, doing her best to ignore the three beady eyes. "Apologies that I'm late."

Chafed was the first to come over to her. He was thin and his eyes were sunken. The months had not been kind. Still, he held out his arms to give her a hug, then stopped himself and gave a Protocol-perfect bow. "Your Highness."

"Father. It's good to see you." Then she opened her arms and they hugged. "It's really good to see you."

"Good that one of you thinks so," he whispered.

"Pardon?"

"Not now." He released their hug. "Condolences on Bënnïë-Änn's passing. She was a grand old gal. I really liked her, and I know your mother trusted her. I thought she was an inspired choice as first advisor."

"Thank you. I'm certainly going to miss her." She lowered her voice. "Especially here at this thing."

He also kept his voice soft. "You'll be fine."

"You think so? I'm not so sure."

He gave a one-shoulder shrug, which was more truthful than any words he might have said. "Go say hello to your sister, then I can introduce you to the others, if you need."

"Sure."

He gave her arm a last squeeze, then she walked over to where Johanna stood with de Coluber coiled on a nearby seat. Her fraternal twin wore a practical, indigo gown, her curly hair was tied back but not braided, and unusually for her, she wore eye make-up that emphasized her dark color, and from what Eloise could see, tried to hide a lack of sleep. Johanna's expression was blank, and Eloise had no idea if she'd be welcomed or scorned.

The snake was stoic and cold, but deigned to bow as she approached. "Queen Eloise. A delight as always."

"Thank you, Ambassador de Coluber." She looked at her sister and nodded. "Queen Johanna."

Johanna nodded back. "Queen Eloise." Frosty as a snowbank in mid-winter. "Condolences on your loss."

"Thank you. First Advisor Thëjëts will be missed."

"I didn't really know her. She was the big woman who said, 'flopping' all the time, right?"

"That's right."

"Right. Well, again, sorry. I think I only met her once or twice."

"She was a good soul."

"I'm sure she was."

They stood there awkwardly, a sisterly familiarity between them, but no warmth. They each glanced around the room, neither wanting to hold eye contact.

Eloise wanted to shout, "What are you doing talking to that snake? He's evil!" But it seemed too early for brickbats, so instead, she said, "Tell me something. I don't understand the number of people at this gathering. I thought it was just going to be ten of us—five monarchs and five observers—but Queen Aglandau is missing and yet there are a dozen of us here."

Johanna rolled her eyes. "You missed a minor bun fight."

"Oh?"

In unspoken agreement, the two of them moved several steps away from the snake, and Johanna pointed discreetly across the room. "Our host, the khan, is being attended by that woman."

"She's the dream wife. I don't know her actual name."

"Yes, that's how she was introduced." Johanna lifted her chin to indicate the horse behind the khan. "Khan Nergüi insisted that all proceedings be observed by that one."

"Oh, right. That's the herd rememberer. I sort of met him before, although mostly what he does is lurk in the background and memorize everything."

"It was actually sort of funny. The khan said he wanted him there, and Queen Aglandau questioned his ability to recall accurately, so the khan turned to him and said, 'Two-and-a-half years ago at the equinox that had the full moon, my brother-in-law made some comments about me. What did he say?' And the Rememberer horse said, 'He made a disparaging remark about your mental capacity.' The khan frowned at him and said, 'What did he say, exactly?' And the other horse got all embarrassed and said, 'It would be unbecoming of me to place my khan in a negative light in public by speaking it out loud.' And the khan growled, 'Just say it,' and I think the herd rememberer flushed, if a horse can flush, and said, 'Your brother-in-law described you as "a few rhinestones short of a tiara" and then later, "two pustules short of a plague." The khan said, 'And?' The herd remember then launched into a lengthy diatribe that covered three dozen faux pas that the khan had allegedly committed, all of which contributed to the 'lessening of the herd's integrity and standing in the realm.' It really was an impressive display of memory. Awkward, but impressive."

Eloise laughed. "I'm sorry I missed it. But how did that affect the number of people here?"

"Well, Queen Aglandau allowed that the herd rememberer could observe silently, then made a stink, because having the herd rememberer attend meant that the khan's delegation would have three people and everyone else only two. The khan countered that the herd rememberer was there for everyone, not just him, since there were no scribes, and the queen insisted it introduced a disadvantage to the others. So we all agreed to expand each realm's delegation by one silent observer."

Eloise looked around the room. "I only see you and Father. Who's your silent observer?"

"Father."

"What? So who's your advisor?"

Johanna tipped her head sideways in the smallest possible gesture toward the snake.

Eloise furrowed her brow. "Father isn't your advisor for the gathering?"

"Nope."

"Really? Care to—"

"Nope."

"Are you—"

"Nope."

A long silence followed, and both of them returned to surveying the room. Eloise glanced at de Coluber, who watched them carefully.

After several long moments, Johanna broke the tension, saying, "Here. Come with me. I'll introduce you to the Easties."

"The *other* Easties, you mean."

"Please. Don't make this more awkward than it already is. You can get that part of the intros over with. I think you know the khan's clan and the Southies, so you can say hello to them on your own."

"Sure. And thanks."

The twins walked across the room to the food table. There, a young, blonde woman in a pale Eastie-green dress had her back to them. She was piling a plate high with a bit from each of the serving dishes. Eloise noted that she avoided the plate of olives.

Next to her was an older Eastie gentleman who held a plate at the ready but seemed to want to keep his distance from the woman.

They waited a few moments, but when the woman did not turn around or notice them, Johanna looked at her, an odd expression on her face.

Eloise looked at her sister, and an idea bubbled up. *I know that look*, she thought. *That's the look she gets when faced with a particularly interesting or puzzling plant. How odd.*

Finally, Johanna cleared her throat lightly, and said, "Pardon us."

"Oh!" The woman startled and jumped. She bobbled her plate, but managed a miraculous recovery, spilling nothing.

"Sorry, we didn't mean to surprise you," said Eloise. "That was an impressive save with your plate. Do you play hockey sacking?"

The woman turned around and laughed. "Oh, Çalaht, no. I'd be lost on a hockey sacking pitch."

Eloise smiled. "From the looks of it, you'd be a natural."

"Give me a library any day. At least there I have a knack for finding interesting things. Not so on an outside field. Have you seen the library here? It's supposed to be amazing."

"No," said Johanna.

"Not yet," said Eloise. "I've only just arrived."

"Of course, of course. The Sibling Superior has promised me a personal tour of the Rarities and Antiquities section. I can't wait." Then, realizing she'd forgotten something, she balanced the plate in one hand and gave a Protocol-perfect curtsy, save for all the food. "Queen Eloise."

Johanna stepped in. "I present you Princess Coratina Frantoio Patrinia Ponentine, daughter of Her Imperialness, Queen Aglandau Gaeta Cerignola Ponentine."

Coratina straightened. "Wow, you remembered my middle names. And my mother's. Impressive."

"My middle name is 'Umgotteswillen.' I tend to be sensitive about these things."

"Well, good for you." Coratina laughed again and lightly squeezed Johanna's arm. She stiffened in response, but the Eastie princess didn't seem to notice. "I don't think I'll remember your middle name by the time I finish this sentence."

The man next to her coughed slightly.

"Oh, sorry," said Coratina. "May I present our silent observer, Seer Throumbolia, my mother's Court Seer."

Eloise noticed the bearded man was looking at her quizzically, like he couldn't figure something out. He met her eyes, realized she was watching him, and bowed, breaking her gaze. "Your Highness."

Eloise nodded. "Nice to meet you."

"I hadn't meant to draw attention to myself. Princess Coratina, you might mention Her Imperialness."

"Oh, right, right, right. My mother sends her apologies for not being here. She is... She's indisposed."

Eloise figured this was code for "She can't be bothered," but kept the thought to herself.

"And..." prompted the seer.

Coratina looked at him. "What?"

"Condolences?"

"Right. Of course." She turned to Eloise. "My condolences on the passing of your mother. I said something to Queen Johanna earlier, but it slipped my mind that I should say something to you as well. So sorry."

Throumbolia's cheeks tightened. "Actually, I meant her recently-deceased first advisor."

"Oh, that, too. Right." Coratina bowed again, plate still in hand. "My condolences for that loss as well."

"Thank you."

Small talk ensued, and Eloise noticed Johanna was as reserved as Coratina was effervescent. Normally, her sister was comfortable in this kind of setting. Maybe she was stressed. Maybe she was out of practice. Or maybe she was a queen now, and everything about her had changed. Who knew? But it was out of character, as far as Eloise could tell.

A few minutes later, Eloise interrupted the princess's description of a rare scroll from Lipid the Elder that she hoped to see while at the seminary. "I shall have to excuse myself. I need to greet the other monarchs. Lovely meeting you, and I'm sure I'll see you again shortly."

"Tah tah," said Coratina. "I'll just keep bending Queen Johanna's ear until she can't stand it anymore. Or until Seer Throumbolia steps in and attempts an intervention." She chuckled at her own joke.

Eloise sent Johanna a quick, subtle message using the secret sign language that they'd developed when they were girls. *Can we catch up later?*

Johanna shrugged, but didn't sign back, leaving Eloise to wonder if the gesture meant "Sure, whatever," or "Not a chance."

Eloise waved a goodbye, and crossed to where Her Majesty Onomatopoeia sat with two others from The South. Eloise realized she recognized one of them—the wheat-haired, plainly-clothed harried functionary who'd led Eloise, Lorch, and Jerome from a waiting room in Her Maj Ono's castle to the throne room. She'd been clipped and efficient in her dealings with them, and looked like she'd be the same now. The second woman looked to be halfway between Eloise's and Ono's age. Her braided hair and dress were both bright red, as was her complexion, and her expression seemed to say, "I'd rather have my tonsils removed by a lobster than sit here any longer."

Eloise approached and curtsied to them, starting with the queen. Ono was slight, and at least two decades older than her late mother had been. As she had when Eloise first stood before her seeking clemency after spending more time than she cared to remember in a Southie jail, Queen Onomatopoeia wore a purple robe that covered most of her olive skin. Eloise wondered for the first time if this coloring betrayed Eastie blood in her heritage (not that it mattered). Either way, Her Maj Ono remained a striking beauty, and a few decades earlier, she would have been an absolute knock-out. "Your Majesty. How lovely to see you again."

"Queen Eloise." Onomatopoeia extended a hand without standing. With the other, she held a small plate populated with bitter and sour foods—an arugula and kale salad, pickles, a stewed mix of cranberries and rhubarb, and chunks of ginger.

The queen patted a chair next to hers. "Join me, little songbird."

"I'd love to."

The chair was one of the most beautiful Eloise had ever seen. Its thick upholstery was embroidered with ornate flowers on a navy background. In between the blossoms were elaborate depictions of Çalaht's thumb-stretching tribulation, which she found somewhat blasphemous on a chair. She lowered herself onto it, and found that this gorgeous piece of furniture was easily the most uncomfortable thing she'd ever sat upon. It was so unevenly stuffed and sprung that it qualified as its own kind of penance. Eloise perched on the edge, trying to avoid the worst of it.

"Thank you again for helping to make this happen," said Eloise. "I'm truly grateful."

"As difficult as getting all of us here was, the hard part remains in front of us. You'll note that one of us did not bother to join this gathering."

"I did notice, yes."

"Perhaps the story that she's not feeling well is true. Perhaps not. We'll see if she joins us in the morning."

"Mother?" said the redhead.

The queen picked a chunk of ginger from her plate and popped it in her cheek to suck. "Hmmm?"

"Perhaps you can introduce me?" She glanced at the functionary. "I mean, introduce us."

Onomatopoeia set her plate on the coffee table and gestured for them to stand. "Queen Eloise, may I please present my silent observer, who, as my daughter, tends not to be so silent, Princess Onomatope Barre Lúüùderming. And my advisor for the Grand Council of the Realms, Administrator Féëèlïïícïïïtÿ Sáäàráäàh-Lÿnnéëè Jóöòhnsóöòn."

Eloise accepted their curtsies. "Pleasure to make your acquaintances."

Princess Onomatope looked like she'd swallowed a whole persimmon, but forced a smile. "Pleased to meet you, too, Queen Eloise."

"Queen Eloise," said Administrator Jóöòhnsóöòn. "I feel I owe you an apology."

"Oh?"

"Last time we met I was less than kind. I did not know who you were, nor did I believe you when you declared yourself."

Eloise waved this off. "I was a stranger with no paperwork who arrived unannounced with a chipmunk and two horses who did not know your ways, with a tale that must have sounded extremely unlikely. It would have been negligent for you to have taken me at face value, and I consider it my good fortune that I'm not still moldering in a dungeon."

"It is generous of you to say so. But I know suffering goes on in there. Deliberate suffering. I hope yours was not permanently scarring."

"I don't think I'll be inviting many chiggers to tea any time soon, but otherwise, I'm OK. But maybe someday, one might speak about reforms that might be considered. A perspective of rehabilitation might be helpful."

"Reforms? Rehabilitation?" scoffed Her Maj Ono. "That's the talk of youth. The whole point of the jail system is to punish. And to find out who needs to be punished."

Their discussion was interrupted by the limping approach of the khan, followed by the dream wife and the herd rememberer. Eloise and the two younger women stood and curtsied, but Onomatopoeia did not.

"Your Alacrity," said Eloise.

"Your Highness," said the horse.

"Thank you for hosting this august gathering. I'm grateful that we are all able to meet on the sacred lands of the Us."

The khan gave the horse equivalent of a shrug. "Dundad Baigaa Ter Tseg is perhaps not as sacred as other places in the realm. I do not ascribe to the Çalahtist claptrap that takes place here. But we tolerate it so long as it does not become odious. And the facility suffices for this kind of purpose. Now, ladies, I must depart. The day has been difficult for me and we have an early start tomorrow. Queen Eloise, allow me to express my sympathies. Do you need me to send a messenger to your encampment so a replacement advisor and a silent observer can be brought up to the seminary?"

"Oh. Right," said Eloise. "With everything going on, I hadn't thought about that at all. But yes, I will want to fill out my contingent. Let me think about it for a few moments."

"Inform the dream wife. She will organize it." He bowed to the four of them. "I'll see you in the morning."

"That you will," said Onomatopoeia. "And it will no doubt be interesting."

The horse gave a low nicker. "If no blood is spilled, I'll consider it a success."

Eloise had no idea if he was serious or if that was what passed for humor among the Us.

She hoped for the latter.

✾   53   ✾

CUT. TURN. CUT. TURN

The next morning Eloise woke from long habit at her usual early time, ready for her Balancing Way training. But Silvia wasn't there, and Lorch and Jerome hadn't arrived yet, so she was on her own. She dressed, took her practice staff and wooden sword, and went looking for a private spot where she could practice.

She discovered a small courtyard that was big enough for the swing movements she needed to make, and after stretching, began the slow, deliberate forms. Fifteen minutes later she was sweating and breathing hard.

"What *are* you doing?" It was Johanna, standing at the far side of the courtyard, nibbling a croissant. "It looks like you're practicing for a pantomime."

"I've been studying with Sylvia."

"Mother's Sylvia?"

"Yes. Sylvia Cloisterfeld. I've been learning the Balancing Way. I like it."

"Huh. Well, I'm not one to begrudge someone's pastimes. Not everyone likes sticking their hands in dirt the way I do."

"True." Eloise put down her practice sword and picked up her wooden staff. She began moving into the eight direction cuts of the celestial lotus. As she swung, she said, "Can I ask you something?"

Johanna found a low wall and sat on it. "I guess. I don't promise to answer, but you can ask."

"What happened with Father?"

"Father and I have not been getting along as well as we did at first."

"I gathered." Cut. Turn. Cut. Turn. Cut. Turn. Cut. Turn.

"It started out just fine. I really needed him at the beginning, and he seemed to come out of his blackness. For a time, anyway. He helped me start finding my feet as queen."

"And?"

She pointed at her shoes. "There they are. I've found them. Both feet. All ten toes are there. I know I may not be a perfect queen, but I'm getting the hang of it all. A bit of schmoozing here, a life-altering decision there, a queen's judgment on Monday, and a budget decision on Friday. Father collapsed back in on himself, emotionally. Which, truly, I understand. His world was shattered. I get it. But when he couldn't poke his head up through his black clouds, his usefulness as an advisor waned."

"That's... That's sad." Cut. Turn. Cut. Turn. Cut. Turn. Cut. Turn.

Johanna reached for a leaf on a nearby plant and gently rubbed it. "He also kept treating me like his little girl. And more than once, he disagreed with what I was deciding, which in itself isn't a problem, but he'd say, 'If it was your mother, she'd...' That started to make my skin crawl. I love him, but he is driving me spare. I thought about replacing him."

"With the snake?"

"Çalaht no. With Theoplonkilis."

"Theoplonkilis. The trade representative?"

"Yes. He's pretty canny with the ways of the world."

"How did Father take it?"

"I didn't go through with it. He's still First Advisor. There's just not a lot of advising going on."

Cut. Turn. Cut. Turn. Cut. Turn. Cut. Turn.

Eloise remembered feeling completely floored when their father had taken up the first advisor role for her sister. She'd felt abandoned, betrayed, and completely hurt.

Now, not so much.

Cut. Turn. Cut. Turn. Cut. Turn. Cut. Turn.

There was another question that was bothering her, but she wasn't sure she wanted to ask it.

Cut. Turn. Cut. Turn. Cut. Turn. Cut. Turn.

"Jo, I have to ask something else."

"No, you don't."

"Yeah, I do."

"No, you really don't."

Eloise stopped swinging her staff. She put it in front of her, and leaned against it, catching her breath. "Why did you do it?"

"Do what?"

"What do you mean, 'Do what?' You know what I mean."

"No. I don't."

"You do."

Johanna hopped off the wall. "I don't. Clarify."

"Why did you take her coin? For that matter, how can you have that snake act as your advisor to this conference?"

"OK, you're right. I did know what you meant."

Eloise waited.

Johanna considered her words. "As for the coin, it seemed like a reasonable solution to some of my problems."

"Uh-huh."

"What 'uh-huh?'"

Johanna's casual tone was starting to irk Eloise. "A reasonable solution to some of your problems."

"Yeah."

"There weren't other factors to consider?"

"Like what?"

"Like what was going on elsewhere. You knew she'd taken Flachberg. You knew what she was capable of." Eloise felt her pulse pounding.. "How could you? How could you do that to me?"

Johanna's eyes went wide. "Do that to you? I didn't do anything to you. Have you seen my realm? Have you seen what an unmitigated disaster Uncle Doncaster left behind? The place is falling apart and there aren't two brass eighths of a coin to rub together in the counting house. It's not like you said, 'I've been to the Half Kingdom. I know what you're up against. Here's a bit from the Western Lands and All That Really Matters to get started with.' So yeah, I took Aggie's coin. Tell me I was wrong to do so. Go ahead. Tell me."

"It was wrong. You shouldn't have."

"Splurgle you," snapped Johanna.

"No, splurgle you. Twice!"

"I did what I had to do. If you took two seconds to think about it, you'd realize you'd have done the same. I have a queendom that needs to not collapse. It still may do so, Aggie's coin or not. There's nothing there. *Nothing.* Nothing at all. What little there was, Uncle D put in his hookah and smoked, or spent on himself." She switched to their sign language. *Kiss my nethers and leave me alone.*

Then Johanna threw the remaining bit of her croissant at her sister.

Eloise batted it away with the end of her staff, and watched as Johanna turned to return to the building, a backwards, one-fingered salute high in the air.

"I need to tell you about the snake."

"The snake is not your concern," snapped Johanna, not bothering to turn around.

"Please, Jo. I need—"

"Stop. Just stop."

"Jo. He's—"

Her sister kept going. "I. Don't. Want. To. Hear. It." And then she was gone.

❧ 54 ❧

PASS

When the horological cuckoo called 9:00 am, Eloise was sitting in a hexagonal room with five doors, one on each side. There were five tables with two chairs each, one for each monarch and their advisor. There was also a chair behind for the silent observer. By design, there was no clear head table.

Eloise's table had a simple white cloth with the Gumball family crest embroidered on it, a bowl of grapes, and a pitcher of water with two mugs. Jerome sat to her left and Lorch stood at attention behind, rather than sitting. She had wondered if someone else might be a better advisor than Jerome, or a better observer than Lorch. Tiberius de Sphenodon, maybe, since he was over a century old and had seen a lot. But no one in her entourage had Bënnïë-Änn's diplomatic experience, so she decided to keep it simple and went with her best friend and her champion.

Eloise, Jerome, and Lorch had arrived first, and were waiting for the other delegations to arrive. Eloise wore a dark navy dress, which she hoped gave her a presence that said "sober consideration and willingness to discuss." She also wore her travel cloak because it went with the dress, and it made her feel better.

They were the only ones in the room. This struck Eloise as odd, but punctuality mattered in these situations, so they waited quietly for the others to arrive.

"Is there going to be morning tea?" whispered Jerome. "I'm peckish."

"You just broke fast. Also, not what I'm thinking about right now, Jer."

"Right, right, right. Fair enough." He drummed his claws on the table. "The Eastie table has a bowl of olives on it. Do you think they'd notice if I snagged one?"

"Again, not really where my mind is."

"Of course, of course." The chipmunk sat quietly for an entire twenty seconds. "How come the Easties get a small, potted tree on their table and we don't?"

"I assume they brought it themselves. We didn't bring a tree. We just brought a tablecloth with a coat of arms."

"Huh. I guess." Another twenty seconds passed. "I wonder what kind of tree it is."

Eloise looked at him. "Take a guess."

"I don't know. How am I supposed to know that?"

"By deductive reasoning."

"Deductive reasoning? What are you, a detective? What clues are you drawing on?"

"There is one big clue."

"And what clue is that, Detective Inspector Eloise?"

"The tree's on the Eastie table."

His whiskers drooped. "Oh. Right. It's an olive tree."

"Spot on, Junior Assistant Detective Jerome."

The chipmunk went back to drumming his claws. "It doesn't look very healthy."

"No. Not really."

Jerome paused, thinking. "Why would they bring a sick tree with them?"

"I suspect they didn't."

"What, did someone substitute a sick tree for their healthy tree?"

"Try another hypothesis, Junior Assistant Detective."

The chipmunk tilted his head, concentrating hard. "It wasn't sick when they left. But it became sick along the way, and no one noticed."

"Works for me."

"I wonder—"

"Jer?"

"Yes?"

"Sshhh... I need to gather myself."

"Of course. Sorry." He mimed locking his lips and swallowing the key, which didn't quite make logical sense, but at least he was quiet.

Eloise closed her eyes and settled into deep breathing.

The door opened and Sibling Superior Nichtsdestotrotz poked her head in. "Goodness, you're here already."

"We were supposed to start at 9:00. Of course I'm here," said Eloise.

"I see no one told you about the changed start time."

"Ah. OK. No, no one did."

"It's now beginning at 9:30. Queen Aglandau requested a short delay."

"Why?"

"I didn't ask. I just tried to accommodate her wishes."

"Well, 9:30 isn't that far away. We'll just wait here."

"Actually, all of the monarchs are supposed to enter at the same time to avoid any indication of rank or priority. I'll need you to wait outside." Nichtsdestotrotz bowed. "My deepest apologies, Queen Eloise."

"Really? I can't just stay here?"

"I'm afraid not. We're doing our best to keep everything balanced and equal."

"Fine." Eloise stood and headed for the door.

"Just a sec, El." The chipmunk hopped down from his chair, sprinted across the room, and scampered onto the Eastie table. He looked around to make sure no one else was in the room, stepped over to the plate of olives, and pocketed a dozen in his pouch. "That should do me."

"Incorrigible," muttered Lorch, as the three of them left the room. "Simply incorrigible."

They waited the twenty minutes in the hall. Jerome spent the time nibbling his pilfered olives. As the horological cuckoo called the half hour, he looked around for somewhere to put the pits. Not seeing anywhere appropriate, he sighed and tucked them into his breeks pocket.

From inside the meeting room, Eloise heard a trio of trumpets blow a fanfare—an enthusiastic, even stirring, rendition of, "Alright, Stop Dawdling Like You Don't Have a Thousand Things to Do and Get On With It," which had been one of her mother's favorites. The door opened from inside, and Eloise straightened and walked into the room at the precise moment the other monarchs did, each followed by their advisors and silent observers.

Everyone was there.

Everyone, except Queen Aglandau. The Eastern Lands door was open, but no one came through.

"For goodness sakes," mumbled Eloise. "The least she could do is front up on time after she delayed everyone."

The other four monarchs stood at their chairs, not sure what to do.

"Let's sit," said the khan, and they did.

Johanna, Onomatopoeia, Nergüi, and Eloise made themselves comfortable, and Eloise saw that, as her sister had said, Bosana de Coluber took his spot to her right in the advisor's chair.

Unbelievable. Outrageous. Absurd. But, apparently, true.

Hushed voices came from the hallway through the open Eastie door. "I'll get there when I'm ready to get there."

It was Aglandau, sounding peevish.

"Mother, we're late. It's rude."

"Rude is the least of your concerns, Cora. Get behind me, let's go in, and let's get this thing over with so we can go home."

"Yes, Mother."

Moments later, Queen Aglandau strode into the room in a rustle of Eastie green like she was holding court in her own castle. Her skin had a sallow, yellowish hue, and she was so thin she looked like she was giving refuge to a colony of intestinal parasites. Her teeth still had that bizarre greenish-brown color, stained in the hues of olives. Eloise didn't know if this was a cosmetic affection or the result of years of olive eating, but it added to her ghoulish look. In short, the Eastie queen looked like a complete carriage wreck.

"Busy morning," Aglandau said, as if that was adequate explanation for her tardiness. "Have we started yet? No? Good."

She took out a handkerchief, dusted off the cushion of her chair, then plonked herself down, with her daughter next to her and her seer sitting behind. The change in Coratina from the previous night was profound. Gone was the cheerful, talkative young woman. This morning, the princess was drawn in on herself and seemed much smaller.

The queen saw the olive tree on her table. She pointed at Seer Throumbolia and gestured for him to pick it up and put it as far away as he could. Then Aglandau slid the dish of olives over, plucked one from it, then stopped and looked at the bowl more carefully. Then she glared at Coratina. "Some are missing."

Her deep annoyance seemed disproportionate.

"I assure you, I put them all out, just like you asked."

"You counted them?"

"Of course I counted them. I always count them. I know how important that is to you."

"Well, there are ten, no, twelve missing." She dropped the olive back into the dish and pushed it away. Fuming, the Eastern Lands queen looked around the room accusingly. In silence, Aglandau looked from monarch to monarch, locking eyes with each in turn.

Eloise met her gaze and stared straight back at her, keeping her face carefully blank. In the corner of her eye, she saw Jerome's whiskers twitching and his paw slowly move to cover his breeks pocket, but otherwise, he also kept a straight face.

"Shall we start?" said the khan, breaking the tension. "The purpose of this first session is for each of us to give a brief opening statement. The order was decided by drawn lots. Queen Onomatopoeia Lúüù-derming of The South, you're to go first."

"Thank you, Khan Nergüi." Administrator Jóöòhnsóöòn handed Queen Onomatopoeia a long scroll, which she unrolled and squinted at. Even from where Eloise sat, the oversized writing was obvious. She hadn't realized Her Maj Ono had eye issues. The Southie queen remained seated, but her voice was strong and deliberate. "My dear fellow queens, my dear khan, I'd like to thank each of you for making the effort to come to this distinguished and unprecedented gathering. I'd also like to thank Khan Nergüi Nimetuseta for so graciously hosting us, and for setting a tone of civility and positivity. I had my administrator do a little digging, and according to our records..." Onomatopoeia droned on for another ten minutes, saying, essentially, "Wow, it's great we're here. No one has tried to do this in a heck of a long time. I hope we can talk through some issues and resolve them. I know what a stubborn bunch we can all be, so let's try to get past that."

Which was, pretty much, exactly what Eloise had planned to say, if perhaps less elegantly. Not that what she'd planned mattered, since her speech scroll remained safely locked away in one of her late first advisor's trunks.

When the Southie queen finished, Jerome began applauding politely, but was the only one in the room to do so. His clapping trailed off into embarrassment.

"Thank you, Queen Onomatopoeia, for your inspiring words," said the khan. "Next up is Queen Aglandau Ponentine from the Eastern Lands."

Coratina put a scroll in front of her mother.

"Pass," said Aglandau.

The horse looked at her. "I beg your pardon."

"I said, 'pass.'"

"You're not going to make opening remarks?"

"That's what 'pass' means, in this instance." Queen Aggie's voice could have frozen a bonfire.

"I see." Nergüi looked genuinely taken aback. "You sure you don't want to—"

"I. Said. Pass."

"As is your prerogative. We'll move on, then. Next, I invite Queen Johanna Gumball of the Northern Lands to present her opening statement."

Johanna already held a scroll unfurled in her hands. She glanced around the room, let her look linger on Eloise for an extra moment, then let go of the bottom of the scroll so it wound itself back up. "I, too, shall pass."

"Oh, please," said the horse. "You've made the effort to come all this way. Let's make a good faith effort."

"Thank you, but I'll pass."

Eloise didn't know what she'd expected, but it wasn't this.

The khan drew a deep breath. He turned to the dream wife and held a wordless conversation while she continued to knit. Finally, he nodded. "Queen Eloise, would you like to give opening remarks? Or should we move on with the agenda?"

She swallowed. "I feel I'd only be repeating what Queen Onomatopoeia has so elegantly expressed. In the interests of getting to the heart of things, I'm more than willing to cede my time as well."

"As will I," said Nergüi. "We've only just started, so there's no point in adjourning, as had been planned. Let's move on to the discussion of—"

Queen Aglandau rapped her knuckles on her table to get everyone's attention. "I'll go first."

NINNYHAMMERED MINIKIN

Having claimed the floor, Aglandau proceeded not to say anything. The Eastie queen picked up the plate of olives again, frowned like they were coated in pond scum, and placed them back to her right. She picked one, ate it while everyone waited, placed its pit in an empty dish, and chose a second.

If her goal was to spark anger, the look on Her Maj Ono's face showed it was working. "Aglandau, get on with it. Some of us are actually here to try and achieve something."

"Are you now. How *noble*." She picked up a third olive, squeezed it a little, testing its firmness, then dropped it back. "Let's not hide behind niceties. We're here because she..." Aggie pointed a bony index finger at Eloise, "... is having trouble accepting reality."

"And what reality is that?" said the khan.

"That wrongs were committed in the past. Grievous wrongs. And things must be put right—in this case, through the complete surrender of lands."

"History is full of wrongs," said Onomatopoeia. "Wrongs perpetrated by our long-dead ancestors do not necessarily accrue to we who are living."

"I agree with half of that. History is, indeed, full of wrongs. But I think they do weigh on those of us who follow. The difference between me and you is that I'm willing to address those historical wrongs."

"By going to war?" said Eloise. "By seizing territory unprovoked and killing people in the process?"

"Unprovoked?" taunted Aglandau. "Unprovoked! Child, you once again show your ignorance. We went through this when you wasted my time at our parlay. History is a provocation. What your ancestors did to my realm is the definition of provocation. For that matter, the very name 'Western Lands and All That Really Matters' is a provocation—it's a goading insult to every other realm that shares Çalaht's green soils and blue sky."

Johanna tried to jump in. "I think—"

"Shut your gob, you," sneered Aglandau. "You're entitled to an opinion when I give it to you."

Johanna's eyes went wide. "I beg your pardon?"

"You heard what I said."

"That's not—"

"You, you spoony, ninnyhammered minikin, gave up your right to do anything other than nod politely and agree with what I say when you took my carriage loads of coin for your queendom."

Johanna's voice dropped an octave and hardened. "There was no such agreement."

"I can't help it if you're too ignorant to read between the lines, or more accurately, to grasp the import of your choices. Frankly, I'm surprised. I thought your mother would've raised you smarter than that. I mean, I get it about that one." Aglandau pointed at Eloise again. "She's not exactly the brightest taper in the candelabra. But you? I really did think I'd see more nous from you. Now shut up and don't interrupt your betters who actually have something useful to say."

Johanna stood. "I won't be spoken to like—"

Aglandau stood as well. "I will speak how it pleases me. And if you don't like it, that's fine. My carriages will be at your front gate tomorrow morning, ready for you to refill them with my coin. If you're not able to, then I will find some other compensation that suits me, whether it suits you or not. And if you don't think I will, just ask your quarter-wit sister about my resolve."

"That's enough." The khan whispered the words, but they cut across the argument. "This manner of speaking does not serve us. Nor do threats."

The Eastie queen turned on him. "They are not threats. They are promises. They are *commitments*. And they serve to ensure my positions are as clear as they can be." Aglandau sat back down and resumed eating olives, apparently having said all she intended to. Next to her, Coratina looked down at her hands, cheeks red.

Johanna sat as well, fuming, embarrassed, and stifled.

Eloise felt like crawling under her chair and melting into the floor. Having faced Aglandau before, this outburst didn't surprise her. But her hopes for a peaceful resolution through discussion lay in shambles and she had no idea what, if anything, might change that.

❧ 56 ❧

MUSK OX MORNING BREATH

The khan adjourned the session, saying, "I think we need to let tempers calm before we continue. Let's reconvene in an hour."

Eloise watched the other monarchs leave the room, Aglandau first, then the others, presumably to go to their designated break areas. The doors all closed, leaving Eloise alone with Lorch and Jerome.

"Is she always so delightful?" asked Lorch. "My gran would have had a word or two to say about her manners."

"She was pretty awful at the parlay. I'd say this is worse."

"At least you don't have her soldiers trying to capture you, like last time," said Jerome.

"That's a low standard, but yes." Eloise stood. "Let's go outside. I need a walk so I can clear my head."

The three of them headed for the door.

Jerome stopped. "Hold on a sec."

Eloise looked at him. "What?"

"I need to do something childish, petty, and deliberately annoying. Do you mind?"

"Why would I stop you from doing something childish, petty, and deliberately annoying?"

"Exactly. Childish, petty, and deliberately annoying are how I roll. I mean, the day just isn't complete if I don't do something that's beneath us all and lacking in dignity."

She gestured. "By all means. Have at it."

Jerome gave her one of his ornate, hand-wavy bows, climbed back up his chair and hopped onto the table. Taking a running leap, he crossed to the next and then the next, until he landed lightly on the Eastie table. He took one last furtive look around, removed the olive seeds from his pocket, and put them in the queen's pit dish with the ones Aglandau had placed there. He took three steps to the olive bowl, looked over the remaining olives with great care, pilfered another half dozen, then jumped down and returned to Eloise and Lorch.

"You're right. That was childish, petty, deliberately annoying, beneath us all, and lacking in dignity," said Eloise. "Well done."

"Incorrigible," muttered Lorch.

Outside, it was bright and crisp. Without thinking about it, Eloise headed down the path she'd taken the night before, toward where Bënnïë-Änn Thëjëts's body lay. The three of them walked in silence, and Eloise's head filled with memories of her late first advisor; in particular, the discussions they'd had before the parlay about negotiating tactics—things like ambit claims, My Hands Are Tied; Good Night Watch, Bad Night Watch; and Hold It or Drop It. Eloise wondered if that's what Queen Aggie was doing—simply using negotiating tactics to try and get get her own way. Perhaps, eventually, she'd come to some sort of compromise.

It didn't seem like it. It seemed like this was really how she felt, and there'd be no way of getting around it without resorting to armed conflict.

Eloise had hoped that having the other monarchs around might temper Aglandau's manner, or at least her demands. But there didn't seem to be any way to move her. She was as recalcitrant and obstreperous as ever.

Her thoughts drifted to the letter her mother had left her when she'd died, which Eloise hadn't opened until weeks and weeks later. Her mother had said, "If you can avoid it, don't put yourself in a position where you have to go to war. The logic is simple. War is bad. Peace is good. Staying out of war can be an incredibly tricky business. I managed it. Your grandmother did, too, somehow. So have many queens before you. But not all of them. Diplomacy should always be your preference, short of needing to face down a madman."

War is bad. Peace is good. That really wasn't such a hard concept. So, did Aglandau fall into the "madman" category? Was she someone Eloise would have to face down? The prospect made her guts tighten as she remembered the next part of her mother's letter: "If your back is against the wall and fighting is what it comes to, go at it with gusto. With rage and vinegar. With spleen and blood and cunning and steel. Queen Gwendolyn is a good model here. She was fierce, determined, ruthless, and most of all, successful. In war, you must crush your enemies, because doing less than that is to invite disaster."

Had she already delayed too much? Had she already courted disaster?

Gusto. Rage. Vinegar. Spleen. Blood. Cunning. Steel.

She thought she could muster those, and instill them in those around her. But she wasn't sure. And even if she could, it seemed like Aglandau had been preparing for war for a long time, whereas she'd only had a matter of weeks. That deficit might prove fatal.

"Gah!" Jerome stopped in the middle of the path, and looked like he was going to retch. "What is that smell?"

Eloise looked around. They were down by all the little huts. And he was right. Something rank filled the air.

Jerome shuddered. "It smells like a family of skunks living in a midden."

"You're right. It is a bit fetid," said Lorch.

"It smells like a musk ox with morning breath."

Lorch looked at him. "How would you know what a musk ox's morning breath smells like?"

"I'm speculating."

"I'm not sure I believe you."

"Really?"

"Please, you two," said Eloise. "First Advisor's body is in one of these huts. Or it was, last time I saw her. Maybe that's what we're smelling."

Lorch shook his head. "Surely they've taken steps to preserve the body, since, I assume, we'll be transporting it back to Brague. Normal procedures would prevent this kind of smell."

Jerome pinched his nose. "I didn't know you were such an expert on dead bodies."

Lorch shrugged. "On campaign, people died. Not often, but often enough. We always brought them home for burial. So I've seen what people do in that situation. You don't want them leaking everywhere if you have to transport them for days or weeks."

"Thanks for that image."

"Any time."

"I'm pretty sure First Advisor is further down. The last hut, or close to. Would we smell her from here?"

"Again, not if they've followed anything resembling normal steps for a dead human body, Your Highness."

"I see. Well, then it's something else, I guess."

"A stink bug having a belching contest with a polecat," said Jerome. "With a cartload of rotted rutabagas nearby as a prize."

"That one was creative," said Eloise.

"Thank you, Queen Eloise."

"Let's keep moving. I'll need to be back soon."

57

VITUPERATIVE BOMBAST

The monarchs re-entered the conference room and took their seats. Johanna was glowering and her cheeks were crimson. Chafed's face looked the same. They must have had words. The snake slid into his spot without reacting to either, but Eloise could have sworn he wore a sly smile. Queen Onomatopoeia had a determined look on her face, the khan's horsey expression looked deliberately neutral, and Queen Aglandau feigned boredom.

Or, perhaps, she truly was bored.

No one appeared interested in actually being there.

Eloise felt the same.

The khan rapped his hoof on the table as a kind of makeshift gavel. "Let's move on to the next agenda item—"

"I've changed my mind," said the Eastern Lands queen. "I'd like to make an opening statement."

"Don't you think you've already said enough?" said Onomatopoeia.

"No, I don't think so, not given the reactions I seem to have gotten." Without waiting for the general assent of the group or permission from the khan, she slid a thick scroll of parchment from her sleeve and unfurled it. She brought it close to her face and squinted. "Let's see, I can skip that bit, that bit, and that bit, as I don't really feel those things and they were just niceties anyway. OK, here we go." She cleared her throat. "Two hundred and thirty-three years ago, Queen Gwendolyn of the Western Lands entered into naked and unmitigated aggression against the Northern Lands, a deliberate attack that has had repercussions for all the realms, even today."

What followed was the longest list of historical grievances Eloise had ever heard. Many of the events she'd heard of, mostly from her Histories and Hearsay lessons growing up, but many were unfamiliar, and could have been made up for all she knew. By Aglandau's recounting, the Western Lands and All That Really Matters queens were villains, and their actions were crimes. Eloise was used to hearing her ancestors praised for their determination, cleverness, and fortitude. In Queen Aggie's invective, the Western Lands history was nothing but duplicity, underhandedness, and a grasping need for more, more, more at the expense of others. It was strange and jarring to hear history described in this way, and from Johanna's expression, she was having a similar reaction.

Aglandau went on and on. Ten minutes became twenty, then thirty, then forty-five. She enumerated countless slights and injuries, bad faith deals, diplomatic undermining, and political destabilization—over and over across decades. Their mother even got a mention toward the end (there was a particular bitterness in Aggie's voice when she spoke of her), as did Eloise, for deceptiveness at their parlay and her unwillingness to accede to the new state of things.

To make it worse, the queen's delivery was hardly riveting. More than once, Eloise found her mind wandering. To keep her focus, she tried looking around the room through the filter of her blurry eye, but nothing in particular jumped out. Similarly, when she listened with her buzzing ear, she found the Eastie queen muffled, but there was no great sense of wrongness to be heard.

Finally, after a full hour of one-sided vituperative bombast, Aglandau sat down.

The other four monarchs looked at her, numbed by the speech.

Maybe it was the weight of the volume of her words, but Eloise found herself somewhat convinced that there was, indeed, something to what the queen had said. Certainly, part of Aggie's speech was ridiculous, so maybe all of it was. The bit about their parlay struck Eloise as particularly unfair. But something inside of her niggled, like there was a point to be had in there somewhere.

On the other hand, people were people. They were imperfect vessels of divine expression. Eloise couldn't believe that the West's historical actions were as always-in-the-wrong as Aggie had portrayed them. But, the flip side of that particular coin was that there was also no way that the queens on her side of the Adequate Wall had always been right, and had not engaged in behaviors that history should frown on. Gwendolyn the Irritable was the most obvious example. She might be a celebrated figure, but she'd gone to war because she'd been jilted and left in the family way, and she'd sent her champion out to use magic against the Northern Lands so the realm's defenses would be compromised and she could conquer it. There was aggression, and the intent to do harm writ plain for all to see, although Melveeta's role was not known by more than a handful of people.

In the silence that blanketed the room, Aglandau reached for her olive dish, noticed that something was wrong, frowned, looked at the other dish with the pits, scowled, and shoved them both off the table. They clattered to the floor and smashed.

Queen Onomatopoeia shook her head. "Feel better?"

"It's not about feeling better." The Eastie queen snarled the last word.

The Southie queen kept her voice calm. "Well then, do you feel heard now, Aglandau?"

"I'm not here to be 'heard.' Or 'seen.' Or 'acknowledged.'"

"Then why *are* you here?"

"I'm only here to clear an old debt, and by me showing up, that debt is now cleared. I've done what I came to do. I can leave when I want." She pointed a bony finger and swept the room with it. "This is a waste of my time. It's a waste of time for all of us."

"You don't think there's value in us sitting down to talk?" Her Maj Ono spoke with a schoolmarmish tone, which Eloise suspected wouldn't help. "Shouldn't we want to clear up our differences without resorting to swords and spears? Doesn't communication have value?"

Aglandau scoffed. "There are some for whom being on the receiving end of a sharp blade is the purest form of communication."

Eloise felt despair gather. She'd genuinely hoped that meeting face-to-face would alter the course of what she knew would come. She was empathetic enough, and had been briefed well enough, to look below the surface. What she saw under Aglandau's bluster and ranting was a queen suffering some sort of significant health challenge, who led a realm that had real problems—an economy that was tanking due to an intractable, incurable disease that was ravaging their most valued commodity and cultural foodstuff. The death of the olive groves was also the death of the Eastie way of life. That must be hard for her to deal with.

Onomatopoeia spoke again; this time her voice was formal. "Tell me, Queen Aglandau, are you really so intent on war?"

"'War' is such a strong word. What I'm intent on doing is—"

Eloise cut her off. "What would it take for you to stop?"

Aglandau shook her head, like she was talking to a prattleweed-addled child. "What would it take for me to stop? Nothing short of a miracle. Do you have any of those up your bony-armed sleeve?"

Khan Nergüi cut across them. "Again, this kind of discussion does not serve us."

"It must be time for another break," said Aglandau. Without waiting for the khan to gavel the session to a close, she got up and walked out. Coratina and Throumbolia rushed after her.

"Let's come back mid-afternoon, shall we?" said the khan. With a lack-luster rap of his hoof, he adjourned them.

58

EPICALLY. PRODIGIOUSLY. BRAZENLY

Eloise took lunch alone in a room set aside for her use. Lorch brought her a bowl of chunky vegetable soup and a side of brown bread, then went with Jerome to stand guard outside the door.

She didn't feel like food. And this was the plainest fare she'd come across since she'd arrived, which tempted, but she just wasn't hungry.

Eloise began stress eating anyway. *She wants a miracle*, thought Eloise as spoonful followed spoonful into her mouth. *A miracle. Who am I supposed to be? Çalaht? Should I get my thumbs stretched?*

Slurp. Slurp. Chomp. Chew. Slurp.

Brap!

She scraped the bowl with her bread crust, chowed it down, pushed the bowl aside, and stood to pace.

Seven steps in one direction. Seven steps back. Up. Back. Up. Back.

Maybe she should do some iron-ring staring. Try to get a hold of herself.

Good idea. Really good one.

Iron-ring staring was the name she'd given to the mental discipline technique that she and Johanna had been forced to learn during their Thorning Ceremony training when they were just shy of fourteen. Their Thorning Master had them stare at an iron ring on a wall for minutes, and then later, hours at a time to learn self-control and focus.

It had been excruciating. It had been dull. It had been more difficult than sitting there staring at an iron ring had any right to be.

But it had been surprisingly instructive, and ultimately, it had been useful.

Eloise sat on the floor cross-legged, and found a splotch on the wall that she could concentrate on. She forced herself to take long, slow breaths. In through the nose, hold, out through the mouth.

Repeat. Repeat. Re—

A freaking miracle. Oh, sure. No worries. I have a few locked in my dead first advisor's trunks. Wait two ticks while I go break them open and haul one out. Heck, I'll haul out two. You can have your choice—

In, hold, out. In, hold, out.

Repeat, repeat, repea—

This is stupid beyond words. Epically stupid. Prodigiously stupid. Brazenly stupid. When they build a monument depicting stupid for the ages, this is the moment they'll capture.

She got up and resumed pacing. Tried to tell herself it was a form of walking iron-ring staring, but who was she kidding. She just couldn't sit still.

A miracle. Such foolishness.

What sort of miracle would even suffice? Eloise figured she could walk across the Gööödeling Sea without falling in or getting wet, and it wouldn't make a difference to Aggie. "Sorry. That's not what I meant by a miracle."

Would the Purple Haze have counted as a miracle? Was Melveeta the Elusive a miracle worker when she cast the spell that destroyed half a kingdom? It didn't feel miraculous. It just felt destructive, and like a really bad use of strong magic. Eloise was pretty sure that if she sent another Purple Haze to grace the Eastern Lands, Aggie wouldn't say, "Well, there we go. A miracle. I guess we're done here."

She spent the next two hours going in circles, mentally and physically. She worked herself into a state of high anxiety, forced herself to calm down, and repeated that cycle a few times.

By the time there was a gentle knock on the door, she was exhausted.

"Your Highness?" said Lorch. "It's time to go back."

Eloise grabbed her travel cloak and put it on.

59

A SUITABLE MIRACLE

Eloise felt despondent as they made their way back to the hexagonal room. She suspected this would be the last session. There had been little discussion, just posturing and the staking out of inflexible positions. Whatever was going on here, it was not heading toward progress or compromise.

Everyone had returned, and the room had been refreshed—pitchers refilled, olives replenished, seats freshly arranged. Their father sat in his chair behind Johanna, and the snake looked overtly smug. Whatever had been going on in the past few hours with her sister, it had left her seething with rage.

The khan rapped the session into order.

"I'd like to make a statement," began Onomatopoeia. "There are points of historical significance that I think need to be addressed. I'm not saying our esteemed colleague is wrong in her interpretation of things, but there are shadings that strike me as unnecessarily unfavorable."

Aglandau snorted, but Her Maj Ono ignored her.

"Proceed," said the khan.

The Southie queen stood and launched into a note-free discourse covering the same history that Aglandau had covered, but her take seemed much more balanced and nuanced. Or so it struck Eloise. But then, maybe she was just searching for any scrap of positivity.

Unfortunately, Ono's speech was just as long and just as difficult to focus on as Aggie's. Perhaps that was by design, but Eloise had a hard time understanding why Onomatopoeia was doing this. Why stake out this territory?

She glanced at her sister. Johanna sat there like a gravestone.

Despite herself, Eloise's mind wandered. The word "miracle" echoed around in her brain. She kept going back to the question—as hypothetical as it was—of what would constitute a suitable miracle for Aglandau. Feeding a village from a half pot of grits, like Çalaht had once done? Coffers suddenly filled with gold? A plethora of coin? An infinity of olives?

Something tickled in the back of Eloise's mind.

Eloise looked down at the table, thoughts whirling. She saw it with her strange, mixed-up vision, the clear eye seeming to fight with the blurry one.

Then her thoughts lined up, and an idea landed like a boulder on a blancmange. *Splango!*

She stood and raised her hand like she was in a classroom. "Apologies, Queen Onomatopoeia. May I have the floor for a moment?"

"I've made my main points. I'm happy to yield."

Eloise moved to stand in front of Queen Aglandau. "You said you wanted a miracle."

"I was being metaphorical, you besprawling cumberwold. But whatever, I might take a miracle. If you can actually produce one that's suitable."

"Suitable. Right." She turned to the horse. "Khan Nergüi, can we recess for twenty minutes?"

"If you need a break, then, yes, I guess."

Eloise slid on her travel cloak, then waved to her sister as she headed for the door. "Jo, come with me for a minute, please."

Johanna wrinkled her nose, like someone had spit in her almond milk. "No."

Eloise stopped, turned to face her, and tried again. "Queen Johanna, would you please do me the kindness of coming with me for a few minutes so we can speak in private."

"No, Queen Eloise. I won't. If you have something to say, say it here."

Anger flashed through her, and she switched to their secret sign language. *So help me, Jo, if you don't stand up and come with me so I can talk to you in private, I'm going to tell everyone you still sleep with your toy, stuffed rutabaga and then I'm going to give you a wedgie that Çalaht herself will have to help you out of.*

Johanna rolled her eyes and signed back. *Fine. And for your information, Rüüütÿÿÿ sleeps next to the bed, not in it.*

She stood and said, "Please, excuse us."

❧ 60 ❧

LACK OF MALINTENT

Eloise led Johanna out of the meeting hall and into an unused room, one that looked like it was used to teach calligraphy, or perhaps for the copying of texts. Its walls were covered in slates that still had someone's lecture diagrams on them, and chalk scented the air. A decorative mace, like one might use at the opening of an official proceeding, leaned against the wall near the door, a coating of dust testifying to its longevity in that position.

Eloise closed the door, and said, "I know what we need to do."

"Hold on, what? And what do you mean 'we?' I thought you hated me."

Eloise looked at her sister. "I don't hate you. I mean, we've had a rough patch, but—"

"You've been nasty ever since you found out that I took Aggie's coin. It sure seemed like you hated me."

"I wasn't thrilled by that. I thought it was stupid. I didn't understand it. And yes, it made me angry. But I didn't hate you. I don't hate you now. Hold on." Eloise rooted around in one of the inside pockets of her travel cloak, pulled something out, and held it up for her sister to see. "Look."

It was a transparent sphere with a flattened bottom. Inside, preserved in a viscous clear liquid, was a flower of incredible beauty.

"It's the crocus I gave you," said Johanna. "Before I left on the trip with Uncle Doncaster."

"I take it with me everywhere. I love this thing." Eloise stroked the smooth surface. "I love this thing because it reminds me of you."

"I... I don't know what to say, except..." Johanna reached into a pocket and took out a clay figurine with a vaguely dog-like look. It was an "artwork" Johanna had made as a little girl, a molded version of her favorite stuffed toy rutabaga, Rüüütÿÿÿ. She'd given to their mother, who'd kept it in her study. "You let me take this with me."

"To remind you of Mother."

"Which it does. But it also reminds me of you, as you were the one who gifted it to me."

The twins looked at each other, then Eloise opened her arms. For the first time in a very long time, the sisters hugged. "I can't tell you how much I miss you, Jo."

"Me, too. Believe me. More than once I've wished for a device that would let us communicate from afar."

"That would have been helpful," said Eloise, patting her sister's back.

Johanna gave Eloise one last squeeze, then let go. "So, why are we in here?"

"Here's what I'm thinking. If Aggie wants a miracle, we give her a miracle."

Johanna wrinkled her nose. "I'm not sure I get what you mean."

Eloise began to pace among the slanted tables and high stools. "One has to ask oneself, what's going on for Aglandau?"

"She's an embittered, manipulative old hag with weird, blackened teeth and a soul to match."

"I won't argue with any of that, but that's not what I'm talking about."

"So what are you talking about?"

"Her realm is falling apart. You know all her olive groves are dying, right?"

"Yeah. What of it?"

"It's nothing short of a catastrophe for her. The entire Eastern Lands economy, their culture, their sense of identity—it's all tied up with olives."

"And?"

"The dying trees and the failings they're bringing on must be making her crazy."

"Again, and?"

"So, I say, we help her."

Johanna's jaw dropped. "Help her. *Help her?* She can go dig a hole and bury herself in it."

"Jo, I think we can fix the olive tree blight. If we solve it, that relieves the pressure on her, which gives her the space to gracefully retreat from her current position."

"Give her a dignified exit. Mother used to say that you should avoid cornering an opponent to the point that their only way out is to run you over."

"Yes, but we only take on the blight if she agrees to back down, and then, once we take care of it, as a group, the rest of us monarchs have to stand together to hold her to her word."

"Are you prattled right now? Because it sure sounds like you're talking to me from the La La Realms."

"I think it could work."

"Yeah, right." Johanna crossed her arms. "The holes in your plan are so big I could drive one of Lurid Eddie's double-decker carriages through them. Let's start with the tiniest of matters—the blight. How are you and I supposed to conquer a disease that has bested everyone who's tried to deal with it?"

Eloise gave her a ta-dah gesture. "We use magic."

Johanna laughed. Not a snicker or a chuckle, but a full-on belly laugh.

Eloise didn't let it deter her. "Specifically, we use your magic for plants and growing things to cure the ailing trees."

"Are you out of your mind? I can't fix the blight. What am I supposed to do, spend the rest of my life traveling from tree to tree using my weak magic and hoping for the best?"

"No, no, no. You and me—we work together. We use your weak magic for plants, but I help you to make it bigger. More widespread."

"How?"

Eloise patted the box at her hip. "With the Star of Whatever."

"Now I know you've fallen on your head." Johanna stepped back. "Let me just restate to make sure I'm clear. You want me to somehow use my weak magic for growing things in a way I'm not familiar with and combine it with your weak magic for whatever you're going to do—but not throwing in this case—to create something that we haven't tested in any way, and spread it across an entire realm to try to fix a problem that's been ravaging the Eastern Lands groves for years, involving the magical object that enslaved Melveeta the Elusive for more than two centuries."

"Yeah, I think that pretty much covers it." Eloise gave her sister's arm a squeeze. "Come on, Jo. What do you say?" Then Eloise's eyes went wide. "But you're wrong about one thing. It won't be weak magic."

"What? What do you mean."

"It'll be *strong* magic." Eloise could hardly believe she was saying the words out loud. "We'll be casting the first, serious, genuinely strong magic spell in more than two hundred years."

"There. Is. No. Way. I'm. Going. To. Do. This. Absolutely not. Çalaht herself couldn't compel me to do it. No way."

"Way."

"No."

"Yes."

"Nuh-uh."

"Uh-huh."

"How, then?" said Johanna. "How are we supposed to use magic to get to every olive tree in the Eastern Lands?"

"I don't know yet."

"Well, then. End of discussion. See you when you figure out—"

"Wait." Eloise stopped pacing. "What about a fog?"

"I beg your pardon?"

"Like the Purple Haze. We use a fog like the Purple Haze, but with different qualities. We make it a healing mist, instead of one that destroys. And we deliberately make it temporary, not permanent. Here. Look." Eloise found a blank slate on the wall, picked up a piece of chalk, and sketched lines, forming a rough map of the realms.

"You never could draw," said Johanna.

"Nope. I'm terrible at it." She set the chalk back in its tray and considered the map. "Melveeta was able to control the direction of the Purple Haze, as well as what it was able to do. I think I... No, I mean *we*... could do the same." She picked up the chalk again and drew some more lines. "We'd send it eastward toward all the olive-growing regions, but it will be imbued with your weak magical affinity for making plants do what you want them to do. In this case, healing them of the blight."

"Except it won't be weak magic," said Johanna. "It will be strong magic." She pointed at the box on Eloise's hip. "Because of that thing."

"Right."

"And you've done this kind of thing before?"

"Sort of, but, if I'm honest, not really. Certainly not on this scale. But I did use the Star of Whatever to enhance the magical capability of the Orb of Alleged Omniscience."

"That thing you dented when you fell at your Crown Plonking?"

"Yes, that's the one."

"And it has magical qualities?"

"Yes, it does, but—"

"What kind of magical qualities?" asked Johanna.

"Sort of like what it says in the name. I had a brief kind of omniscience. But only kinda. Omniscience was overwhelming. Too much information about too many things. So I had to, I guess, turn my attention to more specific things."

"Huh."

"But that's not what I want to focus on here. My point is—"

Johanna folded her arms. "What haven't you told me?"

"I don't know, Jo. I'm sure there's lots." Eloise really didn't want to go into it. Not just then.

It must have shown on her face.

"I'm waiting."

Eloise took a breath and tried to sort through what was worth talking about, or at least relevant to them being at the Grand Council of the Realms. "I'm almost certain Mother and Queen Aggie were, uh..." Eloise felt her ears go pink. "At their parlay, they..." She gestured, indicating intimacy.

"No!"

"Yes. But, moving on—"

"Whoa! Not 'moving on.' You can't just drop that kind of thing and not expect me to have questions."

"Look, we don't have much time. The others are waiting. I'll go into it all as best I can when we've done what we need to do here. My point is, I've used the Star of Whatever to increase the power of magic once before, and I think I, and we, can do it again. Plus, we know Melveeta used it to increase her spell. Actually, that's not strictly accurate. She didn't make another spell bigger. She just made a really big version of what she knew the thing could already do. I came up with the boosting bit. But, again, that's not really my point just now. My point is that I think this could work, but only if we do it together."

"Mother and Aglandau?" Johanna pressed her palms to her temples. "That's just... That's just... I don't want to think about that."

"Jo, I need you to focus on the matter at hand. Queen Aglandau's over on her side of the Adequate Wall scarfing olives and plotting my destruction. Do you think she's going to stop at the border to your realm when she's done with mine?"

"Mother. And Queen Aggie. The mind just boggles. Was this before Father? It must have been, because their parlay was—"

"Jo!"

"Fine. But we're picking this back up sooner, not later. As to your suggestion that we use magic, there's the small matter of Melveeta becoming a slave to what she'd done and living a painful non-life inside the Purple Haze for two hundred-plus years."

"We'd need to make sure that doesn't happen."

"You think?" Johanna shook her head. "Let me ask another question. Did you have any side effects when you used the Star of Whatever that way?"

Eloise hesitated, then told her about her eye and ear.

Johanna scoffed. "Oh, this just gets better by the moment."

"If it brings peace, then I'm willing to risk it." Eloise touched Johanna's arm, and was pleased that her sister didn't pull away. "Let's think about Melveeta for a minute."

"What about her?"

"Her situation was completely different to ours."

"Yeah, it was two centuries ago. People understood strong magic back then."

"More than that. For one, Melveeta thought she was dying. She had broken bones sticking out of her, and she thought she was a goner. The spell she cast was, she thought, going to be the last thing she ever did in her life."

"I guess."

"More to the point, she had destruction in her heart. Her purpose was malignant in its intent, and was filtered through a haze of deep pain. Remember, Queen Gwendolyn had sent her to sneak up on the Northern Lands castle at Stained Rock and cast a spell that would lower the magical defenses. But she fell down that waterfall and banged herself up. When she realized she wasn't going to be able to fulfill her orders, she took everything she had and put it into one final spell of destruction."

Johanna nodded. "The result was the Purple Haze."

"Melveeta didn't know it, but her spell worked. Gwendolyn went in and beat the crud out of King Brüüütus..."

"And the rest is history. What does this have to do with you and me and now?"

"Our circumstances are completely different. For one, we have a complete lack of malintent. Our intention would be to help, not harm. We wouldn't be working in such desperate pain, and, if I'm honest, I think I know more about the Star of Whatever than Melveeta did. I think my connection with it is better. I'm not an expert, but—"

"Stop right there," said Johanna. "That's the bit that worries me. Surely this is a job for expertise."

"Maybe, but no one is an expert in this stuff anymore. Plus, I do have one thing in common with Melveeta."

"What's that?"

"I'm desperate to achieve this for my realm, and by extension, for Aggie's realm. If we can fix the olive blight, then we're doing something good in the world. Surely that's worth trying."

"The risks worry me."

"Me too. But, it seems to me that we have to try. It's the right thing to do, and it's the only way I can see to change our collective futures by stopping Aglandau. Look at how she just treated you. Look at how she's treated me. If I have to go to war with her, I will. But if I can solve this in some other way that maintains honor and dignity, I'd really prefer that path."

Johanna shrugged. "I don't know. I really don't."

"First Advisor Ligurian—"

Johanna snorted. "He was such a prat."

That took Eloise by surprise. "You thought so?"

"Always. Mother adored him, but I... Let's just say that I was never a fan. The least surprising news I received in the past few months was that you'd had him arrested."

"Wow." Eloise frowned. "I wish I'd known your opinion about him before. It might have saved me some trouble."

"Sorry, I thought you felt the same."

"No. Not really. Or not at first, anyway. But my point is that Ligurian did say something useful once. He said, 'There is a time and place for loud and shouty.' At the time, he was encouraging me to *not* be loud or shouty, but by then, he was fully compromised. Jo, I think this is a time for loud and shouty."

"And doing this magical olive thing fits that category?"

"I sure hope so."

"I agree with you about one thing. We have to do something about her. Give me a sec to think."

Eloise waited as Johanna sat on one of the high stools, closed her eyes, and breathed deeply for a minute, then two, then three. When she opened her eyes, she said, "You really think you can do this?"

"I really think *we* can do this."

"I don't know if this is brilliant or incredibly stupid."

"Could be both."

"You're right about that." Johanna stood. "Let's go see if we can cut some kind of deal." She headed for the door, then stopped. "Question."

"Yes?"

"What did you want to say about Bosana de Coluber?"

"Uh... I'm not sure now's the time."

Johanna walked back to Eloise. "Spill it."

Eloise took a breath. "I'm pretty sure he had our mother killed."

"What?! How could you possibly know that? I mean, it seems like the kind of thing he might do, but that's a severe accusation."

Eloise told her about her experience with the Orb of Alleged Omniscience. Patrinia Tanche the goanna who was a serving wench, the pressure applied to her by someone unseen, her distress at her empty nest and the raw haggleberries where her eggs should be, delivering the fatal slice of pie, the deliberately broken eggs and dead babies, a noose, a life ended, and a final witness—a three-eyed snake, bright blue with a white underbelly, and a satisfied smile.

"It was just a vision," finished Eloise. "But it had the ring of truth. And it answered a lot of questions."

"That's it?" said Johanna.

Eloise nodded.

Johanna didn't say anything else. She turned toward the door, took three steps, snatched up the ceremonial mace, and crashed into the hall at a sprint.

Eloise rushed to follow.

61

ID AND RAGE

Eloise caught up just as Johanna charged into the hexagonal room wielding the mace. Her sister headed straight for Bosana de Coluber and smashed it like a club, pure id and rage.

There was a quiet part of Eloise's mind that critiqued Johanna's technique. Her grip was much too far apart, her swing swooped over her shoulder instead of a true up and down, and her aim was off—Johanna cracked the back of the chair he sat on, missing the snake.

Then again, the miss was by mere weak lengths. Overall, Eloise had to rate it as "reasonably effective," especially if Johanna's intent was to scare scaring, not to harm.

Another part of Eloise's brain chided herself with, "You should have done this the second you saw him here. This is what action looks like."

And yet another screamed, "Noooooooooo!" Because this was not how to solve problems.

The snake reacted to Johanna's attack with surprising speed. He leaped off his damaged chair and skittered across the room to take refuge behind Queen Aglandau's table.

Johanna ran after him, heaving the mace back up, ready for a second strike. Chafed, Lorch, and Seer Throumbolia all jumped in front of her, slowing her down.

"Whoa, whoa, whoa," said her father. "Jo, stop!"

"You killed her!" screamed Johanna. "You killed her, you monster!" She heaved the mace at the snake, but it fell well short, clattering on the floor.

Chafed grabbed Johanna's upper arms in restraint. "Killed who?"

"Mother! Now let me go!"

"That doesn't make sense." Chafed turned to the snake. "Is it true? Did you kill my wife?"

"Of course not," he said. "Why would I do that?"

"Bosana." Aglandau scowled, and her voice was ice. "Did you kill the Westie queen?"

"No, Your Imperialness, I did not."

"Tell them, El," yelled Johanna. "Tell them!"

Eloise stepped in front of her sister. "It's true." She sketched the details of what she'd seen in her vision, without revealing the source.

The snake stared at her. "You can't possibly know that."

"And yet, here we are," said Eloise.

Aglandau stood slowly, towering over the snake. "Bosana, you just lied to me."

"No, Your Imperialness, I did not. You asked me if I killed her. I didn't."

The Eastie queen arched an eyebrow. "Don't spit olive pits in my teacup. You had her killed. It's the same thing."

"Under your orders, ma'am."

"I told you!" yelled Johanna. "Eloise was right. He murdered—"

Chafed let go of Johanna and lunged at the snake. Lorch grabbed him by the coat, holding him back.

Aglandau calmly held up a single hand, calling for quiet.

Eloise suppressed a nervous laugh. Her mother had used that gesture a million times. She'd used it herself often enough, too, and she also remembered Onomatopoeia doing it. Perhaps this was an innately queenlike gesture, something all queens came to sooner or later.

The Eastie queen continued staring down the snake. "I did not order you to assassinate the Westie queen."

"With respect, Your Imperialness, your instructions to me were, and I quote, 'Go to the Westie Court and sow chaos. And for the love of Çalaht, show some initiative.' My queen, I did exactly that."

Aglandau's face scrunched, like she was facing a particularly dim student. "Not like that. Killing Queen Eloise was not 'showing initiative.' It was diplomatic suicide."

"I got away with it," snarled the snake. "And you took advantage of the opening I created. Why else invade Flachberg when you did?"

"Oh, I freely admit I took advantage of the jobbernowl's ascent to the throne. Çalaht herself said, 'Suffer not to tarry, lest opportunity flee.' But..." She looked over her shoulder at Chafed, Eloise, and Johanna. "But I would never order such a thing. I swear, by Çalaht's periodontal plague, I would never do that."

"Your Imperialness," pleaded the snake. "I—"

Aglandau snapped, "Silence. I will deal with you when we get home." She straightened and turned to face the rest of the room. "I assure you that this will not go unpunished. And the punishment will match the severity of the crime. King Chafed, Queen Johanna, Queen Eloise, you have my deepest apologies."

The snake let loose a scream of rage. He reared like a cobra ready to strike. "How dare you," he spat. "I've devoted my life to you. How dare you turn your back on me."

The quiet part of Eloise's mind thought, *He's a python. No fangs. No venom. This is posturing.*

As if to prove her point, the next thing he did was turn and bolt for the door.

Stunned, everyone watched him exit.

Then Jerome shot after him.

And Lorch.

And Chafed.

And the herd rememberer.

Eloise doubted de Coluber would get very far.

62

PIPSQUEAK PROPOSAL

The khan tried to bring everyone back to order, but the moment was chaos, so he called for a quarter-hour break. Exactly fifteen minutes later, he rapped his hoof and resumed the meeting.

Aglandau raised her hand, and stood to speak before the khan had acknowledged her. "I wish to again apologize for the actions of the one in my employ. They were regrettable. And wrong. And as I said, I will deal with him appropriately." She glanced out the door behind her. "That's assuming there's anything left of him when the others return."

The room was silent. Eloise couldn't tell if this was supposed to be a joke or not.

"Be that as it may, it does not alter the fundamentals of why we are here. My positions remain my positions. I see no reason to alter them."

She sat, apparently done.

"Anyone else have something to say before we resume?"

More silence.

"Then, Queen Eloise, you have the floor."

Eloise stood, cleared her throat, and said to Aglandau, "You asked for a miracle. I intend to give you one."

Queen Aglandau snorted. "That is the most ridiculous thing I have ever—"

The khan cut her off. "I suggest you let Queen Eloise have her say. Queen Eloise, please continue."

"My offer is simple. I propose to work with Queen Johanna to cure the olive blight that has ravaged the Eastern Lands groves. We will do this by magical means. If we're successful, Queen Aglandau will cease all aggression toward us and our realms. She will also forgive any debts owed by the Northern Lands, and return Flachberg to my realm."

"First of all, I'm not relinquishing Flachberg," said Aglandau. "Second, I highly doubt you are capable of doing what you say you can. And third, even if you could, that hardly erases centuries of wrongs. It hardly seems like a fair deal to me."

"No?" Eloise walked to the middle of the room, but kept her focus on Aglandau. "What sort of economic impact is the loss of your olive trees causing? What will it be like at your Court when the only olives that exist are those enjoyed by the queen, and no one else has any because the trees have all died? What's the impact when Eastern Lands children can no longer learn to count by putting pitted olives on their fingers? That's just one small example of what would become a large and devastating cultural shift. Surely having your groves returned to health would be of incalculable benefit, both financial and cultural."

The Eastern Lands queen grunted and ate one of her olives. "What makes you think you can actually do this thing you propose?"

Eloise wasn't sure what she was supposed to say to that. There wasn't any value in revealing the Star of Whatever if Aggie was going to knock back the offer. "That's not your concern at the moment. It is sufficient for me to say that I think Queen Johanna and I can do it."

"You 'think' you can do it."

"I, sorry, *we* haven't done it before. It's not like we've been sitting in a laboratory testing our olive-plant healing techniques. But I know what I know, and I say we can do it."

"And how will we know if you've succeeded?"

Eloise managed to not roll her eyes. "Your olive trees will return to health."

"How soon?"

"I don't know?"

"How long will it last? Is it permanent or temporary?"

"Having never done it before, I can't honestly say. But let me ask you a question. How have your own efforts gone? How's the aggregate health of your groves? How many more years will you have them? How long until the last tree perishes?" Eloise sat down, exhausted with the effort of trying to convince Aggie. "That's my offer. That's *our* offer. Let us help you, and in return, you let things go back to the way they were."

"I'll say it again: I'm not relinquishing Flachberg."

"How about we let the good people of Flachberg decide whose rule they'd like to be under? I am willing to acknowledge that Queen Gwendolyn taking the canton two centuries ago could be perceived as wrong, especially by those on the ground. Let's put the matter to those good burghers, and let them make the choice."

"Oh, my goodness. A concession from a Western Lands queen. That's one for the heralds." Aglandau snagged an olive pit from between her gum and teeth, and flicked it into her discard dish. "This is preposterous. Imagine it the other way around, with me making such an outlandish offer to you. You'd think I'd lost my grip on reality. But let me be more specific. Your proposal is too vague. It's too open to interpretation. It's absurdly unlikely to succeed. And from my perspective, it's too likely to end up being a mere stalling tactic. I say no to you. Absolutely not." She folded her arms and sat back in her chair.

Once more, silence ruled the room.

Then it was broken.

"Mother."

It was Coratina, her voice soft.

"What do you want?"

"May I ask, how are you feeling today?"

The Eastie queen scowled at her. "What kind of stupid question is that? You know exactly how I'm feeling. And why. And we agreed not to discuss it here, an agreement you've now broken, which is compromising."

"Exactly." Coratina reached for her mother's hand, but the queen pulled it back. The princess looked hurt, but continued. "I have a request."

"What's that?"

"Don't leave me a mess to clean up."

"A mess? A *mess*."

"You know what I'm saying. At least let them try. You can still do what you think you need to do if it doesn't work. But if it does, well, wouldn't that be better?"

Aglandau shifted in her chair. "I don't know."

"Mother?"

"*What?*"

"I miss Ethel. I miss her a lot. I would have done anything to save her. Anything. Surely we owe it to her kind to try. Nothing else we've done has worked. Nothing at all."

The Eastie queen pursed her lips, but didn't say anything.

Eloise had no idea who this "Ethel" was, but the two women seemed very serious about her.

Aglandau sat frowning and mulling for a full two minutes. Every now and again, she glanced at the sad-looking tree that had been shoved aside when she first arrived.

The others waited, giving her time.

With a last look at the tree and her daughter, she said, "Fine. I agree. We'll let the two pipsqueaks have their stupid little chance at pretending to be mages. But when it fails—and it will—this gathering is over, I'm leaving, and history can judge us all for what happens next."

"Done," said the khan. He turned to Eloise. "When do you two want to undertake this task?"

"Now," said the Eastie queen. "They can get on with it right now. No time like the present."

"Are you amenable to that?" asked the khan.

Eloise looked at Johanna, who gave a "why not" shrug. Eloise couldn't think of a reason not to. She'd be winging it whether it was right then or an hour or a day later. "Sure. We'll need a private room with a pair of comfortable chairs, and I'd like—"

"No, no, no." Aglandau wagged her finger. "Whatever you're about to do, you do in front of all of us. I want witnesses. Lots of witnesses. And I want to see how you're going to attempt what you purport to be able to do."

This wasn't OK with Eloise at all, but it didn't seem like she had much choice. She was about to agree when her sister jumped in.

"After lunch," said Johanna. "We need to talk it through, and I'm not going to do this on an empty stomach."

Before Aglandau could object, the khan rapped his hoof on the table. "We adjourn until the afternoon session."

# ❧ 63 ❧

FAILING FAIL OF A FAILURE

s the room emptied, Eloise caught Johanna's eye. *We should have lunch together and use the time to prepare*, she signed.

Right. Should I bring Father?

Lorch and Jerome have seen me do this kind of thing before, so I'll have them there. Your call about Father.

Do you care?

Father is OK.

Five minutes later, Eloise and Johanna were settled next to each other in a side room.

Lorch came in with two bowls of a sweet potato chili spiced with cumin and ginger, and gave them one each.

"De Coluber?" asked Eloise.

"Handled," said Lorch.

Eloise's champion said no more about it, and sat down with Jerome and Chafed at a table that was out of the way, but still within listening distance.

"OK, tell me everything," said Johanna. "I'd better be as across this as I can be."

So Eloise began talking, and kept going for well over an hour. She started with when they were with Melveeta, and the dying champion giving the Star "unto" her, and went through everything she could think of as quickly as she could—surviving the plunge off Mortimer Falls, the rope throw out of the Whacking Great Hole, the brunch-berry paddock sunflower incident, her experience with the khan and the dream wife, her and Jerome's research, and how she'd used the Star of Whatever in conjunction with the Orb of Alleged Omniscience to see and hear the truth.

"The part that's hardest for me to convey is my connection with Sparky," said Eloise.

"That's the naked mole-rat mental construct you use to represent what you call the spark of something in the Star of Whatever," said her sister.

"He's not a mental construct. He's real."

"But you don't have any external evidence of that." Johanna looked at Lorch and Jerome. "Am I right? Is she doing anything other than chatting with herself?"

Jerome raised a paw like he was in class. "I've never seen evidence, but she always speaks of him as real."

"In my gut, I know he's real," said Eloise. "You're going to have to take that one on faith, I guess."

Johanna frowned.

"What?"

"This just strikes me as monumentally risky. It seems like it could go wrong in about numptizillion ways, and that's assuming we can get it to work at all."

"True."

"And, from everything you've said, it never goes exactly the way you think it will, or it ends up leaving you damaged."

"Uh... I wouldn't put it that way."

"How would you put it?"

Eloise thought for a moment. "You're right. You can put it that way."

"But Aggie is Aggie, and something needs to be done. Since she's agreed to this, I think we have to see it through."

Sibling Superior Nichtsdestotrotz knocked on the door and poked in her head. "Is there anything you need for the next session?"

"Something comfortable we can both sit on," said Eloise. "And a solid chunk of good luck."

Not long after, they made their way back toward the hexagonal room. Halfway there, they passed an alcove. In it was something Eloise hadn't seen there before—a locked cage, so sturdy it looked like you could fling it from a mountaintop into a pile of boulders and it wouldn't dent. The slats of the cage were so narrow, a mouse couldn't escape.

Or, in this case, a murderous snake.

De Coluber hissed at her as they went by, and swore revenge using words her mother would not have approved of. Then he began smashing his head against the iron slats over and over.

Eloise stopped and looked at him. She crossed her arms, considering what retorts she had available. Maybe "You'll get yours, villain!" Too forced. "Justice is coming!" Too romance-scroll-villainish. "Would you like me to send you to The South? They have lovely jail chiggers there." Not very snappy.

She looked at him, pounding against his restraint, and decided to simply ignore him. Eloise turned and walked away.

This enraged him even more.

Good enough.

She might see if she could convince Aggie to let her take him back to Brague, so he could face justice there. But that was a matter for later.

They reached the meeting room, and Eloise hesitated before she went in. Her stomach gurgled and there was a rising sour taste in her mouth. Perhaps having lunch hadn't been such a good idea.

She realized that the box with the Star was still tied to her hip, which meant she'd have to fiddle with her robes and skirts in front of everyone to get it out. Eloise waved the others through the door, saying, "I need a moment to myself."

Johanna shrugged and went, followed by Chafed and Jerome. Lorch hesitated at the door. Eloise patted the bulge that was the box and twirled an upright index finger to indicate he should turn around. He did, and she did the same. Eloise hiked up the way too many layers between her and her undergarments to access the box, and untied its sash. She tucked it under her arm, resettled her skirts, and turned back to the doorway.

"Ready, Your Highness?" asked Lorch without looking back.

"Ready."

"May I say something?"

"Of course."

He turned to face her, and swallowed twice, which was about as much emotion as she'd ever seen him show. "I think you are brave. I think you are a good person. And it is my honor to serve you and call you my queen."

"Oh, Lorch." She reached out and squeezed his arm. "That's lovely." Then she looked at him and saw worry flit across his face. "You're worried I'm going to damage myself and never come back."

"It's possible, yes."

"And you're worried that I'm going to wipe us all out, the way Melveeta did the Half Kingdom."

He pressed his lips together, holding in his response.

"Lorch?"

"Yes, Your Highness. That possibility has also crossed my mind."

"If it's any consolation, I'm also worried."

"Good to know, my queen. I think. It will make you careful. Good luck to you. To the both of you. And to all of us."

"Thank you, Lorch. Truly."

Eloise entered the room just as the horological cuckoo called the top of the hour. Her table was gone and in its place was an overstuffed sofa. Johanna had taken the spot on the left, and patted the cushion on her right. Eloise took a look around the room, saw that all eyes were locked on her, and sat. She settled the wooden box on her lap.

"You ready?" she asked her sister.

"As ready as I'm going to be."

Eloise changed to signing. *Are you really OK with this?*

Not in the least. But that's no longer germane.

True. I'm going to hold your hand, OK?

Johanna reached for her sister and they intertwined their fingers. Eloise gave a little squeeze, and Johanna returned it.

"How are we supposed to know what you are doing?" asked Aglandau. "I can't see very well from here."

"I can't exactly narrate," said Eloise. "You'll have to make do with watching."

Coratina stood and moved her chair closer to her mother's. "I'll let you know what I see."

The Eastie queen snorted and waved a dismissive hand, but let her daughter remain.

Queen Onomatopoeia leaned forward. "What are you holding?"

"It's—"

"Sorry," interrupted Johanna. "Excuse me, Queen Onomatopoeia, but Queen Eloise should probably not split her attention by giving explanations or commentary. What we're attempting is serious, and possibly —probably—dangerous. I suggest questions be held until after, in favor of letting the two of us focus."

The Southie queen nodded. "Fair enough. Good luck and Çalahtspeed to you both."

Eloise gave Johanna's hand another little squeeze, this one a thank you. "Let's close our eyes and focus inward. Let your breathing slow and deepen."

She closed her eyes and could feel Johanna deliberately slowing and lengthening her breaths. She could also feel everyone looking at her, waiting for something to happen, evaluating her. How was she supposed to pull this off with them all judging her every nostril flare?

She reached for the spark of something in the Star of Whatever.

Nothing.

Eloise breathed slow and deep, matching her sister, and tried again.

Still nothing.

She sent the Star of Whatever a simple "?".

Nichts.

I'm all in my head, she thought. *And everyone's watching.*

Another long, deep breath. Another "?".

Nada.

This isn't going to work. I'm going to embarrass myself in front of everyone and Queen Aggie is going to send in her soldiers, and I'm a failure as a queen and a failure as a person, I'm a failing fail of a failure and my nose itches and my collar's too tight and I can feel Johanna's palm sweating and I hate feeling other people's sweat, and—

Eloise flung her sister's hand away, her eyes wide. She could barely suppress her revulsion. She hadn't been that repulsed in months and months—not since she was first riding Hector at the beginning of their journey, when his sweat had soaked her breeks. That memory came flooding back, and years of her habits dominating her thoughts and behaviors threatened to come crashing in on her. Eloise's breathing grew rapid and she wondered which door to run out of.

"El!" Johanna's voice cut through her racing thoughts. "El, what's going on?"

Eloise looked at the sweaty-handed girl and had to get away, had to get away, had to get away, had to—

"It's OK, everyone," said Johanna. "I've seen this before. It's just been a while."

Aglandau grunted. "For the love of Çalaht—"

"Button it," snapped Johanna. "Not a word from you."

The Eastie queen pursed her lips, but held her tongue.

Careful not to touch her sister, Johanna started speaking softly. "El, you're safe. You're safe. It's OK, you're safe. Try to breathe more deeply. You're safe. No one here's going to hurt you. The feelings you're having will pass. They always do. You're safe. This will pass. That's it, try to slow your breaths. Don't look around, look at me. I'm the only one here who matters. El, it's OK. You're safe."

Johanna kept the sing-song up while Eloise came back to herself. It took a few more minutes, but she eventually calmed.

Eloise dabbed her sleeve to her eyes. "Sorry," she sniffed. "I didn't mean for that to happen."

"It's OK, El," said Johanna. "It's not like there's no pressure here or anything."

Eloise smiled at her sister and wiped her eyes again.

Johanna turned and looked at her father, then changed her mind and said to Lorch, "Can you bring her a haggleberry tea?"

"Of course." He moved to the beverage table and picked up a cup and saucer.

Johanna turned back to her sister. "You OK?"

Eloise nodded. "Yeah. I'm OK."

"Do you want to call this off?"

"No. I can't."

"Yes, you can. We can come up with something different."

"No, I want to try. I just... I just had a moment. I'll be OK."

"You don't look like you'll be OK."

Lorch brought over the tea, and Eloise took it from him. "I'll have a tea, then we'll try again."

"OK. Done." Johanna looked at the others. "Five minute break. Don't go too far." She turned back and said, "I'm going to grab a tea as well. Is there anything else you need to make this thing work?"

Eloise thought back to the last time she'd tried this, when she'd used the Orb of Alleged Omniscience. She walked through the steps she'd taken: sitting down, telling Jerome not to look at her, going inside, it not working, opening her eyes, talking to Jerome... "Oh," she said.

"What?" asked Johanna.

"Queen Onomatopoeia?" said Eloise.

The Southie queen was across the room talking to her two advisors. She looked up. "Yes?"

"Do you happen to have any prattleweed with you?"

�֍ 64 ֎

MIGHT BE A NEED FOR
BUCKETS

"What a ridiculous question," said Onomatopoeia. "I'm a Southie. Of course I have prattleweed." She waved to her daughter.

Princess Onomatope stood and brought her mother a large travel bag. Her Maj Ono opened the main section, then untied the drawstrings of a sectioned-off compartment. From this, she drew a five-sided box and brought it over.

"Your prayer star," said Eloise.

"Ah, so you recognize a prayer star now. Interesting," said the Southie queen. "This one was my grandmother's. She gave it to me when I came of age."

"It's beautiful," said Eloise. "And it is a deep honor that you would consider sharing some of its contents with me."

The queen lifted a shoulder. "Not to worry. The little songbird seems like she needs it."

The box was made of teak, and the carved outside panel depicted some of the scenes from Çalaht's many tribulations—agonized representations of the Popping of Her Pubescent Pimples, the Burden of Her Boils, the Ignominy of Her Ingrown Toenail, and, perhaps worst of all, the Snagging of Her Torn Thumb Cuticle (which always made Eloise wince).

Onomatopoeia lifted the lid and revealed the five triangular sections that radiated from the middle, four of which contained a different part of the plant (the leaves split down the mid-vein, the purple and pink flowers, stringy shreds of brown bark, and a mound of speck-sized black seeds). The fifth section contained a large wad of downer down, fluff from the seed head of the sober flower that could be used to bring someone out from under the prattleweed's influence (if one could keep the foul-tasting stuff in their mouth long enough).

Johanna eyed the box. "You didn't mention prattleweed before."

"Sorry, I probably should have."

"My experiences with the stuff have not been, as you know, exactly wonderful."

"No. I remember."

"I almost ended up married to Uncle Doncaster."

Eloise shuddered. "That still gives me the yucks."

"Me, too."

"Not much threat of marriage in this context."

Johanna shook her head. "No, thank goodness."

"The prattleweed has helped me do what I've done in the past."

Johanna squinted at the box. "Are you sure I need to take it as well?"

"I don't know. I'm inclined to say yes, but it's up to you."

"Fine." Johanna looked at Her Maj Ono. "May I?"

The Southie queen held the box so she could reach it. "I suggest you—"

Johanna plucked up an entire dried prattleweed flower bulb, popped it in her mouth, chewed and swallowed. "That should do me."

"That should do you and five other people," said Ono.

Johanna shrugged. "Good enough then."

Onomatopoeia held the box in front of Eloise. "Do you need any advice?"

"No, I'll just..." Eloise looked around. "Is there a clean spoon or something?"

"What are you going to choose?" asked the Southie queen.

"The seeds."

She bobbed her head from side to side. "That's what you did at the devotional house last time we were together. Are you sure about that, little songbird?"

"It's what I know has worked."

"As you wish. Traditionally, one just licks one's fingertip and touches the pile. You then ingest one of the seeds that sticks."

Eloise did what the queen said and touched a very small part of her dampened index finger to the black seeds. Three of them came away from the mound.

Her Maj Ono continued holding the box near her finger, ready to catch any that fell or which Eloise wanted to put back. "The potency of this strain is—"

Eloise put her index finger in her mouth and ate all three.

The Southie queen frowned. "I see. Well, this will be interesting, if nothing else." She looked at Lorch. "There might be a need for buckets. Could you see if our hosts could provide us with a couple, just in case?"

"Yes, Your Majesty." He bowed and left the room.

"By Çalaht's dilated pupils, I hope I don't need a bucket," muttered Johanna. "I hate throwing up."

"Me, too," said Eloise. "Although there's an assumption in your statement."

"What, that the buckets are for throwing up?"

"Yep."

Johanna grimaced. "That's just disgusting. And now I can't stop thinking about it."

"There's nothing we can do about it now." Eloise extended her hand to her sister. "It may take a few minutes, but let's be ready to try again."

"Good idea."

Eloise entwined her fingers with Johanna's, and took a last look at the monarchs, advisors, and silent observers intently watching them. Then the two of them closed their eyes and leaned back into the sofa, deepening their breaths.

❦ 65 ❦

"!!!"

Eloise's thoughts began chattering again, going to the same kinds of places. *Everyone is watching. My wrist is sore. Why would I possibly think that this might work? My hair is weird.*

And then her mind gave her three words that were actually useful: *iron-ring staring.*

Good idea, she thought.

Eloise lowered her eyes and picked a spot on the parquetry floor about two arm's lengths in front of her. She began a version of iron-ring staring that focused on her breathing. She slitted open her eyes, kept her lids low, and chose a stain to focus on.

Breathe in. Breathe out. Breathe in. Breathe out.

Keep it steady, girl, she thought. *The stuff will kick in soon enough.*

But what if it doesn't? she replied to herself. *I'll just be sitting here like a lump. A lump and a chump. A lump and a chump sitting in a slump on a bump.*

It will take effect, she assured herself. *It has every other time. Why would this be any different?*

Because this time is this time. I could be here for days. Maybe I've built up a tolerance. Maybe Her Maj Ono's seeds have lost their potency. Or they could have been the wrong kind.

Eloise shushed herself.

Breathe in. Breathe out. Breathe in. Breathe out.

This is as dull as ever. As boring, as tedious, as tiresome. I look like a fool, a jester, a buffoon.

There it is! she thought. *The use of repeated synonyms. I'm definitely feeling prattled. Good.*

Eloise extended her senses toward the spark of something in the Star of Whatever, and sent a "?".

A moment later, she perceived a "!" in return.

She sent a "!!".

And got "!!!" back.

Eloise took the inner journey to the naked mole-rat's green-lit underground space. "Hey, Sparky."

"Loulou! Good to see you. How are you?"

"I know that you know that I know that you know you don't actually have to ask that, since you have access to all my thoughts and feelings."

"You're nervous, huh?"

"Yep." Eloise sat down cross-legged across from him. "How're you doing?"

"Same old, same old." Sparky waggled the tuber. "Shouldn't we be getting on with things?"

"I guess. Shall we?"

"Shall we what?"

"What do you mean? If you have access to all my thoughts and feelings, then you already know why I'm here."

"True. Or mostly true. I need you to articulate exactly what you want, so we're super clear."

"Did you do that with Melveeta?"

"The one you called Melveeta, who I came to refer to as For the Love of All That's Holy Stop Yammering All That Nonsense—she and I had a very different relationship."

"Oh?"

"Much less communicative. She poked and prodded with her mind, but never connected the way you have. She grew more talkative after casting her spell, but by then, her bats had well and truly flown her belfry. Her lucidity waned significantly."

"I see." Eloise hesitated, not ready to get down to it yet. "My sister is with me."

"I sense her presence." The naked mole-rat's eyes got a faraway look. "Hmmm. I see her etheric body. It looks familiar."

"Well, she's my twin."

"It's not that. I've met her before." He tapped the tuber against his cheek, thinking. "At our first encounter. When I encountered you."

"Yes. That's right. She was there."

"See?" The naked mole-rat stood and bowed. "I never forget an aura."

"Well, there you go. So, Sparky, can I please get some help?"

"Sure, Loulou. What do you want help with?"

"We're back to that?"

"Yep."

Eloise paused, gathering her words. "I want to cast a spell, supported by you, that sends healing to all the olive trees in the Eastern Lands and cures the blight. We don't have to limit it to just the Eastern Lands, for that matter. It could go wherever olive trees need it."

Sparky chewed his tuber. "Uh-huh."

"Some specifics. I do not wish for me or my sister or anyone to be tethered to the spell we create. I don't want to spend two centuries like Melveeta did."

"We discussed this. Early on. Melveeta absolutely wanted to be part of her spell. She cast it with every weak weight of her being so it would be as strong and as long-lasting as she could make it. She gave herself utterly and completely to it. I only did what she induced me to do."

"I remember you talking about that. So if I don't do that, then you don't do what you did to her?"

"Again, I didn't do anything to her. She did it to herself."

"Point taken."

"I have a question. How is this olive tree cure supposed to come about? It's not what you know. And I can't conjure it from nowhere."

"That's where Johanna comes in. She has a weak magic for working with plants."

"Ah. I see. You'll need her to be here with you for that to work."

"I don't know how to get her—"

Behind Eloise, there was a thunking sound, like someone had tripped coming down a long set of stairs and landed at the bottom. "For the love of—"

"Jo," said Eloise. "Is that you?"

"El! What in the name of Çalaht's punctured pancreas is going on? Where are you? Where am I?"

"That's a bit hard to explain. Come toward the green glow and meet Sparky."

Her voice came closer. "Am I hallucinating? It this just the prattleweed making everything weird?"

"Maybe. I'm not quite sure of the mechanics."

Johanna emerged from the darkness. "Nice place you've got here. Lovely catacomb ambience." Then she saw Sparky. "Hey there. What are you, like a bald hamster or a gerbil or something? What's up with your teeth?"

Eloise clucked at her. "Jo, don't be rude."

"Come on, El. Are you telling me I have to be polite to my hallucination? Well, sure. I can go with that." She stood, and gave an absolutely Protocol-perfect curtsy. "G'mid-arvo, Master Sparky. I am Queen Johanna Umgotteswillen Gumball of the Northern Lands. Pleased to make your acquaintance."

The mole-rat stood and bowed to her in return, all grace and exaggerated tuber waggling. "I am the one your sister calls Sparky. Care for some tuber?"

"No thanks on the tuber. But pleased to meet you, Sparky." Johanna sat next to her sister. "Why Sparky?"

"To be honest, I don't remember." Eloise patted the ground next to her. "Come. Sit. We have a spell to cast."

"Not yet, you don't," said the naked mole-rat. "If she's going to be here, she needs a name."

"I have a name. Johanna, like I just said."

"He means a nickname. He calls me Loulou. I call him Sparky. Something like that."

Sparky tapped the tuber against his cheek. "Nothing is particularly coming to mind."

"When we were girls, I used to call her Johanna Banana," said Eloise. "Or Juana the Iguana."

Johanna poked her sister in the arm. "And what did I say when you called me either of those?"

Eloise put on a mock thinking face. "If memory serves, you offered to remove my bones from my body and scatter them to the seven winds."

"That offer still stands."

"Noted."

"Jonnis?" suggested the naked mole-rat. "Johannita? Johanna-chan?"

"Stop it," said Johanna. "If she's Loulou, you can call me Jojo."

Sparky nodded. "Done."

Johanna leaned forward, elbows on knees. "How is this supposed to work?"

"We'll get you to conjure something that'll heal the olive trees, we'll send it out like a wave or a fog, we'll let it do its work, then we'll bring it to an end. Does that work for you, Sparky?"

The naked mole-rat shrugged. "A bit light on details, but it's a good start."

"Don't we need something to make it work?" asked Johanna.

"Like what?" said Eloise.

"I don't know. A wand? Magic words, maybe?"

"No wand needed." Sparky leaned toward her and lowered his voice. "But there is a magic word. It is secret and ancient, and must be used with great care."

"Oh. That's exciting. I get to learn a secret, ancient, magic word." She leaned toward him. "What is it?"

He leaned in closer and whispered. "You already know it."

Johanna wrinkled her forehead, then looked at Eloise. "I already know it?"

Eloise nodded. "The magic word is—"

"No, no. Let me guess. Uh... Hmmm." She rested her chin in her hand and tapped her cheek with her index finger. "I already know it. I already know it. I already know it."

"Jo—"

"Hold on, I can get it. Is it something like 'sim sim salabim' or 'hokey-pokey' or 'hooley-dooley?'"

"Jo—"

"Maybe 'higgledy-piggledy?' 'Hurdy-gurdy?' 'Harum-scarum?'"

"You're heading in the wrong direction," said Eloise. "What did Lady Seneschal say to us when we were girls? 'What's the magic word?'"

Johanna put her face in her palm. "You're kidding."

"No."

The magic word is 'please?'"

"Yep."

"That's just... That's just... disappointing." Johanna sighed. "And you're sure we don't need a wand or anything?"

Eloise pointed at Sparky. "We already have a magical object."

"Of course, of course. Sorry. Forgot."

Sparky gave a dismissive wave of his tuber. "Not to worry."

"Hey, how long have we been here?" asked Johanna. "Are the others starting to prepare our bodies for burial or something?"

"Time works differently here," said Eloise. "They're unlikely to be antsy yet. They're probably just looking at us being slack-faced."

"I hope I'm not drooling."

"Best not to think about it."

"Ladies, you're dawdling," said the mole-rat.

Eloise reached out her hand to her sister. "Let's cast a spell."

66

EAT THE TUBER

Eloise felt her sister take her hand. "So what do we do?" asked Johanna.

"I'm not exactly sure. Let me ask you a question. Let's say you had an olive tree with the blight in front of you and you wanted to heal it. How would you do it?"

"That's kind of hard to explain. You could say, I sort of sense it into health. Or project it into wellness."

"I don't understand."

"Give me a sec. I've never tried to verbalize this before." Johanna closed her eyes and Eloise felt twitching in her hand, like her sister was running through a physical process. She opened her eyes and said, "Think of it this way. I feel my way into the plant to detect where I get a sense of wrongness. Maybe I'll put my hands in the dirt to connect to the roots or I'll cup some of the leaves in my hands to give that part of the plant my focus. Then I build a picture in the ether of the ideal state of the plant. I've always felt it easiest to create healing there, rather than down here in the physical. I mean, we're not in the physical here, but you get my meaning. Once I have a sense of the ideal state, I sort of nudge the sick plant toward its ideal."

"Nudge?" said Eloise.

"Well, I can't force the plant. But I can encourage it. I can entice it. I can make the plant think that getting better is its own idea, or would be to its benefit. So, yeah, I nudge. If I can get the plant to move toward its perfect form, then it gets better."

Eloise gave her hand a squeeze. "So that's what we're going to do now."

"But I don't have a plant. Without a plant, it's all theory."

"You have a plant. There's a plant in the room we're in. Fix that one, and then we'll send that cure outward to all the others."

Johanna tilted her head, considering. "I'll see if I can make that work. I think I can sense the plant, even though I'm not touching it."

"Good. Let's get to it. Jo, do your thing, and let me know when you're ready."

Johanna closed her eyes again, and the twitching of her hands resumed. Minutes ticked past.

Eloise waited.

"OK. I think I've got it."

"Good. Hold onto all of that." Eloise looked at Sparky. "Sparky, can you please help us—"

"No, no, no," said the mole-rat. "This isn't quite right."

"Huh?"

Johanna slumped and looked at him. "What do you mean?"

He scratched at the pit beneath his forearm. "I dunno."

"You 'dunno?' You can't say, 'I dunno.' You're you."

"I dunno." Sparky shook his head. "This is a big thing you're trying."

"So?" said Johanna.

"So it needs extra oomph."

Eloise narrowed her eyes. "And how do we get oomph?"

"I dunno."

Johanna let go of Eloise's hand and crossed her arms. "Melveeta did a big thing. How did she get her extra oomph?"

"We don't want to go there," said Eloise. "She got her oomph by falling down a cliff, breaking a bunch of bones, and knowing in her soul that she was about to die and this was the last thing she'd ever do."

"So, that's not something we can easily replicate."

"No."

The naked mole-rat thought for a moment, then smiled. "I've got a solution." He held up his frayed, slobbered-on, half-chewed tuber. "You can eat some of this."

"What?"

Johanna shuddered. "That's disgusting. You've been gnawing on that thing since I got here. What is it even?"

"This, Jojo, is a tuber. Tubers are my favorite."

"Ugh. Just ugh." Johanna shuddered. "I really, really don't want to eat that."

"Sparky," said Eloise. "Is it entirely necessary?"

"Absolutely not," said the mole-rat. "But then, neither is casting a successful spell."

"But we want to cast a successful spell."

Sparky took a step toward her and his gaze bored into Eloise's. "Then. Eat. The. Tuber. Loulou." He held it out, close to her mouth.

"Fine." Eloise took it from him. "I'll eat the stupid tuber." She chomped down on the frayed end and chewed off a chunk. "Ugh. This is like munching on a hunk of hemp rope."

Johanna pursed her lips. "What's it taste like?"

"Like a spit-covered raw potato, with hints of horseradish, cilantro, and rust." Eloise handed it to her sister. "Go ahead. Eat the tuber."

Johanna made a gagging motion, but took it. She flipped it around, chomped off a big hunk from the unchewed side, and handed it back. "Blech."

Eloise nodded. "Perfectly said." Mouth still half full, she took another bite and offered the tuber back to Sparky.

"No, no. You two finish yours." From nowhere, another tuber appeared in his hand. "I'm good. I have this one."

Eloise furrowed her brow. "You mean, we could have had a fresh one?"

Sparky looked at her, then at his tuber. "Yeah. I guess so." He shrugged and took a bite, then gestured for them to continue.

The twins devoted a good ten minutes to chewing, swallowing, and gnawing off further chunks.

When she'd choked down her last bite, Johanna shook herself, then stuck out her tongue. "Foul. Just foul. The least you could have done was make it taste good."

Sparky looked offended. "What are you talking about? It's delicious."

"Allow me to rephrase. The least you could have done was make it taste good to humans."

"Oh, that's no problem. What flavor would you like?"

"Blueberries," said Eloise.

"Chocolate," said Johanna.

They looked at each other, then together said, "Chocolate-covered blueberries."

"As you wish." Two more tubers appeared, and Sparky handed one to each. "Down the hatch, Loulou, Jojo."

Eloise bit into hers. As promised, the flavor was chocolate-covered blueberries, but the texture was still wretched. From Johanna's expression, hers was the same.

Bite, chew, swallow. Repeat. Repeat. Repeat.

When they finished, he handed them a third. Then a fourth. And a fifth.

When she'd eaten that last one, Eloise said, "I don't feel any different. Maybe my jaw's a bit sore, but nothing else."

Sparky hefted his half-chewed tuber. "You won't."

"We won't? Why not?" said Johanna. "Why wouldn't a magical tuber make you feel different?"

"Magical tuber?" scoffed Sparky. "They're not magical."

The twins gaped at him, then practically yelled, "What?!"

"I said, they're not magical."

Johanna looked like she was going to be sick. "Then why did we just scarf all those?"

"The tubers served one purpose only: to get you two to be quiet and take some time to think through what you're about to do."

"Oh," said Eloise.

"Did you?" asked Sparky.

The two women both nodded.

"Well, there you go." The naked mole-rat applauded. He seemed genuine in his praise. "Now then, it's time to get started. Loulou, you take the lead."

"Right." Eloise drew a deep breath. "Jojo—"

"He's allowed to call me 'Jojo.' You're not. It sounds weird coming from you."

"I can respect that. Jo, go back to what you were doing before, gathering your olive tree healing image thingo."

Johanna took Eloise's hand, closed her eyes, and before long, there was that twitching in her hands again. It wasn't long before she said, "OK, I've got it." Tears slipped from her closed eyes. "This poor, poor plant. It…No, *she*… She's so tired, so listless. She's really suffering."

"What does the tree need?" whispered Eloise.

"Oh, El." Johanna's voice was racked with sadness. "She needs a lot of love and care." Johanna paused, then raised her palm so it faced upward. "And she needs this."

A spark of green emerged from Johanna's palm. The spark floated just above her open hand, gathering and growing.

Eloise gasped at the intensity of it. "That's it. Sparky. That's it. Please, please help me send that out into the world."

"Sure. Both of you, lean forward."

Still holding hands, they did.

"Ready?" he asked.

"Ready," they both said.

The naked mole-rat smacked them simultaneously in their wisdom eyes with tubers.

There was a *flash!* as a magical, green flare burst forth in all directions.

Then everything went black.

67

SCREAMING AND WEEPING

Darkness remained.

Time passed.

It was unclear if it was normal time or the weird non-time time that happened when Eloise was with Sparky.

Perhaps both.

At some point, enough of the darkness dissipated that Eloise could vaguely perceive a certain amount of screaming and weeping going on somewhere not too far away.

She very much hoped it wasn't her doing the screaming and weeping.

But she couldn't be sure.

The darkness enveloped her again.

68

UNCOMFORTABLY NUMB

Eloise blinked open her eyes.

Her thoughts were muzzy. Unfocused. Nebulous. Vague, vague, vaguity vague.

The room looked familiar enough, even if she couldn't quite place where she was.

Hexagonal.

Tables.

Chairs.

Half blurry.

People. About a dozen, roughly. Her mouth was open. She closed it. Was that drool on her chin? She tried to lift her arm to wipe it with her sleeve, but that seemed like way too much effort. It could stay where it was.

She needed a nap. A very long, very deep nap. Nap, nap, napinoo.

Eloise became aware of her chair. No, not a chair, a *couch*. Now there was a word she liked—couch. Short. Simple, but nuanced. A hard sound at the beginning, and a softer sound at the end, but not too soft. Lots of rhymes available to it, like grouch, slouch, ouch, pouch, and bowtch (which, come to think of it, might not actually be a word).

She became aware that the inclination to think something like, "couch, sofa, davenport" was not there. That was interesting, because she'd used prattleweed seeds. She remembered their taste.

Did that mean she was no longer prattled?

How long had it been?

She noticed that the taste of jalapeño-flavored soldier sock was absent from her mouth. That meant no one had used downer down on her. Thank Çalaht for that.

There was someone on the couch to her left.

The person even looked a bit familiar.

She wore nice clothes. Smelled familiar. Was sleeping or mind-numb or something, Head back, mouth open. Not such a flattering look.

Her name... It had something to do with bananas.

Oh! It was her sister. Right, right, right. Banana Gumball.

No, that wasn't quite it.

It would come to her eventually.

Eloise's head drooped forward. That was much easier than raising her arm, since she was taking advantage of gravity instead of working against it.

Oh, look, she thought. *Banana and I are holding hands. That's nice.* She looked at their entwined fingers a second time and scrunched her nose.

Her hand—the one that held Johanna's (that was her name! Johanna. Not Banana. Banana was a bit of a silly name, and, to Eloise, carried an inexplicable note of threatened violence)—was numb.

Yep, definitely, her hand was numb. Completely, irrefutably numb.

She couldn't feel anything at all with it.

Uncomfortably numb.

Having a numb hand was odd. Very odd.

More than odd, it was unsettling.

But, if she was being honest with herself, having a numb hand wasn't—as she was coming to perceive more and more of what was going on around her—the most unsettling thing at that moment.

A small chunk of clarity clanged into place.

Eloise worked out where she was (way the heck away from home in the Central Carbuncle). They "why" and "with whom" were still wooly.

But what wasn't clear yet was who was there with her, besides Banana/Johanna, and what in the name of Çalaht's twelve gangrenous toenails had happened?

She tried to blink her eyes into focus. It sort of worked.

She made out the Eastie seer. (What was his name? Throm-something. Thrombosis? Thrombone?) The older man openly sobbed into his beard. His were wet, sloppy, snotty tears—strange, because her sense of him was that he was reserved. Wait. Wasn't he supposed to be a silent observer? Was there such a thing as a blubbering observer?

Her gaze wandered over to Queen Onomatopoeia's daughter. Princess Ono-something-or-other sat on her chair with her legs drawn up and her knees hugged to her chest. She rocked back and forth, making a kind of "Hyungah, hyungah, hyungah" noise. Was she damaged some-how? In shock?

Neither Throm-something's crying nor Ono-whatever-her-name-was's babbling provided useful clues as to what had happened.

A man's face loomed into view, cutting off the scene unfolding in the room. He gingerly took her free hand in his. "Ëëëlöööïïïsëëë, are you OK?"

"Hey, 'Ëëëlöööïïïsëëë,'" she muttered. "That's what my father calls me."

"It's me, Ëëëlöööïïïsëëë. I'm your father." Chafed gave her hand a small squeeze. "Are you... Are you OK?"

"Father? That's right. You're here, present, in this place." Eloise blinked. Apparently she was still somewhat prattled after all. She'd better be careful or someone would shove some of that foul-tasting stuff in her mouth. She leaned forward. "Can I tell you a secret?" Her words were half-slurred, but that was the best she could do.

"Sure, sweetie."

"We cast a spell. Me, Jojo Banana, and Sparky."

"Yes. We worked that out." Chafed hesitated. "Who are Jojo Banana and Sparky?"

"It was a biiiiiiiiig spell."

"I think we worked that out as well."

"The biggest in a long, long time."

"Very possibly." Her father shook his head. "I certainly felt it."

Eloise's eyes went big. "You felt the spell?"

"Yes. We all did."

"Wow. That's interesting, absorbing, fascinating. What did it feel like?"

"I can't speak for the others, but for me, it felt like I was hugging a stun eel for a quarter hour."

"That would be a long time to hug a stun eel."

"Yes, sweetie, it would."

"Father?"

"Yes."

"Could I please have some water?"

"Of course."

He went to the Northern Lands table to pour her a drink.

Eloise looked down at the hand that held Johanna's. She tried to wiggle her fingers a little, but not so much that it would disturb her sister.

Still numb.

I'm so very, very tired.

Eloise closed her eyes and let mind-numbness claim her again.

69

FWOMPS

Eloise came to awareness again.

She was in the same room on the same couch, but now she had a blanket over her. Johanna was still next to her, but now she was sitting forward with a blanket over her shoulder, holding a mug of what smelled like rice malt-sweetened cocoa in her left hand. She was looking at her right hand, annoyed, and was flexing her fingers. She also looked somewhat groggy.

"She's awake," said someone.

Eloise turned toward the voice. It was Queen Onomatopoeia, her face a mix of worry and relief.

With a few dragged-hoof clops, the khan came nearer. Next to him was the dream wife, who looked at her, not with worry, but... was that pride? Maybe admiration? "Queen Eloise, can you hear me?" asked Nergüi.

"Yes, I can hear you. Is everything OK?"

The khan and Onomatopoeia exchanged a glance. "We might talk through the event before we say."

Coratina Ponentine bounced forward and knelt in front of the couch. She held her hands clasped in front of her chest and her face beamed. This was not sitting-mouselike-next-to-her-mother Coratina. It was on-her-own-at-a-party Coratina. "You two did it. You. Did. It. YOU DID IT!"

She threw her arms around Eloise's legs and hugged her, then did the same to Johanna, who stiffened, and struggled not to spill her drink under the onslaught.

"I don't know how you did it, but look!" She ran back to the Eastie area, where her mother sat expressionless, heaved up the potted olive tree that had previously been put to the side, and brought it over. She held it out for them to look at. "It's incredible!"

"I'm not sure what I'm supposed to be seeing here," said Eloise.

Coratina moved it closer to Johanna. "Queen Johanna? What changes do you see?"

"I only glanced at the plant earlier, so I can't make much of a before-and-after comparison. However, the leaves are glossy, there aren't any blight spots, and if I'm not mistaken..." Johanna's eyes went wide. "Are those flower buds?"

"Exactly. The tree should be budding this time of year, and it is! Strong, healthy buds. It's incredible! It was like *fwomp!* I looked over and the tree looked like this."

"Fwomp?" said Eloise. "What kind of fwomp?"

Coratina mimed being buffeted by a gale force wind. "Fwomp! But no actual wind or anything."

"Huh," said Johanna.

"Yeah, huh," agreed Eloise. "Why is your seer crying?"

"I suspect it was the fwomp," said Coratina.

The khan rapped his hoof on the table. "Can we please come to order? I'd like to discuss what we've just seen."

"We can talk fwomps later," said Coratina. She gave an awkward curtsy, still balancing the plant. "Thank you, both." Then she went back to her table, put down the olive tree, and sat next to Aglandau.

Johanna leaned over to Eloise. "I don't think I'm ready to move. Can I stay here with you?"

"Absolutely. I'd much rather you did."

Johanna wiggled her wrist. "My right hand is weird."

Eloise lifted hers. "My left one is too. Numb."

"Yep. I assume it's because of..." She waved her good hand vaguely.

"Seems like it."

"I hope it's temporary."

"Me, too." But the buzz and blur in Eloise's ear and eye weren't temporary, and she feared her hand would be the same. "I guess we'll see."

The khan turned to the Eastie queen. "Queen Aglandau, would you like to say something?"

She shook her head. "Someone else can go first. I'm not ready to speak."

"I think it would be appropriate for you to be the one who begins."

"Excuse me," said an unexpected voice. It was Seer Throumbolia, who stood and stepped forward. "I know I'm supposed to be a silent observer, but I beg your leave to make a statement."

The Eastern Lands queen looked at him, wary. "I don't think so."

"My queen, I think I have expertise that's relevant to understanding what we all just witnessed."

She waved reluctant permission.

Throumbolia looked around, and when the others nodded their assent, he took another step forward. "Simply put, that was the most profound experience of my life." Saying this brought renewed tears to his eyes. He slid a linen handkerchief from his sleeve and dabbed at his face, then continued. "I have spent my professional life engaging with the Unseen, which by its nature, intersects with the realm of weak magic. That was, without a doubt, the most acute magical event in my lifetime. I have thousands of questions I want to ask, although I know they'll have to wait, for now. But I stand by my assessment of what just happened, and..." He pointed to the potted plant next to Coratina. "And we can see its results, surprising as they are. I can't say whether the effects were felt beyond the walls of this room, but I'll be deeply surprised if they weren't." He looked at the monarchs, and apparently decided that was all he had to say. "Thank you for letting me speak." The Eastie seer returned to his chair.

The dream wife rose from her place next to the khan. "May I, Your Alacrity?"

The horse nodded.

"Seer Throumbolia's experience matches my own. 'Profound' is exactly the word I would use. That's all I have to say."

She sat.

"Anyone else?" said the khan.

Silence.

He turned to the Eastie monarch. "Queen Aglandau?"

"What?"

"You will honor the agreement you made?"

"There are considerations to take into acc—"

"Let me say it differently. You *will* honor the agreement you made."

Aglandau stiffened. "You're in no position to say what I will or won't do."

"Perhaps not. But the four of us, together, are." Painfully, the horse heaved himself to standing. "There will be peace between the realms.

You abide by your word, and there will be no need for us to marshal our collective forces."

The queen looked like she'd eaten a persimmon. "There's not—"

"I'm not done speaking," interrupted the khan. "I agree with Dream Wife's statement, and that of your own seer. We've seen a profound use of magic today, done in good faith for *your* benefit and for the benefit of those you rule. You will honor that, keep your word, and maintain peace. I don't need to state the obvious. That which has been done can be undone. That which is beneficial, can also be rendered the opposite."

"I will ignore the fact that you just threatened me." Aglandau heaved herself up from her chair. "I'll keep my word if the olive groves have, indeed, been cured—and if they remain so. However, we won't know if that's the case until we return and survey our groves. For now, I grow weary of this gathering. We'll leave in the morning." She left the room, with Coratina and Throumbolia trailing behind her.

When she was gone, Nergüi let out a sigh. "She's always been difficult, hasn't she?"

"That she has," said Onomatopoeia.

"I think we'll have another break," said the khan. "The Western and Northern queens look like they need a rest. Shall we reconvene for dinner?"

Onomatopoeia stood, and her daughter began gathering their things. "Sounds good."

Eloise and Johanna remained where they were, both exhausted. When the khan and the Southie queen were gone, their father charged over. He pointed at them. "You. And you. That was the most dangerous thing I have ever seen in my life. Dangerous and stupid."

"Father—" began Eloise.

His hand sliced the air. "No. Follow me. Now. We have to talk."

70

INTOLERABLE

Chafed stormed out of the Northern Lands door, leaving Eloise and Johanna to follow.

"Do you know what this is about?" asked Eloise.

"No. Not at all. He hasn't spoken to me with that kind of tone since my Crown Plonking. And he hasn't looked that engaged or sharp for weeks. Months."

"You'll excuse us," Eloise said to Lorch and Jerome.

The twins went after their father and caught a glimpse of him barging into a room on their right. Checking that she and Johanna were alone, Eloise took a few seconds to put the Star and its box back on her hip, under her skirts. Then the twins stepped through the doorway into some sort of a deserted games room. There were tables with chess boards inlaid, tables set up for card games, and one table set up to the side with a game that Eloise didn't know but which had miniatures made of silver or pewter in the shape of a shoe, a thimble, a carriage, a horse, a dog, and a strange, tall hat.

Their father started yelling. "That was stupid. Unbelievably, undeniably, incredibly, and irrevocably foolish."

"Please, Father," said Johanna. "Don't spare our feelings. Tell us what you really think."

"Don't cross me, girl. I never spanked you as children, but by Çalaht's hemorrhoidal backside, I'm willing to start."

"Father, stop," said Eloise. "What's going on?"

"What's going on? *What's going on?* You just hung big signs around your necks that read, 'Go ahead, kill me.'"

Johanna put up a palm. "Stop. You're overreacting."

"No," said Chafed. "If anything, I'm under-reacting."

"Care to explain that?" said Eloise.

"Your lives are in danger."

Johanna scoffed. "There's no need to exaggerate."

"You think I'm exaggerating? Really? Let me describe to you what I just experienced. My two daughters sat down in a room with the three other most powerful people in all the realms, and out of nowhere, displayed a capability, a power, a *force* that's beyond what any of them have ever encountered. Do you think they're going to react with, 'Well, that's nice?' No. They're not. That will have scared the beçalahtus out of them."

"Why? We helped them, and we helped Queen Aggie in particular," said Eloise. "We healed a blight that's been wreaking havoc for years."

"That's great. There's no question it was an astounding thing. And good for you. I'm not trying to take that away from you. But what you did is not the problem."

"What's the problem then?" asked Johanna.

"What comes next. That's the problem."

"Explain, please."

Chafed folded his arms. "What you two can do is no longer a secret, and the people who know your capabilities are, like I said, the most powerful people in all the realms. They will find the fact that you have this available to you, and only you, completely intolerable. Maybe not the khan—the Us live in their own little world most of the time. But Queen Aglandau, and I suspect Queen Onomatopoeia to a lesser degree, will be eating their own livers right about now."

"How do you know that?" said Eloise.

"Because I've lived with these people all my life. No, that's not saying it right. I *am* these people. I grew up as one of them, married one of them. I know how these people think. I certainly know what your mother would have thought."

"I think Mother would have been proud of us," said Eloise. "She was always a fan of novel, positive solutions to challenges, even if she didn't come out and say it that way."

"True. And if she were here and the situation was that her two daughters had joined forces to do something like what you did to the benefit of her realm, she would have been beaming." Chafed frowned. "But imagine a variation on that scenario. She shows up and daughters from the Eastern Lands queen cast a spell, beneficial or not, that is so far beyond her ken that it leaves her jaw hanging."

"Jaws were hardly dropped," said Johanna.

"Trust me, jaws were dropped. You two were just too mind-numb to see it." He paused. "Any jaw that was not dropped is currently clenched, and that person is frantically trying to figure out how much of a disadvantage they're facing. Look at it from their perspective. This huge question hangs over everyone: what will you two do with that power next?"

Johanna sat down on one of the game table chairs. "Nothing. Nothing at all," she said.

"People in their right minds don't mess with magic," said Eloise. "And they certainly don't use it for ill."

"Gwendolyn the Irritable did," said Johanna. "Melveeta the Elusive did. And what she did wiped out half a realm."

"If there's a better example of what not to do, I can't think of it." Eloise shuddered. "Plus, that was two centuries ago. It's not like it is fresh in anyone's memory."

"For monarchs like Aglandau and Onomatopoeia, what Melveeta did might as well have happened this morning. Institutional memory is long."

"I don't want anything to do with this kind of magic. It's freaking dangerous." Johanna flexed her right hand and looked at Eloise. "What about you?"

Eloise was less sure about wanting nothing more to do with it. For one, she had a relationship with Sparky that she valued and enjoyed. She wasn't in a hurry to give that up. And if she was honest with herself, she still had an acute curiosity about the magical arts, and about Sparky's capabilities in particular.

But Johanna was right. Eloise's encounters with magic had been uniformly dangerous, to which the buzz in her ear, the blur in her eye, her broken wrist, her dislocated shoulder, and now, the numbness in her hand attested.

And what had her mother said in her letter to Eloise? "Don't meddle with magic." She'd been unequivocal.

"El?" Johanna snapped her fingers in front of her sister's face. "Come back."

"I'm here, I'm here."

"Look, this isn't a hard question. Surely, you're not—"

"No, you're right. It isn't a hard question. And I'm not anything." Eloise hoped her expression showed less ambivalence than she felt. "I have no plans to repeat that kind of magical act. For that matter, I hadn't planned on using magic this time, either. If Aggie hadn't backed me into a corner and demanded a miracle, I wouldn't have even considered it. But she did, so I did."

"You're both missing the point." Chafed pulled some more chairs over, and the three of them sat facing each other in a triangle. "What either or both of you might or might not do is immaterial. The other three monarchs—one of them definitely, and the other two possibly—are, as we speak, spinning up scenarios in their heads that range from 'those two are a worry' to 'doom and loss are nigh.' You have a power they don't, and they don't know how they can get the same for themselves, which means they'll try take it from you instead, or do something else to rebalance the scales."

"That doesn't sound good," said Eloise.

"You've introduced a massive asymmetry. A colossal unknown factor. It will be utterly unbearable to them that there is this force, this potential threat, and one of such magnitude, that is outside their control. Their jealousy will eat at them. Whatever they show you to your face, they will, without doubt, fear you. They may try to coddle you, harass you, or fight you. But whatever direction their reaction takes, it will never stop."

"This is getting better by the minute," mumbled Johanna.

"The best-case scenario I can think of is that they will come to you with an arrangement where you will be expected to fulfill whatever magical requests they might have—when they want, and how they want. The worst-case scenario... Well, I can think of all kinds of worst-case scenarios, which makes none of them the worst. But one way or the other, you will be hounded to the ends of your days."

"Father, that's just grim," said Eloise.

"Let me say it again. No one will tolerate you being the only ones with that kind of power. No one."

"Then they don't understand the situation correctly." Eloise pointed to her ear, her eye, and her hand. "I've been repeatedly damaged from using that power, even for what seems like smaller things. Everything I've come to understand about this magic tells me that there are only so many times I could use it before there's nothing left of me that remains functional. It's ruining my body one piece, one spell, at a time."

"But they don't know that, do they?'" said Chafed.

"Then I'll tell them. *We'll* tell them."

"Let's say you do. How are they supposed to know that you wouldn't be willing to inflict further physical cost on yourself to achieve a political or territorial end?"

"I just said, I wouldn't do it. I'd be willing to swear to that in front of them. Jo's already said she wouldn't use the magic again, and she can be very convincing. She can convince them, if they don't believe me. Aggie likes her more than she likes me. She'll listen to her. Look at it this way: we don't have a problem of reality. We have a problem of perception. It's merely some kind of hypothetical that may or may not be running around in Aggie's noggin."

Chafed nodded. "That's my point, exactly."

"Father's right," said Johanna. "Imagine it was Aggie who'd showed up here and done something like what we just did. You and I would be panicking. For that matter, if you'd done it without me, I can imagine I'd be having a few frantic thoughts right around now. Plus, they don't know how much of this was you, how much of it was me, and how much of it was that green rock. That's a lot of question marks."

"I guess." Eloise shifted on her chair. She wondered if bolting from the room and escaping back home might be an option.

Johanna folded her arms, mirroring their father. "Answer me this, El. What sort of magic have you considered doing with that thing?"

"None."

"None? Balderdash. I don't believe you for a second. You're not oblivious, and you were under attack. There's no way you wouldn't have considered options."

Eloise had, in fact, considered various possibilities. Over and over. That was the whole reason she'd sent Jerome diving into Gwendolyn's archives. She'd wanted something in her back pocket just in case things went badly with Aglandau, even if using the Star petrified her.

Chafed spoke before she could answer. "Let me ask you this." He reached out and gave her shoulder a gentle squeeze. "Would you be willing to hand over the Star of Whatever to someone else? Perhaps to a neutral third party that everyone trusted? The khan, maybe. Or the Mages' Guild."

Instinctively, Eloise turned her hip so that her body was between him and the box.

Chafed gestured with his chin. "I think that tells us everything we need to know."

"Khan Nergüi seems trustworthy enough," said Johanna. "But you have to worry about the khan who comes after him, and the one after that. I trust Eloise more than any of the others. As for the mages, I'd trust the Mages' Guild about as far as I could toss a stack of anvils."

"I'm with her on that one," said Eloise. "The mages know nothing, and don't know that they know nothing, which is about as dangerous as it gets."

The three of them sat there, silent.

"Where does that leave us?" asked Eloise. "And where does it leave me, in particular?" She rapped on the box at her hip. "And what am I supposed to do about this?"

Chafed shook his head. "As the late, great Bënnië-Änn Thëjëts might have said, 'I have abso-flopping-lutely no floppingly flopping idea.'"

Eloise couldn't have agreed more.

71
PULL

Eloise stood. "I need some air. I have to think this through."

Johanna also got up. "Well, think fast, because we have a session in about an hour, and if what Father says is true, we, and especially you as the possessor of the Star of Whatever, are going to have to deal with this head-on."

"Excellent. I have an hour to get ready for a reign-defining moment."

"Go have a break," said Chafed. "Clear your head."

"I'll cover for you until you get back," said Johanna. "Just don't make it too long."

"No, I won't be long." Eloise kissed both of them on the cheek, turned, and headed for the door, trying to ignore the continued numbness in her hand.

Ten steps down the hall, she found Lorch and Jerome waiting for her.

"My queen," said her champion. "Are you alright?"

"Sort of, I guess. Why?"

The chipmunk put a paw to his forehead. "Holy Çalaht darning her wholly holy socks, El. What you did with Queen Johanna…" No more words came out.

Eloise couldn't remember the last time she'd seen Jerome speechless.

"Jerome is right," said Lorch. "That was… That was quite something in there. Do you need anything?"

"Other than a solution to all my problems, no, I think I'm good." She gestured down the hall. "I'm going for a walk."

"We'll come with," said Jerome.

"You can shadow me if you feel you must, but, please, no chattering. I'm in need of quiet."

Jerome mimed tying his snout shut in overly-elaborate detail, then gestured for her to lead the way.

The afternoon air was unexpectedly crisp. Eloise hugged herself for warmth. Lorch silently gestured with the corner of his cape, but she declined his offer. "It's OK. I'll warm up."

For the second time that day, she headed away from the main seminary and back toward the line of huts, where in the last one, her former first advisor still lay. The route was becoming familiar, and since she didn't have to worry about where she was going, she could focus.

What *was* she supposed to do? Everything her father had said seemed accurate. The power imbalance represented by her having the Star of Whatever wasn't going to make inter-realm relations smoother. But what was she supposed to do? Share it around? Take magical requests from the other monarchs, evaluate them on their merit, and execute the worthy ones? Not likely, if the toll on her body was any indicator.

"Gack! There it is again." Jerome looked like he was going to be ill. "That smell. It's like a platoon of beavers ate a bushel of garlic, onion, and horseradish, then set up a belching contest."

"It really is an impressive smell," said Eloise.

378

"It's not First Advisor Thëjëts," said Lorch. "She's presumably still down that way."

Jerome's nose twitched. "It reminds me of something, but I can't quite put my claw on it."

Eloise let go of her nostrils and sniffed, took a couple of steps, turned in a different direction, and sniffed again. Lorch saw what she was doing, and did the same. Reluctantly, Jerome joined in. The three of them sniffed carefully for a full minute, until Lorch said, "If I'm not mistaken, I think it's coming from there." He pointed to a tiny hut that looked exactly like the one First Advisor was in, tucked just off the pathway in a copse of elder trees.

Eloise sniffed, took half a dozen steps toward the hut, and sniffed again. "Agreed." She considered the hut. "Huh."

"Huh?" asked Jerome.

She stood there, thinking about it. Something was wrong. No, not wrong. "Wrong" was the wrong word. "Alluring" wasn't right, either, but was heading in the right direction. "Beckoning." That was it. The hut was somehow beckoning her.

"Queen Eloise?" said Lorch.

She held up her hand, asking for quiet, and continued looking. There was definitely a "come unto me" vibe emanating from that direction. Odd.

Also, oddly familiar, somehow.

Eloise took a dozen steps in the hut's direction, then stopped. "Oh."

"What?" said Jerome.

"This reminds me of how I felt when Johanna and I were in the Purple Haze. There was a kind of tugging, a pull to go in a particular direction. I'm feeling something similar now. But that was more physical. This is more..." She wafted her hand around her. "More ethereal."

Jerome stepped ahead of her. "Do you want El Lorcho and me to go check it out?"

"Give me a sec." Eloise covered her good eye, and concentrated on looking at the half-hidden hut with her blurry one. She gasped. Seen that way, the whole building was lit up, glowing like a bonfire—not in a way that screamed danger, but like there was some kind of force inside that couldn't be contained.

Eloise uncovered her eye. "You two wait here." She strode toward the hut and the source of the stench, ignoring Lorch and Jerome's protests.

"Queen Eloise, please. You can't—"

"El, wait!"

She turned back to them and did a perfect imitation of her mother, holding up her hand to stop them. "Please. Wait. Here. If you hear me scream, by all means come in. But give me ten minutes. No, make that twenty. I've got a feeling. Grant me that?"

Both nodded their assent, but neither seemed happy about it.

Eloise walked to the front door and knocked.

The door swung open at her first rap, revealing darkness.

She stepped inside.

❦ 72 ❦

NOT FOND OF THAT

The one-room hut was built from roughly hewn boards. A single, guttering candle more or less lit the space, which was filled with a miasmic fug so dense and foul that it was almost liquid.

The pull Eloise had felt was even stronger now that she was inside. She paused to let her eyes adjust. Squinting into the dimness, she could make out a hulking, indeterminate form sitting at the back wall, mostly hidden in shadow.

"Please come in." The voice rumbled like boulders being ground to dust by a glacier.

"Thank you." Eloise took a second, then a third step into the hut. The form resolved itself into a human shape, but not like one she'd ever seen before. He was massive, a fill-the-room kind of bigness. Eloise had gotten used to large people, working with Bënnïë-Änn Thëjëts, who had outstripped her in every direction. But this person—a man, it seemed—made her first advisor look like a toddler. How had he even gotten into the room? He was bald and dressed in a formless black outfit, including a black scarf that covered his head to the temples.

"I'm Gordon," he graveled.

"Gordon? Are you..." Eloise hesitated. There was the smell. The covering over his ears. She suspected she knew who he was, but wasn't sure. "Are you possibly Gordon the Noisome?"

"Yes, I am, although I can't say I'm very fond of that nickname."

"Oh. I'm sorry. I don't mean to offend."

"How would you like to be known as Eloise the Fetid?"

"Point taken." She paused. "So, you know who I am."

"Yes. I do."

A memory pinged in Eloise's head. Seer Maybelle, months and months before—that first time Eloise had been sitting on the Listening Throne in the Receiving Room. The old chipmunk had tried to convince her to marry Jerome, an idea that had been preposterous from the word go. Seer Maybelle's justification included her consultations with the Unseen. But she'd also conferred with Gordon the Noisome and the predictive twitches of his earlobes. Eloise remembered, because the chipmunk had said it had taken a week to get the stench out of her fur.

Standing there with Gordon, Eloise now understood what she meant.

The big man continued. "I know who you are. I also know when and where you are."

Eloise raised an eyebrow. "I don't understand."

"I don't get out much. But I've traveled for over three months to be here to see you. Or, probably more accurately, for you to see me. And speak with me."

"That doesn't make sense. Three months ago, I had no idea I'd be here."

He looked at her.

"Oh. The Unseen. You're... You're like Seer Maybelle."

He nodded.

"But Seer Maybelle can no longer see me in the Unseen. I am opaque to her. It has vexed her greatly, although she does her best not to show it."

"I feel for her. She's a good and capable seer. But that would limit her value as Court Seer, would it not?"

"Yes. It has," said Eloise. "I'm not opaque to you?"

"No. You are blurry compared to what you once were, but my connection to the Unseen is strong, a strength gathered across decades. I can still sense you." He patted a bench. "Come. Sit. I am ready to listen."

"Not speak?"

"I am not averse to speaking." He patted the bench again. "Light another couple of candles, if you'd like."

Eloise wasn't sure she could stomach getting closer to him, but she steeled both her will and her stomach and walked forward. She picked three candles from a box on a table, lit them, melted them to the table in lieu of candlesticks, and sat on the bench.

Up close, Gordon looked even bigger. His proportions seemed normal, and he didn't seem particularly dirty or travel worn. But that smell! It emanated from him, like he was decaying from within.

"It's my age," said Gordon.

"What is?"

"It is obvious from your face that my odor is disquieting."

"I'm not disquieted—"

"Queen Eloise, if we are going to use our extremely limited time together effectively, honesty and directness are crucial."

"OK, you're right. I find the... ambience... off-putting. There's no doubt that your moniker, unkind as it is, has its origins in the effect of your... presence."

"My 'presence' has worsened with the years. Apologies." He chuckled a little.

"What's funny?"

"Your way of speaking reminds me of your great-great-grandmother. She'd make up word salad sentences that sounded like something you'd hear spoken at Court, but didn't actually say anything. I knew Ameli when she was about your age."

"Are you talking about Queen Amelianna Zahnschmerzen Caltrop Gumball?"

"Yes, I am. But she was a princess at the time." He smiled at the memory. "What a scamp. A real card."

Eloise frowned. "May I ask, just how old are you?"

"Oh, I lose track. I was already well over a century old when I had the pleasure of serving Amelianna's mother as Court Seer. She was my last queen, though. Life took me in a different direction after that."

"Wait. That would make you..." Eloise scowled. "That doesn't seem possible. That would mean you were alive during the reign of Queen Gwendolyn. Did you know her as well?"

"No, no, no. I was an apprentice during the early part of her reign. They never let the likes of a lowly apprentice anywhere close to her."

"Did you know Melveeta the Elusive?"

"In person? Only as a bad taste in the mouth. The way she extracted the queen's tithe from subjects wasn't exactly friendly. Or polite. My family—everyone's family—suffered any time she arrived at the village green."

"If it's any consolation, she spent two centuries in pain from a broken body and enslaved to the spell she cast."

"I don't wish anyone ill—to do so is bad for one's soul. But I came as close to it with her as with anyone. If her path led her to suffer for a few decades, let me just say that I'm not surprised."

"What about in the Unseen? Was Melveeta visible to you there?"

"At times, sure."

"What do you mean, 'at times?' Isn't she either there or she's not?"

"It's analogous to the physical world. Do you know every person who strides the realms? Does everyone everywhere occupy your attention?"

"Of course not. One has to choose where to put one's focus."

"Exactly. It is the same when I experience the Unseen. My attention might be drawn to a particular person, or it might be directed there by a request. By the time the Purple Haze had become an indelible part of life, the fact that Queen Gwendolyn's champion had disappeared was old news. No one asked me to look for her, and I had no cause to have my attention drawn to her. It was like that for decades. Centuries. That is, until..." He trailed off, his eyes getting the same look that Seer Maybelle's did when she contacted the Unseen.

Eloise leaned forward. "Until?"

"A surprisingly Melveeta-shaped essence flared in the Unseen, then was gone," said Gordon. "That was just a few months ago. I suspect you might know something about it."

"I do."

"She was not alone when it happened."

"You're right," said Eloise. "She wasn't."

"I can't tell you what a surprise it was that, after two centuries, there she was, burning brighter than ever with the support of not one, but two, other entities. Queen Johanna, I presume, in retrospect."

"Yes."

"And then, poof. Gone." Gordon made a fist, then flared out his fingers, like a stage illusionist. "And with her, the spell that powered the Purple Haze. I would say that it caused quite a stir in the Unseen, but that would be inaccurate. The Unseen just is. It does not stir or gossip. And there were very few on the physical plane who would have had the capacity to witness the event, and even fewer who might have been in touch with the Unseen at that particular moment."

"But you did."

"Yes. I did. I don't mind saying, I was absolutely fascinated." He gestured to the hut around him. "Indirectly, and then directly, it guided me here to this place at this time, where I have waited for you and the stone you carry."

"You know about the Star of Whatever?"

"How could I not? It shines in the Unseen like a bonfire at your hip. It hadn't moved for two hundred years, then suddenly it's bobbing around the place like an apple in a waterfall."

"I didn't know it could be perceived in that way."

"No, you wouldn't. That is not your gift." The big man shifted on his bench. "We should get down to the heart of things. Your champions are worrying about you."

A knock at the door confirmed his words. "Queen Eloise?" asked Lorch, cracking open the door and struggling to keep a straight face against the smell. Eloise could hear Jerome, just out of sight, coughing and gagging. "Are you OK? Twenty minutes have passed."

"I'm fine, thank you. But I'm not quite done here. Perhaps you can tell the others that I'm temporarily indisposed?"

"I don't suggest you do that," said Gordon. "The Eastern Lands queen already chafes to leave. What I've seen would indicate that you should return to the others sooner rather than later. But you're right that we're not done here yet."

"Right. Lorch, can you tell the others that I'm conferring with an advisor and will be there shortly. But tell Johanna the truth. She'll help you cover for me."

"And what truth is that?"

"This is Gordon the... Gordon the..." Eloise looked at the big man. "Uh, sorry. How about, 'The seer formerly known as Gordon the Noisome?'"

He lifted his shoulders. "That will do for now."

Jerome poked his head around the door jamb, claws pinching his nostrils. "Gordon the Noisome? *The* Gordon the Noisome? Çalaht serving succulent succotash! I thought I recognized the odor. This is amazing. My mother thinks you're awesome. I mean, so do I, obviously. I'm a big fan. Big, big fan. The biggest. You're right up there with Lyndia Thrind in my scroll of all-time favorites. Wow! Gordon the Noisome!" The chipmunk stepped in front of Lorch. "What are you doing here in the middle of nowhere? Aren't you supposed to be hidden away in the Elder Swamp drawing Twigs of Fate from the Bag of Kismet? Oh, can I get you to autograph a bit of hemp parchment or something?" He looked at Eloise. "You don't have parchment and a quill on you, do you? I—"

"Jer. That's enough."

"What? Enough? It's *Gordon the Noisome*, El! The Notorious Big G. Gordino the Noisommissimo, himself! In the flesh. Did you know he still holds the realm-wide record for most prognostications in a day that came true within a month? One hundred and twenty-three. One hundred and twenty-three! Astounding."

"That was a long time ago," rumbled Gordon. "I had a good day."

"I'll say. Hey, Gordo, you've got your earlobes covered. Is that to keep the prognostications from leaking out? Or is it more like a sign that you're off the clock?"

"That'll do, Jer. I really don't have much time."

"Right, right, right. Sorry. Of course. But how did you know he was in here? Apart from the smell, I mean. Like, that smell could have been anything. Beaver halitosis. Baboon armpits. The locker room of a team of rhino professional wrestlers. No offense intended, of course."

"Jerome Abernatheen de Chipmunk."

Jerome stopped in his tracks as his brain finally registered what his mouth had been saying. "Apologies, Your Highness. I forgot myself."

"Not to worry. Can you and Champion Lacksneck find a way to gain me another half hour without the others hauling tuchus out of here?"

"Of course, Your Highness. We'll do that." Jerome bowed to her, face expressionless. "We'll await you at the meeting room." He turned and bowed to the seer. "Again, my apologies. It is an absolute honor to have met you. If you ever find yourself in the vicinity of Castle de Brague, my mother and I would love to offer you hospitality."

"It would be a pleasure to visit with Seer Maybelle once again. And you. But I don't envision that it will happen any time soon."

"No?"

He gestured meaningfully to the ether around him, but also to his own body. "No."

"Right, right, right. Got it. Well, the invitation is there if, you know..." Jerome imitated the gesture in the air, but managed not to point to the man himself. "Just if."

Gordon nodded. "Thank you."

Lorch bowed to Eloise and Gordon separately. "We'll leave you to it. Queen Eloise, we'll ensure no one leaves before your return."

"Thank you, Lorch. See you soon."

The door clicked closed, leaving Eloise with the seer. "So, what are we supposed to talk about?"

"I think you already know."

"I do?"

He nodded. "Yes, you do."

So Eloise began speaking, words spilling out of her like the water tumbling over Mortimer Falls.

UNDERESTIMATED

Eloise let loose her pent-up thoughts and worries, filling in the bits of her story that she felt he might need to know. From her encounter with Melveeta the Elusive and how she gave the Star of Whatever "unto" her before she died to her calamitous Crown Plonking Ceremony. From her use of the Star of Whatever and the resulting lingering effects on her eye, ear, hand, wrist, and shoulder, to the disaster that was her parlay with Queen Aglandau. From the annexation of Flachberg Canton to her attempts at a peaceful resolution, it all came out. Every now and then, Gordon interrupted briefly to clarify a detail, but mainly, he listened for ten minutes, then twenty, then a full half hour.

Finally, Eloise said, "Which brings me to this bench in your hut." She slumped back against the rough-hewn wall. "So, tell me. What should I do?"

Gordon laughed—a full body, belly-shaking guffaw that filled the hut with a nauseating new wave of his breath. "Oh, Queen Eloise," he gasped. "Oh, my goodness." A fresh cackle bubbled up and consumed him for a full minute. Eventually, coughing took over, and he rasped out, "Apologies. Truly, I wasn't expecting that." The big man wiped tears from his eyes with the heels of his hands. "Whoo. Sorry."

"That was funny, then?"

"I just wasn't expecting it from you. Surely you have sufficient experience with seers to know that's completely the wrong question to ask."

"Uh, not really. I didn't have much access to Seer Maybelle's services when I was a princess, and as I said before, her use now that I'm queen is not as one in touch with the Unseen." Eloise straightened up. "Let me frame it differently, then. I feel like I have a very narrow set of options. I can take the Star of Whatever, go back to my realm, hide it away and never use it. I can take it home and try to figure out how to use it to the benefit of my realm at some unknown expense to my physical well-being, either with or without using it against one or more of the other realms. I can share its capabilities with the other realms. Or I can somehow lose control of the Star completely, either by having it taken from me by force or by agreeing to surrender partial or total control of it. That last option probably puts me and my queendom at greatest risk."

"That's all your options?"

"Have I missed something?"

"I think you have."

Eloise sat quietly, looking at Gordon, and considered what he'd just said. He waited like he had all the time in the world—which might well have been the case.

She shook her head. "I've got nothing else." Eloise enumerated on her fingers. "I have it and use it. I have it and don't use it. I share it. I don't have it."

"There's at least one more option."

"Tell me."

He didn't.

She looked at him.

He looked back.

She waited.

He waited longer.

Then it hit.

"Oh," said Eloise. "I have it and use it. I have it and don't use it. I share it. I don't have it." She paused. "Or no one has it."

Gordon nodded. "That's the one I had in mind."

"I'm not sure I'm happy with that choice."

"It wouldn't be an easy one to make."

"I'm not sure how the Star of Whatever could be made to disappear, never to be found again."

"I'm not sure it would have to be hidden."

"No?"

"No. There's a different option."

Eloise went back to looking at him, her mind searching, looking for a possibility that fit what he said. She shook her head. "I'm stumped."

"What has happened in the two-plus centuries since Melveeta cast her spell?"

"You're referring to the weakening of magic."

"I am. Queen Eloise, I have lived a long time. This body, this mind, date back to Back When, to the time of strong magic," said Gordon. "The things I've seen." Melancholy settled across his face. "When I was younger, I witnessed those with strong magic ruling the realms. But more than that, magic imbued the world. Not everyone had access to it, and there were injustices that came from it, but magic was woven into the day-to-day, just as air and water are. The interaction with magic was integral to who people were. I was one of those fortunate to have a strong affinity with it."

"I've often wondered what it was like back then," said Eloise.

"It was, if I may say so, nothing short of magical. But also, it was completely normal. It was simply how things were."

"Just like you said—like the air and water."

"Exactly. And then, slowly, slowly, slowly, I was witness to magic leaching from the world. I felt what was once powerful and core to my being become as wispy as smoke. Then later, it was even less substantial than that." He shifted his great weight to lean on his right leg. "I knew something was going on. I could feel the magic fading from everything around me, from my body. Those with shorter lives came and went, not seeing the change from day to day, year to year, lifetime to lifetime to lifetime."

"But you did."

"Yes."

"Did you find that things got worse in the world? I imagine they did, but it's hard to tell from the historical scrolls what the lived experience was."

"I don't think better or worse is the right framing. Things were simply different. People are people. They adapted."

"I guess so." Eloise hesitated, not wanting to offend. "I'm sorry, but I'm not sure where this discussion is heading."

"My point is that it wasn't immediately clear what caused the decrease in magic."

"It was Melveeta's spell, of course."

"There was no 'of course' about it. How was anyone to know that it was her spell? No one knew what happened to Melveeta the Elusive. She was a secretive figure at the best of times, and then she was just gone. The queen's tithes were collected by someone else, and there was a lot of distraction from the ongoing war between Gwendolyn and Brüüütus. When the Purple Haze first appeared, there was no way to know what had caused it. The mechanism of its creation and sustainment was opaque on this side of the fog. And it was menacing and clearly deadly. No one wanted to go near it."

"So, what happened?"

"At first, nothing. But, eventually, I figured out the puzzle, more or less."

"How?"

"Observation, mainly. I saw two different ships sail into it. I was there when the birds were trying to see if they could fly into it, and learned that it was a one-way trip. I watched countless foggings to see what I might detect. In the end, I figured it out more by process of elimination than active discovery. It was sort of like looking at an object's shadow across a month of days, and deducing what it is that's blocking the sun. Eventually, it became clear to me that there were only one or two approaches that could have created such a huge phenomenon, and I settled on the high likelihood that it was a magical object combined with a massive harnessing of talent and will. I conferred with colleagues, and even brought my theorizing to the mages in the Mages' Guild."

Eloise wrinkled her nose. "Aren't they basically useless?"

"Less so then. There were still some older ones who were only one generation away from Back When. On the whole, they tended to think that I was probably right, but as decades had passed, no one was really all that interested in the origins of the deadly fog anymore."

"It had become a fact of life, like you said."

"Yes. The really frustrating thing was, once I thought I understood the process by which it came into being, there wasn't anything I could do about it. *No one* could do anything about it, even if they'd had the inclination to, which they didn't."

"Because the Purple Haze kept everyone out. There was no way to go in and affect what was going on inside there."

Gordon nodded. "All I could do was stand back and watch all the magic creep out of this world."

"That must have been terrible."

"It was. Agonizing. Or it was for me, anyway, given the blessing and curse of time." He took a deep breath and blew it out. Eloise did her best not to flinch or gag at the smell. "But, it turns out everyone was wrong. Everyone. There was a loophole. The one you found."

"I wouldn't call getting thrown to my death in the Purple Haze and somehow not dying finding a loophole. I didn't find anything. It was far from deliberate."

"Perhaps. But you did find the crack in the spell that no one else had. More to the point, you saw it for what it was. And even more to the point, once you discovered it, you did something about it. Not everyone would have done that."

Eloise shrugged. "I guess."

"Don't sell short what you did."

"I just felt a pull and followed an instinct."

"Queen Eloise, please. Breaking the spell that caused the Purple Haze is the most significant event in two centuries."

"Don't balance kreplach on my nose."

"I'm not flattering, nor am I trying to mislead. *Everything* will change from here—the relationships between the realms, the scope of trade, the number and types of resources available—everything. I understand that the Half Kingdom's justice system has already changed. Because of what you did, we are in very, very interesting times."

"I guess. I hadn't thought about it that way."

"If you take a moment to do so, you'll find I'm right. But, while that's important, we're heading away from my point, not toward it."

"What point is that?"

"Let me ask a question." Gordon leaned his bulk toward her and whispered, "Where did all that magic go?"

"What do you mean?"

"What I said. Where did the magic that existed Back When go?"

Eloise scoffed. "How am I supposed to know? Look, I really need to be getting back—"

Gordon's eyes unfocused for a moment. "Your companions are handling it. The small one, especially. He has a way, doesn't he?" His attention refocused. "This is important, Queen Eloise. Think about it. Where did the magic go?"

"Well..." Eloise pursed her lips, and moved them side to side. This was a question she'd asked when she was a child, almost from the time she'd learned there *was* a Back When. Along with wondering what it was like in the time of strong magic, she'd asked people where it went, but no one had any kind of answer. Once she was older, it became a question that didn't have much usefulness, like why are cooked lima beans slimy or why does the root of the jointed charlock weed smell of turnip? "I'm not sure."

"Let's take a step back, then. Why did Melveeta the Elusive cast her spell?"

"Because Gwendolyn the Irritable told her to."

"But to what purpose?"

"Gwendolyn was attacking Brüüütus's realm. She thought it would help her win."

"How?"

"By suppressing the Northo magical defenses."

"Did it work? Was it successful?"

"I mean, to the extent that you can call a murderous fog like that a success, sure, I guess."

"There." Gordon pointed at her. "That's the problem. Right there."

"What?"

"Your use of the world 'murderous.'"

"It is murderous. Or it was, anyway."

"No. You're wrong. People disappearing into it and never coming back was a side effect."

"A side effect? There was a whole judicial system set up around it."

"Still, a side effect." The huge man's eyes got an intensity to them. "What was the Purple Haze meant to do?"

"Suppress magic."

"Did the magic just vanish?"

Eloise shook her head. "I don't think so, no. Things tend not to just vanish."

"I agree. So what happened to it?"

"It might have been consumed."

"What do you mean?"

"The way a fire consumes a log. Something happens to the log and it sort of..." She waggled her fingers. "It disappears into heat and light and ash."

"Is that what you think happened?"

"Again, I don't know. It's possible."

"I agree. It's possible. But what else is possible?"

"I don't—"

"Think!"

Who was he to speak to her like that? He wasn't her parent. He wasn't her tutor. He was just some random, massive, semi-mythical prognosticator with a dreadful stench and weird ears. She was tempted to leave.

Or you can sit here and work with him, she said to herself. *Maybe you'll learn something useful.*

"Fine. I'll think."

Eloise closed her eyes and tried to clear her mind. The first thing that popped up was something that her mother had said in her deathbed letter to her. "Don't meddle with magic," she'd written. "The weakening of magic is one of the blessings of our age." That had struck Eloise. Her mother's attitude must be, in part, why neither she nor Johanna had been given even rudimentary training in magic. Both of their parents had been taught rudimentary spelling, and had participated in spelling bees. But no spells for their daughters.

In retrospect, this seemed like an oversight. Having some grounding in magic would have been useful.

Eloise then turned her thoughts to the problem of the Purple Haze. She thought about the Star of Whatever and Melveeta at the spell's core. Then she pictured the lavender fog itself, and recalled what it had felt like to be in it. There was that horrible, annoying buzzing, the fine powder everywhere, and all the bones. She tried to imagine magic coming in contact with the edge of the Purple Haze, and combusting like a log on a fire. She pictured it like players on a hockey sacking field. The left flutter carrying the hockey sack represented magic, and she was hurtling down field right at the opposing team's defensive girder, who was the Purple Haze. They slam into each other and both burst into flame.

A little gruesome, but maybe this was a useful way to look at it.

So that was one possibility. What were others?

In her mind, she changed the quality of the fog from something wafty to something hard, then pictured magic coming in contact with it and bouncing off. The left flutter slams into the defensive girder, and they go *boing! Oof!*

What if the fog was sticky?

In her mind, the left flutter slams into the defensive girder, and they splat together, like two bagel halves slathered in rice syrup.

Huh.

What if the fog was absorbent?

The left flutter slams into the defensive girder, and she sort of melts into him, like a sponge in a bathtub.

Eloise's eyes snapped open. "Sponge."

Gordon nodded. "Go ahead."

"Another possibility is that the Purple Haze absorbed the magic."

"Keep going. Where's the magic?"

"In the Purple Haze."

"Maybe. Where else could it be?"

Eloise gasped and put her hand on the box at her hip. She swallowed once, twice, and said, "You know, ever since Melveeta gave the Star of Whatever unto me, I've considered it the most dangerous thing in all the realms, because of what she used it to do."

"And?"

"And now I'm thinking I underestimated it. Deeply, profoundly, wildly underestimated it."

Gordon the Noisome shifted his bulk again, leaning back against the hut wall. "I think, Queen Eloise, that you might be right about that."

❄ 74 ❄

ALWAYS A PRICE

"So where does that leave me?" asked Eloise.

"It leaves us circling back to the earlier question in our conversation."

"Sorry, which part of the conversation are you referring to?"

"Where we started, more or less," said Gordon. "Your options for what to do with the Star of Whatever."

"I can't see that's changed." She counted on her fingers again. "I have it and use it. I have it and don't use it. I share it. I don't have it. Or no one has it. We haven't uncovered a new possibility."

"I think we might have." Gordon once again listed to one side, letting his heft settle on his other side. "We were talking about what that last option might mean. You were saying you didn't know how you could make the Star of Whatever disappear, never to be found again."

"That's right," said Eloise. "And you said you weren't sure it would have to be hidden."

"I still think that. The other option is one that's the polar opposite of the last one you were considering."

399

"What? The opposite of 'no one has it'—wouldn't that be that everyone has it?"

"That's exactly what I'm saying."

"That's irrational." Eloise stood, her face reddening. "What are we supposed to do? Hand around the most dangerous object in all the realms from person to person? 'Here, it's Tuesday. Your turn with the Star of Whatever, humble peasant.' How's that supposed to work?"

"That's not what I meant. And I think you know that." Gordon looked like he wanted to stand as well, but there wasn't room. "I ask you again, Queen Eloise. Where did all the magic go?"

"You're saying it's in the Star of Whatever."

"Does that still make sense to you?"

Eloise thought about it again. "Yes. Yes, it does."

"Then what would it mean that everyone has magic?"

"You're saying go back to what it was like Back When." Eloise instinctively turned her body so the box at her hip was away from him. "You're saying... You're saying that the magic should be..." She could hardly get the words out. "It should be let back out into the world."

Gordon nodded. "It would be a clear and obvious way to deal with your problem."

"The magic is released from the Star, which means no one can use it against anyone else." Eloise sat back down. "But what..." Her mind raced. "But what would that do to the realms?"

The huge man shrugged, a motion that seemed to fill the room. "There's no way to answer that."

"Would it destroy everything?"

"It was in the world before and didn't destroy everything. I suspect that just as everyone learned to live without magic, they would learn once again to live with it."

"But it disappeared slowly," said Eloise. "The change, the acclimation happened over decades. If all floods back into the world, who knows what would happen? People might use it accidentally. They could hurt themselves. It could be a true disaster."

"Or," countered Gordon, "they could learn to use it for the betterment of their lives. They might find talents augmented. Weak magic is still with us. There's still magic around. It would just be..." He waved his hands in the air. "More around."

"I have to think about this. This is big. Very big."

"Take your time." His eyes went unfocused again. "Your chipmunk friend has them quite bamboozled at the moment. I don't think they're going anywhere anytime soon."

Eloise's mind raced. Gordon's suggestion did seem to solve a problem or two. If each of the monarchs had equal access to whatever magic was in the world, then she would no longer be an obvious target. That would take some of the pressure off. For that matter, she could imagine Queen Aggie spending the rest of her seemingly numbered days trying to find out about it and harness it. That would also take pressure off. She'd have to convince them that it was happening, because, Çalaht knew, they wouldn't take her word for it. But that was a detail.

Plus, there was something in the justice of releasing the pent-up magic, the equality of it, that appealed to her. It felt wrong to her that magic might be hoarded the way it was in the Star. Surely it was meant to be shared by all.

It would certainly breathe new life into the Mages' Guild, those old fuddy-duddies.

Eloise looked at me. "You're telling me it can be done safely?"

Gordon chuckled again. "I said no such thing."

"But... But it was your idea."

"I planted a seed. You're the one who has the connection to the object. It'll be up to you to work out how to do it safely."

She didn't like the sound of that.

"And you'll need to be mindful of the price."

"The price?"

"With magic, there is always a price."

"You're demanding a price of me? That's outrageous. Wouldn't I be doing it for the common good? Why would you charge me for that?"

"Me?" Gordon's huge body suddenly shook into a mild convulsion. Eloise realized he was laughing uproariously. It unnerved her. "I don't demand a price," he rumbled. "Do you know nothing of magic? It is the magic itself that demands to be paid. Someone always pays. It is just that with the magic being so weak for so long, the price was so negligible, it could be ignored." He stretched his back. His vertebrae popped from disuse. "I think you know of what I speak."

She realized that she did. There was Melveeta the Elusive and the terrible price she paid in centuries of pain. Then there was Turpy. She remembered his face as they fell in the depths of the Whacking Great Hole, and how the Star of Whatever sucked the very life and soul from him when he tried to control it. It went without saying that Eloise had paid a price every time she'd used it, whether it was a dislocated shoulder or the numbness that now afflicted her hand. "Yes, I think I do know what you're talking about."

"There is no escaping the cost of magic, so you must be ready to pay it."

"What will it be in this case?"

Gordon frowned. "How could I possibly know that? I am not you. I do not have the Star of Whatever. You'll have to either work it out beforehand or simply ante up after the fact."

"I'd rather know up front, thanks."

"That might be possible."

"Really? How?"

"You said before that you have a connection with the object, yes?"

"Yes."

"Then connect with it." He pointed to an adjoining room. "I haven't been in the bedroom. Feel free to use it, if it would help."

75

BASICALLY GOOD, BASICALLY BAD

She headed for the bedroom and closed the door behind her. The sparsely furnished room had a bed with a headboard made of walnut, a maplewood vanity, and a rocking chair of walnut. The pieces were clean, but looked like they'd been assembled from the unloved items stored in someone's barn. A single small window had the shade drawn. With the door closed, Gordon's odor was somewhat mitigated, if still present.

Eloise hiked her skirts and untied the sash at her hip. She settled into the rocking chair, put the box with the Star of Whatever onto her lap, and with a small nudge of will, clicked it open. She cradled the emerald-colored stone in her palms and nestled the orb onto her lap. Closing her eyes, Eloise reached out to the spark of something in the Star of Whatever with a simple "?".

No answer.

That wasn't so unusual. The first attempt often went without response.

She tried again with a little more mental force: "??"

This time, she got "^-^" back.

That was new. What was that even supposed to mean?

She sent him another "?" and waited.

"..."

That was odd. Had he done that before? She couldn't remember it if he had.

Sparky must be in a weird mood. Perhaps he had an inkling of the discussion she had in mind. She had no idea how he might react.

A moment later, she perceived a "." of assent.

She found Sparky, like she always did, in his naked mole-rat form. He waved her forward with a chewed tuber. "Hey, Loulou. Nice to see you. Come in, come in. Pull up a rock."

"Good to see you, too." Eloise settled down across from him. "How are you?"

"Splendiferous."

Another odd note. "That's great."

He produced a deck of cards. "Whist?"

Eloise felt rushed. All the other monarchs were presumably waiting for her. But then, time worked differently when she was with Sparky. "Whist sounds great."

"Play to fifteen points?"

"Sure. Go ahead and deal first."

"Got it." The naked mole-rat shuffled, let Eloise cut, then dealt thirteen cards each. He put the remaining deck between them, and flipped the top card face up—a seven of cups. "Cups are winners."

"Yep." Eloise looked from her cards to Sparky and back, trying to figure out what card to play first, and if something was going on with her friend. She played the ace of coins. "Are you sure you're OK?"

He looked into her eyes, expression neutral. "What do you think?"

Eloise thought about it for a moment. "I think you have full access to my thoughts and memories. I think you know why I'm here, and what I want to talk about."

He nodded.

"Is that a problem?"

Sparky gave a mole-rat shrug and played his two of coins, letting her take the trick. "Not at all. But I think that, with respect, the question indicates a certain cluelessness about the conversation topic."

"Cluelessness?" Eloise leaned back. "Wow. OK." She gathered the two and the ace, took the winner card from the top of the pile, and let him take the next one down. She then played her queen of swords. "Perhaps you could do me the kindness of clueing me in?"

Sparky looked up from his hand. "Ask me a question and I'll answer."

"Alright." Eloise folded her cards together. "Is my understanding correct, that the Star of Whatever—you, in other words—has absorbed all the magic that was once out in the world?"

"Not all. But most of it, yes."

Eloise waited for him to elaborate.

He didn't.

"'Most of it, yes.' That's it? That's all you're going to say?"

"It was a simple question. There's a simple answer. No point in wasting words." He twirled his forepaw in a "keep going" motion.

"The idea I'm tossing around is to release all the stored magic back into the world."

"I gathered that, yes."

"Is it possible?"

"Yes."

He hadn't hesitated. It was another blunt, simple answer. That was interesting.

Eloise leaned forward and lowered her voice. "Is letting go of all that magic a good idea?"

The naked mole-rat didn't answer. Instead, he played the king of swords, taking the trick and the top card. When he played his queen of cups, Eloise laid down her four of that suit, letting him take that trick as well.

They traded tricks until the first part of the game was done and there were no cards left in the pile. Sparky was ahead seven tricks to six. Even though she was losing, playing the game helped Eloise relax.

As they started the second phase of the game, the mole-rat played his king of coins and said, "That's not something I can answer."

It took Eloise a beat to realize he'd gone back to the question she'd asked ten minutes before—whether or not it was a good idea to release the magic. She put down her jack of coins. "You can't? Why not?"

"Hammers don't have relevant opinions on the world in which they are swung."

"You're not just a hammer, Sparky, and it annoys me when you say that kind of thing."

"Fine, Loulou. Semi-mythical magical objects don't have relevant opinions on the world in which they exist."

Eloise scowled. "Stop that. You're you. A some*one*, not a some*thing*. That means a lot to me. You know that."

"Be that as it may, my point stands. This decision is for you to make."

"I know that. Believe me, I understand." Eloise looked down at her cards, spread them, considered her next move, then folded them again. "You really can't give me advice?"

He played his queen of swords. "Nope."

His answer made Eloise wonder why she'd bothered to visit him this time, with everything that was going on out there. She flipped down her eight of swords.

Sparky took the trick with a nine of swords, then reached over and patted her knee. "Would it help if I talk it through with you?"

"I guess. It's better than zero."

"So run me through it." He placed his ace of coins between them.

She countered with her five of coins. "Right. OK." Eloise put her hand on the ground face down and stood. "You already know everything. What can I add?"

"Talk to me like I was your new first advisor and you need to get the salient points across in a rush."

So she did. She talked about the world without strong magic, the implications of what having just used magic on the olive trees seemed to be, what her father had said, what Gordon had said, her worries about how putting all that magic back into the world would change things, and the uncertainties that introduced, and on and on.

She found that talking to him helped her order her thoughts. When she'd said everything she had to say, she sat back down and looked right in his eyes. "What do you think?"

"Still can't say. But here's what I heard you say." He picked his tuber back up and gestured with it. "You're trying to figure out what's more dangerous—having what you're calling strong magic be limited to just you or just whoever has control of..." He waved the tuber around, indicating their surroundings, then pointed it at himself. "Control of me, or if it is more dangerous to give everyone access to magic, the way it used to be."

"That's not how I said it, but I guess that's more or less it."

"So what's the answer? Which is more dangerous? Exclusivity or broad availability?"

"How can I possibly answer that question?"

"Exactly." He leaned back against the wall, put his cards in a stack in front of him, and bit off a chaw of his tuber. His left cheek puffed out with the wad of fibers. "You can't."

"So how do I make that decision?"

"You ask yourself one simple question."

"What question?"

"Who do you trust?"

"Who do I trust?" She shook her head. "What does trust have to do with anything?"

"Do you trust yourself?"

"Mostly, yes."

"Do you trust your sister?"

"Again, mostly, yes."

"What about the other monarchs?"

"I trust the khan. I pretty much trust Onomatopoeia. I'd trust Aggie as far as I could fling her." She paused. "Actually, less. My throwing is pretty good."

"But you can't just think about the other monarchs as they are now. You have to think about those who will come after them. And those who represent their interests. Or those who might use magic on their behalf. Do you trust them?"

"Again, that's something I can't possibly know, since I don't know who they are or who they will be, beyond the obvious existing offspring."

Sparky nodded. "Exactly." He fixed her with a direct look. "How about this one: do you think people are basically good or bad?"

That question surprised her. "I don't know."

"Think about it."

She thought about all the different people she'd interacted with, even just since she'd become crown plonked, or in the year or so before then. There was such a huge range of people, of species, and of behaviors. How could she compare, say, Läääcy de Aardvark and First Advisor Thëjëts to First Advisor Ligurian and Queen Aglandau? Or the soldiers she'd met who put their lives on the line for her, to the three-eyed snake who'd most certainly been a malign force. Or people like her father and her sister to her Uncle Doncaster and his jester Turpy.

"It seems to me that some people are good and some are bad. Or, more accurately, some people behave with goodness in their hearts and others behave with bad intentions. It's better to talk about how they act than how they are, since how can you ever know the full measure of someone across their lives? Only Çalaht can do that."

"But if you were to place them all on one side of a balance scale or the other, which side would weigh more?"

Eloise felt surety fill her. "On the whole? I think people, no matter their species, are good. You see so much more good in the world, so much more good in most individuals, than bad. Maybe the bad things get more attention, or have an outsized presence. Maybe most people are just trying to get from one end of the day to the other, without much thought of good or bad. But if you consider everyone, in aggregate, the good side of the scale would be the heavier one. And I think by a lot."

He waggled the tuber. "Can you see where I'm going with this?"

"What? With the tuber?"

"Very funny."

She took a moment to arrange the words. "Basically, you're saying that if I trust that people are good, then letting the magic back into the world would mean that more good people will have access to it than bad people. That if I trust people in general, then I should trust that they'll engage with magic in a good way. That if I can't rely on my fellow monarchs to be good, then I'm better off trusting people as a whole to be good."

"Something like that, yes."

"But what about the bad people? What about the damage they might do?"

"What's it like now? Aren't there what you'd call bad people already? Or, to go with the term you used just a minute ago, aren't there already bad behaviors?"

"Yes. Of course."

"So what's the difference?"

"The difference is in the extent of the tools they have available to them. There's a reason one keeps machetes away from toddlers."

"So that's your worry? That you're going to be giving a whole bunch of machetes to a whole bunch of children?"

"Metaphorically speaking, yes," said Eloise. "Machetes, axes, ice picks, sharp sticks, swords, scythes, truncheons, clubs—the works—to people across all the realms who haven't had them for a couple hundred years and have no idea the damage they can do."

"You know what?"

"What?"

"If you do this, it is a certainty that there will be people who will get hurt. At some level, you're right. An unfamiliar surge of magic will be disruptive. There's nothing you could do about that. Even a page of hemp parchment can hurt you if you do the wrong thing with it. But let me ask you this. Did you ever use your weak magic for throwing in a positive way?"

"It helped me get out of the Whacking Great Hole when I was at the bottom of it. And I freed an indentured chameleon with it by winning a carnival game."

"And did you ever hurt anyone with it?"

"Not deliberately." She paused. "Actually, that's not true. I tried to hit my parents and sister with grapes when I was a girl." Another memory came up, and Eloise pursed her lips. "And I did bean Turpy with an apple at Castle Blotch when he had us hostage. That was deliberate, and done in anger."

"On the whole, have you used it more for good or ill?"

"Good, I guess. Neutral to good."

"So, there you have it," said Sparky.

"Have what?"

"You tell me."

"Good and bad, with the balance toward the neutral side of good. But not everyone will be like me."

"Which is why I asked what you thought the overall nature of people is."

"If I believe people are basically good, then I can trust them to use magic in basically good ways. And if I think people are basically bad, then I can't." She shook her head. "And what about the outliers? What about the Melveeta the Elusives? Or the Gwendolyn the Irritables who might direct them? For that matter, what of all the mages who acted with magic to promote the interests of their monarch or realm?"

"What of them? Good or bad?"

"Both."

"Even Gwendolyn? Even Melveeta? Melveeta perpetrated a spell that killed half a realm."

"I'd never defend her," said Eloise. "But she was acting in what she thought was service to her sister, the queen." She sat back down and picked up her cards, but didn't look at them.

"It's a dilemma you face, Loulou. And you know what?"

"What?"

"There's no single, right answer. You can, as you have, argue it either way. So what does it come down to? What's the core of it?"

"Whether releasing the magic solves my problems or not, and whether or not doing so will have a net positive or net negative effect."

"That sounds about right."

She fretted on this for what felt like a very long time, then finally said, "Yes. I think... I think letting it back into the world is the better answer." Having voiced her decision, a sense of relief came over her.

"There you go, Loulou."

"What about the practicalities of doing it? How do I release the magic?"

"Just like the other times you've engaged in it. You focus your will and apply it toward an outcome."

"You'll be able to guide me, though, right? Just like you have before?"

"Of course." Sparky smiled.

"Good. Thanks." She looked at her cards. "I should probably be getting back."

He picked up his cards and stared at her. There was something in his expression that Eloise couldn't quite read. Maybe he was just about to play a winning trick.

"We can finish this hand, I think," said Sparky. "I'm sure you've got time." He laid down the deuce of swords and smiled. "Your turn."

76

SPOKEN FORCE

Eloise rushed back to the hexagonal room, and found the gathered monarchs sitting at their tables looking confused, and not a little bored. Jerome stood on Eloise's table, babbling, "... as clearly described in the Scrolls of Çalaht, in the 53 Malformed Malapropisms, where it says, 'And lo, for the kidney bean sacrament shall be—'" He stopped when he saw her standing in the doorway. The chipmunk's shoulders slumped in relief, and he turned toward the khan. "Your Alacrity, I yield the floor to my queen."

Eloise stepped into the room and walked along the back wall, brushing past Johanna. She moved to stand in front of her table and faced the khan. "Your Alacrity, I request permission to address the gathering."

"I object," said Aglandau, her voice dripping with irritation. "Her..." She flicked her hand toward Jerome. "Her whatever-he-is has wasted too much of this gathering's time—"

"It was a stalling tactic," said Eloise. Was it the first time she'd interrupted Aggie at the meeting? Maybe. It felt good. "It was a blatant stalling tactic to gain me a bit of time. But now I'm here, and I'll have my say." She gave a small bow to the khan. "With the chair's permission."

"Queen Aglandau," said the horse. "Queen Eloise has yet to address this gathering in the same way that you have, when we all listened to you with politeness and attention. She deserves equal respect and opportunity."

"Fine." Aglandau rolled her eyes. She flicked a go-ahead-and-talk gesture toward Eloise, and dragged her plate of olives in front of her like she needed something useful to do.

Eloise shook her head. The hand flick was the last straw. "Queen Aglandau, with all due respect, you really are a piece of work."

"Listen, you cumberwold—"

"No, you listen. You don't like me. I get that. You've made it abundantly clear that I'm far from your favorite person in the world. And it's hard for me to tell if the sniping, the insults, the dismissiveness, and your ever-present sense of being aggrieved are an act, or if that's how you really feel. I've reached the point where I don't actually care. But my sister and I just saved your precious olive trees. We saved your realm. We saved *you*. And you can't muster the decency to even say thank you."

Aggie glared, but said nothing.

Eloise let her tone veer toward sarcasm. "So, *you're welcome*, Queen Aglandau. Long may you flourish in the sacred olive groves of your realm."

The Eastie queen kept quiet, but dropped her gaze.

"And stop calling me names. It's unbecoming." Then Eloise turned her back to the Eastie table. "Now, everyone, I have a proposal. You've seen what magic can do when used for good. Rather than keep sole control of it for myself or the Western Lands and All That Really Matters, I suggest that it be given to everyone." She quickly ran through her history with the Star of Whatever, then told them what she had in mind.

When Eloise finished, Aglandau took an olive pit from her mouth and said, "That is, without a doubt, the stupidest thing I've ever heard in my entire life—and that includes the parlay you and I had. Your proposal is idiotic beyond words."

They all looked at her. The words were as harsh as any she'd spoken, but her manner was less arch.

"What?" She gave a one-shouldered shrug. "It is lunacy incarnate. Surely you see that."

"Perhaps you can clarify your perspective," said the khan.

"Really? It isn't obvious? Then let me spell it out." Her voice took the tone of one explaining the nature of water to a school of particularly dim fish. "The world has changed in the past two centuries. We have what we have, and we know what we know. Your suggested course of action will do no less than unleash complete chaos into the realms. It is rash and foolhardy. It would be much better to take turns with the object so that it could be used with focus and purpose."

"I couldn't disagree with you more," said Johanna. "I don't want anything to do with it." She jabbed a finger toward Aglandau. "And I certainly wouldn't trust you with it. I reckon that Queen Eloise has the right idea. She has my support."

"Queen Johanna," said Onomatopoeia. "Can you vouch for Queen Eloise's story?"

"Yes, I can. Certainly for the parts where I was there—how it came to be in Eloise's possession, the ending of the spell that caused the Purple Haze, the magical capability of the Star—all those bits. And I trust her for the rest."

"And it doesn't worry you to have the magic let loose back into the realms?"

"Of course it does. Queen Aglandau is right about one thing—this is a massive unknown. But the Star of Whatever, the way it is right now? That thing is dangerous. Dangerous, unpredictable, and represents far too much power concentrated in one place." She held up her right hand. "This went numb when we used the Star's magic this morning. I still can't feel anything with it. That scares the stuffing out of me, and I

416

can only pray that the feeling comes back some day. But I'm not holding my breath." She shook her hand, frowned, and continued. "Let me tell you what it was like inside the Purple Haze. It was awful. Just awful. Not just all the skeletons and all-pervasive dust, which were bad enough. But the feeling of it. There was a deep malevolence. A fierce wrongness. It was truly vile." Johanna shuddered at the memory. "So, yes, I agree with Queen Eloise. The greater risk is to have the Star of Whatever the way it is. I support Eloise's proposal, even with all the unknowns and unknowables."

Onomatopoeia pondered for a moment, then said, "I'm not entirely convinced."

"Nor should you be," said Aglandau.

"But I'm inclined."

Aggie snorted. "Of course you are."

"What's that supposed to mean?"

"It means you're being soft-headed if you're swayed by the mooncalf and her eighth-wit sister."

Onomatopoeia heaved herself up. "I suggest you remember yourself."

Aglandau rose as well. "I remember everything, Ono. Every word, every gesture."

The two queens devolved into argument, their vociferousness and rudeness steadily rising. Eloise got the feeling there was more being hashed out than the actual matter at hand, but couldn't tell what it was. Those two had history. That much was clear.

"If I may?" The soft voice cut through the harsh words.

It was the dream wife.

She'd barely said two words during the entire gathering, having spent her time next to the khan, knitting.

Nergüi tilted his head and looked at her with one eye. "Are you sure?"

"Yes, Your Alacrity."

"As you wish." He addressed the others. "Dream Wife will speak."

She set aside her knitting and came to her feet. She brushed the tangled ropes of her hair over her shoulders, laced her fingers in front of her, and got a faraway look for a moment. "I speak as the dream wife of the Us," she began. "And all that I say shall be true."

The words had the ring of ritual, and the khan and herd rememberer both gave a sing-song response, "So it has always been, and so it shall always be."

Aglandau rolled her eyes again, her snide "how quaint" implied but unspoken.

"I have been in touch with the Purity all my life," the dream wife said. "I've connected with it in the service of the Us since my girlhood ended. I had years of training with the dream wife who came before me, and through her, inherited lore and tradition much older than that surrounding Çalaht. This is what I say to you: the world is out of balance, and has been out of balance for centuries."

"Out of balance for centuries," whispered the khan and herd rememberer. Their expressions were intent, like they might have to recite her speech verbatim.

"When you consider the six elemental aspects of the world, there's air, earth, fire, water, ether, and what, in our tradition, we refer to as the 'spoken force.'"

"Spoken force," repeated the two horses.

"This spoken force, which you call weak magic, was so sacred to the Us that it was, traditionally, discussed openly and often, from before one foaled to at one's death rites. 'Spoken' referred not just to how the force was invoked, but its central place in the society of the Us."

"Society of the Us."

"Or so we are taught. What was is no more. For generations, across two centuries, the spoken force has waned. Now, it is almost nothing.

418

Certainly nothing to speak of. We glance at it peripherally, seeing its echoes through our contact with the Purity." The dream wife looked wistful. "In my training with my predecessor, I was told stories of the strength of the spoken force. My teacher conveyed how the spoken force would pool and gather force in certain people, places, and objects. By the time this knowledge came to me, it was like I was being told a child's fables. Or maybe it was like a bad romance scroll, a story tinged with sadness and loss."

She walked to Eloise's table and reached out her hand. Eloise extended hers in turn, and the dream wife took it and kissed her palm. "My lineage owes you a debt of knowledge."

The khan and the herd rememberer both gasped, then repeated, "Debt of knowledge," but this time at full volume.

Eloise tilted her head. "What do you mean, a debt of knowledge?"

"You have explained how the spoken force left our world. I might not have believed you, had I not witnessed what you did this morning for the olive groves. When you came to our lands before, we knew from the Purity that you were the Light Bearer. I realize now that this has two meanings, for you carry the stone of light, but you've also brought an enlightenment of understanding. For that, I place myself in your debt."

"No," said Eloise, taking her hand back. "That's not necessary."

"I enter into that debt with gratitude." The dream wife placed her palms together and bowed. "I hereby obligate myself and the lineage of my successors to somehow try to meet this debt of knowledge. I'm not sure we can, but we will try."

Eloise tried to wave her off. "I don't want you to be in my debt. I yield that knowledge freely."

The khan broke in. "The debt is an honor for the dream wife to give. And it is an honor for you to take it on. Please, Queen Eloise, I ask you to accept it in the spirit in which it is offered."

Eloise didn't like such an open-ended obligation, but also didn't want to give offense. She mirrored the dream wife's pressed-palm bow and said, "That's very kind of you. I'm grateful."

The dream wife smiled. "The debt can be negotiated later. But for now..." She turned back to the others in the room, "let me be clear about what I am saying. The world was wrongly changed. When the spoken force was removed, it was an aberration, a transgression against all. Without that force, all of our realms are out of balance. All of life is out of balance. To bring balance back, there is only one path forward, and that is the one proposed by Queen Eloise. I implore you to agree." She moved to the center of the hexagonal room. "I've heard you discussing, quibbling, and worrying. And you are right to consider the uncertainty of what you're deciding. But I suggest you treat this not as a matter of knots to be untangled. Cut through to the core of the matter. Releasing that which is bound in the Star of Whatever isn't just the politically safe thing to do to maintain balance between your realms. It is the right thing to do to restore balance to the world's forces."

"Balance to the world's forces," whispered the horses.

One by one, she looked at the queens, and held each one's gaze. Then she walked back to her table. "Those are the words of the dream wife," she said. "All that I have spoken is true. So be it."

"So be it," said the khan and the herd rememberer. "So be it."

The dream wife sat and picked her knitting back up. The only sound in the room was the quiet clack of her needles.

Her Maj Ono finally spoke. "I am compelled by the dream wife's words. And Queen Eloise's. And Queen Johanna's. I worry about it, but I agree that the magic should be released."

Khan Nergüi nodded. "I agree. I say, release the magic. Queen Aglandau? You are the only one who has not expressed a consensus on the matter."

Queen Aggie gave a weary sigh. "It's not like I can stop the addlepate... Apologies. Habit. It's not like I can stop Queen Eloise from doing it. And I acknowledge that it appears the olive trees have been helped. So, go ahead. Do it, I guess."

"Then we're decided," said the khan. "Queen Eloise, what are the next steps?"

"I guess I'll need a private room so that I can—"

"No," said Aglandau. "If you're going to do this, I want to see it for myself. You're right, Queen Eloise. I don't like you and I don't trust you. I will witness this act, and I suggest the rest of you do the same."

Eloise pressed her lips together to keep all her retorts inside. "Fine. I'll do it in front of everyone, although I don't know how much there will be to see. Give me half an hour to prepare."

77

THE LOVE OF HAMMERS

Half an hour later, Eloise settled back on the comfy couch with the Star of Whatever on her lap. A glance around the room confirmed everyone was there.

She'd never used prattleweed twice in one day, and still felt a little befogged from its earlier effects. Even so, she waved Queen Onomatopoeia forward and the Southie queen offered her the small, black seeds once again. Eloise dampened her index finger, poked it into the dish, and came away with five. "Sorry, I've taken too many."

"In most devotional houses, it's considered rude to put them back." Her Maj Ono extended her palm. "I'll take them."

Eloise brushed two off her finger, then, ignoring her trepidation, ate the rest. *Here goes nothing*, she thought.

Except, it wasn't nothing. It was everything. If she really did succeed in releasing the magic back into the world, it would likely be the first line of every history scroll ever written about her.

No pressure.

She closed her eyes, and readied herself to head back down to see Sparky. She was glad he was going to help, aid, assist. He really was a good friend, pal, chum.

Synonyms. Already? That seemed awfully quick.

She sent a "?" toward Sparky.

There was an immediate "!!" in response.

Down she went into the green-lit, underground space, where the naked mole-rat munched a tuber. Except this time, there was a difference. He was dressed up in a mole-rat's version of court finery.

"Looking sharp, Sparky," she said.

"It's a big day." He waved his tuber, and the light in the little room changed from green to white. Then he turned around so she could take in his outfit. He wore a green linen tunic and matching green breeks, tailored to a perfect fit. These were matched again by a tricorn hat that was expertly proportioned to his body. What caught the eye, however, was his cloak—an ornately embroidered masterpiece that would have had Seamstress Linttrap's jaw on the floor. The cloth was forest green that swirled out as he rotated, its gold stitching glinting in the light.

Eloise moved closer so she could see better. A moment later, she giggled.

"What?" But he was grinning, so she suspected he knew why.

"The embroidery on your coat."

"Yes?"

"It is stitched in the shape of tubers. That's delightful."

Sparky gave a Protocol-perfect bow that included a sweeping wave of the tricorn. "At your service, Loulou."

"It's perfect. You scrub up well."

"Glad you think so."

"Shall we get started?"

"Sure. Let's."

Eloise smoothed her skirts to settle on the floor, but Sparky shook his head.

"Hold on," he said.

With a flick of his tuber, the light flashed, returning the space to its usual green. Eloise blinked, eyes adjusting, and saw there were now two chairs facing each other, one with an extra pillow on it. Their emerald green blended perfectly with Sparky's outfit, and the chairs and pillow all had matching tuber-shaped gold embroidery.

"Very cute," she said. "And are you telling me we could have had chairs down here the whole time? We didn't have to sit on the floor?"

"All you had to do was ask. Can you help me up?"

"Of course." Eloise extended a palm and he danced a jig as he moved toward her, then hopped up. She placed him on the pillow. Sparky patted it, settled, and gestured for her to sit.

She did. "Oh. Oh, my." Eloise stood, looked at the chair, and sat again.

"What?"

"This is the most comfortable chair I've ever sat in." She wiggled a little and leaned back, sighing. "This is amazing."

"Glad you like it."

"I do. I wish my throne was this comfortable."

"You're queen. It could be."

"I suppose that's true." She closed her eyes, memorizing the feel of it and relishing the comfort a while longer. "So good." Eloise drew a deep breath and said, "Shall we start?"

"If you're ready, sure. I need you to clearly state what you're trying to do."

"Like I said last time, the idea is to let the stored magic back out to restore the proper balance in the world. It took a lot of discussion, but everyone seems to agree that it's the right thing to do for the greater good. So that's that. I'll mention that I think we need to be careful how we do it, because we don't want things to explode or burn or anything. What we did this morning was a bit harsh on the people who were nearby."

"Got it. And you know what to do?"

"Judging from what we've done in the past, I need to hold a clear intention, and specifically ask you for help, remembering the magic word, 'please.' You may or may not whack me in the vision eye with your tuber. I'm not really sure if that's part of it or not."

"That all sounds good," said Sparky. "We'll leave whether or not the tuber is whacked as a surprise."

"That's OK. I can't tell if it actually does anything or not."

"It does. Or, it has in the past."

"Fair enough," said Eloise. "How will I know if it is actually happening?"

"You'll be able to tell." Sparky gestured around them with his tuber. "The light in here will change. You'll want to pay attention to that."

"OK, good. What will you be doing?"

"I'll just be sitting here, Loulou, watching the light with you."

"Got it."

"That is, until I disappear."

Eloise's heart missed a beat. "What do you mean, disappear? You're not going anywhere."

The naked mole-rat shrugged. "What do you think I am, Loulou? What do you think is going to happen to me when you release all the magic back into the world?"

Eloise rocked backwards in her chair with a gasp.

There it was.

The price.

Gordon the Noisome had said there was always a price.

And here it was.

"No," she whispered. "No way. No Çalaht-benightedly way. I can't do that."

"Yes," said Sparky. His voice was soft, comforting. "Yes you can, Loulou. You've already said that you and the others agreed it was the correct course."

"I..." A lump formed in Eloise's throat. She had to force the words out. "I can't do that to you."

"Sure you can."

She blinked away tears. "I don't *want* to do that to you. I can't have you not be there."

Sparky waggled the skin where his eyebrows should have been. "Obviously, it's your call." He shifted on his pillow, getting more comfortable. "I'm just a naked mole-rat, sitting in front of a girl, asking her to do the thing she's already decided to do. But it's your choice. Completely."

Eloise stared at him. Sparky truly didn't seem to care one way or the other.

"You're more than just a mole-rat to me," she said. "A lot more."

"I'm a hammer, Loulou. Nothing more than a hammer. And if a blacksmith needs his hammer to have a different shape, you know what she might do with it?"

"What?"

"Melt it down. Chuck it in the forge and start over."

426

"What if she wants to keep her hammer? Maybe she can get a second one."

"In this metaphor, there's only going to be one hammer. She has to melt it."

"But she might miss that hammer. A lot." Eloise wiped her eyes with the heel of her hand.

"That's true," said Sparky. "People do get attached to their hammers."

"Some people love their hammers."

"You know what?"

"What?" sniffed Eloise.

"Some hammers love them back."

The two of them looked at each other.

What had Sylvia Cloisterfeld said about sacrifice? That sometimes, that which must be sacrificed is precious beyond words. Such is the Balancing Way.

Well, stuff that. Stuff the Balancing Way, stuff Aglandau, stuff being queen, and stuff the world.

But Eloise knew that she wasn't considering the whole idea. Sylvia had said that sometimes, that which must be sacrificed is precious beyond words, and yet, it must be yielded because one knows it is the right thing to do. Such is the Balancing Way.

The thought echoed in Eloise's mind: "Because one knows it is the right thing to do."

And as much as she hated to admit it, she knew that was the case.

Stupid Balancing Way. Stupid life. Stupid duty. Stupid right thing to do.

Eloise opened her arms. Sparky crawled into her lap, and let himself be embraced, hugging her forearm. She let her emotions flow free, her sobs rocking both of them. The mole-rat allowed himself to be embraced, and he patted her arm gently, saying, "There, now. There, now."

They stayed like that for what might have been an eternity, but Eloise knew she'd remember it as more like an instant.

When she was all cried out, Eloise relaxed, and Sparky released his grip. She looked him in the eyes and said, "So, we're doing this?"

He grinned a lop-sided smile at her. "Still not my choice, Loulou. You were the one who said it was for the greater good. You have to do what you think best."

"If I'm being honest and not selfish, I still think it's the right choice. But, oh, Sparky. Isn't there some other way?"

"Think about it. There's just one way to let out the magic, and that's to let out the magic."

She paused, letting the finality of her decision settle onto her heart. "I'm going to miss you. A lot."

"I'd say the same, but..." He gave a palms-up gesture. "I'll be gone, so, in truth, I won't feel the same because there won't be anything left to feel. But if I *was* still around, I would. Does that count?"

"I guess. So, you'll help me make it happen?"

"I already said I would."

Eloise stroked the back of his head, and Sparky leaned into it. His skin was surprisingly warm, and much smoother than she would have expected. He made a small, chirping noise that Eloise assumed was the naked mole-rat equivalent of a purr.

A few minutes later, he gave her knee a final pat. "You OK?"

"Yeah. I think so."

Eloise sighed, not wanting their time together to end. Not yet. "I'm not ready."

"No time like the present, Loulou. I'd suggest one last game of whist, but we'd just be putting off the inevitable."

"Goodbyes are hard."

"Some goodbyes are hard, sure."

"This goodbye is hard."

"I can imagine."

They sat looking at each other, Sparky with infinite patience, Eloise with infinite sadness. She held on to the moment as long as she could. Then, with a deep breath, she said, "I'm ready."

"Good."

Eloise turned her mind to the vision of the magic stored in the Star of Whatever gently oozing out into the world, wafting across the realms, and seeping into and through every nook, corner, cranny, and crack.

"Is that right?" she asked him.

"That's it," said Sparky. "That's right. Just keep going."

"You OK?"

"Yes. I am." There was a hint of surprise in his voice.

Eloise saw herself there with him, the surrounding green-hued light pulsing, shifting and growing lighter by degrees. At the same time, she saw herself from above, in the hexagonal room, a young, white-haired woman, her eyes closed, a green stone on her lap pulsing at the rate of a heartbeat and bathing the room in its emerald glow. She was surrounded by monarchs, advisors, and observers, all of them locked on to her, intent and curious, their skin and hair tinged jade and mint.

The strange, overlapping feeling of being in two places at once made no logical sense at all, and yet at the same time, complete sense. Most of her was with Sparky, and only a tiny part was in the conscious realm.

But as the magic flowed out, Eloise could feel a change in the balance between the two, moving inexorably away from Sparky.

"You still OK?" she asked every few minutes.

And each time, Sparky replied, "I sure am" or "Yep" or "Doing fine."

Until he didn't.

"Hanging in there?" Eloise asked.

There was a particularly bright series of pulses, but no response.

Her stomach tightened, and she perceived that she was now much more in the hexagonal room than underground with him.

His lack of reply lasted much longer than any of the previous gaps.

"Sparky?"

Nothing.

Eloise sent him a "?".

And got a sluggish "?" back.

Relief. He was still there. She acknowledged him with "??".

He replied with a faint "...".

So Eloise waited.

Then a while later, there was an unprompted "—" from him.

And then silence for a long time.

The Star's pulsing continued, as did Eloise's shift away from Sparky's underground home. More and more, her sense of herself was in the meeting room, her eyes closed, the glowing stone on her lap.

After what seemed like forever, Sparky sent a "?", weak as a wheeze.

"?"

"♥"

"♥!" Eloise replied. "♥♥!!" Wetness tracked down her cheeks.

The stone's pulsing gradually slowed from the beating of a heart to the yawning of a sloth, then the dripping of treacle in mid-winter.

After what seemed like forever, there was the weakest hint of a "♪" from Sparky.

Then nothing.

In that moment, Eloise's sense of the spark of something in the Star of Whatever slipped from almost imperceptibly faint to gone completely.

She opened her eyes in time to see the emerald glow pulse one last time, then wink out for good.

Sparky was gone.

Gone forever.

A sob escaped Eloise's throat as the dull, cold rock crumbled into pieces in her cupped hands. She stared at the fragments, not wanting to make eye contact with any of the others. "It's done," she whispered. "He is no more."

78

ADJOURNED

Oblivious to those around her, Eloise put the broken fragments back into the box that she'd worn on her hip for so long. It felt like interring remains in a coffin. Maybe she'd put the box in the family crypt. There was a slot down there ready for her remains. She could let what once housed Sparky's spirit rest in eternal peace, hanging around with the bones of her ancestors until it was Eloise's time to join them.

She closed the lid and, by reflex, reached for the sash to tie it on, then stopped. No point. There was nothing there to keep close and protect.

It would take a while for her to get used to its absence.

Eloise took a steadying breath. She felt no sense of accomplishment. The realms were changed irrevocably, and it left her spent and empty.

She needed to grieve the loss of her friend. Eloise found a handkerchief in a pocket, dabbed her eyes dry and blew her nose. She took a deep breath to settle herself.

"El? Are you OK?" Johanna's gentle question brought Eloise's awareness back to where she was.

"No. Not really. But I will be."

Johanna switched to their sign language. *That was something.*

Was it? asked Eloise.

Yeah. Look around.

Eloise did. It was so different to their reaction that morning. This time, there was no screaming or weeping. Just stunned silence.

But something was wrong.

No, not wrong. Different.

It was their hair.

Everyone's hair was white. Johanna's and Eloise's, of course, had been white since the Purple Haze had stolen their natural color. But looking at Aglandau, Coratina, and Onomatopoeia—white, white, white. Their father's salt and pepper was now pure chalk. Same with the dream wife lanky knots. But most striking were the khan and the herd remember-berer. Their coats would now give them perfect camouflage if they were sneaking through a snowfield.

How very odd.

As she gawped at them, something else niggled at the corner of her awareness, tugging for recognition.

No one was bleeding, so that wasn't it.

They seemed a little dazed, or perhaps amazed. That wasn't it either.

She glanced again at Johanna, who was flexing and shaking out her right hand like she was testing it. Eloise did the same with her right hand. Nothing odd there. She tried it with her left.

Oh.

Her left hand was no longer numb. She wiggled it, fluttered it, flicked it.

It felt normal.

Which meant...

Eloise quickly covered one eye, then the other, looking through each in turn.

Her vision was the same.

She poked a finger in her left ear, then her right. The ambient sound in the room stayed constant.

No numbness. No blur. No buzz.

By Çalaht's ghastly, gargantuan goiter, her magical maladies had been cured.

No, "cured" was the wrong word. Their source had been removed, so their symptoms had faded as well.

Part of her hoped Eldridge the Apothecary was still alive when she got home so she could tell him about it. But another part felt a wave of grief. Not having the blur and buzz was going to make remembering Sparky that much harder. The return to normal perception was welcome, but it was tinged with sadness.

She suspected there would be a lot of that kind of sadness for a while.

The khan broke the silence. "Is everyone OK?" His tone was tenuous.

"I'm—" Onomatopoeia's voice cracked. She cleared her throat and tried again. "I'm OK. That was... That was profound."

"Queen Aglandau?" asked the horse.

The Eastie gestured "yes" with her fist, but looked like she couldn't speak.

Eloise wondered what it had been like for them. Why "profound?" She'd have to ask Johanna or Her Maj Ono when she could. But right now, the effort seemed too much. All Eloise wanted was a bed and a few hours to nap.

"I suggest that the work of this Grand Council is finished for now," said the khan. "If you agree, then let's take a recess. I invite you to be my guests at a closing dinner starting at sundown. Dress casually, as we've all had quite the day." He clopped a hoof on the table. "With that, we are adjourned." The horse hobbled out of the room, his herd rememberer and the dream wife trailing behind.

Eloise slumped back in her chair and closed her eyes. She listened to the rustling of people leaving the room, testing that her hearing really was restored.

Soon enough, she was alone.

Emotions swirled inside her. She didn't know whether to laugh, cry, swear, pray, or pass out.

Through her eyelids, she saw a body loom in front of her. "Queen Eloise?"

It was Lorch.

"Queen Eloise?"

That was Jerome.

Couldn't they just leave her alone for a few minutes? "Yes?"

"Can we help you to your room so you can recover?" asked Lorch.

"I think I'd like to stay here for a year or two, if you don't mind."

"As much as we'd like to let you do that, there's still the dinner to attend," said Jerome. "At some point you'll need to get ready."

Eloise put on a petulant child's voice. "I don't want to."

There was a longish pause. Eloise could picture the looks that Lorch and Jerome were exchanging, a non-verbal discussion of "What are we going to do with her?" She hoped they'd continue for a long while.

Eventually, Jerome spoke. "Did I mention that I brought a small store of one of my favorite haggleberry teas?" he said. "It's from a rare harvest that took place two years ago. A group of haggleberry bushes on a north-facing slope of Blaggard's Bluff had a rare combination of rain, frost, and sun that led to haggleberries that, when correctly prepared and brewed, taste of smoke, malt, a spring day, and what I can only describe as hope."

"You're offering me a cuppa as an incentive to open my eyes and get out of this chair?"

"Yes."

"Sold." Eloise pried opened her eyes. "Oh. Oh, my. Your hair. Your fur." She lifted her chin at one, then the other. "Lorch, you look like you stepped in from a blizzard. And Jer, you look like an arctic hare, or one of those white tree squirrels."

"I think what you're trying to say is, 'My, that white coat sure makes you look distinguished,'" said Jerome. "And for El Lorcho here, I'm thinking, 'That premature whiteness certainly looks dashing.'"

"Distinguished and dashing. Got it." Eloise struggled to stand up. "I'm sorry, you two. I really am. I didn't know that..." She trailed off, knowing nothing she said would make a difference or make them feel any better. When the Purple Haze had bleached her own hair, it had taken her weeks and weeks to stop being surprised and shocked every time she caught a glimpse of herself in a mirror.

Lorch took her elbow and steadied her. "Queen Eloise, if hair like this is the price of peace between the realms, then it is one I happily pay."

"What he said," echoed Jerome.

"I guess that's a good way to look at it." Eloise cradled the box that held the Star fragments in her elbow. "Now, let's get me to my room so I can rest up for the evening and figure out what I'm going to wear. Or if I'm going at all."

"You're thinking of not going?" asked Lorch.

"Do you think I could beg off? I certainly don't feel like an evening of trading barbed nothings with Aggie or yakking with one of Ono's hangers-on with whom I have nothing in common."

"You sound like someone who needs a bath and a nap," said Jerome.

"Correct on both counts." Eloise leaned on Lorch and moved to leave the hall. "Let's go. I'm curious now what a spring day mixed with hope actually tastes like."

79

NO DIFFERENCE

Eloise emerged from her room right on dusk, bathed, napped, coiffed (or as coiffed as her still-short hair allowed), and dressed in one of Seamstress Linttrap's more glorious designs, a navy-blue long-sleeved, side-laced cambric kirtle that struck Eloise as the right combination of comfort and not-too-formal.

She found Lorch and Jerome waiting for her.

"Looking good, Queen Eloise," said Jerome.

"What he said," said Lorch.

"Thanks, guys. I think there's still time for me to bail, if you think I can get away with it."

Jerome indicated her outfit. "You're up. You're dressed. You may as well make an appearance."

"I suppose it would be churlish to spurn the khan's hospitality."

Lorch nodded. "There's that, yes." He gestured down the hall. "After you, my queen."

Eloise turned and led the way. "To be honest, I can't say I'm expecting all that much from this evening, it being hosted by the Us and all."

"I certainly wouldn't," said Jerome from behind her. "I mean, we've spent time with the Us. Their austere lifestyle is certainly suited to discipline, training, and the spare existence required of warriors. But it doesn't exactly scream, 'Let's throw a party!'"

"No, it doesn't," said Eloise. "Nor does it say, 'Let's impress people with our fine cuisine.'"

"Mark my words, we're in for an evening of nuts, berries, and grass. I'm almost relieved that Lorch and I will almost certainly be relegated to a spot at the back of the room where no one will notice if we aren't eating."

With her expectations appropriately set, Eloise arrived at the entryway to the seminary dining hall.

"Oh," she said.

"Oh, indeed," agreed Jerome.

"That's really something," added Lorch.

The seminary dining room was decked out with a splendor equal to anything Eloise had ever seen at home. Banners and bunting draped the walls in a shade of ochre that matched the splotch that the Us wore on their wisdom eye. The banquet tables were laid out with silver and starched linen finery that was distinctly incongruous to the seminary's overall sense of diminished wealth and repair. Eloise had expected the usual setup—one long, formal banquet table that demanded a hierarchy of seating and facilitated speechifying and toasts. That was exactly what she'd been dreading.

But it wasn't the case. Instead, the table arrangement was more like an intimate conversation club, each seating only four and placed around the room like the goal was conviviality. This might be a good or a bad thing, depending on who the other three at her table were. If her group included Aglandau, it would be a very, very long evening.

Or she'd make a quick exit and make it a very, very short one.

Looking around the dining room, Eloise realized they were one of the first to arrive. Great. She'd be sitting by herself like a bump waiting for everyone else to show up. But before she could walk away to come back later, Sibling Nichtsdabei stepped over and bowed. His black tonsured hair was now the same white as her own, and everyone else's. "May I show you to your seat?"

Eloise forced a smile. "That would be lovely."

He nodded to Lorch and Jerome. "Someone will be here in a moment for you." Then he led Eloise to a table across the room, where there was a place setting with a name card reading, "Her Majesty, Queen Eloise Hydra Gumball III, Sovereign of the Western Lands and All That Really Matters" in a fancy, curlicued, handwritten script that barely fit all the letters in the space available.

The dream wife already sat in the chair to Eloise's right. Eloise saw that she was counting stitches on her knitting needle, a look of fierce concentration on her face like the fate of the universe depended on her getting it right. The woman's ropey tangles of now-white hair practically glowed in the hall's candlelight.

Eloise glanced at the name at the setting to her left. It was one of the Southie advisors, someone she only knew in passing. This non-hierarchical seating struck Eloise as being consistent with the ways of the Us. Egalitarian. Not enamored of rank. Or maybe they just wanted to spread the monarchs around to give more people a chance to rub elbows with royalty—a thought that made her vaguely ill.

"Good evening," Eloise said.

The dream wife jerked like she'd been zapped by a shock eel and dropped her knitting in her lap. "Çalaht's bunions!" she gasped. The old woman saw it was Eloise, took a breath, composed her expression, and bowed from the waist while remaining seated. "Apologies. I was a million strong lengths away. Good evening, Queen Eloise."

"I'm sorry. I didn't mean to startle you."

"It's fine. Sometimes when I knit I go somewhere... else. Apparently, that just happened. Anyway, you are well?"

"Well enough, thank you. May I join you?"

"They are assigned seats, but it's kind of you to ask. Please."

Sibling Nichtsdabei helped Eloise with her chair, then said, "I have to start with an apology; we're somewhat short on serving wenches. My fellow siblings and I will act in that role for you tonight. Can I bring you something to drink while we await the arrival of the others?"

"What would you recommend?" asked Eloise.

"Your choices this evening are a yucca root tea, which is a lowland, desert import, or an aloe vera slurry. That's a healthy mix of aloe vera juice, rolled oats, baby kale, baby chard, baby spinach, a bit of cucumber, some blueberries, a banana, and seasoned with cinnamon and cayenne pepper. I must say, I'm rather partial to it. We grow all the ingredients here in a greenhouse and make it on site."

"If you like the slurry, then I'll give that a go," said Eloise. "I'm not a fan of yucca."

"Very good, ma'am." He turned toward the dream wife. "Ma'am? A beverage?"

"I'll have the yucca root tea, thank you. With rice malt, if you have it. Lots."

"Very good, ma'am." Nichtsdabei headed for the kitchens.

The dream wife picked up her knitting again, and checked that she hadn't dropped any stitches. When she was happy that all was in order, she wrapped the cotton yarn around her index finger and resumed looping the needles. "So, Queen Eloise. If I may ask a personal question, how are you? Truly?"

Eloise picked up a spoon with her left hand, and for the dozenth time since the end of the Star and Sparky, confirmed that any numbness was totally gone. "I'm a jumbled mix of things. I'm sad. Desperately sad.

I'm exhausted. I'm hopeful that the situation with Queen Aglandau has resolved well."

"It does appear that we have an appropriate resolution to the conflict, which is why we're all here. So that's good." The dream wife paused. "Anything else?"

"I'm grateful that…" Eloise gestured to her ear and eye. "I'm grateful that these seem to be better. The blur and buzzing are gone. So, that's something, I guess. I have to admit that I'll miss the touch of weak magic they gave me access to."

The dream wife waved a dismissive hand. "You'll have to look and listen with a different focus going forward. And who knows what it will be like once the world adjusts to having all the spoken force around once again. Perhaps you'll be able to do the exact same thing you could do before, or at least something similar, by drawing on a different source of magic. We have no idea what the world will be like."

"You think?"

"Absolutely. For those of us interested in such things, there's a lot to be curious about now."

"Curious? About what?"

The dream wife looked Eloise directly in the eyes. "Like, how accessible will the spoken force now be? How strong? How will it affect our ability to connect with the Purity? Will the spoken force be an even layer over everything, or will it eddy and pool in particular locations like it used to? And if so, will it map to spots where that was the case before the Purple Haze robbed the world, or will it go somewhere new?"

"Goodness. Now I want to know all that as well. What else?"

"Will those with what you called weak magic have those abilities enhanced? Reduced? Changed? Augmented? Will a former affinity for the spoken force help or hinder with channeling it in this new era? Will more people be able to access the spoken force? Will the ability to use it be generalized the way it once was, or remain oddly specific, the way it was with your weak magic?"

"That's... That's a lot to think about."

"It is," said the dream wife, her smile sly but genuine. "If you're inclined in this direction, the times won't be boring, by any stretch."

"I worry about the unknowns, and the unexpected consequences. Speaking of which, I'm sorry about the..." Eloise indicated the whiteness of the older woman's mass of hair. "I had no idea something like that would happen. Maybe I should have, since..." She indicated her own hair. "But I didn't."

The dream wife lifted one shoulder. "Just one more thing to try to figure out. The 'why' of it completely escapes me, but it is something I'd like to work through."

The two sat sipping their drinks, each lost in thought for a few moments.

Eloise set down her cup. "May I ask something?"

"Certainly."

"What was it like?"

"What was what like?"

"When the magic all came out. I perceived it from the inside, but what was it like from the outside?"

The dream wife's face softened. "It was different. Very different."

"Different how?"

"When you used the spoken force earlier in the day to heal the olive groves, it was like sitting next to a blasting oven. Or maybe more like standing under an avalanche. It was massive, directed, and had an overwhelming, unstoppable sense of purpose. I could barely stand to be that close to it. And if I'd known what it would be like, I might have chosen not to be anywhere near you. You saw how it affected those in the room."

"I feel like I need to apologize again."

"Don't. You were pushed into a corner, and you provided a service to the Eastern Lands queen that she…" The dream wife looked around to see if anyone was listening. "That, to my mind, she didn't deserve, and still doesn't. But you did it, which I admire."

"I didn't do it for her. I did it for the olive trees. I did it for her people. And I did it for a strategic result, which by extension, means I did it for myself and my people."

"You did it with good intention and in good faith. That's enough." The dream wife took another sip of her yucca tea, grimaced, and added another heaped spoonful of rice malt. "The olive tree healing was an intensely profound experience, ten times, maybe one hundred times stronger than anything I'd ever experienced before. That includes when I've connected with the Purity with vision herbs. And I've been doing that for decades now. If your magical act of healing of the olive trees had been the only direct experience of the spoken force I had here, I'd have been changed forever."

"But it wasn't," said Eloise.

"No. It wasn't," agreed the dream wife. "If that first use was akin to a rockslide, the second was more like what I've heard the Gööödeling Sea is like. I can't remember having ever seen it, although my predecessor dream wife said I did when I was a baby. That was before I came to the Us."

"It's spectacular. You should go sometime."

"Those of us who dwell in the Central Ranges are disinclined, but I'll think about it." The dream wife picked up her needles and knitted a few stitches while she thought about what to say next. "I know I advocated for the release of the spoken force from the stone you carried, but if we're being honest here, I had absolutely no idea what would happen when you did."

"None of us did."

"I didn't know if it was even possible, but you're a surprising young woman, so I took you at your word that it was. But I don't mind admitting that I had trepidation about being a witness to it."

"You did?"

"Yes. But there was no question that my khan was going to be there as witness, which meant there was also no question that I'd be by his side. Mentally, I prepared myself for another nigh-intolerable onslaught of the spoken force. In truth, I was prepared to die."

"Really?"

"Really."

"That seems extreme."

"It wasn't."

"I... I didn't know," said Eloise.

"I assumed you didn't, but we're here to tell the tale. That's good enough. Now, you asked what it was like." She closed her eyes, calling back the feeling. "It was waves of power, ebbing and flowing and crashing in on itself. I had my eyes closed, but the waxing and waning light shone through my eyelids. Flow and crash, flow and crash. It was intense but, in the end, bearable. And not lethal. So, bonus." The old woman took another sip from her cup and grimaced. "This is most foul. I should have gone with the aloe vera slurry."

"It's pretty good. Would you like a sip?"

"Thank you, but no."

"May I ask you something else?" said Eloise. She gestured to the air around them. "Does it feel any different to you? Can you sense more magic in the air in any way?"

"Not really. But, to be clear, I haven't tried connecting with the Purity yet, or not with vision herbs, anyway. There hasn't been time. My guess is that it will be like humidity, and we'll just feel it. I suspect we'll have to seek out the differences."

"That makes sense."

"What about you?" asked the dream wife. "Any differences?"

Just the gaping loss of my friend, Eloise thought. *Just the bereft knowledge that things will never, ever be the same for me. Never, ever, ever.*

"No," she said. "No difference at all."

80

LIPIDS

From the corner of her eye, Eloise saw Princess Coratina Ponentine enter the room led by one of the serving siblings, who took her to a table across the room. The princess frowned, shook her head at something the server said, then when the server's back was turned, picked up her name card and strolled toward Eloise and the dream wife. She paused at another table, picked up a second name card, and carried it to where Eloise and the dream wife sat. "Good evening," she said, and put her name at the seat to Eloise's left. The other pilfered card staked out the setting opposite. She then picked up the two displaced names, said, "Back in a moment," and sauntered off to complete her rearranging.

Eloise watched her go. "It would not have occurred to me to usurp the seating chart."

"You probably have no need to."

"True. I don't think I do." Eloise paused. "What need do you think she has?"

"To avoid her mother, maybe?" The dream wife had kept her head down and her focus on her needles, but the corner of her mouth crooked upward.

"That could be a need I share with her."

"Could be. I might also share it. Such a disagreeable woman I've never met before. It makes me grateful, once again, that my life has taken me to live among the Us."

Coratina returned just as Sibling Nichtsdabei came back to the table. He looked at her, looked at the name at the seat, looked over to where she was supposed to sit. He met her eyes, then chose to pretend nothing had changed. "May I help you with your chair, Princess?"

She sat, and he asked for her beverage preference.

"My choices are yucca tea or aloe vera slurry?" said Coratina. "How ghastly."

"We do have olive leaf tea."

"Oh, no, no, no. By Çalaht's divine delusions, I'd rather stab myself in the eye with a spork. Would it be possible for me to have a mint tea?"

"Oh, of course, ma'am," said Nichtsdabei. "What kind?"

"What do you have?"

"Spearmint, peppermint, field mint, apple mint, water mint, banana mint, chocolate mint, lavender mint, slender mint, less-slender mint, not-slender-at-all mint, horse mint, donkey mint, echidna mint, strawberry mint, grapefruit mint, Çalaht's tribulation mint, and licorice mint."

"Do you have ginger mint?"

"I'd have to check."

"I'll have that, if you've got it. Otherwise, a combination of the Çalaht's tribulation, chocolate, and not-slender-at-all mint. Equal thirds."

"Yes, ma'am."

As soon as Nichtsdabei was gone, Coratina turned to Eloise and gushed, "You were amazing today. Really amazing. I don't think I could ever do what you did."

The young woman's enthusiasm caught Eloise by surprise. "That's, uh, those are very kind words. Thank you."

"You deserve them. What you and your amazing sister did was amazing. I mean, I really hate olives. Deeply, deeply hate them. But you made an amazing difference to the lives of a lot of people today. And then, to top it off, you did that whole thing with the—" Coratina gestured pulses with her hands and made a kind of whooshing, exploding sound. "Just amazing."

Eloise was struck by just how complete the contrast was between the version of Coratina who appeared when her mother was in the room and the version when Aggie was absent. She supposed it made sense. Eloise had always held herself back when her mother was around, not wanting to make mistakes or embarrass her in any way. "Again, thank you. But it remains to be seen if it will be a 'good amazing' or an 'uh-oh-that's-worrying amazing.'"

"Fair point, fair point. Still, I've had the most truly amazing day. After all the—" She made a flashing sound, then another whooshing explosion. "After all that, Sibling Superior Nichtsdestotrotz took me to their Bibliotheca de Çalaht."

"How was it?" asked the dream wife, not looking up from her clicking needles.

"Amazing! Truly amazing. Did you know that in their Rarities and Antiquities section, they have what must be the most complete collection of writings dealing with Çalahtist-inspired napkin-folding in all the realms?"

"Is that so?"

"Yes, ma'am. It is."

"And did you see them?" asked Eloise, bracing herself for an impromptu treatise on the religious use of serviettes.

"I was supposed to, but I didn't quite make it."

"No? Why not?"

"There's this thing that happens when I go into libraries. I tend to get waylaid by unexpected things that I accidentally discover. I call it a knack, although my mother calls it a 'propensity for malingering,' or sometimes, 'Stop being such a stampcrab, you dew-beater.'"

"Stampcrab? Why does she think you're clumsy?" said the dream wife. "You don't strike me as such."

"It's the way I find those unexpected things."

"What way is that?" The clicking needles paused. "And what do you mean by unexpected? Unexpected, like the way maple syrup tastes good with sweet potato fries, or unexpected, like finding a drop off a cliff in the fog?"

"'Unexpected' in that it is just things of interest to me, which is a pretty broad category. And surprisingly, the unexpected items always end up being of interest to whoever is with me." Coratina giggled and shrugged. "As to how I find them, I literally stumble into them. I can't make myself do it. I can't pretend to trip. That doesn't work. But if I do slip on a rug or lose my footing or whatever in a library, what I land on or dislodge is always well worth the time to look at."

To Eloise, this sounded like a kind of weak magic. She wasn't sure that weak magical abilities were a topic that Easties spoke of in polite company. It hadn't been in Eloise's household growing up, so caution had her keep the thought to herself. "What did you find?"

"Thank you for asking. It was amazing! I stubbed my toe on a book-case, sort of staggered a little, and broke my fall against a library shelf. This jostled it, but it didn't fall over, thank Çalaht, as that would have been really embarrassing. Three dust-caked scrolls toppled from the top of the shelf unit. They clearly hadn't been looked at in decades.

Probably longer. And you know what? They were works by Lipid the Younger."

"Who's Lipid the Younger?"

Coratina's face lit up like a centenarian's birthday. "I'm so glad you asked. You've heard of Lipid the Elder, of course, right?

"Uh..."

"Come on, *Lipid the Elder*. He was a gifted thinker and wonderful scholar, and he's famous for his Boredom Penance Principle, the somewhat heretical notion that says that if Çalaht deems you unworthy to stand with her in the afterlife, you are not sent to an eternity of torment."

"No?" said Eloise. "I thought eternal torment was pretty much a given."

"Not according to Lipid the Elder. He says that, instead of everlasting anguish, you are sent to an eternity of boredom. He postulates that the soul has a better chance of repentance and improvement if it is given the space for contemplation and reflection, rather than writhing in metaphoric and literal pain."

"I see." Eloise had no idea where this was heading.

"Lipid the Younger was his son. He's a lot less well-known, which is unsurprising. I mean, how can you compete with Lipid the Elder? Most people don't think much of Lipid the Younger's scholarly contributions as there aren't a lot of them and those that do exist are generally thought of as derivative and reflective of a lesser mind. But the scrolls that dropped from the shelf?" Coratina almost bounced out of her chair. "They were—I can almost guarantee you this—the first known, original, and most importantly, *novel*, contributions to Çalahtic thinking to emerge from Lipid the Younger."

"That's... good, I guess?"

"They revealed what the younger Lipid called his Paternus Penance Probability."

"What's that?" asked the dream wife.

"The Paternus Penance Probability shows that Lipid the Younger took a much less sanguine view of what happens to the soul after we pass on. He was of the firm opinion that, if Çalaht decrees you are unworthy to spend eternity standing at her side, then severe punishment is called for."

"So we're back to eternal torment," said Eloise.

"Yes," agreed Coratina. "But Lipid the Younger writes that the eternal torment takes only one form: being sentenced to spending one's eternal existence having to listen to his father rave about the redemptive value of being bored. Unworthy souls go to a replica of his childhood home where they must sit in uncomfortable chairs and listen to his father's endless, hectoring lectures. They're forced to endure his 'banging on and on and on forever and a day'—that's a quote—about his Boredom Penance Principle." Coratina shuddered. "Lipid the Younger's view of the afterlife is just so very dim." Her gaze drifted off as she pictured it. "Such a horrid fate."

Eloise wasn't sure how to respond. She didn't think much of either Lipid the Elder's or Lipid the Younger's perspectives, but there was no doubt that Coratina had been profoundly affected by her discovery. "How very interesting," she managed.

"For the Us, it is much less complicated than that," said the dream wife. "One simply disappears back into the Purity. No more. No less. And no standing with Çalaht. There's no one passing judgment, and no possibility of eternal pain. No judgment. There's just a reabsorption in that which came before and that which shall endure after."

"I didn't know that," said Coratina.

The moment was interrupted by the reappearance of Sibling Nichtsdabei, who led Johanna into the room. He took her to one of the spots at a different table, then furrowed his brow and looked around, confused. Coratina waved them over and patted the seat to her left, across from Eloise. "You're here, Queen Johanna," she bubbled. "Come join us. We're talking about the afterlife."

Eloise saw her sister hesitate, glance at the chair then at Coratina, then look resigned. She let Nichtsdabei help her into her chair and was served yucca tea.

"You're talking about the afterlife?" said Johanna. "Whatever for?"

"Princess Coratina made a discovery in the library," said the dream wife. "She's helping us understand what she found."

"And what was that?"

Eloise held up two fingers. "The short version is that, in the unfortunate case that you don't get to stand with Çalaht after you cark it, your destination is either a) endless boredom, as described by Lipid the Elder, or b) an eternity of torment listening to Lipid the Elder jammer on forever about boredom, as put forth by Lipid the Younger."

"Goodness," said Johanna. "If that's not an argument for living an upstanding life, I don't know what is."

"My thoughts exactly." Coratina touched Johanna's forearm and smiled. "I'm not sure I agree with either of them, but I love the exercise of thinking about it all."

Johanna took a sip of her yucca tea, looked like she wanted to gag, and pushed the cup away. She waved over a serving sibling. "Do you think I can get haggleberry tea?"

"Yes, of course, Queen Johanna."

Eloise raised her hand. "I'd love one as well."

"I still have some of my ginger mint," said Coratina. "But haggleberry sounds amazing. I'll have some as well."

The dream wife raised her index finger in agreement.

"Haggleberry teas all around," he said, and with a nod, headed for the kitchen.

The four of them relaxed into the evening. Around them, the hall hummed with contented chatter and the clink of cutlery on dishes. Eloise saw that Lorch was in polite conversation with Princess

Onomatope. Jerome seemed to be having a deep and meaningful with Seer Throumbolia, and she suspected they might be comparing notes on the role of a seer.

At Eloise's table, the discussion ranged widely, from Coratina's experiences of Eastie court life, to the dream wife's role among the Us, to Eloise and Johanna recounting some of their experiences slogging their way through the Purple Haze. Eloise was surprised by just how comfortable and congenial it was.

The food was as delicious as their conversation was scintillating. It started with an appetizer of salad à la Lower Glenth (scroll-thin slices of radish and cucumber, mixed with chickpeas and spiced with dill) plus finger-food-sized servings of tempeh-wrapped potato scallops with a paprika sauce made from coconut cream. Next came a main of braised broccoli and chili-flavored butterbeans stirred through a risotto. The khan gave a short, unremarkable I-guess-we're-done-here-thanks-for-coming speech, then to top everything off and round out the evening, there was a choice of desserts—chocolate avocado mousse or green apples with salsa, a combination that Eloise had never even considered before. She asked for a serving of both.

Eventually, Coratina scraped the last of her mousse from its dish and set down her spoon. "The food has been amazing."

"Agreed," said Johanna.

"And it has been lovely chatting with you young ladies," said the dream wife. "I don't get to speak with humans all that often. It's been a nice change."

"Agreed," said Johanna again. "It's been fun."

"I'd love to do it again sometime, somehow," said Eloise.

"We could have another Grand Council of the Realms next year," suggested Johanna. "This one has gone well enough. We could do it again."

"I don't think I can wait a whole year to see everyone again," said Coratina. "That's such a long time." She hesitated, looking momentarily shy. "Would it be too forward of me to invite you to the Eastern Lands, subject to my mother's approval? You could see how the olive trees are doing."

"Would your mother really have us?" asked Eloise. "Or more to the point, have me?"

"Good point," said the princess. "That might be a hard sell."

"We could meet at Flachberg," suggested Johanna. "There are olive trees there. I know it's disputed territory, but your parlay was there, so there's precedent."

"Ooh, that's clever," said Coratina. "I'll float it with Mother."

Eloise thought for a moment. "I have another idea." She drew herself to her full height and put on her most regal air. "Whether we meet in Flachberg or not—I hope we do, but either way, I hereby officially invite all of you to my formal coronation, to be held... Oh, I don't know for sure... Let's call it two months."

"How delightful!" Coratina turned to Johanna. "You'll come, won't you? And you, too?" she said to the dream wife.

"It would be an honor," said the dream wife. "Subject, of course, to the khan's permission."

Eloise nodded. "He'll be invited as well, of course. I see no reason not to invite everyone in this room."

Coratina leaned in. "Maybe not my mother. Or invite her, but say, 'You or your representative.' That will give me enough to work with so that I can attend."

"Done," said Eloise. "And when you come to Brague, I'd love to show you our Bibliotheca de Records and Regrets. I'd love to see what you run into there."

Coratina beamed. "It would be my pleasure."

Eloise raised her teacup in a toast. "Until we meet again, then."

"Until we meet again," echoed the others, and they clinked cups.

81

PEBBLE

It was close to midnight when Eloise left the dining hall, her head full of the evening's conversation and her stomach pleasantly sated. "I need a moment's air," she said to Lorch and Jerome, who'd come up to shadow her. "Care to come with?"

"Yes, Queen Eloise," said Lorch.

"Sure," said Jerome.

Eloise knelt and extended an arm for Jerome to climb onto. He settled on her shoulder as they headed for the door.

The evening air was crisp, the smell of conifers sharp, and countless stars lit the night sky. They walked once again down the path toward the hut where she'd found Gordon the Noisome earlier. She had a notion to stop in and thank him.

As they approached the hut, Jerome's whiskers twitched and his nose tested the air. "You smell something?"

Eloise sniffed. "No. Not really."

"Exactly. No stench."

Gordon the Noisome was gone. His hut was dark and empty, the hearth cold, and the air was free of all but the most lingering of noxious odors.

"I guess he was done here," said Eloise.

Lorch peered into the side room. "No trace. It seems you're right."

Eloise wondered if she'd ever see him again. She both hoped she would, as he was fascinating, and hoped she wouldn't, as she suspected he didn't tend to arrive when tidings were good. If that was the case, once was plenty.

They drifted around the seminary grounds enjoying the night. There was an amiable silence between them, which was such a contrast to the last few days. Or months. Ever since she'd gone off after Johanna, her life had been nothing if not fraught.

"Let me ask you two something," Eloise said. "Do either of you feel any different since..." She made a whooshing, exploding noise like Coratina had. "Since all this happened today?"

"Not me, Queen Eloise," said Lorch. "But then, magic isn't really part of my life like it has been for you. What were you expecting?"

"I have no idea. I just thought that maybe things would feel different with magic released back into the world. What about you, Jerome?"

"It's been incredible. Visions. Prognostications. Seeings. Knowings. All of that stuff all over the place."

Eloise plucked him off her shoulder and faced him toward her. "Really?"

"No. Nothing. I was just kidding. I feel no difference at all. Not a niggle."

"Right. OK."

"What about you, Queen Eloise? Anything?"

"The ear buzz and eye blur are gone, and the numbness in my hand as well. Other than that, not really."

"Have you tested it?" asked Lorch.

"What do you mean?"

"I mean, you could run a test." He reached down and, after a moment of searching, picked up a large pebble. It was smooth, fairly evenly round, and about the size of an oversized grape. He brushed off the few flecks of dirt sticking to it, rubbed it on his breeks to give it a polish, and handed it to Eloise.

"What am I supposed to do with it?"

Lorch mimed throwing it.

"Oh. That makes sense," said Eloise. "Good idea."

She looked around, and picked a direction where she wouldn't be throwing toward any of the buildings, and where the stone might land safely. Eloise felt the weight of it in her hand, summoned her intention the way she did when she was throwing the hammer, like she had when she'd thrown the rope out of the Whacking Great Hole. Full focus, full force.

Eloise wound out and let the pebble fly with a mighty throw.

It went a long way.

A very, very, very long way.

So far that they couldn't hear it land.

The three of them stood there and watched where the pebble had shot through the night sky.

"Huh," said Lorch.

"Huh," said Jerome.

"Huh," agreed Eloise.

❋ 82 ❋

OLIVACEOUS AND OLEAGINOUS

wo months later...

Olivaceous and Oleaginous was a sprawling olive grove just on the Eastie side of Flachberg. Its trees dated back centuries, and the current proprietor, one Arbosana Tanche, was trying very hard to speak, but was crying too much to make himself understood.

"Ibbuh nubbuh shubbhuhuhhuhhuh ubbuh mirubuhulubub," he blubbered from the other end of the long table, where he sat close to Queen Aglandau and Princess Coratina.

Somehow, Jerome was able to understand him. "It was nothing short of miraculous," he translated. The chipmunk listened to more garbled crying, then added, "We faced ruin. My family was days away from moving to Gordal in desperate search of work. But then, like a breath of healing from Çalaht, the trees recovered. No more Verticillium wilt. No more olive knot. No more fruit mummification or leaf spot. By Çalaht's pustulant palms and sacred sacrum, we were saved."

Lorch leaned close to Jerome and asked, "How can you decipher that from the noises he's making?"

"Talent, I guess."

The three of them were under an ancient olive tree in the middle of the orchard, where a semi-formal spread had been laid out and enjoyed. Halfway along the table, Johanna sat with a retinue that would have included their father, but he'd come down with a summer cold and begged off from the trip, promising to meet up with them in Brague the following week for Eloise's formal coronation.

Jerome's translation continued: "My family and I are honored to act as hosts today, and humbled to be a small contributor to the prosperity of the Eastern Lands."

Lorch leaned over to Eloise and whispered, "Does it annoy you?"

"What? This property was always in her queendom."

"You know what he means," said Jerome. "That Flachberg voted to remain with the Easties."

"It would be hypocritical of me to be annoyed." Eloise pursed her lips. "And yes, it does a bit. But I'll live."

Aglandau stood, thanked Tanche and his family, and invited those present to wander the groves and enjoy the day's warmth.

Johanna stood, stretched, and came over to them. "I couldn't understand a word that man was saying."

"He was talking about you," said Eloise. "He sounded like he was going to propose. How do you feel about living near Flachberg?"

"Ha ha ha. That's hilarious. Stoofy should be worried you'll take his job as jester."

"Jester is a life position. I'll have to wait until he goes to stand with Çalaht before I can take his place."

Johanna held out her hand. "Walk with me."

Eloise stood. "Back in a bit, guys. I won't go out of eyesight." She took her sister's hand and they walked down a row deeper into the grove.

They stopped at a tree that looked especially old.

"I'm glad it worked," said Johanna. "Look how glossy the leaves are. And the fruits seem to be coming along beautifully."

"That's Hollace," said a voice from behind them. The twins turned and saw Princess Coratina approaching them. She curtsied to Eloise, and then to Johanna. "Hollace is a Meslalla. She bears green olives. Meslallas usually go to olive oil production, but Hollace is a special old girl." She put a hand on the trunk like she was greeting an old friend. "Her olives are kept aside to be pickled in garlic and hot peppers. And if you're lucky, someday you might have the honor of enjoying some of them in a sweet potato and lentil tagine."

"Sounds yummy," said Eloise. "Thank you again to you and your mother for hosting this informal gathering. It's been lovely, in part because it's been so low-pressure."

"I agree," said Johanna. "I'm grateful to not be faced with solving all the problems for a couple of days."

"I'm so glad you could both make it," said Coratina. "Mother has been..." The princess looked around to see if she might be overheard. "She's not been well. She's hanging in there, because she's a tough old gal, and that's what she does, but it will be a blessing if she makes it to Yule."

"That seems hard," said Eloise.

"It's definitely complicated. And I'm trying not to think about it too much. Hey! Let me introduce you to Darindra. She's just a couple of rows over, and she's magnificent."

The women walked toward another spectacular olive tree. After introducing Eloise and Johanna to it, Coratina said, "I'm so looking forward to your formal coronation, Queen Eloise."

"I'm glad you'll be able to make it."

"Nothing could keep me from it." The princess frowned a little. "I can't say I'm looking forward to the trip, though. Since Mother's not going, I'll be spending the travel time in a carriage with Seer Throumbolia. I've done that before." Coratina leaned in and whispered. "Between you and me, he drools when he sleeps. Still, it will be fun when I get there."

"How about…" Johanna hesitated. "How about you ride with me? I've got room in my carriage, and I'm heading there anyway."

The princess brightened. "Really? Oh, I'd love that, Queen Johanna. That would be amazing. And you can tell me all about the Western Lands and All That Really Matters as we go through it, since I've never been there before. And you can tell me about the Northern Lands, since I've never been there, either. I'll have to make sure Mother is OK with it, but that sounds amazing. Thank you."

"That's settled then," said Johanna. "Your seer can drool in the privacy of his own space."

They strolled through the trees for another quarter hour, chatting about not much. Eloise saw Queen Aglandau sitting alone at the table where they'd eaten. She touched Coratina on the arm. "I might go pay my respects to your mother. We haven't really spoken since I've been here."

"Do you think it's safe?" asked Johanna.

"It probably is," said the princess. "She didn't really say it earlier during the speeches, but she's both grateful and relieved that the olive trees have bounced back so beautifully. There's been a lot more calm in the queendom since then."

"Good to hear," said Eloise.

"Just don't tell her I said so. As she would say, 'One must keep up appearances.'"

"Thanks for the warning."

Eloise detached herself and made her way to the Eastie monarch. She approached from the front so she wouldn't surprise her, and gave a polite curtsy (unnecessary, even wrong, by the standards of Protocol). "Queen Aglandau. May I join you for a few moments?"

"I suppose." Aggie gestured toward a chair.

"Thank you so much for hosting this gathering. I'm very grateful to see your groves looking so lush."

Aglandau looked like she was trying to figure out what to say to that. Eventually, she landed on, "It would be churlish of me not to say thank you," said the queen. "So, consider it said."

"You're welcome. May it never be needed again."

"From your mouth to Çalaht's ears."

"I have a question, and I don't know how to work my way toward it, so I'd like to ask your indulgence in allowing me to ask it directly."

"I can tolerate a question," said Aglandau. "Just know that I won't feel obligated to answer."

"Fair enough." Now that Eloise was in a position to pose her query, she wasn't sure just how to put it. "At our parlay, I asked you what happened between you and my mother, and you declined to say. The relationship between your realm and ours under my mother's reign was smooth, but, if I may say, frosty. Is that a fair characterization?"

The queen lifted a single shoulder and let it drop. "Fair enough."

"Why did you hate my mother so much? Because... Because I suspect she felt the opposite for you."

"Are you prattled again, child? Why would you possibly say that?"

"Are you familiar with *The Most Torrid Trials and Tribulations of Goodwoman Mountebank*?"

"I do not relish the frivolity of romance scrolls, and I can't imagine how my answer to that might be relevant."

Eloise narrowed her eyes. "Is that a yes or a no?"

"It's possible that I've come across Goodwoman Mountebank at some point in my past. Not that particular scroll, though. The one I knew was *The Most Memorable Mistakes and Misadventures of Goodwoman Mountebank*. Oh, and there was *The Most Scorching Scandals and Scurrilousness of Goodwoman Mountebank*. And *The Most Ribald Rivals and Revelations of Goodwoman Mountebank. The Most Capricious Contretemps and Confessions of Goodwoman Mountebank*, also. But, otherwise, no."

Eloise did her best to suppress a smile. Unbelievably, she'd found a point of commonality with Queen Aglandau—a fondness for romance scrolls. "Well, I found a copy of *The Most Torrid Trials and Tribulations of Goodwoman Mountebank* among my mother's things, and read it on a whim. Toward the end of it, there was a note."

"What kind of note?" asked Aglandau.

"A marginal note, definitely written in my mother's hand. I suspect it pertained to you."

"Why? Why me?"

"Because it read, 'Just like at the parlay with Aggie. To give one's self so completely, and then be cast aside. How mortifying. I was so young and stupid.' There might be an infinite number of ways to interpret that," said Eloise. "But I don't think so."

To Eloise's surprise, the old queen's cheeks flushed an odd shade of olive-pink. "Well. Well, well, well." She then went silent. A full three minutes of silence passed, while her gaze went somewhere else. Just when Eloise suspected that four "well"s was all she was going to get, the queen said, "Well, well."

Six "well"s then.

Eloise continued to wait.

"She was a striking young woman, your mother," said Aglandau. "And had a mind like a lightning bolt. I was expecting absolutely nothing from her, so was completely taken by surprise. We got along pretty well. But then, you'd already more or less worked that out." She took a sip from her glass of water, which had a single green olive in it. "I was a lot younger then, and more inclined to be swayed by such matters. But then we left the parlay, and, well, I was embarrassed. Plus, I knew it would never lead to anything, so I needed to shut it down. I cut off all but the most perfunctory of contact." She got another distant look. "Maybe I could have handled that a bit better. But I didn't." She shrugged. "I didn't mean for her to feel mortified. I felt my own share of that, if it's any consolation."

"Thank you for sharing that with me," said Eloise. "You didn't have to. I appreciate it."

"One doesn't have to carry all of one's secrets to the grave."

"I'm sure that will be a long time from—"

"Don't blow smoke, child. They're practically digging the hole as we speak."

"I... I'm sorry."

"Bah. Don't be. I'm not gone yet. But I will ask you a question now."

"Of course."

"When I'm cold and in the ground, will you check in from time to time on Cora? You seem to have this queen thing down, more or less. I'm worried she won't. Can you do that?"

"It will be an honor, Your Imperialness."

Aglandau nodded once, and nothing more was said.

❧ 83 ❧

ARE YOU READY?

A *week after that...*

For the second time in her life (and, barring some sort of resurrection in the future, the last time), Eloise knelt on a prayer kneeler while the Venerable Prelate Herself held aloft the Gumballic Heraldic Crown and monotoned her way through a tedious invocation. The old, berobed tapir gestured, as usual, with her prehensile snout, waving it about in holy benediction. The hoof-like toes on her front feet pressed against the crown in lieu of gripping, and to her credit, she didn't seem in danger of dropping it any time soon.

Also for the second time (and she desperately hoped it was the last), Eloise found herself pondering whether tapirs in general, and the Venerable Prelate Herself in particular, had armpit hair beneath all those vestments.

She suspected the answer was yes, but had no idea what it would take to confirm or disprove the supposition in a way that would not give offense.

She guessed it was a mystery never to be solved.

Just as Eloise had at her Crown Plonking, she wore the Raiment of the Queens. The gown was still musty, uncomfortable and a skin-crawlingly disgusting, clashing, hodgepodge of colors and styles, but she'd had Seamstress Linttrap alter it so that it actually fit despite its hideous design. It didn't hurt that it no longer needed to accommodate a hidden box at Eloise's hip. Most important of all, the echidna had raised the hem several weak lengths so the odds were now significantly lower that Eloise would trip and face-plant in front of the largest crowd ever crammed into the largest devotional house in all of Brague.

As a bonus, she'd managed to convince the seamstress to remove the embarrassing collar ruffle that was several decades out of style. Linttrap had argued for leaving it in place. "It's tradition," she'd said, gesturing with one of the plucked quills she used for her sewing work.

Eloise hadn't said a word in reply, but instead had merely begun ripping the collar off. Seamstress Linttrap had gasped and conceded the point before more damage could be done.

So, the Raiment of the Queens looked as good as it was going to, which made it tolerable. The other thing that rendered the outfit tolerable were the shoes. Eloise had insisted on comfy shoes, as both her mother and father had separately suggested, and they were making all the difference in the world.

The ritual that the Venerable Prelate Herself recited was the same as the one she'd used at the Crown Plonking. Eloise had more or less memorized it, so only paid it half a mind, knowing she wouldn't have to say anything for a while. She took a few moments to glance out at the crowd.

There in the front pew were Johanna, her father, Lorch, Jerome, and Seer Maybelle, all nattily dressed and wearing big grins. Also in pride of place, but over to the side, were Hector, the Nameless One, Läääcy de Aardvark, and Odmilla de Platypus. They, too, all wore fancy outfits and huge smiles.

To the other side, looking simultaneously nervous and proud, was Helda, who'd done an incredible job with organizing the coronation.

The goose wore an exquisite gold braid collar down her long neck, and she checked her parchment of notes every fifteen seconds or so.

Representatives from the other courts enjoyed front-row seats. Her Maj Ono had made the trip, as had Princess Coratina (but, thankfully, not Queen Aggie). The khan had sent the dream wife in his stead with apologies for not being able to travel such a distance anymore.

Looking farther into the room, she spotted RoyLee scrunched in between Master Shovelhovel and Seer Bunkerhunker, who sat in the middle of the whole gang of Wombanditos (or, was it Pillagiarists?). Across the aisle from them, she spotted a very spruced-up Cäääsëëëy Liïïss. The chameleon wore a top hat and had his skin tinted to make it look like he wore formal robes. His tail was entwined with an extremely comely chameleon that Eloise didn't recognize, but the two of them radiated happiness.

How lovely.

Before she knew it, the Venerable Prelate Herself had set down the Gumballic Heraldic Crown and was rattling into the call and response with the crowd, asking if they'd accept Eloise as their queen. The responses were distinctly more enthusiastic than they'd been at her Crown Plonking.

That was also lovely.

Next, there was a lot of standing, sitting, and kneeling as Eloise promised to be a good queen (or that's how she paraphrased it in her head during rehearsals) and an appropriate figurehead as the head of the Çalahtist faith. After that, she kissed the opening verse of the Scrolls of Çalaht and signed the oath scroll with the quilliest quill Eloise had ever seen—it looked like it must have come from an albino peacock.

The Venerable Prelate Herself anointed Eloise with symbolic oils in the pattern of a Western Lands kiss (right cheek, left cheek, forehead). Then macaques, led by the Crown Jeweler, adorned Eloise with the royal regalia. First was the Queen's Robe, then the Orb of Alleged Omniscience (which had been very nicely repaired so that one barely noticed it had been horribly dented). Finally they handed her the Scepter of This is Much Better than the Stick They Used to Use, the Coronation Spork, and the Scimitar of Great Bodily Discomfort If Employed According to Specification.

All this went off without a hitch.

The Venerable Prelate leaned toward Eloise, and whispered, "Crown time. Are you ready?"

Eloise figured the question was probably rhetorical, but she paused and actually thought about it for a few moments. She'd been queen several months, and somewhere in there had also turned the corner from seventeen to eighteen years old. It felt like a myriad of years since the Gumballic Heraldic Crown had first been dropped on her head, and so much had happened since then.

She hadn't been a flawless queen. Eloise felt far from perfect. But she knew this about herself: she wanted to be as close to perfect as she could be. She wanted to make her queendom a better place for every-one. She wanted to improve the lives of those under her rule. And she had a pretty good idea that she could do a decent job of muddling through the uncertainty and make choices that would achieve those ends.

Eloise looked the Venerable Prelate Herself right in the eyes, and said, "Yes. I'm ready."

The tapir smiled. "Good. I think so too," and she placed the crown on Eloise's head.

Heavy weight and all, it felt right to have it up there.

❧ 84 ☙

SEED

The formal coronation ended with a lot of people cheering, "Behold, our queen!" and "Honor to the queen!" Eloise made it up the aisle of the devotional house without incident (thank Çalaht). Instead of riding a carriage back to the castle, she rode on Hector's back (a deviation from Protocol that would feed the gossip heralds for days, if not weeks).

The first order of business that the now-formally crowned Queen Eloise the Third wanted to conduct was to fulfill a request made by her dying mother. She made her way to the Culpability Courtyard, where Johanna stood waiting for her. "Shall we do this?"

Her sister pulled a silver hand spade from a robe pocket and waggled it. "It will be my pleasure."

Eloise held the envelope for her sister to take. Inside was an ironwood tree seed pod with five seeds in it. It was one of the items the late queen had left Eloise in a box that she'd called a birthday gift, but in fact was a letter of advice and warning, along with a few symbolic items. Her note had included a paragraph about the seed pod that read, "It's my wish that you plant one somewhere prominent. I'd like to be remembered with a living thing. Maybe you can fashion a memorial plaque. The five seeds should give you four to spare, in case you need to try again, given you don't have your sister's gifts in the garden."

But her sister was there, which meant that one seed was all they'd need.

Johanna took the envelope and poured the seed pod into her palm. "I like your idea of planting Mother here in the Capability Courtyard. It's prominent, which she wanted, and you can think of her when you do your morning runs."

"I'd like that, I think. What should the plaque say? I was thinking, 'Solid as an ironweed was Queen Eloise Hydra Gumball II.'"

"Maybe. But sometimes, it's best to keep these things simple. Perhaps, "In loving memory of Eloise Hydra Gumball II. Always in our hearts."

"I like it. Do you want me to help?"

"Actually, I do. Do you remember when we planted that acorn as a memorial to Melveeta the Elusive?"

"How could I forget?"

"What did I do with the acorn before I planted it?"

Eloise replayed the moment in her mind. "You put it in your mouth."

"That's right, to give it some of my essence." Johanna cracked open the pod and removed one seed from it. She put the remaining pod and seeds back in the envelope and returned it to Eloise. Then she placed the seed in her sister's palm. "You first. Tuck it in your cheek, and give it all the intention you've got."

Eloise poked the seed in her mouth. Saliva flowed, and she imagined soaking the seed with her life force. Johanna let her do this for a full two minutes, then put out her palm. Eloise removed the seed and gave it back. Her sister popped it into her own mouth.

Eloise wrinkled her nose. "That's a little bit disgusting."

"You and I went through the Ceremonies of the Stone of the Ancestors together. It's no worse than that."

"That was also disgusting."

She shrugged. "It sure was. But this is the way it has to happen, so I do it. Now let me focus." Johanna closed her eyes and concentrated on the seed in her mouth for the same two minutes.

She removed it from her mouth and wrapped her fingers around it, then handed Eloise the shovel. "Dig a hole about the width and depth of the spade, and think of Mother as you do it."

Eloise did just that. A protective cloth had been laid on the ground, and she knelt in her post-coronation dress. It took about thirty seconds to dig, and brought to mind the happiest moments she could recall with their mother—spinning season in the dervish elder forest. Her family had gone on a trip to the Kestrel Mountains, near the border with the Central Ranges, a journey that had been timed so they'd be there when the dervish elders released their rain of winged seeds, which spun like tops in the wind. Eloise would never forget standing with her mother, father, and Johanna, each holding a protective parasol and grinning with delight as a spinning cloud of seeds descended all around them.

Johanna knelt down beside Eloise, placed the seed in the divot, and mounded the loose soil on top of it. Using her fingers, she dug a small, circular channel around it to catch rain. "Place your palms flat on the earth, like this. Now, close your eyes, and cast your mind forward to a time when there is a mature, healthy, venerable ironwood tree that's grown from this seed. See the sheen of its leaves, feel the roughness of its bark, and picture the roots thrusting into the ground at a depth that mirrors the tree height."

"Got it."

"Good. Now, I haven't had much time in my garden since I got back from the Midpoint of All the Realms, but I've tested a couple of things. Leave your hands where they are, and watch this."

Johanna's expression went unfocused, and a look of serene, but intense, concentration came over her. A full minute later, she smiled, stood, and held out her hand to help Eloise up. "We'll want to take a couple of steps back. Oh, I forgot." Johanna used the watering can to drizzle a light rain into the shallow trench surrounding the seed. "There."

The sisters held hands and looked at the ground.

"What are we—" started Eloise.

"Sshhh. Not much longer."

Eloise felt a gentle vibration from the ground through her comfy shoes.

"Here we go," said Johanna.

A tendril pushed up through the ground, worming its way skyward. Stems branched out, and leaves sprouted and grew. Over the course of about three minutes, the seed became a knee-high sapling.

Eloise squeezed her sister's hand. "That's incredible."

"Thank you."

"How did you do it?"

"It's more or less what I did with the haggleberry bush when I got it to grow here, but with a little more oomph."

"Why not make it a full-grown tree?"

Johanna lifted and dropped a shoulder. "It didn't work. I mean, I could get the tree to happen, but they didn't survive more than a day or two. This approach, as far as I can tell, is just enough help to let the plant emerge and establish itself quickly, which gives it more of a chance to take over on its own and thrive over time."

"I think Mother would have been happy with this."

"I like to think she would have as well.

Eloise handed the envelope back to Johanna. "Take these. Plant an ironwood in her memory at Stained Rock."

"I will, but I only need the one seed. Why don't you give Her Majesty Onomatopoeia, the dream wife, and Princess Coratina the remaining three. That way, there'll be a little of Two in each of the realms."

"She'd have liked that."

They stood there for a few minutes holding hands, staring at the new life emerging from the soil, and remembering their mother.

A soft voice broke their reverie. "Queen Eloise? Queen Johanna?" It was Helda de Anatidae.

"Yes, Helda?"

"They gala and concert are in an hour. You need to get dressed."

"We'll be right there."

❧ 85 ❧

THERE'S A LADY

The coronation's celebratory gala and concert, like the rest of Eloise's coronation, took to heart the rule expressed by her previous Lady Seneschal, Älphonsinä Póöòmáäàdéëè, who'd said, "You need to have the coronation that you want to have. You don't want to look back with regret."

Working with Headlong Helda and Läääcy, she'd done her best to put that maxim into practice. The decorations in the ballroom were primarily white, from the bunting to the candles. The floral arrangements on the tables featured her favorite flowers—daisies—giving everything a fresh, clean look, which she hoped would be appropriate for a new reign. While the crowd allowed for visiting dignitaries and those from Court who had to be invited, she did her best to skew the guest list and the seating arrangements to ensure that those she loved most were both included and sitting closest to her. In practice, this meant that there was undue prominence given to her Assistant Court Seer to the Court Seer, who sat to her left at the raised head table, and her champion, who sat to her right.

Eloise wore a white, sleeveless evening gown and an ornate, yet simple, crown of silver and jade. It filled her heart to see the packed hall

475

buzzing with excitement. As serving wenches scurried in and out with platters piled with delicacies, couples made their way to and from the dance floor, gyrating to the latest gavottes. Eloise looked forward to joining them after the concert.

The musicians finished the last pre-concert dance, and servants rushed to blow out candles and light ones that illuminated the stage. A panda in a sequined tunic and breeks with a matching sequin bow tie strolled into the spotlight. It was Martin de Ursidae, the MC from the Velvet Cask Cabaret. "Good evening, ladies, gentlemen, and all points in between. Welcome to the Royal Command Performance in celebration of the coronation of our new queen, Eloise Hydra Gumball III!" The crowd applauded. "We have a full program's entertainment for you, with performers who've come from near and far. I've seen them all rehearsing, and I can tell you that you're in for a treat. So, let's get started with our first act. All the way from..." He pulled out a scroll from a pocket and checked a note. "All the way from Ultimate Realization of Numinous Transcendence, it's the percussive stylings of Bongos de Bongo!"

A family of bongos clattered onto the stage in high spirits—a mother and father with lyre-shaped horns and their four kids still sporting antler buds.

"Oh, wow. Look who it is," whispered Lorch. "It's great to see them again."

"I know, right?" said Eloise. "I asked RoyLee if he could get someone to find and invite them, and he handled it like a champ."

"I hope they don't ask me if I've been practicing my bongos. I haven't had time."

"Me either."

The bongos took their positions, and began hammering out complicated rhythms on their bongo drums. This blended into a sophisticated and syncopated introduction to their cover of the song "Papa's Got a Slightly Used Sack," with the mother, Prééëcĩĩíóòòúüùs de Bongo, doing the singing and the father, Fortitude de Bongo, providing harmonies. Next, they performed "Seven Realm Army," and ended their three-song set with a version of "All Along the Adequate Wall of the Realm's Turrets."

Eloise, Jerome, and Lorch joined the rest of the crowd in wild applause.

"That last one was a complete rave-up," said the chipmunk. "And now I'm going to have 'Seven Realm Army' stuck in my head."

After the Bongos de Bongo came the Juggling Jerboas. They wore lavish, tailor-made costumes, all sequins and tassels, and they juggled everything from hoops and clubs, apple cores, and folded socks to burning hoops and clubs, burning apple cores, and burning folded socks. It was another spectacular showing.

Eloise leaned over and said, "What do you think, Jer? Does their act seem like they used a weak magic for juggling? Because it is even more incredible than what they did when we last saw them."

"I suspect they do," said the chipmunk. "But it could also be sheer talent." Jerome paused. "Should we still be saying 'weak magic?' Should we start just saying 'magic' from now on?"

"I have no idea."

The stage was cleared for the next act, and out came Sylvia Cloister-feld. Having spent so much time with her as her Balanced Way master and military advisor, Eloise found it strange to see her glammed up in low-cut frills and fripperies. It suited her like her sword did, but in a different way, and she absolutely lit up the hall with torch-hot rendi-tions of "Limping Up That Mound," "I Wanna Dance With Somebody (Who Is Reasonably Fond of Me)," and "Killing Me Softly With His Canticle."

Act after act followed. There was a duck who did a one-person comedy sketch about being Çalaht's next door neighbor. A contortionist who crammed herself into a half-sized pickle barrel. A children's troupe that danced to a medley of popular galliards.

And on and on—each personally approved by Eloise, and each a thrill to watch.

At intermission, Eloise fanned herself and said, "I need a breath of air. I'm going to pop outside for a minute."

"Yes, Your Highness," said Lorch. "Shall I come along?"

"No, I'm good. But I know you'll be there in the background anyway, so do what you need to do."

"Yes, Queen Eloise."

She made her way toward a side door, where she found Helda bossing a bevy of serving wenches. "Drinks, drinks, drinks," said the goose. "Quick! Refill those glasses while there's a break." Then Helda saw Eloise. "Your Highness. I trust all is well?"

"Yes, thank you." Eloise leaned forward and said, "Helda, you have been amazing. An absolute, Çalaht-sent miracle. The party is perfect. Just perfect. I'm so incredibly grateful for all you've done."

The goose straightened her neck, pleased. "Thank you, Queen Eloise. It's been my pleasure."

"If you'll excuse me, I'm just going to get some air." Eloise nodded a goodbye and ducked outside. She made her way into a barely lit private garden at the side of the auditorium. She strode along a flagstone path and enjoyed the cool feeling of an evening breeze on her face and neck.

A movement caught her eye.

There, in a dark alcove, several paces ahead and to her left, was an indeterminate shape. It was moving a little, and there was the sound of what might have been a struggle coming from it.

Eloise took several cautious steps toward the form. The sounds continued.

She was about to ask, "Are you OK?" when the shape resolved itself.

It wasn't a hidden form in a darkened corner. It was two hidden forms in a darkened corner.

One of them was her sister.

The other was Coratina Ponentine.

The noises weren't struggles.

They were kisses.

Oh, thought Eloise, smiling a somewhat puzzled smile to herself. *That's nice.*

She hadn't exactly expected it, but it made sense, now that she'd seen it.

Eloise slowly backed away, leaving them to their huddled privacy.

Her mind whizzed through the possible implications of such an alliance. It might bode well for inter-realm relationships—so long as they didn't end up like Queen Gwendolyn the Irritable and King Brüüütus.

But neither of them struck her as the kind of person to resort to realm-threatening revenge.

Well, once upon a time, maybe her sister would have burned down a realm in spite. But that was before... Before everything. She seemed much happier now.

So, yeah. An assignation between the queen of the Northern Lands and the heir to the Eastern Lands throne might not be such a bad thing.

Eloise made her way back to the ballroom and retook her seat, mind still racing.

Jerome caught her expression. "What?"

"What what?"

"You know." He gestured to her face. "What what what?"

"What? Nothing."

"Nothing? No way, nothing. What what what what?"

Eloise was saved from having to explain by Marty the MC reappearing on stage to begin the second half of the show. The quality of performance was as weird and varied as the first half.

And then out walked a man in a natty outfit and a neat beard.

"Oh!" Jerome tugged at Eloise's sleeve. "Oh, oh, oh, oh, oh! You didn't tell me he was coming."

"I thought you might like the surprise."

"Oh, oh, oh, oh, oh, oh, oh, oh, oh, oh!"

"Good evening," the man said. "My name is Jaminity Delgado Blister—"

The crowd (led by Jerome) exploded in cheers and applause. Shouts of "The Jammer!" (a nickname Eloise knew he didn't like) rocked the hall. Jaminity looked nothing like the maudlin, road-weary, disappointed shell of a person Eloise had first laid eyes on in a hamlet called Name Goes Here, eating crackerbread and playing for a pittance. Instead, there was a sparkle in his eye and a palpable zest for life.

He grinned his appreciation and waved to quiet the audience. "Thank you for that. It's an honor to be chosen to close off this Royal Coronation Command Performance. But first, let me start by saying..." Here he bowed toward Eloise's royal box. "Congratulations on your coronation, Your Highness. Long may you reign."

This got another round of cheering, and Eloise waved him a thank you.

"Most of you probably don't know that I met Her Royal Highness not that many months ago in a clapped-out inn called the Name Goes Here Something Something Arms. I don't mind saying that things weren't going well for me, but somehow, meeting a certain young princess led me to apologize to someone who deserved it, and to breathe new life into a career that, let's just say, wasn't going to prompt any bards to write a song about it. So for that, Your Highness, thank you very much."

This got another round of applause.

"I'd like to play a song that one or two of you may have heard before. But before I do, I need to bring out my partner in music, who our beloved queen introduced me to. Ladies and gentlemen, boys and girls, arachnids and birds, rodents and reptiles and everyone else, I give you the musical genius that is Alejandro Diego Ferdinando Felipe Esteban Iglesias Desoto de Lugo!"

A gold and blonde palomino Andalusian stallion, his thick mane and tail brushed and flying wild, pranced forward from the back of the auditorium calling, "Hola! Hola, everybody!" He reached the stage and leapt onto it. He bowed to Eloise, bowed to Jaminity, and bowed to the crowd. Then he cleared his throat, and said, "Good evening. I am Alejandro Diego Ferdinando Felipe Esteban Iglesias Desoto de Lugo, but you can call me Al."

The duet's reputation must have preceded them, as Al got as big a reception as Jaminity.

"Good evening, good evening, all," said the horse. "And congratulations, Señorita Princesa—oops, I mean Señorita Reina Eloise on the occasion of your coronation."

Another pause for applause.

"My good friend Jaminity and I treasured our time with you, and how you brought us together. We'd like to perform a song for you that we wrote."

Jaminity said, "It's called 'My Western Lands and All That Really Matters Rose.'"

"Aw, that's sweet," whispered Jerome.

And it was. The two blended their voices in a poetic ode to Eloise that made her sound rather good, which was nice.

They followed this with "Burlap Bag of Rain," "Straight Outta Lower Glenth," and "Mr. Bombard Man."

When the clapping tapered off on that last song, Jaminity leaned forward and spoke conspiratorially. "There's another song we want to do, but I think we need some help to do it." He turned to the horse. "Alejandro, my friend. Do you think we need help with the last song?"

"I don't know," said the horse. "You're the one who wrote the song. I shall defer to your expertise."

"I think another singer might be nice. And there's one woman who took my song and made it her own."

Jerome grabbed Eloise's sleeve. "No!"

Eloise patted his forearm. "Yes."

"Ladies and gentlemen," said Jaminity. "Please welcome to the stage the most divine diva to ever tread the boards—Lyndia Thrind!"

"No, no, no!" squealed Jerome.

"Yes, yes, yes." Eloise glanced at him. "Don't faint, Jer. You'll miss her."

Lyndia Thrind burst onto the stage, her robes a sparkling purple, her teeth a blazing white, her hair a tower of curls, and her smile like a full moon on a clear night. She waved to the crowd with both arms, looking half her 80 years. "Hello, hello, hello, my darlings. Darlings, I'm so honored to be here to celebrate our new queen." She turned to Jaminity and Alejandro. "Would you boys mind if I joined in the song?"

Alejandro bowed to her. "It would be an honor and a privilege."

"Thank you so much, darling. And I have a few more friends I need up here to help us so we can get the harmonies right." Lyndia then waved toward a side curtain, and out came Sylvia Cloisterfeld and Prëëècîïíóöòúüùs de Bongo. Then someone else eased onto the stage with them—a hulking figure muscled like a warrior gone soft: Gouache Snotearrow McCcoonnch. Eloise was surprised to see Gouache up there, but thinking about it, it made sense.

Lyndia turned back to the audience. "You all know this one. I want everyone to stand up. Right now, ladies and gentlemen, stand up. You, too, Your Highness. We're all doing this together."

The crowd did as she asked. Eloise smiled as she, Jerome, and Lorch stood as well.

Lyndia Thrind extended one hand to Jaminity, and put her other on Alejandro's wither, and the three of them led the packed auditorium into the song.

"There's a lady who knows all that glitters is groats..."

Eloise, who never, ever, ever wanted to sing in public, opened her mouth and contributed her voice, as the room filled with the most glorious version of "Three Bags of Groats for My Sweetheart" that had ever been sung in all the realms.

❧

Thank you for reading *The Magic of Last Resort*. I really appreciate the fact that you've come through the whole journey with me.

Want to read more about Eloise and Jerome? Six months before the start of *The Purple Haze*, they
played hooky from Court and headed out for a stolen adventure. It goes well. And then it really doesn't. Claim your copy of *The Wombanditos* today to find out what happened!

❧

And if you're wondering just what exactly happened at their Thorning Ceremony that caused Eloise and Johanna to go from being as close as twins can be to as estranged, then you'll definitely want to check out the standalone prequel novel, *The Thorning Ceremony*. I promise you, you'll never guess what caused the rift.

THANK YOU

Thank you for reading *The Magic of Last Resort*. Reviews are crucial for helping other readers discover new books to enjoy. If you want to share your love for Eloise, Jerome, and all the gang, please leave a review. I'd really appreciate it!

Recommending my work to others is also a huge help. Feel free to give this book and the whole series a shout-out in your favourite book recommendation group to spread the word.

ACKNOWLEDGMENTS

It is always joy to get to say thank you to those who have helped me bring this book to the world.

Tamsin Dean Einspruch, our daughter, has from the word go been my first port of call for ideas, perspective, and thoughts on words. She is my first reader, and has been with this story and the whole series every step of the way. Over and over she has helped me stay headed in the right direction. Thank you, sweetie.

Many, many thanks also to Cheryl Hannah, Olivia Martinez, and Brian Busby for their beta reads. Cheryl has been, for each of these books, the first person outside my family to read the manuscript, and her encouragement always gives me the heart needed to keep going. Olivia brings an always-keen eye to the words, and she and Brian provided very different perspectives to what they read. Valuable and valued input all.

Thank you to my editor, Vanessa Lanaway, and my proofreader, Abigail Nathan. Sharp eyes and red pens, both. Y'all rock. It's that simple.

Thank you to Maria Spada for the wonderful cover. This one is absolutely one of my favourites.

As always, a massive thank you to my bride, Billie Dean, who reads and gives incredible input on everything I write, who has encouraged me forever, and who believed in my creative soul much, much earlier than I ever did. I love you and I thank you. L^3.

And finally, thank you to you, whoever you are, for picking up this book and this series, and having a read. I appreciate it very much.

ABOUT THE AUTHOR

Andrew Einspruch is fond of the wordy, the nerdy, and the funny, which means that if you arranged for him to have lunch with Weird Al Yankovic, Tom Lehrer, William Gibson, and any of the Monty Python guys, he'd be your friend forever. Visit his web site for a complete list of his books at andreweinspruch.com.

Andrew is an ex-pat Texan living in Australia, and is the co-founder of the not-for-profit charity the Deep Peace Trust, which fosters deep peace and non-violence for all species. With his wife and daughter, he runs the Trust's farm animal and wild horse sanctuary. (You can see why there's the odd animal or two in his books.)

If pressed, he'll deny he ever coded in COBOL for a bank.

If you haven't done so yet, use the QR code below to claim your copy of the standalone prequel, *The Wombanditos*.

www.ingramcontent.com/pod-product-compliance
Lightning Source LLC
Chambersburg PA
CBHW050103120726
47904CB00004B/1192